Kilgart

Kilgarthen

Gloria Cook

CANELO

First published in the United Kingdom in 1995 by Headline Book Publishing

This edition published in the United Kingdom in 2020 by

Canelo Digital Publishing Limited
Third Floor, 20 Mortimer Street
London W1T 3JW
United Kingdom

Print ISBN 978 1 78863 806 7
Ebook ISBN 978 1 78863 646 9

Look for more great books at www.canelo.co

Printed and bound in Great Britain by Clays Ltd, Elcograf S.p.A.

With love and affection to my daughter Tracy and her husband Anthony, a super young couple of whom I am really proud.

Chapter 1

As her husband's coffin was lowered into the cold, wet, black earth, Laura Jennings was thinking about how much she'd come to hate him. Let his flesh and bones rot here, in the place where he'd been born and bred, the little moorland Cornish village that he had loved so much, the place he had always refused to take her to.

Laura would never grieve like the villagers of Kilgarthen over their 'local boy made good'. The mental cruelty that Bill Jennings had inflicted on her throughout the five years of their marriage had left her totally numbed. She felt as bleak and lonely as the granite and slate headstones that stood guard over the graves at her feet. She felt as cold and raw as the persistent winter winds that swept over the brooding, exposed, sometimes dangerous moorland, part of the eastern flank of Bodmin Moor, that made up the stony horizon of the village. A tor dominated the skyline; Laura knew its name, Hawk's Tor, and she felt it was frowning down upon her.

Daisy Tamblyn, Bill's aunt, whose homely face Laura recognised from his weekend holiday snaps, came to stand beside her at the graveside. She gave Laura a sympathetic smile but Laura kept her face rigid. All around her people were sobbing, but Laura took them for fools who didn't know, or indulgent dimwits who chose to ignore, the truth of their hero's character.

Rather than listen to the burial committal, Laura eyed the mourners through the net of her smart black hat. Her shoulders had developed a slightly dejected stoop, her eyes tended quickly to look down, she was inclined to feel guilty even when something bad that had happened was not her fault, but she felt superior to the people here whom she thought of as simple villagers. Except for one woman in a matching fur coat and hat, compared to the other women in their square-shouldered utility suits and plain hats and boring headscarves, Laura was a striking sight in her large-buttoned full-skirted Dior coat. Her three-inch heels, which brought her model's figure and bearing to nearly six feet, made her a few inches taller than the average Cornish man in attendance.

Laura knew who some of these people were, Bill had talked about them often. The middle-aged couple with suitable funereal faces on the opposite side of the grave must be the stern schoolmaster and his wife, Cecil and Barbara Roach. Laura took an instant aversion to Cecil Roach. She recognised similar traits to herself in Barbara Roach; there was no spark of life about her, her eyes were dull, mouth taut, complexion unnaturally pale, like her own. Next to them, his legs squashed against Bill's parents' headstone, was a broad, whiskery man whose solemn expression could not disguise his cheery nature, making him the pub landlord, Mike Penhaligon. The little woman with her arm linked through his was his wife, Pat.

Bringing her eyes round to Daisy Tamblyn, Laura was also able to pick out Bunty Buzza, Daisy's best friend and next-door neighbour; two dumpy ladies in their late fifties, in black today but usually in drab dresses and overalls. On Bunty Buzza's other side was Marianne Roach who had placed herself as far away as possible from her school-master father and in a good position to ogle the tall, handsome, rather amused-looking Harry Lean, a rich estate agent. The woman in fur, standing straight-backed and aloof, was his elegant mother, Felicity; she was probably thinking it a shame she had to dirty her snakeskin shoes in the damp grass. Marianne Roach took her eyes off Harry Lean for a moment and glared at Laura.

The vicar brought Laura back to the matter in hand by gently shaking her arm. The interment was over. 'You have my deepest sympathy, Mrs Jennings. If there is anything I can do, please do not hesitate to call at the vicarage.' He pointed to the left of the large granite church; fifteenth century in origin, it seemed to Laura too large to accommodate the little village. 'It's just round there. I'm so very sorry I can't stay for the wake but I have an urgent meeting to attend.'

'I understand, Vicar,' Laura murmured, looking at the ground and moving away from him. She was in no mood for handshaking. 'Thank you for taking the service.'

Shrugging his thin shoulders, the Reverend Kinsley Farrow signalled to Daisy Tamblyn to take over from him. He left the graveside with his robes flapping in the wind.

'Mrs Jennings, I'm so pleased to meet you at last,' Daisy Tamblyn said, looking unsure of herself as she secured Laura's reluctant attention. 'Although not in these circumstances of course.' Daisy sniffed into a large white handkerchief and looked sorrowfully down into the grave.

'As I didn't know what you wanted to do after the service, I took it upon myself to arrange for refreshments to be served in the village hall. Billy was very popular here, you see, there would be too many mourners to pack into my little house at the back of the shop, and I didn't think you'd want them in Billy's cottage.' Daisy owned the village shop which doubled as a post office. She put her hanky in an old flattened black handbag and looked expectantly at Laura. There were many curious faces around them waiting for Mrs Bill Jennings to speak. 'The train journey down from London must have been long and tiring. You'll at least be glad to have a hot cup of tea, I'm sure.' Daisy seemed eager to please.

'I have to get back to London, Mrs Tamblyn,' Laura replied in a cool, brisk voice, her educated London accent, which she'd deliberately heightened, a stark contrast to Daisy's broad burr. 'I haven't got time to stop. I just want to spend a little time freshening up in Bill's cottage then I'll phone for a taxi to take me back to the railway station.'

'Oh!' Daisy flinched, clearly disappointed. She was about to open her mouth again but Laura wasn't going to be persuaded.

'Good afternoon, Mrs Tamblyn. I too am sorry that we had to meet like this.' She walked away as fast as her heels, which were biting into the rough turf, allowed. She heard the remarks muttered at her back.

'You'd think she'd at least spend a few minutes in Bill's birthplace.' This came from Bunty Buzza. 'At least stop and have a word with you, Daisy.'

3

'Yes,' a male voice uttered disgustedly. 'She refused to come here while he was living. Must think she's too good for us just because she comes from money and looks like a film star. It's too bad her behaving like this, and with Spencer Jeffries not bothering to show up at all.'

Someone else added loudly, 'Stuck up madam! It's a disgrace.' Daisy began to sob, but Laura was unmoved. These people had loved and respected Bill but they had never really known him. Well, she had done her last duty by him, brought him back to this little backwater village to be buried as he'd wished.

Harry Lean made to block Laura's way out of the churchyard but her ice-blue eyes and steely demeanour quickly made him step aside. She walked up to the funeral directors, thanked them, and promised them there would be a cheque in the post. Bill's cottage was directly across the road, the newly whitewashed one with hanging baskets under the eaves, quaintly named Little Cot. She searched about in her handbag for the key and cursed inwardly when her clumsy gloved hand let it drop to the ground. To her consternation Harry Lean picked it up.

'Allow me, Mrs Jennings,' he said, dropping the key into her outstretched hand with an exaggerated flourish. He was smiling. Laura instantly distrusted him; she had seen that sort of smarmy expression all too often on Bill's face, there was no sincerity in it, it was designed to get the man his own way.

Harry Lean doggedly kept eye contact with her yet his dark active eyes were sweeping the whole scene before him. He had careless good looks, was well built with a three-dimensional fleshy circle in the centre of his chin that some women would find endearing. Laura found his ready smile offensive.

'Thank you,' she said stiffly, vexed that she'd been helped by someone from this village.

'The name's Harry Lean,' he drawled. 'It was a pleasure to meet you, Mrs Jennings, albeit for just a few moments.'

Laura was aware of some of the villagers gawping at her over the churchyard wall. All she wanted to do was to get away from this place as quickly as possible, but first she needed a hot drink and the use of a bathroom and telephone. She wouldn't allow Harry Lean to delay her.

'Goodbye, Mr Lean.' She moved away and looked to the left and right before attempting to cross the road.

'No need for that,' he said, coming up to her side. 'Hardly any traffic passes through the village, even without petrol rationing – few of the villagers have cars. Things are very different down here to London. Mine and the hearse are the most to be seen together in a long time.'

'Really?' Laura retorted, angry that he had made her feel a fool.

His face still seemingly full of hidden amusement, Harry Lean turned on his heel and ambled up the hill to his sporty car parked outside the Tremewan Arms, one of the places in Kilgarthen that Bill had enthusiastically spoken about. Laura warmed a little to Harry Lean; apparently he had no wish either to go to the village hall and pick regretfully over Bill's bones.

She crossed the road and unlocked the cottage door. Lifting the misshapen latch which had been there for decades, she stepped straight into the sitting room, which Bill had called the front room. He had told her in detail the changes he'd made to the cottage; she was never meant to see them, telling her about them had been part of Bill's spitefulness.

Like all the dwellings in the village, the cottage had extremely thick walls to combat the cold winds. When Bill had been brought up here, the cottage had been dark and bleak and no more than functional. He had decorated it himself in warm colours and furnished it comfortably with a tapestry-covered three-piece suite and wooden rocking chair, not at all like the modern lines he had insisted on for their home in London. A large ornament of a sleeping ginger cat lay inside the brass fender at the hearth. Pictures of wildlife adorned the walls and horse brasses hung from the black beams of the low ceiling. The stairs came down into the front room and Bill had changed the banister to one of thick dark oak with an ornately carved newel post at the bottom; it gave a charming effect. The room was spotlessly clean and smelled of lavender; Daisy Tamblyn checked over the cottage and cleaned it about twice a month.

Bill had put in every modern convenience – to show the villagers he had made something of himself, no doubt, Laura thought bitterly. He had installed a generator for electricity in a shed in the garden, but there was no telephone; Bill had not wished to be disturbed in his holiday hideaway.

Laura entered one of the two bedrooms at the front of the cottage and looked out of the window. She could see past the pub up to the top of the hill down which the hearse had driven to reach the churchyard. The village was sheltered in a valley and near the top of the hill in the opposite direction nestled the little Methodist chapel. Roughly halfway between the church and chapel, the public telephone stood out like a red beacon. In a little while she would go there to phone for a taxi to take her back to Liskeard railway station. A tawny pony and jingle stood close by and Laura watched, somewhat amazed, as an enormously fat woman in a huge tartan cloak and black bonnet awkwardly dismounted and approached the telephone box. She had difficulty opening the heavy door. Despite her size and strange mode of dress, Laura couldn't place her from Bill's reminiscences. But why be interested in anyone from Kilgarthen now?

Across the road no one was left in the churchyard. Apart from herself and Harry Lean, the rest of the mourners must have trudged along the gravel path and passed through the gate at the end of the churchyard to the village hall, a modern, grey, rectangular building. Judging by the remarks just thrown at her back, the villagers thought she'd refused to come down here. Bill must have told them that. According to him, some of them were narrow-minded, they'd never forgive her – not that she cared about that. She was glad she couldn't actually see Bill's grave from here.

She didn't go into the main bedroom. There would be many of Bill's personal things in there and she wasn't up to looking them over. Some day she would have to decide what to do with the cottage. She could sell it but had thought about giving it to Daisy Tamblyn who had served Bill faithfully over the years since his mother, Daisy's sister, had died.

Laura used the bathroom, the only fully furnished one in the village; Bill had had it built on from the kitchen. She looked in

6

the mirror over the sink. She ripped off her hat and took out the combs that restrained her shoulder-length blonde hair and shook it free. She wore no make-up and the clear skin of her face was white, transparent looking, and stretched over her high cheekbones. Her eyes were dull, making her look slightly older than her twenty-three years.

In the kitchen she opened a window and listened to the gurglings and rush of the Withey Brook that ran the length of the back of the village. She kicked off her soiled shoes and took off the black coat which she'd bought for her father's funeral two months ago; she hadn't wasted valuable clothing coupons on anything new for today's event. The generator had not been switched on but the cooking range was lit, and she put half a kettleful of water on the hottest spot to heat for coffee. She hunted through the cupboards and found Bill's favourite biscuits. She felt guilty at first then realised he wasn't here to tell her she mustn't eat them. She'd only meant to spend a few minutes in the cottage, but he wasn't here to say how long she could stay. She was free at last to do as she pleased.

Her life with Bill had been hell from the moment their honeymoon began after their whirlwind courtship. She had quickly found out that she had only been the route to a seat on the board of her father's successful construction company. Bill had left the village for London in 1940 as a twenty-year-old youth, not to do something for the war effort as he'd been unable to fight due to an eye defect, but to better himself. He'd got himself a carpenter's apprenticeship in Laura's father's construction company, but with little need for building due to the bombing, Colin Farraday had diverted his wealth and energies into munitions. Like most of the workforce, Bill had lost his job but he hadn't been dismissed altogether. Colin Farraday had liked the youth's drive and energy, his determination to get on and his apparent loyalty, and had kept him on as a 'runner' between his businesses. Bill had made himself indispensable and at the end of two years had been promoted to office manager.

Laura had met him in the office when, as an impressionable girl of eighteen years, fresh out of boarding school, she'd worked as her father's personal assistant. Bill had quickly wormed himself into her affections and she had fallen for his apparent good nature and ready charm. Her father's health had been deteriorating for some time and he was beginning to allow Bill to make serious decisions for him. He had no real objections when Bill asked for Laura's hand in marriage, and believing the three of them would have an excellent working relationship, Laura had allowed herself to be rushed into wedlock.

Bill had made it clear from the start, however, that he expected her to stay at home and keep house, only allowing her out to work in the soup kitchens and canteens. That had set the pattern for the next five miserable years. When the war ended, Farraday Construction was resurrected to rebuild parts of the bombed-out capital city and by then Bill was chairman of the company, one of the biggest in South London. No wonder the good people of Kilgarthen thought he'd done well for himself.

Now, seven years after he had left the village, the wretched existence Bill Jennings had imposed on her was finally over, finishing not tragically as reported in the newspapers from suffocating in a fire while lying innocently in a hotel bedroom; Andrew Macarthur, the family solicitor, had managed to keep quiet the two high-class call girls who had died with Bill. And Laura was free of Bill in a way neither of them had been planning. A divorce would have upset her father but when he'd died she'd made up her mind to leave Bill, then she'd found out he'd been about to leave her for the wealthier daughter of a minor title.

She finished her snack, washed the cup and saucer, tidied up the kitchen and was locking up the cottage to make her way to the public telephone when Daisy Tamblyn waddled up to her, looking agitated.

'M-mrs Jennings. I've just been called away from the village hall. I was told my telephone has been ringing and ringing. Anyway, I went home and there's a London gentleman on the phone for you. He says it's urgent and can you come to speak to him right away.'

Daisy was red-faced and out of breath and Laura felt guilty about her earlier unfriendly behaviour. 'I'll come at once, Mrs Tamblyn. Thank you for coming to fetch me.'

As she walked beside Daisy up the short steep hill to the shop, Laura made amends with a lie. 'I should have explained more fully about wanting to go back to London immediately. There's a very important meeting tomorrow. Bill would have wanted me to be there in his place.'

'Yes, I do see,' Daisy replied breathlessly. 'It must all have been a terrible shock to you, Billy dying like that, so young, bless him. Twenty-seven's no age to die, and him doing so well too. Yes, he would have wanted you to look after the business, what with you losing your father only a couple of months ago. You've had a very tragic time.'

Laura didn't want to talk about Bill. 'Did you ask who was on the telephone?'

'A Mr Andrew Mac-something,' Daisy puffed out obligingly.

'Andrew Macarthur. He's the family solicitor,' Laura explained, feeling Daisy was owed this knowledge after having her afternoon upset twice on her account.

'Must be something important then.'

'Yes.' Laura smiled to herself. Andrew was also a friend and probably wanted to know how she was faring. He'd been concerned about her insisting on making the long journey straight back. It would be good to hear his familiar voice.

Daisy showed her into her snug sitting room and left her there. Laura picked up the big black telephone, which stuck out like a sore thumb on a highly polished sideboard. She could hear Daisy talking to Bunty Buzza in the kitchen.

'Hello. Andrew?'

'Laura! Thank goodness I reached you before you left Kilgarthen. Listen, I've got some serious news for you. I think you'd better sit down.'

'Sit down? Whatever for?' She lowered her voice. 'Has the press found out about those women who died with Bill?'

'It's nothing like that, Laura.' Andrew Macarthur's usually quiet voice was so grave that Laura eased herself down onto a chair. Her hope of finding a little comfort from him was slipping away.

'What's happened?'

'You remember how jittery Bill was several months ago, just before your father died?'

'Yes, what about it?'

'I've found out why. Bill was involved with some shady characters—'

'I've always known that,' Laura interrupted impatiently. 'He was up to his neck in underhand deals. He made money for the company through them. Dad never knew why the profits were so high but he trusted him.'

'There was more to it than that, Laura. He'd got in with some big boys, the Morrison brothers, a particularly nasty firm that likes to be paid on time or off come your toenails. Bill was worried out of his mind – well, you know that by the way he treated you when you refused to sell your grandmother's jewellery. Bill couldn't come up with the money he owed after a deal went wrong. Then he procured the ten thousand your father left you personally in his will and that kept the Morrisons quiet for a while.'

'The swine!' Laura gripped the chair arm in rage. 'I... I thought that money was safely in my bank. It was my escape route if I ever left him. I don't mind admitting to you, Andrew, I was about to use it.'

Andrew Macarthur made a sympathetic sound then went on with his distasteful news. 'Bill got himself out of that jam but promptly put himself into another. He over-committed himself on a housing project which it was rumoured the government was going to build. He borrowed twenty-five thousand pounds from the Morrison brothers but the government decided to build somewhere else. And now that Bill's dead, the Morrisons have pulled the plug. They want their money back and so do several other major creditors. I'm sorry to tell you this, Laura, but this will mean the company will go bankrupt. By the time the receiver's finished, there won't be a penny left. I thought I ought to tell you now, Laura. I was afraid you might commit yourself to selling the cottage or something, which might not be wise in the circumstances. Laura, are you still there?'

Laura felt numb, in the way she would have done if she had buried a husband today whom she'd loved. She had lost something very dear to her after all, the company her father had built up from nothing, which he had wanted her and the grandchildren he'd hoped she'd give him to inherit, the company which he had entrusted Bill to look after for her lifetime needs.

She took a deep breath. 'G-go on, Andrew.'

'I've done some figures for you, Laura. By the time the Morrison brothers are paid off, and they've got everything wrapped up legally, and the other commitments are met, all that you have left is your grandmother's jewellery, a few hundred pounds in a bank account which Bill didn't touch, and his cottage in the village which he didn't put up as security. At least you have something to tide you over with for a while.' Andrew's voice was echoing with regret and concern. 'Laura, are you still going to travel back now? Shall I meet you somewhere? Would you like me to come down and collect you?'

'No, no. Listen, Andrew. I need a few minutes to think things over. Can I ring you back in about half an hour?'

Laura put the receiver down and sat very still. The numbness began to wear off to be replaced by a strange and terrible anger which was seeping into every part of her body. Bill had unexpectedly changed her future for a second time. He had robbed her of her inheritance, the company which he had cockily called his own for over two years, his prize acquisition, his undeserved reward for clawing himself up from nothing. And now another sensation was assailing her; because there was no company left for her to run, she was freer from Bill than when his body had been lowered into the village dirt. Tears of bitterness and, for a moment, a sense of peace mixed together and ran down her face.

When her tears stopped, she felt drained, rather fearful and a little excited. Apart from a few friends, she was all alone in the world and somehow she had to make a new life for herself.

She became aware of the voices in the kitchen. What would Daisy Tamblyn say to what her precious Billy had done? Laura crept to the kitchen door and was about to go in but hesitated over something she overheard.

'I know what Billy was like, Bunty. I loved him dearly, but I won't hide behind pleasant memories and not admit his bad points as well, specially to you. He must have led that poor young woman in there a dog's life. No wonder she didn't want to come to the hall and wants to go straight back home. Who would blame her if they knew the truth?'

Home. Laura didn't have a home now, except for the one where she'd eaten Bill's favourite biscuits. She kept her ear to the door. So Bill's aunt knew his real character.

'He could be cruel even as a small boy,' Bunty agreed. 'Just like his father. William Lean was a cruel devil and no mistake. He deserved his sticky end.'

William Lean? Laura gulped back a sudden cry. Had Bill known this? Bill's father had been called Ron Jennings. He had worked as a groom for William Lean. She forced herself not to go charging into Daisy's kitchen and ask what Bunty Buzza had meant. William Lean had been the local big landowner, a tyrant according to Bill's account. He had been Harry Lean's father. Bill had been dark and similarly built to Harry Lean. Could the amused-looking man at the funeral be Bill's half-brother? There was no facial resemblance. Bill had been bull-necked, his teeth had been crooked, his skin sallow, eyes intense, his eyebrows had met in the middle over heavy brows. His pale eyes had stared from the thick glasses he'd worn for reading.

''Tis no wonder Billy turned out like he did,' Daisy said sadly. 'It wasn't really his fault.'

Not his fault? Laura fumed. For being callous, manipulative and unforgiving?

'S'pose we shouldn't be surprised that Spencer Jeffries didn't come to the funeral.' Bunty was speaking. 'He and Bill hated each other, and Spencer had good reason, too, if you don't mind me saying now we're speaking so plain.'

Who was Spencer Jeffries? This was the second time his name had been mentioned. If he hated Bill, then Laura wanted to meet him, they had something in common. Laura was suddenly curious about the villagers, who in the main seemed to hero-worship her late husband. Yet despite her love for her nephew, Daisy admitted his faults to her friend and confidante. Why did these ordinary people love and revere Bill so much? True, he had given them money, her father's money and part of her squandered inheritance. It had built the village hall, it had paid for the chains that had been put round the war memorial she had passed by in the churchyard, it had supplied a generous donation towards the church organ fund even though Bill had rarely stepped inside the church. He had obviously been different when among the people of Kilgarthen.

Laura felt shaken by the double revelation, that Bill had bankrupted the company and that he'd been fathered by someone other than Daisy's sister's husband. After several days of feeling nothing over Bill's death, her newfound freedom and the depth of her various and complicated feelings overwhelmed her. She didn't feel like returning to London, she couldn't face the long journey alone so soon. There was nothing she could do for her father's company that Andrew Macarthur couldn't do anyway.

She considered staying in the village overnight, and even a day or two longer. She could try to learn something more about Bill, then perhaps she could purge her soul of some of the effects of his cruelty, free herself from the feelings of bitterness for her lost years as his wife when he'd made her feel worthless, less than a human being. She had no idea what her future might hold, but learning something about Bill's past might make it easier to begin afresh.

Chapter 2

Laura tapped on the kitchen door and went inside. The two women were sitting in small comfortable armchairs either side of a cream-coloured range in the fireplace. The kitchen was warm and they were a cosy sight. Laura felt a pang of loneliness. She'd thought Bill's tales of village life were quaint but he had known the comfort of belonging to a close-knit community. Was that the reason he had spent so many weekends here? The two women were smoking and hastily stubbed out their cigarettes.

'I've decided to stay in Kilgarthen overnight,' Laura told Daisy and Bunty, raising her chin in challenge.

Daisy smiled kindly and put her chubby hands together, 'Oh, we're delighted, aren't we, Bunty?'

'Yes, indeed,' Bunty answered emphatically. She took off her winged glasses and polished them on a towel hanging on a nearby hook but she was gazing at Laura keenly.

'I was wondering,' Laura said, feeling awkward, 'do you think the villagers will be offended if I go to the hall? I feel awful about leaving the churchyard so suddenly. You see, I was so upset, and not knowing anyone here...' She thought the best way to find out more about the side of Bill she didn't know was to lie. Daisy and Bunty were taken in. They might have known his true nature but they accepted that she'd loved Bill like they had and was grieving over him.

She made a quick return telephone call to Andrew Macarthur, which Daisy would not allow her to pay for, then the three women set off down the hill. The sky was overcast and the wind was picking up. It was bitingly cold.

Laura wasn't embarrassed by the sudden turn of heads and the hum of shocked whispers her unexpected arrival caused in the hall, the 'Bill Jennings Hall' she read on a brass plaque over the door on her way in. The people inside were proud of the building, a good size thanks to its benefactor's generosity. It was strongly constructed to withstand the harsh weather coming off the moor behind it.

'Mrs Jennings has decided to join us after all,' Daisy chirped up in the hush the mourners had lapsed into. 'She was too upset before and needed to go to Bill's cottage to compose herself.'

Laura realised she was confronting a variety of personalities. Some people genuinely offered her their sympathy, others were ingratiating as if she was some sort of celebrity, probably hoping she would keep up Bill's tradition of spending money in the village. Those who'd made unkind remarks about her were unforgiving and looked away.

Laura looked for the people she had noticed at the graveside and they were all here except for Marianne Roach. A tall, thin woman with a high bosom and wearing a severe straw hat over an iron-grey bun bore down on her and Daisy whispered to Laura that she was about to meet the village gossip, Ada Prisk.

'Such a terrible tragedy, such a loss to the village, Mrs Jennings.' Ada Prisk had a sharp, grating voice and looked Laura straight in the eye. 'What will you be doing with the cottage? You could rent it to someone local. We're a bit remote here for holidaymakers, although we get some who like to go pony trekking over the moor, and last year we had a family down for their holiday from Liverpool whose kiddies had been evacuated down here. We don't want any foreigners living here among us.'

'I hardly think Mrs Jennings wants to think about things like that now, Mrs Prisk,' Daisy said grittily, taking Laura's arm and steering her away. 'If you'll excuse us…'

Laura smiled at Daisy. She was a comfortable person to be with and Laura sensed she felt loyalty towards her. 'Call me Laura.'

'Oh, yes, that will be nice. If you like, call me Aunty Daisy. Now, my dear, from what I can see, not many people have gone home yet, which is good. Perhaps you'd like to be introduced to a few people.'

A number of the mourners were looking at her with something approaching reverence and Laura realised she must appear a bit of a lady to them. But not Mike Penhaligon. He held out his large warm hand and shook hers enthusiastically. From Bill she knew he was Cornish but not a born 'n' bred villager and she took to him at once. He had a friendly face with twinkling pale eyes, a bumpy forehead, broad nose and red cheeks.

'Come to the pub tonight, Mrs Jennings. We're seeing Bill off with a drop of good brandy.' He grinned, making his brown whiskers crawl up his florid face. 'There'll be a good turn-out.'

'Leave her be, Mike.' Pat Penhaligon laughed kindly as she brought Laura a cup of tea and a plate of food. She was small and neat and looked at her big jovial husband adoringly. 'He isn't happy 'less he's got a drink in your hand, gets you a little bit merry and singing your head off.'

'It sounds good, Mrs Penhaligon, but I don't know about coming to the pub tonight. I'll have to think about it. I want to spend some time with Aunty Daisy.' To Laura's surprise it was the easiest thing in the world to slip into calling her Aunty Daisy.

'She'd love a drop of drink.' Mike roared with laughter, wiggling his whiskers about. 'Bring her along too!'

'Quieter, Mike,' Pat scolded. 'You're at a funeral, remember.'

'The vicar'll come,' Mike asserted, nodding as he pictured the scene. 'He's a good'un for an up-country vicar. Lead the singing 'n' all, he will.'

Pat made a 'what can I do with him' face at Laura. 'It's men only,' she whispered. 'We women like to keep our decorum.'

As Laura tried to drink the tea, served in thick white crockery, Daisy introduced her to the Methodist minister, the Reverend Brian Endean. A short, portly, elderly man in dull clothes, he held her hand for some moments. 'Bill wasn't one of my flock but he wasn't slow to put his hand in his pocket when I put out an appeal for funds to repair one of the chapel windows. I didn't know him well because I don't live in the village but he was a well-liked and respected man. I know you're not chapel but if I can ever be a help to you, please do not hesitate to contact me.' The Reverend Endean seemed a little shy of her and he quickly withdrew after Laura thanked him but she sensed his sincerity.

The tea was stewed and lukewarm but Laura swallowed it down and devoured the two ham sandwiches, clotted-cream scone, a sausage roll and piece of Victoria sponge on her plate.

'Will you have a yeast bun?' Barbara Roach offered in her soft hesitant voice. 'Mrs Tamblyn made them. She always does the yeast buns for village occasions.'

'They look and smell delicious.' Laura felt a kindred spirit in this woman. Bill had told her that Cecil Roach was 'a sodding bully and led his poor cow of a wife a dog's life'. The woman was looking down at the wooden floor. Her colourless eyes had dark shadows under them, her nervous hands were constantly fidgeting. Laura nodded pleasantly. 'I think I've just enough room left for one.'

'It's wise to keep up your strength at a time like this,' Barbara Roach returned, her sad eyes brightening a little in her thin, pale face. 'I do offer you my deepest sympathy. Bill will be a great loss to the village. I'm Barbara Roach, by the way, wife of the village schoolmaster.'

Unlike the others whom she had met, Barbara Roach did not point out her family to Laura. Cecil Roach was talking, in a formal manner, to another man and had his back to her. It occurred to Laura that he'd had his back to her all the time.

'Thank you for your card of sympathy, Mrs Roach, it was comforting to receive it. Let me guess, you were responsible for the sponge cake.'

Barbara was delighted. 'Yes! Yes, I was. How did you guess? I do the sponge cakes for all the village events.'

'It takes a light hand to make a lighter than average sponge, Mrs Roach.' Laura could see she had won a friend for life. If Cecil Roach was as dour as his hard, lined face and stiff clothes suggested, and she recalled Bill telling her he'd been caned often by 'Old Cesspit', Barbara never received compliments on her baking from her husband.

Laura found herself monopolised by a group of villagers and Felicity Lean left before she could exchange more than a polite nod with her. Laura would like to have spoken to her. Did the elegant woman know that some people thought her husband was Bill's father? She heard Harry's pleasant tones filtering through from the doorway and a sudden hearty laugh. Evidently he had come back to collect his mother. Had Mrs Lean told her son the widow was staying in the village after all?

Finding herself temporarily left alone, Laura responded to a mellow voice at her elbow. It came from a calm-faced man with such gentle brown eyes that Laura felt an immediate flicker of warmth towards him. Aged about thirty, he was dressed in a rather shabby suit which fitted in only a few places on his wide shoulders and otherwise lean frame. His hair was dark and curly. The few lines around his softly formed mouth and strong nose were made, Laura guessed, from kind and gentle smiles.

He introduced himself quietly. 'I'm Ince Polkinghorne, Mrs Jennings. I'm a farm labourer. I work on Rosemerryn Farm for Spencer Jeffries. I knew your husband quite well. I pray that the Lord will bless your future.' He shook her hand in a warm grip.

'I don't recall my husband mentioning a Spencer Jeffries. Will you tell me something about him, Mr Polkinghorne?'

'Rosemerryn Farm has been in his family's hands for centuries. 'Tis about halfway between the village and the main road. The lane that runs past it is called Rosemerryn Lane. You passed the farm on your way into the village.' Ince looked deeply into Laura's eyes for a moment and she wondered if he, too, had known what Bill had been really like. Then he gave her the merest smile, it was shy and withdrawing and Laura realised he was about to depart. 'If you'll excuse me, Mrs Jennings, I have to get back to work.'

'What an unusual man,' Laura remarked to Daisy as she watched Ince leaving the hall.

'It's unusual for him to speak to anyone without they speaking to him first. He's very quiet, very religious and very nice.' Daisy looked at Laura pointedly. 'There are some nice people in the village.'

Laura admitted ruefully to herself that perhaps there were. 'He was telling me that he works for Spencer Jeffries on Rosemerryn Farm. What's this Spencer Jeffries like?'

'He's even quieter than Ince, practically a recluse.' Laura looked Daisy straight in the face. 'From what I've heard, he didn't like Bill.'

Daisy flushed and busied herself clearing up the tables. 'They fell out years ago, but Spencer's rarely seen in the village anyway. I thought I'd come to the cottage after this and light you a nice fire. Must be cold in there. Be freezing through the night.'

'I didn't notice before.' Laura thought about Bill's home, a place so personal and private to him that there was no evidence he had taken any of his conquests there. A lump rose and stuck in her throat. His belongings were there, perhaps things from his childhood, possessions which had given him the background he had chosen to stay in touch with. Now his body lay just up the road. She shivered, suddenly feeling rejected all over again and very lonely. She couldn't face a night on her own in Little Cot.

'Aunty Daisy...'

'Yes, dear?'

'I don't want to spend the night in Bill's cottage. Could I stay at your house tonight? I've brought an overnight bag and change of clothes with me so I don't need anything.'

Daisy put her arm round her waist and hugged her. She looked overcome with emotion and her eyes filled with tears. 'Course you can stay, Laura. I'd love to have you. I was going to suggest it anyway.'

For a fleeting moment Laura felt she would like to rest her head on Daisy's shoulder. She was her only source of comfort in an alien world. If Bill had had any redeeming features, they would have come through Daisy Tamblyn's influence.

—

Although exhausted by the long journey and wearied by her jumbled feelings and the revelations of Andrew Macarthur's telephone call, Laura couldn't sleep. It felt strange lying here in Daisy's spare room listening to the wind thrashing the moor, instead of being several miles back on the journey to London. Bill had told her about the moods of the moor, how it could be enchanting and peaceful one moment, savage and perilous the next, and the many sounds the wind made, beguilingly gentle and breezy, or shrieking through buildings and trees, moaning and wailing as if it was a form of tormented life. She'd been captivated by his tales when he'd courted her, fully expecting to come down to Cornwall with him to see and hear for herself and walk the moor with him. But he hadn't wanted her to come near his homeland. Now she could stay here as long as she liked. She could stay in his cottage, invite people there, speak to his friends, explore the lanes and moorland.

Her thoughts, triumphant, bitter, merging into spitefulness and wanting revenge, made her toss and turn into the early hours of the morning.

When she woke up it was pitch dark, the curtains were heavy and there were no street lights in the village. She lit the bedside lantern and picked up her wristwatch to see the time. It was nearly seven o'clock. She could hear Daisy downstairs, raking the ashes out of the range. It was a comforting sound, reminding Laura of how her mother used to get up early to prepare breakfast for her and her father, the only job her mother did before the daily help arrived. Laura had not shared a congenial breakfast table for the last five years. She put on her dressing gown and went down to the kitchen.

Daisy was dressed, her grey hair in curlers and hair net, humming softly and cutting bread at the table. 'Good morning, dear. Hope you slept well. You warm enough?'

'Yes, thank you.' Laura felt like a little girl; yesterday's feeling of superiority was all gone. She was on Kilgarthen home ground and although this woman was kindly and a relative by marriage, she was a virtual stranger. 'I, heard you moving about. I hope you don't mind me coming down like this. I'm not in your way?'

Daisy stuck a doorstep of white bread on a long, three-pronged toasting fork. 'You're welcome to do anything that takes your fancy, Laura. Make yourself comfy in Bunty's chair. The fire's picked up nicely, though it never gets cold in here overnight, the embers keep the room warm. What you need is a bit of looking after. Lost your mother many years ago, didn't you? Got no one left, but…'

'But you, Aunty Daisy?' Laura snuggled up in Bunty's chair with her feet curled under her. 'It's good of you to say that after I upset you yesterday. I am sorry.'

'It's you I was upset for.' Daisy angled the fork so it was wedged in the grill of the range to toast the bread.

Laura's eyes were on the embers and she watched the bread rapidly toast golden. She wished she could talk openly to Daisy about Bill. 'I would have liked to have met you before,' she said tentatively.

Daisy nodded. 'I knew it was Billy's decision not to bring you down here. I often said to him, "Why don't you bring that pretty young wife of yours down to stay? I'd love to meet her." I'd have thought he'd love to have showed you off to everyone, but there was a side to him that needed to be private.'

He might not have found it so easy to lord it about down here with me around, Laura thought bitterly.

'As you probably know,' Daisy went on, 'Billy's mother was my younger sister, Faith. I reared him when Faith died and I knew his ways better than anyone, except for you, of course, and I want you to think of me as flesh and blood. Bacon and eggs, toast and cereal? Just toast? Right then. That's ready now.' Daisy took the toast to the table and spread it thickly with creamy butter. She put a dollop of dark marmalade on the plate with a knife and passed it to Laura.

'I only ever saw one photograph of you,' Daisy said, pouring the tea, 'on your wedding day. I was some upset that he invited none of us from the village to your wedding. He said it was rushed, so we all thought you were...'

'Pregnant?'

Daisy's face wore an overcoat of embarrassment as she stabbed another doorstep of bread.

'Well, when no baby was mentioned, I asked Billy if he intended to start a family and he said, "No ruddy fear, I hate children." I told him off for saying that. I said, "I hope you're not giving Laura the runaround. I know what you can be like." He just laughed and said you had everything you needed.'

'I did,' Laura said bitterly. 'Except a loving husband and a baby.' She wondered if she'd gone too far and looked at Daisy for her reaction, but Daisy just shook her head sadly.

'I'm sorry, Laura. But it's no good dwelling on the past. You're still young, you're lovely and there's plenty of time to have a family.'

'After what I've been through,' Laura said, 'I don't ever want to get married again.' She wanted to ask Daisy about Bill's childhood but Daisy changed the subject.

'Look,' she said, 'I hope you won't be offended but I had an insurance out on Billy. I'd like you to have it to help pay for funeral expenses.'

Laura knew the money would help after Bill's elaborate funeral and her changed financial circumstances but she felt she couldn't take it from Daisy. She would have to cut into her small bank balance. 'There's no need for that,' she insisted. 'Everything has been taken care of.' Daisy might be disarmingly frank about Bill's character, but this wasn't the time to tell her he was a swindler too.

–

Later in the morning, wrapped up in a scarf and gloves and wearing warm lined boots borrowed from Daisy to offset the wind that only a barren sweep of moors could make so harsh, Laura strolled through the village. Unlike many other villages in Britain where dwellings and church were grouped round an ancient village green, a road ran through the middle of this one. Houses and cottages, a few of them charmingly thatched, were straggled about in roughly equal numbers either side of the road.

What she saw and heard today would help her make up her mind about how long she would stay here. She avoided the churchyard and its new mound of earth. She walked over to admire the communal pump which she had noticed yesterday. It was used regularly because few dwellings here had piped water. It was made of ornate cast iron and stood on a granite mount. Its water was crystal clear and pure – if it hadn't been so cold Laura would have pumped up some water and drunk it.

She stopped again outside the Tremewan Arms and realised with a start that it had Christmas lights and decorations up at the windows. Was it so near the end of the year already?

Pat Penhaligon, who was returning laden with shopping bags from Daisy's shop, hailed her. 'See you're dressed up nice and warm. Be careful if you go on the moor,' she said as she dumped her shopping in the pub doorway and took a key out of her coat to unlock the cellar door – the pub was awaiting a delivery. 'It can be very dangerous. Don't you go out there on your own.'

'Bring the maid in here!' bellowed Mike Penhaligon, poking his head through a window. 'A tot of rum in a mug of hot milk is what she needs on a day like this. 'Tis what we always have for elevenses in winter.'

Laura smiled and glanced at her watch. 'It's a bit early for elevenses.'

''Tis never too early for he,' Pat laughed, taking Laura's arm and leading her inside.

It was warm inside the pub with a pleasant olde worlde atmosphere; the lingering smells of alcohol and tobacco weren't as strong as in Laura's local drinking places. Two large oil lamps stood either end of the bar top and more were suspended from the beams; candles set in old spirit bottles covered in graying trickles of wax sat on every table. Holly, ivy and mistletoe were extravagantly draped everywhere.

Laura thought the pub would be a good place to start finding out something about Bill. The Penhaligons were friendly people. They might not have lived in Kilgarthen as long as most of the villagers but they would probably know all the gossip.

'Did you know Bill well?' she asked when she was cradling her rum and milk in her hands.

'Not really,' Mike said, peering closely at a glass he was polishing behind the bar. 'He'd left the village a couple of years before me 'n' Pat took over the pub. Little Cot stayed empty until Bill got on and bought it off the Leans, then he did it up bit by bit, did a lot of the work himself.' He picked up another glass. 'He loved that little place, wouldn't let hardly anyone step over the doorstep. 'Twas all his and his alone, he used to say. He came into the pub with Daisy most nights he was here. Sometimes he had a drop too much but usually he behaved like a real gent. Could be a miserable bugger though, if you ask me.'

'Mike,' Pat scolded.

'It's all right,' Laura said. 'Bill had his moods. Little Cot was owned by the Leans, you say?'

'They used to be the big money round here then, not so much now. They only have a big house and stables on the edge of the moors left now. Hawksmoor House, it's called, be worth taking a look at it. Felicity Lean's a charming woman, don't think she'd mind you looking round.'

'Harry certainly wouldn't,' Pat said. 'He's got an eye for a pretty face.'

Mike looked down at Laura's feet, let his eyes ride up to her waist, then winked and gave his great head a jaunty toss. 'He's like me, a leg man.'

'Mike!'

'I don't mind, Pat,' Laura smiled.

'See, she's got the measure of you already,' Pat laughed at her husband.

Laura sipped her hot drink. 'I met Harry Lean yesterday. I noticed he only went to the village hall after the funeral to pick up his mother.'

'Harry and Bill never got along, so we've heard. Bill went to the village school and Harry to boarding school but they fought like cat and dog in the holidays, apparently. Bill resented being poor and living in a tied cottage – well, that's what we reckon, reading between the lines. People round here were proud of Bill Jennings leaving the village and getting on so well, but then you probably know that.' Mike looked at Laura curiously and she knew he'd like to ask her some questions too. All the villagers must be curious why she had never come among them until yesterday.

Laura didn't want to talk about herself. 'Aunty Daisy said Bill didn't get along with a man called Spencer Jeffries either.'

'That's a different story altogether. They wouldn't have been friends anyway. Spencer Jeffries is about ten years older than Bill was.'

'Oh, I was picturing three boys of the same age growing up at the same time.'

Laura didn't learn anything else that was enlightening from the Penhaligons and after a convivial half-hour braced herself to face the cold again. She walked up and down the village, slipping into the few short side roads, but no one else seemed eager to be out in the cold morning air except for an elderly man in a flat cap, greatcoat and gaiters, wearing a chestful of medal ribbons and walking a Jack Russell.

'The name's Johnny Prouse,' the man said, pointing proudly to his medal ribbons. 'Late of the King's Navy in the Great War, having been sailor on a string of important ships, and this is Admiral my faithful companion. Didn't get a chance to speak to 'ee yesterday, Mrs Jennings. Had to get back home for Admiral. He's some old now, nearly fourteen year, and has got a wheezy chest.'

Admiral was well trained and not on a lead but eager to carry on with his walk, so the old sailor bid Laura good morning. If Johnny Prouse patronised the Tremewan Arms, she thought it likely a pint or two would secure something of what she wanted to know.

As she approached the school, she could hear children singing. It was a small, bleak building and the two playgrounds, one for the boys, one for the girls, were grey with a few forlorn leaves blowing around them. The song inside had a merry tune but the singing sounded regimented.

Moving on to the schoolmaster's house which stood on the other side of a high dividing wall, she saw white sheets and pillowcases flapping on the washing line. No one else had put washing out in the bitterly cold weather with the darkening sky threatening a shower of rain. Having lived under Bill's strict regime and knowing Cecil Roach's hard reputation, Laura wondered if Barbara had a choice in the matter. She could well imagine Cecil baulking at having washing drying in front of the kitchen fire. She noticed the three white beehives from which Bill had stolen honey as a child.

Laura was getting colder but wanted to seek out more information about Bill before going back to the shop for the midday meal. It was only ten thirty. Daisy had said she could borrow her bicycle and Laura decided to explore the lanes. It made sense to have a look at Hawksmoor House and hopefully meet the sophisticated Felicity

Lean, then perhaps she'd find out why there was no love lost between Harry and Bill. But she was more curious to learn something about this man Spencer Jeffries, and soon she was riding along the lane that led to Rosemerryn Farm.

Chapter 3

Buffeted by strong winds tearing across the exposed land, Laura slowly cycled the narrow twisting lanes which were splashed with cow dung and mud from cart wheels. There was rugged granite upland on all sides. Hawk's Tor rose steeply on part of the moor called Hawkstor Downs. It provided a rugged backdrop to the village.

She passed pathways and tracks leading off from the lane. One wide track had a signpost sticking out of the hedge, a weathered piece of wood with Tregorlan Farm painted on it in faded black letters. Laura pedalled on, unsure if she was travelling along the part of road the locals called Rosemerryn Lane yet, looking for a signpost that would disclose the location of Rosemerryn Farm.

She had to pull into gateways and laybys three times to allow other vehicles to pass by, including the pony and jingle driven by the curious old woman in the cloak and bonnet she'd seen at the telephone box, who acknowledged her with a curt nod. The third time was for Ince Polkinghorne on a horse and cart and she responded to the smile on his peaceful face. He pulled up and jumped down to speak to her.

'Good morning, Mrs Jennings. So you've changed your mind about staying on in the village.'

'I became curious about the place Bill loved so much, Mr Polkinghorne,' she replied. 'I don't remember the road being this narrow yesterday – the hearse didn't have to pull in for other traffic once.' A sudden gust of wind smacked at her face, bearing with it tiny freezing raindrops, and she thought she was going to lose her balance. Ince put out a hand to steady her.

'They would have pulled in for the hearse and stayed there until they were sure all the mourners had passed by,' Ince said, smiling lightly. 'The name's Ince, by the way, no one calls me Mr Polk-inghorne.'

'It's an unusual name – Ince,' Laura said, turning up her collar and wanting to linger and chat to this quiet, unassuming man. She was also hoping for a hint as to how far it was to Rosemerryn Farm.

'It was my mother's maiden name. I would have preferred a good solid Biblical name like Daniel or Joshua, but there it is.' He looked at Laura closely for a moment, that same deep gaze he'd given her in the village hall yesterday as if he wanted to convey something to her without words. 'Some things we can't help.'

'No, I suppose not. You're not working in the farmyard today then?'

'No, I'm off to put fodder down in the fields. The cows in calf in particular need some extra help in winter.'

She thought it too forward to ask if his boss was at home; Ince would wonder why she wanted to meet him and she didn't really know herself now. She looked up at the dark grey sky. 'Do you think we're about to have a shower of rain?'

He shook his head. 'Probably just a few drops this morning but it'll tip down this afternoon.'

'That's good. I don't want to turn back yet.'

'All the same, I shouldn't go too far from the village, Mrs Jennings. You might get lost.'

'I'll take your advice, Ince. Well, I'd better let you get on with your work.' She hadn't known this man for long but felt he was one person she wanted to be on friendly terms with. 'Please, call me Laura.'

He smiled and nodded, got back on the cart and waved to her before moving off. Laura felt some of the bitterness and anger melting away from her heart. She had met some very kind people since the funeral. All these people had known Bill, in some ways probably better than she had. She realised that she was seeking a way into Bill's heart and mind. He still had a hold over her and she wanted to break it; perhaps most of all she wanted to find out if it was her fault that he had been so horrible to her.

When Laura reached the end of the long lane, she realised she must have passed the turning to Rosemerryn Farm. Since meeting Ince she had noticed only one turning that was more than a path; that must have been the way to the farm. She cycled back. If she found the farm she'd say she wanted to buy some eggs or something; having reminded herself that Daisy had said Spencer Jeffries was a recluse and he and Bill had hated each other, she was losing her confidence.

She found the opening again and turned down it to find herself bumping over a muddy track with high hedges on either side. Her legs and the bike were soon hopelessly splashed. Why didn't these farmers tarmac the way to their farms?

Like all moorland farms, Rosemerryn Farm was carefully sited in a natural dip and sheltered by tall wind-vexed trees and bushes. Laura dismounted and leaned the bike against a granite stone wall, her eyes sweeping round the yard as she picked her way over the cobblestones. Her overriding impression was that everywhere was extremely muddy; a glance at her boots and she despaired of ever getting them really clean again.

Bill had told her a lot about the local farms and this one owned everything she was expecting to see, barns, outhouses and hayricks, a pigsty, a few scratching chickens, granite animal troughs, spare granite gateposts, discarded horse implements, an old corn binder, a roller, a heap of mangolds and turnips, and a plough. She couldn't see the cow shed but wrinkled her nose at the strong steamy smell of the dung heap that would be beside it. In the middle of the yard was the farmer's most prized possession, vital to his work, a grey Ferguson tractor. The wheels were caked with mud but the bodywork was well cared for; a can of paraffin, a tool box and bundle of rags were lying beside the vehicle ready for some maintenance work. It was parked on a reasonably clean part of the cobbles, close to a somewhat neglected Ford saloon.

Hearing a sudden noise, which she first thought was a wail of the wind, she noticed a big black horse, which had whinnied to her in greeting, looking over the stone wall of a field. Laura made her way to the horse and stroked its splendid head. The horse was doubtless ridden to inspect the herd of cattle; Laura knew that cattle used to this sort of herding would ignore anyone trying to drive them on foot if they wandered into the lanes. After several moments she left the horse for the farmhouse in search of its master.

She knocked on the door of what looked like a very old but well-kept building and conjured up a picture of the interior of the house as rustic and cosy. She was standing inside a wide sheltered porch with healthy potted plants on shelves either side of her. She thought she heard a movement inside but after several moments no one had answered. Must be out working in the fields, she thought, or perhaps in one of the outbuildings.

She rounded the house and saw a little girl riding a tricycle in the yard. Laura stopped in her tracks and stared, utterly captivated. She had never seen a more beautiful child. Long wispy curls of white-gold hair drifted down her slender back from her red wool hat. Her skin was honey-toned and flawless, her small features perfectly proportioned in a delicate heart-shaped face. Her eyes shone like sparkling blue gems as she pedalled furiously in a wide circle.

Laura held her breath. She was bewitched. She had dreamed of having a child like this one.

'Hello,' she said softly.

The girl was startled by her voice and fell off the tricycle. Shocked at what she had done, Laura rushed to her and helped her to her feet. 'Oh, I'm so sorry. Did I frighten you? Are you hurt?'

The girl clambered quickly to her feet. Then she smiled so broadly, impishly crinkling up her face, that Laura wanted to gather her up in her arms and kiss her cheeks. 'I'm tough, you know,' she said pertly, keeping one eye narrowed.

'Are you, darling? I hope your trike isn't damaged.'

'Daddy will mend it,' the girl said brightly, then looked over her red and blue tricycle. 'No, it's not hurt, just a little scratch, but that doesn't matter. Daddy's got lots of scratches on his tractor.'

'I'm Laura. Will you tell me your name?'

'I'm Vicki. Have you come to see about me going to school? I'll be five soon and old enough to go to school,' Vicki said proudly. Her voice was a pleasure to listen to, clear and tinkling.

'No, Vicki, I'm not connected to the school. I'm staying in the village for a while. Do you live here, on the farm?'

'Course I do. Are you a holidaymaker?'

Laura wanted to stay and talk to this little beauty. She lowered herself down and put her hands gently on Vicki's waist. 'Do you know the lady in the shop? She's my Aunty Daisy.'

'She's a nice lady. She gives me an extra sweetie when Daddy buys me dolly mixtures.'

'Who's your daddy?'

'I am,' came a gruff voice almost on top of them. 'Take your hands off my daughter.'

Laura turned to face a man with the coldest eyes she had ever seen, yet when he smiled at Vicki they were full of gentleness.

'Run along inside, pipkin,' he said to Vicki. 'I'll see what the lady wants.'

'Goodbye, Laura.'

Laura looked from the man to his daughter. 'Goodbye, Vicki. I'm very pleased to have met you.'

Vicki skipped happily to the back door, sat down just inside it and pulled off her boots. Laura couldn't take her eyes off her and returned the wave she gave before disappearing inside the house.

'Well, what do you want?' Vicki's father asked her, folding his arms and standing across the doorway as if he was guarding his home and family. 'Are you lost?'

'No, no,' Laura blustered, her eyes now rooted on the man who had passed on his looks to his daughter. 'I, um, thought you might have some eggs for sale.'

'Did you now?' he asked suspiciously, his lower lip twisting into a sneer. 'I only sell my eggs to the village shop. Ask your late husband's aunt for a tray to take back to London with you.' As far as he was concerned, his business with her was over and he made to follow his daughter.

'You know who I am then?' Laura challenged him, raising her voice to detain him, angry at his bluntness. 'How?'

He looked at her disparagingly. 'Dressed like that in a farmyard? Who else would you be?'

'Are you Spencer Jeffries?'

'That's none of your business. Leave now. I don't like people on my property and I don't like strangers talking to my daughter.'

'I meant her no harm,' Laura persisted stubbornly. 'She's a charming little girl. She obviously didn't get her good manners from you!' Laura knew she had no right to be here or to say what she just had, but this man made her see red.

He looked at her gravely for a moment, then gave a high-pitched whistle which made her jump. A big scruffy border collie ran round from the side of the farmhouse and took up a menacing stance in front of her. 'If you don't go now, Barney will make sure you will.'

'You'd set your dog on me? I only wanted—'

'Make sure she goes, Barney,' he grunted and with that he went indoors.

-

'Spencer Jeffries is the rudest man in the world,' Laura complained to Daisy when they were sitting across the dinner table.

Daisy looked up in surprise from her bowl of oxtail soup. 'You've met Spencer?'

'I have if he's a tall, fair-haired man with a gorgeous little daughter called Vicki,' Laura admitted guiltily. 'I was curious about him and drove to his farm.'

'So that's why you came back so muddy,' Daisy said, breaking off a piece of fresh crusty bread. 'What did you want to see him for?'

'I told you, I was curious. His name kept coming up yesterday and he sounded rather mysterious. I suppose I was looking for something to take my mind off burying Bill and—' She stopped there. She was still reluctant to tell Daisy what Bill had done to the company. It would upset her so soon after his funeral. Perhaps she never would.

Daisy let out a girlish giggle. 'I bet Spencer sent you away with a flea in your ear.'

'He did,' Laura said crossly. 'He threatened to set his dog on me. He whistled to fetch the lumbering great brute into the yard and all the while I was getting back on the bike I was dreading the sound of another whistle to send the dog after me to tear my leg off. It followed me all the way back to the lane,' she added indignantly.

Daisy laughed, much amused. 'Spencer'd never go that far. And Barney wouldn't harm you.'

Laura looked peevishly across the table. 'You seem very friendly with the man.'

'There's a special bond between me and Spencer. I delivered Vicki. Natalie was in the shop that day, only seven months gone, when she suddenly went into labour. She thought she'd been having wind all day. Anyway, I brought her in here and because she had problems and was s'posed to go into hospital I phoned for the ambulance, but we'd had snow and the ambulance had trouble getting through. It wasn't long 'fore things were speeding up and I had to get Natalie upstairs. I banged on the wall for Bunty and between us we calmed Natalie down and I delivered little Vicki. What a day that was. Bunty was panicking – she's never married and has no children but I've had three, they live all over the world now, and things came natural to me.

'The birth was straightforward but with Vicki coming so early, that was the worrying bit. She were so tiny. I remembered what my old midwife had said once and I wrapped her up in cotton wool and towels and put her in a shoe box. By this time Spencer had come searching for Natalie. I'll never forget the look on his face when he first saw Vicki. He's adored her ever since. She's just like him to look at, though his hair's darker and his eyes are grey and not blue. She's got Natalie's eyes. When the ambulance finally got through, Natalie and Vicki were rushed to hospital. Spencer was so grateful to me and Bunty, and we've got on well ever since.'

'I didn't meet Natalie, Vicki's mother,' Laura said, returning to her soup, now gone cold after the long tale.

Daisy looked down mournfully at her plate and sniffed back tears. 'She… she died three days after the birth.'

'Oh no! What a sad end to the story.'

'Spencer took Vicki home when she was strong enough and has practically brought her up single-handed. Most of the help he has comes from Ince. We all offered, of course, and she usually stays here a few hours each day during the hay making, but for the most part that little girl's had the love of two doting men.'

'I don't think I've seen anyone as beautiful as Vicki Jeffries,' Laura said wistfully. 'I wish I could have spoken to her for longer. Her father will miss her when she starts school.'

'Be good for her, though,' Daisy said, taking things off the table.

'It doesn't explain why he's so aggressive.'

'He's been like that since Natalie died. He always did keep himself to himself, but now he's over-possessive and over-protective of Vicki. He adored Natalie, you see. Without Vicki I think he would have gone to pieces. He's probably afraid of losing her too.'

He should think himself lucky he's got someone he's afraid of losing, Laura thought bitterly. She said, 'Why did he and Bill fall out? It was obvious he despised me because I'm Bill's widow.'

'I don't know, Laura,' Daisy mumbled, looking over her shoulder as if there was something that needed attending to on the range. 'But with Billy lying down the road, what does it matter now? What would you like for afters? I've got some yeast buns and cake left from the funeral.' Laura frowned. Why was Daisy being evasive? While she was fetching the cake tin, the telephone rang and Laura went into the sitting room to answer it. Andrew Macarthur was on the other end of the line.

'Laura, are you starting for home today?'

Without hesitating, Laura found herself saying, 'No.'

'You're not?' Andrew sounded surprised.

When Laura had arrived in Kilgarthen yesterday she thought she'd hate Bill's home village. But she was beginning to find Kilgarthen interesting and although Bill was buried here she couldn't bear to go home and get involved in the mess he had left of her father's company; she would feel his presence there more than here. She knew she could go to friends in London, there were some who would be glad to have her until things were settled, but she wanted to stay with the kind-hearted woman who in a few short hours she had come to call Aunty Daisy – and she couldn't get the shining little face of Vicki Jeffries out of her mind.

34

'You can see to everything, can't you, Andrew?'

'Yes, of course, if that's what you want. I thought you might like to go over things with me. You were your father's personal assistant before you married.'

'Do you think we can salvage anything?'

'No, the bank won't co-operate. Bill's pulled too many fast ones over the years and the business world's lost confidence in the company.'

'In that case I'd rather not pick over the bones. Do what you have to, Andrew. At least I have the comfort of knowing I'm not destitute and when I'm ready to face the world again I'm sure I can get a job. I haven't forgotten what I learned with Dad.'

'Are you hiding away down there, Laura?' Andrew asked sternly.

'Of course not,' she said emphatically. Andrew was a very close friend but he wouldn't understand why she wanted to stay here.

'Are you sure you're doing the right thing?' This was Andrew the friend, not the family solicitor speaking now. 'I didn't think you'd want to stay down there with...'

'Bill buried here?'

'Yes. You were upset, of course, but when you left here you said you couldn't wait to get rid of him, to leave him there. You've had quite a change of heart.'

Andrew Macarthur had disliked and distrusted Bill, and Bill had hated Andrew. There had been many clashes between them over the years. Because Andrew was a young, attractive, somewhat debonair man who had served his country with distinction during the war, Bill had been jealous of his friendship with Laura.

'It isn't because he's got a hold over me from the grave, Andrew,' she replied, although this wasn't strictly true.

She could tell by a sigh that he wasn't convinced. 'What then?' he asked.

'I don't know. Bill's aunty has been so kind and... I can't explain it really. Look, I'll ring you in a couple of days.'

'That was my solicitor again,' Laura told Daisy as they tucked into yeast buns while sitting either side of the fireplace.

'Worried about you, is he, dear?'

'Yes. He wanted to know when I'm going back to London.'

Daisy set her brown eyes on her shrewdly. 'What did you tell him?'

'I told him I'd ring him in a couple of days.'

'Good. I'm glad you're not going yet, Laura. I hope you're going to stay with me. You're very welcome.'

'Thank you. That's very kind of you. I'd rather have some company at the moment. I will go down to Bill's cottage and sort out his things. There must be some keepsakes you'd like.' Laura gathered up the crumbs in her lap. 'You can talk to me about Bill, you know. I want to leam about his life here.'

'That your main reason for staying here then?'

'Yes. Bill was so horrible to me. I want to know why the people here thought so much of him. I suppose it's obvious really. Bill did well for himself and people revel in reflected glory and he was very generous to the village which he never forgot, and—'

'I shouldn't go asking too many questions if I were you,' Daisy blurted out. 'Like I said before, 'tis best to let sleeping dogs lie.'

Daisy looked so fierce that Laura was silenced. Was there something more to be found out about Bill Jennings than his being Harry Lean's half-brother?

–

When Laura put her coat on to take another walk through the village, Daisy climbed up on a chair in front of a built-in cupboard and took out a square locked box. She carried the box upstairs. Taking the bottom drawer completely out of her dressing table, she put the box in the space on the floor. She put the drawer back in and when she straightened up she saw her reflection in the mirror. It was filled with guilt.

Chapter 4

Vicki Jeffries was sitting in her nightie, slippers and dressing gown crayoning on the kitchen table. Ince was watching her, his sleeves rolled up, exposing his long, muscled arms which were resting on the table. Spencer was making her night-time cocoa. This sort of scene could be found nearly every night on Rosemerryn Farm.

'Didn't you like that lady this morning, Daddy?' Vicki suddenly piped up, her face puckered with concentration as she coloured vigorously.

'What lady?' Ince got in first.

Spencer poured hot milk on the cocoa. 'Do you want a biscuit with this, pipkin? She's talking about Mrs Bill Jennings,' he told Ince with a look of distaste on his handsome face.

'Mrs Jennings? What was she doing here?' Ince demanded.

'Nosing around.'

Vicki put her hands on her hips and said aggrievedly, 'No, thank you, I don't want a biscuit. I was talking first. I asked you a question, Daddy.'

Spencer fondly ruffled her silky hair. 'She was a stranger, pipkin, and I don't like strangers suddenly turning up on the farm. Put your crayons away and drink your cocoa. It's way past your bedtime.'

Vicki made a long face and gathered up her crayons and pencils and dropped them into their box. 'She had a face like a fairy princess and long golden hair. Look, I've drawn a picture of her.'

Ince turned the picture round to him. 'So that's who this is.' The drawing consisted of a matchstick woman in a brown coat and blue skirt, the colours Laura had been wearing that morning, and long straight yellow hair, standing beside Vicki's tricycle. 'I thought it didn't look like you.'

'I'd like to be like her when I grow up,' Vicki said, pushing her box of colours away.

'No, you wouldn't,' Spencer said sharply, picking her up and carrying her to a chair by the hearth and sitting her on his lap. He passed her the cocoa. 'Drink up before it gets cold.' He kept his eyes on his daughter's back. Ince was staring at him and he knew he would get a ticking off from his close friend and farmhand when Vicki was tucked up in bed.

'Mrs Miller said that lady who was here this morning is beautiful,' Vicki remarked before putting her full red lips to the mug. She sipped and swallowed. The two men watched her, they were fascinated by everything she did. 'She told me her name was Laura.'

'Maybe she did,' Spencer said, breathing out heavily. He kissed the back of Vicki's head. 'But if you see her again you must call her Mrs Jennings.'

'Why?'

'Because for one thing I said so and for another it's good manners.'

Vicki twisted round to look at her father. 'Has she got bad manners then?'

'Get out of that one,' Ince murmured, turning his head so Vicki couldn't see him smiling.

Spencer grunted and reddened. Ince was going to have a field day with him. He was always exhorting him to be more sociable, less abrasive, more ready to turn the other cheek.

Ince had moved into the farmhouse when Natalie had died, to take more of the workload from Spencer so he could visit his daughter in hospital and then so he could give Vicki the care she needed when he brought her home. Spencer had been adamant he wanted no more help than what Ince and Joy Miller, the daily help he employed from the village, could provide. Spencer greatly respected Ince and would be lost without him.

Spencer moved about uncomfortably. He could curse Ince at times for making him feel needlessly guilty. 'It's your turn to put Vicki to bed, isn't it?' he asked on a soft note.

'Yes,' Ince said eagerly, holding his hands out to, Vicki. 'You finished, princess? When you've cleaned your teeth and I've read you a story, Daddy will kiss you goodnight.'

Vicki went upstairs happily with Ince, enjoying the alternate bedtime ritual she shared with the two men.

Joy Miller had left the ageing kitchen spick-and-span that morning, the furniture well polished, the ornaments and ormolu clock dusted on the high mantelshelf, the huge oak dresser tidy, the floor linoleum washed, mats brushed and put straight and Vicki's numerous toys packed up in the corner. Vicki had only wanted her drawing book tonight so everything was still tidy. Spencer washed up the supper dishes thinking about the ceiling-high Christmas tree he would get for Vicki, how he would take her into Bodmin to choose some new decorations, and he thought sadly that after Christmas his beloved little girl would be starting school.

He was ready to face Ince when he came downstairs. 'Don't go on at me, mate. I'm not in the mood.'

'It's not Laura Jennings' fault what her husband was like,' Ince said quietly. 'She seems a good sort of woman to me.'

'Don't tell me you've fallen for her pretty face?' Spencer returned, his voice edged in sarcasm.

Ince kept his usual calm. 'Vicki's said her prayers. She's waiting for her goodnight kiss.'

Spencer walked to the door that led to the hall. Before leaving the room, he stated, 'We can't all be as forgiving as you, Ince.'

–

Laura and Daisy went to the pub that evening and were immediately joined at their table by Harry Lean and asked what they'd like to drink. Laura ignored his smiles but accepted his offer, asking for a gin and orange, while Daisy had her 'usual', a milk stout.

'Cheers, Mrs Tamblyn, Mrs Jennings.' Harry raised his whisky and soda, seating himself with them without being invited. 'Nice to be drinking with you,' he said to Laura.

'Thank you, Mr Lean,' she returned, keeping her face straight. Harry Lean had the sort of smile that was all too easy to reciprocate. She thought if he wanted to get familiar with her he wouldn't take her recent widowhood into account.

'Shame about Bill,' he said, looking sympathetically at Daisy. 'We despised each other but it's terrible to die so young.' Then turning his dark eyes on Laura. 'And in such a terrible way.'

'Why didn't you like my husband?' Laura asked bluntly, looking Harry straight in the eye and making Daisy tut-tut.

'Class barrier, my dear,' Harry drawled, the corners of his thin wide mouth smirking.

Daisy turned her head away to show her disapproval at the turn of conversation, but Laura wasn't going to be put off 'In this day and age?'

'Naturally. What makes you think it's disappeared? It's very apparent in a small place like this.'

'Perhaps you didn't like your family property being sold off Mr Lean,' Laura said harshly. She wasn't taking Bill's side; she didn't like this cocky, self-assured, dark-haired young man and wanted to put him in his place.

Harry's eyes moved slowly up from his whisky glass and burned into hers, yet there was still that hint of amusement; he wasn't a man easily rattled. 'I've heard that your husband has done an excellent job of disposing of yours.'

Laura gasped and looked hastily at Daisy who jerked her head round. 'What's he talking about, Laura?'

'Something he knows nothing about!' Laura snapped at Harry.

'You might as well come clean with Aunty Daisy, my sweet. Word gets round a village faster than a summer gorse fire.' He got up and went to the bar and beckoned to Mike Penhaligon.

'What was he talking about, Laura?' Daisy demanded again. 'Whatever it was, it looks like he's telling Mike now.'

A red flush of anger coupled with embarrassment crept up Laura's neck. She could have got up and thumped Harry Lean between the shoulder blades. If her financial situation reached Ada Prisk's ears it would be all round the village in an hour. 'I didn't want you to know yet, so soon after the funeral. Bill has bankrupted the company. I'm sorry you've found out like this. You see Bill wasn't quite as—'

'I know,' Daisy said, sniffing into a handkerchief. 'I know what Bill was like. Has he left you penniless?'

'No, I've got some money, the cottage in the village and my grandmother's jewellery which is supposed to be worth a fortune.'

'I'm sorry, Laura.'

'It's all right, Aunty Daisy,' Laura said, slipping her hand into Daisy's. 'I've got you and I don't think Bill could have left me anything better.'

Daisy looked embarrassed, a little overcome and flattered. 'But you hardly know me, dear.'

'But I know you intimately, Aunty. Bill told me everything about you. What I'd like to know is how Harry Lean knows about the business.'

'Didn't you know? Harry's a local estate agent but he's got contacts in London.'

'So he would have heard about it on the grapevine,' Laura murmured. She shot a look filled with contempt at Harry's back as he shared a joke with Mike. 'I don't like him any more than Bill did. What a bighead!'

'Never mind him,' Daisy said firmly. 'I'm telling you something, Laura, and I'll have no argument on it. You're having the fifty pounds I had insured on Billy. I took it out when he left the village in case anything happened to him. Well, now it has, and it will go a long way to seeing him rest in peace without being a burden on you.'

Laura felt it would be selfish and insensitive to argue and she accepted the money with gratitude.

Johnny Prouse came in with Admiral and parked himself at their table and Laura and Daisy were treated to his Great War memories. After a couple of drinks his mind was sharp and his tongue well oiled. If Laura had been alone she would have picked his brains about the villagers of Kilgarthen, confident he would have spoken freely about Bill.

Others drifted in and out as the evening wore on, some from outside the village who liked the beer and friendly atmosphere. A man in his late fifties, built like an ox and wearing shabby clothes, came over to their table and introduced himself as Jacka Davey, owner of Tregorlan Farm. He offered his condolences and apologised for not being able to attend Bill's funeral, explaining that urgent work on the farm had prevented it. He looked acutely embarrassed and as soon as he had said his piece he took himself off to drink in a quiet corner. Daisy told her he was hard-working but had fallen on bad times.

The Reverend Kinsley Farrow popped in at nine o'clock. He was astonished to see Laura there.

'Mrs Jennings!' he exclaimed, picking up her hand and pumping it up and down. 'I do apologise. I had no idea you were still in the village. How are you? Is there anything I can do for you? You're not stranded or anything?' He sat down too and Pat Penhaligon brought him a half pint of mild.

'Aunty Daisy is looking after me, Vicar,' Laura assured him. 'I've decided to stay here in Bill's birthplace. I don't know for how long.'

'Splendid, splendid,' Kinsley said, sipping his ale and leaving a trail of froth over his upper lip.

He had an interesting face. Laura found herself studying it, moving her head in time with his quick movements. His clear-cut features were animated, his jaw looked as if it was constantly chomping, his expressive large eyes as if they were whirling pools of dark liquid. Laura realised she had taken no notice of him yesterday. If she hadn't seen him again she wouldn't have been able to describe one single feature about him. He was about forty, younger than she expected in a clergyman, with thick hair the texture of bird's feathers.

'You must meet my wife, Roslyn,' he said. 'She'd love that, wouldn't she, Johnny?' He patted Admiral's small head. 'She's always on the lookout for new blood, so to speak, for our annual village events, concerts, dramas, sports days, church socials, that sort of thing. No matter how long you're here, she'll have you involved in something.' He sipped again, adding to his frothy moustache. 'Do you sing, by any chance? We could do with a couple more sopranos in the choir.'

'I wouldn't be any good for a choir but if I'm around when one of your events comes up I'd be interested to join in, Mr Farrow,' Laura replied giddily. She felt one could get quite exhausted listening to the vicar.

'Will you be keeping your husband's cottage on for your holidays?' Kinsley asked. 'I'm sure you'd enjoy visiting down here regularly. Roslyn and I are only "furreigners" – you have to live in Cornwall at least forty years to be considered a local – but my flock are generally very good to us.'

'I'm sure they are,' Laura said, making Johnny nod approvingly. She realised that Harry Lean was eyeing her with his ever-present smirk. She couldn't imagine that individual being good to the vicar.

When Harry Lean left the pub half an hour before closing time he flashed Laura another bright smile. She dropped her head and gave Johnny her attention but a few moments later glanced out of the window. She saw Marianne Roach, the schoolmaster's daughter, her face heavily made up, her hair frothily curled in front and wearing a coat that was obviously new, getting into Harry's car.

Chapter 5

Laura was in the kitchen curled up in Bunty's chair. She was in her nightdress with a few of Daisy's curlers in her hair. Her head was bent over the morning newspaper which had been brought by the postwoman on her squeaky bicycle.

She heard someone coming into the room and without looking up she said, 'Good morning, Bunty. I'll get up and you can have your chair.'

'Where's Daisy?' came a harsh voice.

A bright red flush shot up Laura's neck and face and she put up a hand to hide her curlers. Spencer Jeffries was glaring accusingly at her from the doorway.

'She... she's preparing to open the shop.'

'No, she isn't. She must have popped round to Bunty's for a moment. So you've decided to stay on, have you?'

Laura visibly bristled. 'That's got nothing to do with you.' She added on a high tone, 'Can I help you?'

He tossed a piece of paper on the table making Laura blink. 'I've brought my monthly order, don't lose it.'

'Why should I lose it?' Laura was offended but her nightdress and curlers kept her meekly in the chair.

He turned to go but Laura couldn't resist asking him, 'How's your dear little girl today? Have you brought her with you?'

'Vicki's waiting for me, with Ince Polkinghorne on the cart,' he said defensively, as if he was asserting that he looked after his daughter properly. Then he left.

After being pinned to Bunty's chair by Spencer Jeffries' ice-cold grey eyes Laura couldn't concentrate on reading the newspaper. She went upstairs to get dressed. Although she didn't want to, for Daisy's sake and in keeping with what the villagers expected a grieving widow should wear, she dressed in her black clothes. She wouldn't gain their confidence if they thought she didn't care about Bill. She combed her hair in its usual flowing shoulder-length style and put on very little make-up. Then she went downstairs into the shop. She'd said last night she wanted to contribute to her keep and Daisy said she'd be delighted to have her work in the shop for a couple of hours; in that way she could meet the villagers too.

At eight thirty Daisy still hadn't returned from Bunty's so Laura turned the sign round on the door to 'Open' and unlocked the door. Through the advertisements on the glass she could see the Rosemerryn horse and cart. So the crusty-mannered recluse was still in the village, was he? She hoped he'd come back to the shop and bring Vicki in for her sweets ration.

Laura had a good look round the shop. Bill had told her that his mother's parents had owned it and had left it to Daisy, their elder daughter, when they died. Laura wondered if that was because they knew Bill had been fathered by the tyrannical William Lean and not Ron Jennings. The shop, small and dark and permeated with a variety of homely smells, had seen no changes since Daisy's parents' day. Laura found the half-packed shelves, high wooden counter, and ancient cash register fascinating. Biscuits were sold loose from big square tins, fat brown eggs were laid out in gingham-lined baskets. Christmas decorations were on sale next to some medicinal herbal remedies. The items on the next shelf read like a miniature pharmacy: bile beans, syrup of figs, Sanatogen, cough linctus, Eucryl toothpaste, Nivea cream. Two pairs of nylons took pride of place in the window with small stacks of dummy packets. In a corner a roll of linoleum, which had been ordered from a catalogue, was awaiting collection by a Mrs Miller.

Laura was about to go into the kitchen and get Spencer Jeffries' shopping list, curious to see what his monthly requirements were, when there was a terrible screeching and grinding sound outside, then an almighty bang which shook the shop windows.

As Laura rushed to the shop door, it was wrenched open.

'Here,' Spencer Jeffries said urgently, thrusting a pale-faced Vicki into her arms. 'Look after Vicki. There's been an accident. I'll have to use the phone. Get away from the windows, it's not a pretty sight out there.'

When Spencer had dialled the emergency services for an ambulance and a fire engine, Laura faced him in the passage with Vicki clinging to her. 'Did she see it?' Laura whispered. 'She's terrified.'

'I'm afraid so,' Spencer replied grimly; stroking Vicki's hair and kissing the top of her head. 'I'll have to go back outside and see if I can do anything. Will you keep her in here, try to take her mind off it, please?'

'Of course. What happened?'

'It's a delivery lorry. It was heading for the shop when old Johnny Prouse's little dog suddenly dashed out in front of it.'

'Is—'

'I'll have to go,' Spencer said, striding away. 'I'll tell you later.'

Vicki had her face buried deep in Laura's neck. 'Where's Daddy gone?' she asked fearfully.

'Not far away, darling. He thought that as I came to see you on your farm yesterday that it's your turn to visit me today. What would you like to do? Shall we go into the kitchen and have some milk and biscuits? I could read you a story.' Laura had noticed a box of toys and children's books Daisy kept in a corner.

Vicki looked up, her eyes shining like they usually did. 'Will you read me *The Gingerbread Man*, please? It's my favourite.'

As Laura was saying she would, Daisy came running in breathlessly, a hand clasped to her full breast. 'Thank goodness the little one's all right. That's right, you go along into the kitchen with her.' She patted Vicki's shoulder. 'I'll bring in some dolly mixtures for you, my handsome.'

Laura read the story, enjoying the closeness of having Vicki on her lap. She was on tenterhooks wondering what was happening outside, if old Johnny Prouse was hurt. She felt useful comforting Vicki and keeping her occupied. Two days ago she had felt life wasn't worth living, that she had little to look forward to, but now she was already playing a part in the lives of a community that had meant nothing to her those same two days ago. How quickly life could twist and turn, she mused. Needlessly she retied the big red ribbon that held back the hair on the crown of Vicki's head.

She and Vicki were playing teasets with a doll, the little china teapot full of milk, with dolly mixtures and bits of broken biscuit on the plates, when Daisy came into the kitchen and went to her airing cupboard. With a grim face she took out a large white sheet.

'What's that for?' Laura mouthed the words over Vicki's head.

'Bandages,' Daisy mouthed back.

In this way they communicated so Vicki couldn't hear. 'Is it bad out there?' Laura asked.

Daisy nodded. 'They're trying to get the driver out of his cab. His head's bleeding. A piece of metal pierced Ince's hand and Mike Penhaligon's cut his hand on broken glass.'

'What about Admiral?'

Daisy shook her head and Laura wiped away the tears which sprang to her eyes. She'd only met Johnny Prouse twice but it was obvious how much Admiral had meant to him.

'And Johnny?'

Daisy's eyes filled with tears. 'He went after Admiral. He's under the lorry, the fire engine will have to—'

'What are you two whispering about?' Vicki said, looking eagerly into their faces.

'Oh, we were wondering if your daddy would let you have dinner with us today, Vicki,' Daisy answered quickly. 'Would you like to stay?'

Daisy knew at once she'd made a mistake mentioning the little girl's father because Vicki wailed, 'I want my daddy. A big lorry frightened us.'

'He'll be here in a little while,' Laura said, automatically holding out her arms. 'Shall we have another story? There's lots of books in the box and I haven't heard their stories yet.'

Vicki was comforted and sat on Laura's lap holding as many books as she could clutch.

'Looks like you'll be running out of breath,' Daisy smiled before leaving.

Laura raised her voice as she read when a persistent ringing announced the arrival of the ambulance and fire engine within two minutes of each other. A third noisy bell spoke of someone having rung the police too.

Daisy popped in and out of the kitchen, making up Spencer's order. There'd been only a few customers to the shop, most preferring to surround the grisly scene outside, watching from a safe distance.

It was nearly two hours before Spencer returned. Vicki ran to him to be picked up. He, too, had cut his hands on broken glass as he'd tried to help the wounded and clear up the wreckage; strips of sheet were wound round them.

'Thank you, Mrs Jennings,' he said quietly, kissing Vicki's cheeks. 'Have you enjoyed yourself playing, pipkin?'

Laura noticed he did not ask Vicki if she'd been a good girl, which was the usual parental question. This pleased Laura; after all, Vicki hadn't asked to be suddenly put into the care of a virtual stranger, so why should the emphasis be on her behaviour?

'Are we going home now, Daddy?'

'In a short while,' he replied, ruffling her hair. 'I'm waiting for the road to be cleared,' he explained to Laura. 'The workmen have just arrived. I don't want Vicki to see...'

Laura nodded. 'Of course. And Johnny?'

'Not good,' he replied in a whisper.

'The driver?'

'Should be all right in time.'

'Why do grown-ups always whisper?' Vicki asked peevishly, making a petulant face before snuggling in against her father's strong neck.

There was a sudden buzz in the shop as it filled with customers, all come to talk about the accident. Ada Prisk could be heard talking nineteen to the dozen.

'I'd better see if Aunty Daisy wants any help,' Laura said, thinking that Spencer would prefer to be left alone with Vicki.

48

Bunty reached the doorway before she did. ''Tis all right, m'dear. I'll help Daisy, though I don't think many in there want to buy anything. Could you make some tea?'

Laura said she would and Bunty closed the door and the noise of the chatter died down.

'Would you like some tea?' Laura asked Spencer, suddenly feeling unsure of herself in his presence. She hadn't forgotten his hostility towards her the day before.

'Yes, please,' he said, sitting down in Daisy's chair with Vicki held tightly to him.

The kettle on the range was always close to the boil and Laura felt self-conscious as she looked in the cupboards for the things needed to prepare a tray.

'Is Aunty Daisy your Aunty Daisy too?' Vicki asked her, following her movements.

'Yes, that's right, Vicki.' Laura was cross with herself for blushing because Spencer was looking at her. His expression wasn't hostile as it had been yesterday and earlier this morning, it was just a steady gaze, and rather stern. She was glad when Vicki claimed his attention again, but only for a moment.

'Daddy doesn't like you,' Vicki said with the innocence of her years.

'Vicki!' Spencer had the grace to look embarrassed. 'I told you that Mrs Jennings just took me by surprise, that's all.'

'Don't worry,' Laura said coldly, putting a tray down on the table with a thud. 'I won't be surprising you again.'

'Where's Uncle Ince?'

'He hurt his hand. The doctor is looking at it. He'll be along in a minute.'

Vicki gingerly touched the bandages on her father's hands. 'Did the doctor look at your hands too?'

'Yes, but they're not badly hurt. I'll be able to take these pieces of cloth off later today.'

Laura listened to them talking. There was obviously a very strong bond between father and daughter and, probably because she had spent so much of her nearly five years among two adults, Vicki's speech was clear and articulate.

49

Laura asked Vicki if she wanted some more milk and when Vicki shook her head, Spencer reminded her to say no thank you politely; Vicki was still a little shy of her. Laura put a strong mug of tea for Spencer on the little table Daisy kept handy by her chair. She asked him if he wanted a biscuit.

'No, thank you,' he said, only glancing at her as he tucked Vicki's blouse more comfortably into her trousers and pulled down her warm jumper. Feeling even more out of place, Laura sat opposite them and tried to start a conversation.

'I understand you and Bill didn't like each other.' She was getting used to asking questions, and forthright ones too, about Bill and one slipped out before she knew it. She instantly realised she'd picked the wrong subject.

Spencer said tightly, 'It's hardly the sort of thing to discuss in front of a child and, anyway, I never talk about my private affairs.'

Laura got up quickly. Vicki watched her with curious eyes. Laura turned away from them, her feelings following the direction of her eyes as they sank down to the floor. 'If you'll excuse me, I have things to get on with.'

'Find out if the road is clear, will you?' Spencer muttered.

Laura flinched. It had sounded very much like an order. She felt browbeaten. The little confidence she had attained deserted her. She left the room thinking that with the exception of Ince Polkinghorne, she heartily disliked the younger men from this village. None of them seemed to have any manners or feelings of respect where women were concerned.

Chapter 6

Barbara Roach cringed as her husband scowled over his lunchtime meal. He did this every day and every day it made her cringe. He sat in his stiff formal clothes at the table in their dining room and no matter what she put in front of him, he found fault with it. She wished he would do what other schoolmasters did, eat with the staff and children, but Cecil thought this was beneath him.

'Terrible about that accident this morning,' she commented as she put sardines and poached eggs on toast in front of him. 'It nearly killed Spencer Jeffries and his little girl. That poor driver, and poor Johnny Prouse. He'll be some upset when he learns his dog was killed, if Johnny doesn't die himself.'

The hard lines on Cecil's dour face deepened into cracks and his prominent Adam's apple danced about in his thin, ragged throat. The skin over his long hooked nose stretched, making the narrow ridge of bone that ran almost to the tip stand out. 'Must you talk about these blasted villagers! It's bad enough having to live amongst them, having to try to stop their horrid offspring from saying things like "some upset" without hearing you saying it too. It's so upset. So!'

'Yes, dear.' Barbara meekly poured out his cup of tea, her eyes on the cup, making sure it was just the right strength and colour.

Cecil suddenly paled. 'What lorry was it?'

'Rowe's, the fruit and vegetable.'

He looked visibly relieved. 'Oh, that's all right then.'

Barbara thought this was an odd thing to say but she dared not ask him what he meant.

'I want your help this afternoon.' Cecil chomped noisily on his food, tomato sauce squelching at the corners of his mouth. 'I want the school to do me proud at the village Christmas concert. I'll drill the choir. You can help Miss Knight with ideas for Class Three's costumes. I've written them a little sketch.'

'Yes, dear.' She placed the tea on the precise spot he demanded it on the table. He moved it a fraction of an inch. Barbara checked her hair in the mirror over the fireplace, ensuring every strand was in place. If just one was astray Cecil would go wild; it wasn't in keeping with his position in the village if his wife wasn't immaculately groomed.

'These eggs are rubbery. I hear that Jennings woman is still in the village. I wonder why she's stayed on.'

Barbara's heart sank. She'd have to find out exactly why Laura Jennings hadn't gone back to London and woe betide her, one of her husband's favourite sayings, if her account differed from anybody else's.

'Did Marianne get up in plenty of time to catch the bus to Launceston?'

'Yes, dear,' Barbara lied. Marianne had left it so late she'd had to run for the bus that came into the village every morning at eight ten for the workers who had jobs in Launceston, the nearest town.

'You let that girl stay out too late.'

Barbara was facing the other way and raised her eyes to the ceiling. As if she had any say in what their rebellious daughter did. Eighteen-year-old Marianne was usually polite and co-operative when her father was around. Barbara received nothing but cheek and tantrums. Barbara was caught between a rock and a hard place in her own home. Cecil would never forgive her for not giving him a son and Marianne was antagonistic towards her for providing her with a miserable, strait-laced father.

'She's got a good job as secretary at Hobson's Drapery. She ought to appreciate it, work hard to make something of herself like I have.'

Oh, yes? Barbara thought ironically. I thought this little village school wasn't good enough for the great Cecil Roach's talents. None of these children will amount to anything, you keep saying. Bill Jennings was an exception – and you thought he was a braggart. It helped her to bear her husband's constant complaints and nagging to admonish him inside her head.

'Have you burnt that low-cut dress Marianne brought home, like I told you?'

'Yes, dear,' Barbara lied again. She could do this if she kept her face rigidly straight and she had perfected a stony expression over the years. The dress, an evening gown, its style accentuated on the bosom, had been secreted out of the house and was hanging in a wardrobe belonging to one of Marianne's friends, ready to be put on for the next dance. Marianne's only lament was that dances were few and far between and then there were usually no decent men at them.

'She shouldn't waste her clothing coupons. I won't have a daughter of mine dressing like a common trollop.'

'Nor will I, dear.'

'Pardon?' Cecil's fork clattered on the table.

Barbara's few words of agreement had sounded almost like sarcasm. She flushed and took off her glasses to wipe her eyes. 'No, dear.'

He glared at her hard for a few minutes. Barbara held her breath. After what seemed an eternity he pushed his cup and saucer towards her for a refill. She was glad she was out of his reach. He often hit her.

'Make the next one stronger. I'm going to get someone from the *Cornish Gazette* here to take photos of the children in the concert. I have to show that this school, though its pupils are small in number, counts for something. There are no more than thirty-seven on the register and only Victoria Jeffries and Benjamin Miller starting next term. The local authorities might decide to close the school and send the children on to Lewannick or even bus them into Launceston. We'd find ourselves out of position and home then. They could close the school, you know, they're beginning to shut down the smaller ones round the county,' Cecil ended gloomily. 'Where's that damned cup of tea, woman?'

–

Laura had been quiet and pale-faced since the Jeffrieses had left the shop.

'Why don't you go out for a little walk?' Daisy suggested. 'There's no need for you to work in the shop and you'll feel better for a breath of fresh air, but don't wander over the moor alone.'

'I must admit I don't feel like meeting any more people today,' Laura said dejectedly.

She went up to her room. Her bruised feelings spilled over into a fit of bad temper and she yanked the black dress off over her head and threw it onto the bed. Damn Spencer Jeffries! How dare he speak to her like that, and after she had done him a favour too. And damn what the villagers expected her to dress like. She wouldn't pretend to grieve over that other blasted swine lying in the churchyard.

Wearing her blue skirt, an Aran knit jumper and Daisy's warm outer clothes and boots, she tramped to the top of the village hill, passed the few cottages and houses on the outskirts of Kilgarthen and carried on along the road. She stumped along looking down on the ground, following the turn of the lanes which were beginning to become familiar to her. She'd been walking for fifteen minutes when she realised the way she was heading would lead towards Rose-merryn Farm. She'd meant to go the other way and take a look at the Methodist chapel and the outskirts of the other side of the village and then walk on to Hawksmoor House. She grunted in annoyance, although she wouldn't have minded seeing Ince Polkinghorne.

She knew she was very near Tregorlan Farm, its sign in the hedge was not very far up ahead. She thought about the two farms and reasoned that their land must border each other, divided only by the road. She walked a few yards to a gateway, climbed over it, and took a tentative step onto the turf. It was coarse and springy but felt firm. She'd wander over Jacka Davey's land and hope he wouldn't angrily evict her as she was sure Spencer Jeffries would.

A few more steps and the starkness and beauty of the scenery, which she'd ignored in her anger, sank into her mind. Bill had told her the moor as a whole was steeped in history and legend, that something of significance had happened on it in every age, from the settling of Bronze Age men who had left evidence of their homes, tools and burial mounds, to tin and copper mining in the nineteenth century, to an American aircraft crashing on it in the last war. Laura sensed a deep feeling of timelessness, as if any of these events could occur now.

From the ground at her feet to the peak of Hawk's Tor everything looked windswept but hardy and strong. The rough fields had been cleared for grazing and elsewhere the grass and fern was dying back as winter approached. The sweeps of bracken with their many shades of russet, red and brown were turning dun and grey like the stony horizon. Only the bud-like flowers of the gorse bushes, standing ready for the winter storm blasts, retained a little yellow here and there. Granite boulders, which looked as if they'd been dropped at random from a great height, stood out purposefully among the foliage.

The landscape made her feel vulnerable. Its very exposure to the elements seemed in some way to expose her hurt, and yet a strange feeling was stirring inside her, as if something living and able to maintain mastery of a constant struggle was calling to her. She knew it wasn't a good thing to bury her feelings deep inside. Bring it to the air, expose it to this vibrant light and wide expanse of Nature, a voice inside seemed to be calling to her. The feeling of peace she found here filled her with a warmth, a feeling of belonging to it, as if it had seeped inside her and become a part of her. Two days ago she wouldn't have believed this possible.

She walked on, watching her steps carefully, testing the ground in case it was saturated and boggy, keeping away from the marshy edge of one of the many streams that coursed the moor and watered the livestock. She kept looking behind her; if she kept the road in sight she wouldn't get lost. She climbed a small hill and found herself looking down into a valley with another, higher hill on the other side. A few cattle were grazing, dotted about down in the valley, one or two on the lower hillsides.

The figure of a small man appeared on the opposite hill. He was too far away for Laura to see his face, to ascertain his age, but his build told her it wasn't Jacka Davey. He stood and looked in her direction. Laura lifted her hand in a tentative wave. He responded after a moment and stayed where he was, apparently watching her.

'Another friendly native,' Laura said to the wind.

He turned away and disappeared from sight.

Laura called to him to wait but her words were lost on the wind. She wanted to talk to him, to ask him about life on the moor. Was it as lonely as Bill had said it was? So terribly difficult to make a living out of it? Bill had said it turned some people into loners. Had it done that to the small man? Did he have urgent work to do or did he have no desire to meet and speak to her? Laura was overwhelmed by a pressing need to know everything about the people who lived in and around Kilgarthen, not just to search into Bill's soul, but to know them for themselves. Most of all she wanted to get to know little Vicki Jeffries. Meeting her had stirred her greatest desire – to have a child of her own.

She swung round to face the way she had come and made her way back to the road. She would stay here in this village, live in Bill's cottage, for years if she had to, until she was either fed up with Kilgarthen or had learned all she needed to, and cold-hearted brutes like Spencer Jeffries wouldn't drive her away.

She'd return to Daisy's and telephone Andrew and ask him to send down some of her things. Then she'd catch the next bus into Launceston to buy some clothes more suited to moorland living.

–

Laura bought a pair of warm trousers, some thick stockings and a sturdy pair of fur-lined boots. Daisy's old brown coat was serviceable enough for the moorland and she bought a woollen scarf with hat and gloves to match. Loaded down with shopping bags and parcels, she called into a bakery in Westgate Street to buy a treat for Daisy for tea. Daisy had a baker's van call every day at the shop and she sold a variety of cakes and bread. Laura was looking for something different.

'Saffron cake?' the shop assistant suggested, pointing to a shelf filled with the yellow loaf-shaped cakes.

'No, we've had some of that.' Laura bent forward to peer through the glass showcases. 'And hevva cake and scones. As it's nearing Christmas, perhaps some mince pies.'

'May I recommend the fancies,' a voice from behind startled her. 'From this bakery they are excellent.'

Laura recognised Harry Lean's voice. She turned to find him winking at the shop girl. 'I'll choose for myself,' she retorted crossly.

'Then let me hold your shopping while you make up your mind,' Harry offered, extending his arms. He looked handsome and elegant in a dark three-piece suit topped with a dark wool coat. He doffed his hat to her.

Laura wanted to say no and tell him to go away, but because she couldn't carry much more and she wanted to call in at a chemist before catching the bus home, it made sense to accept his offer. 'You can carry these,' she said ungraciously, holding out a couple of the heavier bags and the box with her boots in it.

He took them from her with one of his habitual broad smiles. Laura sighed impatiently when she saw that the shop assistant was gazing at him with admiration. 'I'll take half a dozen mixed fancies,' she snapped.

'Inviting me to tea?' Harry drawled over her shoulder. 'No, I am not,' she hissed back under her breath. This man brought her quickly to the point of exasperation. Why should she explain that although it seemed a lot to buy, Bunty would share them too.

'Don't tell me you and old Ma Tamblyn are going to wolf down the lot? You'll ruin your delectable slender figure.'

'Mr Lean, I would be grateful if you would keep your personal remarks to yourself!'

Laura banged a ten-shilling note on the counter and the shop girl gave her the change with her mouth agape. Harry winked at her. 'Don't worry, she loves me really.' The girl broke into a fit of giggles and Laura marched out of the baker's shop indignantly.

'How dare you say things like that,' she snarled at Harry as they walked along the pavement and through Southgate Arch, part of the wall that had enclosed the market town in medieval days and was a uniquely splendid entrance to the narrow streets. She tried to ignore him by looking at the curious sight of the sycamore tree that grew out of the grey stone of the arch wall.

'Where's your sense of humour?' he laughed.

'I haven't got one, and what do you expect anyway? I've recently been widowed.'

'According to what I've heard from my London colleagues, there was no love lost between you and Bill. I would have thought you must be glad he's dead.'

Laura turned on him in a whirl of fury, almost knocking another shopper off her feet. 'I'm well aware that you know my true circumstances, Harry Lean, but I don't appreciate having them thrown in my face. Maybe I didn't love Bill at the end but his death was terrible and my whole world has been horrendously turned upside down! It's a pity they no longer execute people in Launceston Castle because at this moment I'd like to see you hanging there.' Tears coursed down Laura's face and she tried to grab her shopping from him.

Harry held the bags and parcel up out of her reach. His face had changed from its usual veneer of cynical amusement to embarrassed contrition. 'I'm very sorry for everything I've said and how I've behaved towards you. Forgive me, Mrs Jennings, I've not been the least bit sensitive to your situation. Let me make it up to you. We could put these things in the bus, it doesn't leave for an hour, then let me take you to lunch. You'll feel better with a good meal and some excellent wine inside you. Or perhaps you'd prefer a drink in the Bell Inn?'

'No, thank you. I just want to finish my shopping and wait for the bus to leave.'

He waited for her outside while she went into the chemist's shop to buy hand cream and toiletries. They walked in silence until they reached the bus stop, saying nothing as they put her shopping down on one of the front seats.

'Thank you for your help,' Laura said stonily.

Harry lifted an inquiring eyebrow. 'Are you sure you won't change your mind about lunch?'

'Quite sure. I have things to do.'

'Before I go, Mrs Jennings, I have something for you.' He took an envelope out of his coat pocket. 'I have to drive through the village on my way home to Hawksmoor House. I was going to drop this into

Mrs Tamblyn's letter box. It's from my mother, to you, inviting you to dinner next Wednesday evening, if you're still in the village. I hope you won't refuse because I've upset you.'

Laura took the envelope from him, glancing down at the neat handwriting that spelled her name. 'Thank you, Mr Lean. I'll see if I'm free.'

As the ancient bus trundled the nine and a half miles to Kilgarthen, Laura thought about the sudden change her outburst had wrought in Harry Lean. 'So you have a little bit of heart, after all,' she said to the image of him in her mind. Something Bill, his half-brother, had not possessed at all.

When she got back to the village she took her shopping to Bill's cottage. She intended moving into Little Cot tomorrow and there was no sense in taking the parcels into Daisy's. She dumped everything down on the dining table in the front room and looked at the fireplace. It was cold in here. Before she moved in she'd light the fire and range. She didn't stop to think about what it might actually feel like to live in her husband's beloved holiday home.

She locked up the cottage and turned to walk up the hill to the shop. A movement across the road, by the lychgate, caught her attention. A man, someone she felt sure did not come from the village, dressed in a hunter's hat and long overcoat, was watching her.

Chapter 7

Laura had banked down the front room fire the evening before so Little Cot was warm and aired when she and Daisy arrived there the following morning. Laura brought the few belongings she'd kept at Daisy's, her overnight bag and the clothes and shoes she'd worn at Bill's funeral.

'I haven't got much to put away,' Laura said as Daisy carried a box of provisions into the kitchen. 'You've kept the place in tip-top condition, Aunty Daisy. It won't take me long to settle in.'

'No one's lived here on a permanent basis since my sister and her husband died,' Daisy called out as she unpacked the box, putting things away. 'Billy rented it then bought it off the Leans four years ago. Harry made him pay over the odds, I can tell you. How long do you think you'll be staying here, Laura?'

'I don't know,' Laura said, looking out of the window at the lychgate across the road. 'It depends on a lot of things.' Daisy came back into the front room and joined her at the window. 'What are you looking for?'

'When I dropped off my shopping yesterday there was a strange man staring at me. He was standing over there. He didn't look like he belonged to the village. I found it rather odd.'

'You're a beautiful young woman. You shouldn't be surprised if men look at you. It was probably a holidaymaker. You can find one or two about even at this time of the year. Probably someone who's come here for the peace and quiet, maybe with an interest in the moor, a naturist or something.'

'I think you mean naturalist, Aunty,' Laura smiled. 'A naturist is someone who likes to spend time outdoors in the nude.'

Daisy laughed. 'I hope we don't see any of they round here. Not in weather like this anyway.'

'Yes, it is cold today, the wind was really cutting on the short walk down here,' Laura said, looking beyond the church walls to the rising moorland. 'But thanks to you, it's nice and cosy in here.'

'You'll get used to the weather down here.' Daisy looked meaningfully at Laura. 'This has been a cosy little place since Billy done it up. He got rid of the draughts and had the windows put in. Goodness knows where he got the bits and pieces, what with all the shortages. I think he's done a good job here, don't you?'

Laura looked around the pleasant surroundings of the front room. She sniffed, she listened, she strained, feeling for an atmosphere. After several moments she returned Daisy's searching gaze with an admission. 'I suppose there is a comfortable feeling here.'

'Are you surprised by that, Laura?' Daisy asked gently.

'Yes. It's not in keeping with the character I knew Bill had.'

Daisy looked thoughtful. 'I think Billy saw you as a separate part of his life to what he had here.'

'He must have done.' Laura noticed a photograph of Bill's parents and one of Daisy on the mantlepiece. There were several of Bill in the house but none of her. 'I was only a means to an end. He knew I would have liked it here, how I would have enjoyed the community spirit.'

Daisy put a hand on her shoulder. 'Don't get bitter, please, Laura. Whatever you suffered at Billy's hands, don't let him do that to you.'

'I do try not to. Sometimes I feel hate for him, other times I feel nothing. He stripped me of everything I once had, peace of mind, hope for the future, my father's company which was my inheritance.' Laura's eyes dropped to the carpet. 'Bill never raised a hand to me but his mental cruelty was in some ways much worse.'

Daisy put a hand under her chin and raised it. 'Don't look down, Laura. I've seen you do it so many times in the few days I've known you. Look forward. You're a lovely young woman, you're only twenty-three years old, you have lots of years ahead of you. Believe there's a future for you and it starts now. You'll find real love one day, if you're open to it.'

Daisy looked so serious, so resolute, it lifted Laura's spirit and made her smile. 'Make decisions, that's what my dad used to say when things were uncertain, and that's what I've done. I've decided to move in here. I've telephoned Andrew and he's going to send down some of my things and arrange for my bank account to be transferred down here. I'm going to make a point of meeting all the villagers and after that I'll make a fresh lot of decisions. I want you, Aunty, to feel free to pop in any time you like, and you can tell that to Bunty too. Now, have you got time for a cup of tea?'

Reassured, Daisy kissed Laura on the cheek. 'You put the kettle on, dear. Bunty will be happy looking after the shop a bit longer. I'll show you how to start the generator before I go. Billy showed me how to do it. When you get the hang of the range in the kitchen you'll find that it will warm the cottage through upstairs and in the bathroom. There's plenty of logs in the yard. With the Trebartha plantation so near we don't have the worries of the coal shortage like the rest of the country, nor cuts in electricity,' Daisy laughed ironically, 'seeing as we haven't got none. I'll help you carry some logs through after our cuppa.'

'The villagers must think me lucky having all mod cons here,' Laura remarked when they were drinking tea at the kitchen table. 'The bathroom is lovely. I recognise it from a design Bill was looking at in one of the company's brochures. Are all bathrooms in Cornwall built downstairs?'

Daisy looked at the door that separated the kitchen from the bathroom. 'No. Billy had the back kitchen modernised and enlarged, taking in the little outdoor closet. Some of the villagers would love to take a look at it. Billy wouldn't let anyone but me over the doorstep. Even Bunty hasn't been inside the cottage since Billy's parents died. I'll tell her she's welcome, I expect she'll be down later today. You be careful who you invite in, though. Some will be nothing but nosy.'

'Like Ada Prisk?'

'Especially Ada Prisk. If you're going to make a point of meeting all the villagers, I take it you'll be accepting the invitation to dinner from Felicity Lean.'

'Yes, it should prove interesting. I hope Harry won't be there. His perpetual charm gets on my nerves.'

'It would be wise to watch out for he. A confirmed bachelor that one. Likes to play the field. I can't ever see Harry Lean settling down.'

'I find it curious that a man like him lives in a small village, and with his mother. You'd think he would be attracted to the lights of the big cities and live in a bachelor flat.'

'He did for many years. He came home to his mother after the war because she was ill.'

'He's different from Spencer Jeffries. He's a terrible man,' Laura exclaimed, snapping a biscuit in half and scattering crumbs on the table. 'He shouldn't be allowed to bring up that gorgeous little girl of his alone.'

'Laura, be careful what you're saying,' Daisy cautioned, wagging her finger. 'Folk round here don't care much for Spencer but they're very loyal. They wouldn't take kindly to a stranger saying things like that about him. Spencer is a very good father, he adores Vicki.'

'Sorry. I hope no one will think I've come from another planet.' Laura looked shamefaced but only for a moment. 'But that man gets me so angry. I like Ince Polkinghorne very much, he seems a caring, gentle man. Even Harry Lean must have some good points to care about his mother like that, but Spencer Jeffries, he's a – a fiend!'

'Did he say something to upset you yesterday? I thought it was the accident.'

Vicki Jeffries' sweet little face, frightened by the accident and suddenly being thrust into her arms, came into Laura's mind. 'Oh, he's not important. Have you heard anything more about Johnny Prouse? I know they said he's suffering more from shock than his injuries but Johnny is old and his condition could have changed. I wish I could do something for him.'

'I'll phone again after dinner. I'm-sure Johnny will be all right. He was sitting up and chatting to Mike Penhaligon when he visited him last night. 'Tis a relief to know that old Mr Maker won't be going up to School House and telling Cecil Roach's bees.'

'Telling Cecil Roach's bees? What are you talking about, Aunty Daisy?'

"'Tis an old custom. When someone dies, someone tells the bees.'

Laura was enchanted. 'Why?'

Daisy frowned. 'I don't really know. So they can spread the news around, I s'pose.'

'Well, they wouldn't be flying about at this time of the year.'

'Anyway, Bunty's getting up a collection to buy Johnny some fruit and flowers and the rest of the money will come in handy towards a new coat for him. His was ruined in the accident. You could contribute to the collection, if you like.'

'Ask Bunty to call on me. I'll show her over the cottage at the same time.'

Daisy got up and put her cup and saucer on the draining board. 'I'll have to be going soon, dear. Shall we take a look at the generator and fetch in some logs?'

Laura hadn't unlocked the back door and investigated outside yet but she knew roughly what it looked like from Bill's description and photographs. What Daisy had called the yard began with a good-sized patio. Bill had walled it in and it was a perfect spot for sunbathing. There was a large concreted area with a big shed, half of which was filled with tools, the other stacked up neatly with logs. Another small shed housed the generator. The garden was huge and landscaped with a rockery. A statue of a wood nymph stood in the middle of the lawn.

'Bill did a good job out here too,' Laura remarked, much impressed.

After a couple of false starts, Daisy got the generator working. When the shed door was closed, the vibrating sounds were considerably lowered and with the cottage several yards away, Laura realised she'd hardly hear it indoors. They filled the huge fireside basket with logs and carried it to the hearth in the front room. 'Bill had them delivered,' Daisy said. 'I'll write down all the numbers of the people you'll need to contact for regular deliveries. Anything else you'd like to know about before I get back to the shop?'

'There is one thing I was going to ask you about. I took a walk over a field belonging to Tregorlan Farm yesterday. I saw a small man with the cattle. It wasn't Jacka. Who do you think it was? Has he got a son?'

Daisy opened her mouth to answer but a cheery 'Cooee!' stopped her. The front door was opened a little and an attractive young woman popped her head round it. 'It's the vicar's wife,' Daisy said. 'Looks like you'll have to put the kettle on again, my dear.'

–

Roslyn Farrow took off her bright paisley headscarf, sat down in a fireside chair and took a notebook and pen out of the top of her straw shopping bag. She was a small, neatly boned woman in her mid-thirties and she looked completely at ease. She ran the pen through her thick black hair and rested it on her ear. She grinned rather cheekily as Laura served the tea.

'Thank you, Mrs Jennings. It's good of you letting me in like this but I felt I couldn't just go by, not after Miss Buzza told me in the shop that you were staying on, and with me living nearly opposite. Is there anything I can do for you?'

'I think I've got everything under control, Mrs Farrow, but it's kind of you to ask,' Laura smiled as she took a seat. 'I've a shrewd idea what that notebook's for. The vicar told me you like to get people involved in the village events.'

'Oh, he didn't, did he?' Roslyn clapped a hand to her face. 'Trust Kinsley to open his big mouth. I hope you don't think I'm only here to rope you into something. It's just that I believe it helps newcomers to get to know their neighbours and to feel integrated in the community.' She opened the notebook and held her pen over it. Winking, she asked, 'What can I put you down for? Choir? An act in the concert coming up soon? Or perhaps you're good at needlework and can help with the costumes. Or painting scenery?'

'I was good at art at school and I used to paint for relaxation, although I haven't painted anything in years. I suppose I could help with the scenery. One thing I do enjoy is flower arranging. That any good to you?'

'Is it!' Roslyn exclaimed, nearly jumping off her, chair. 'You're a life saver. Old Mrs Sparnock used to do the flowers every week until she passed away three months ago. She's buried on top of her husband three graves away from your dear husband, so he's in very good company, I hope that's a comfort to you. I'm hopeless at doing the flowers. Mrs Tamblyn and Miss Buzza do them occasionally but I don't like to call on them too often as they're busy sewing the costumes and rehearsing their own sketch.'

Laura raised her perfectly curved brows. 'Aunty Daisy and Bunty are in the concert?'

Roslyn swallowed a mouthful of tea. Her dark eyes were twinkling like stars. 'Oh, yes. They do something in the comedy line every year. They're a great hit with all ages in the audience.' She looked at Laura artfully. 'I don't suppose I could press you to do the flowers this afternoon for tomorrow's service? It's my youngest child's birthday today and I have such a lot to do getting ready for the party. It would be a wonderful help to me. I've got flowers lined up from Hawksmoor House. Mrs Lean kindly sends some over most weeks.'

'I'd be delighted to,' Laura replied truthfully. Bill had told her one reason he wouldn't take her to Kilgarthen was because the villagers were standoffish and would never accept her. He had lied; becoming involved in the village life was easier than she could have dreamt.

'Splendid, splendid,' Roslyn said, repeating one of her husband's jovial sayings and jotting Laura's name down in two places in her notebook. 'There, that's organised that. You'll find everything you need at the back of the church by the font. The flowers are soaking in a bucket of water. When you're finished perhaps you wouldn't mind shoving the scissors and things into the vestry and the waste on the bonfire round the back of the church.' She rapidly drained her cup. 'Now I'd better get off and let you get on with your settling in.'

Laura stood up to let Roslyn out and was startled to see a face peering in at the window. 'Oh! Who's that?'

'Oh dear, it's Mrs Prisk,' Roslyn told her. 'I'm afraid she can be a little bit too curious for comfort. If you let her in she'll keep you talking all day.'

'In that case I'll go to the church and arrange the flowers now,' Laura said, reaching for her coat on the bottom of the banister.

The two women waited a minute but Ada Prisk was lurking about outside when Laura shut the door. She didn't lock it, Daisy never locked her doors, except for the outer shop door, until she went to bed, and Laura found it natural to follow suit.

Roslyn said forcefully, 'Good morning, Mrs Prisk. Are you walking my way?'

'No, Mrs Farrow, I'm on my way to the shop. I'm right out of flour for my apple crumble.' She turned from the vicar's wife and concentrated on Laura. 'Good morning, Mrs Jennings. And how are you today? I know what it's like to grieve for a beloved husband. Mine was a farm labourer and peat cutter. I see you've moved into your husband's cottage. How brave of you, how painful it must be.' The woman's face darkened and narrowed like a metal rod. 'But then you have no choice, have you? I've heard your father's company went bankrupt, despite all the hard work Bill must have put into it. I bet you wish now that you'd taken the trouble to come down to Cornwall before.'

'I wish no such thing,' Laura returned, lifting her chin, her eyes tightening and flashing blue darts of fire. Harry Lean had wasted no time in trying to sully Bill's memory, but if Ada Prisk was anything to go by, it was her father's reputation that was damaged, not Bill's. She added tartly, 'What I wish for now is to have the peace and quiet and the understanding of those around me to allow me to live through my grief.' She didn't mean grief over Bill.

Roslyn was astonished at Ada Prisk's piece of gossip. She had wondered herself why Laura had decided to move into Little Cot now when she had never made an appearance in the village before. She made a wry face at Laura's counter-attack.

'I'll be on my way then,' Ada Prisk sniffed and with a snort of displeasure she stalked on up the hill.

Laura looked Roslyn in the eye. 'My father always advised me to start as you mean to carry on. I won't let a village gossip get the better of me.'

Roslyn put on her headscarf. Slightly embarrassed, she cleared her throat. 'Well, if you ever need anyone to talk to, don't forget I'm only just across the road.'

As she placed the flowers into the pedestal that would stand in front of the raised pulpit in the church, Laura thought over her retort to Ada

Prisk. Before Bill's death she would have been so cowed she would have taken all the old woman had said, and more, without retaliation.

In one way she was grateful that news of the company's bankruptcy was out; it would stop villagers like Ada Prisk expecting too much of her.

—

Laura climbed into the bed that Bill had used on his visits. There were three more bedrooms in Little Cot but she had deliberately chosen his room to prove to herself that she was no longer under his thumb.

Gazing up at the slanted beamed ceiling she tried not to admit she could sense his overbearing presence in the room. Many of his things were here, the war novels he must have read in bed, a half-full packet of his expensive brand of French cigarettes. The sort of clothes a 'country gentleman' would wear were packed in the wardrobe; he had acquired a lot of clothes and luxury items on the black market. His favourite cologne and hair cream stood beside his brush, comb and clothes brush on the dressing table. A trinket tray was full of cuff links and tie pins.

Acting on a sudden thought, Laura, searched under the pillows and came up with a pair of silk pyjamas Bill had bought at Harrods. She tossed them contemptuously on the floor. 'I'll pack up your stuff tomorrow,' she glared defiantly at a photograph of him on the bedside cabinet. 'A charity might be glad of it. Out with your things, in with mine.'

It was over two years since she had shared a bed with Bill, or rather since Bill had come to her bed in the large house he had bought in South London. She had been grateful to be spared his rough, insensitive lovemaking. After the first year she had not thought of it as that, just as doing her duty, and Bill had always criticised her even when she'd tried to please him. She had come to hate it when he had forced himself on her, usually when he was drunk. Apart from her father and chaste kisses from male friends, she instinctively avoided contact with men.

Her one hope had been that she would have a baby, something she had always longed for, to have someone she could love and cherish, who hopefully would soften Bill's attitude towards her. But Bill had hated the thought of having noisy children disrupt his selfish life; he had denied her anything that had meant something to her.

Laura had gone to bed very late, hoping she would be tired enough to drop off to sleep quickly but she lay wide awake for hours. The road ran on this side of the house but she heard only one vehicle driving through the village, at about two o'clock in the morning. Harry Lean taking Marianne Roach home after a night out? She couldn't imagine the dour schoolmaster allowing his daughter to go out with Harry, and so late, even if he was the richest man in the village. Was Marianne slipping out to see the good-looking estate agent secretly? It seemed so after what Laura had witnessed last night.

She thought about the villagers she had met so far. Most of them seemed pleasant and honest. Most of them had liked Bill. But then why shouldn't they? They were ordinary and hard-working, they would not have seen the dark side of him. Most of them seemed to have forgiven her for her abrupt behaviour on the day of his funeral, readily believing her lie that she had become distraught. What would they say if they knew what an excellent liar Bill had been?

But had he lied to them? Perhaps he had genuinely liked them and been happy to provide for the village.

–

'You've done a beautiful job with the flowers,' Daisy whispered to Laura as she sat sandwiched between her and Bunty in a front pew of the church. 'The congregation will be impressed.'

'Arranging flowers is something a businessman's wife is expected to be good at, but I've always enjoyed doing it,' Laura whispered back.

She felt self-conscious. She hadn't really felt like attending a service so soon after Bill's funeral but had thought it a useful place to meet more of the villagers. When she had arranged the flowers yesterday she'd blocked out the memory of Bill's coffin lying on the trestles in front of the altar rail, but now, wearing her black clothes again, the hushed atmosphere, the bowed heads of people in prayer and the rather mournful notes of the organ brought back the raw feelings of her hurt and hate. She felt she shouldn't be in the church while she harboured such feelings of anger and unforgiveness. And she felt she was the one on view to the villagers instead of it being the other way round.

The Reverend Farrow conducted the service of morning prayer in a flowing manner and while Laura switched off to much of what was said and couldn't join in the prayers, except for those said for Johnny Prouse, the service seemed to be over quickly. She stood in the churchyard with Daisy and Bunty protectively on either side of her and received many compliments and thanks from the congregation over the flowers. Ada Prisk sneered at her from a short distance and grabbed another woman's arm and chattered away while looking at Laura.

'You done a proper job in there, maid.' The man doffed his flat cap and greeted her enthusiastically. Laura had to smile. This was Mr Maker, the old man who talked to the bees.

Roslyn lined her three young children up to introduce them to Laura. 'This horrid bunch you see before you are Rachael, Richard and Ross. Ross is the youngest. He was the birthday boy yesterday, he's now eight years old.'

The children squirmed with embarrassment and when they had shaken Laura's hand and said 'Good morning', politely, they ran off to join some other children.

'I can remember hating being introduced to grown-ups at that age,' Laura said, looking after them sympathetically. She noticed a flash of white-gold hair hanging down from a red wool hat and saw Vicki Jeffries being carried out of the church in Spencer's arms. He shook hands with the vicar and Kinsley tweaked Vicki's nose, making her giggle. Then Spencer moved aside to talk to Cecil Roach. Laura watched Vicki. The little girl's eyes were roaming all around the churchyard and they lit up when she saw the group of children.

'Mrs Jennings?'

'Laura,' Daisy pulled on her arm. 'Mrs Farrow is talking to you.'

'Oh, I... I'm sorry,' Laura stammered, coming back to those immediately around her.

'I was just saying it's a pity that Mr Jeffries doesn't let his little girl play with the other children,' Roslyn said. 'He's so protective of her. And she's a bit too old to be carried around like that. He's going to hate seeing her grow up.'

Laura shrugged her shoulders as if she wasn't interested in the Jeffries. 'I'm surprised not to see Ince Polkinghorne here,' she said. 'Didn't you tell me he's very religious, Aunty Daisy?'

'He's up the other hill in the chapel,' Daisy replied. 'He's a Methodist.'

'Oh, I see. There are a few faces I've missed this morning. Does this mean they go to the chapel too?'

'Some of them, not all,' Roslyn replied. 'Mrs Lean from Hawksmoor House comes to church only on the anniversary of her daughter's death. Mr Lean, her son, doesn't go anywhere. The Penhaligons from the Tremewan Arms are Methodists. The Daveys from Tregorlan Farm come here but we don't see much of them, except for Mr Davey, although that's not because they aren't devout. Johnny Prouse goes to both church and chapel, whatever takes his fancy, but no one really minds. Now the hospital says he's over the worst, hopefully he'll be home soon. Kinsley's got the terrible task later today of telling him that Admiral died in the accident.'

'Poor Johnny,' Laura said, her eyes straying towards Vicki who was now looking bored with her face laid on her father's shoulder.

The people began to disperse but Laura hung back until she was following the Jeffrieses out of the churchyard. She smiled at Vicki and the little girl lifted her head. 'Hello, Mrs Jennings,' she piped brightly.

Spencer stopped walking, with obvious reluctance. Laura ignored his bad manners and ill humour. She didn't want to talk to him anyway.

'Hello, Vicki, it's nice to see you again.'

'Uncle Ince said you're not living at the shop now,' Vicki said.

'That's right. I live just across the road. In the cottage with the hanging baskets.'

Spencer muttered something.

'I beg your pardon?' Laura said sharply.

He put Vicki down and repeated very quietly, 'I said we get rid of one only to get another.'

'Another Jennings, I presume you mean,' Laura challenged him.

Daisy shot Bunty a worried look. She took Vicki by the hand and drew her away.

'That's exactly what I mean,' Spencer replied.

'You ought to remember you've just come out of the church,' Laura hissed at him.

Spencer bent forward from the waist so his face was closer to hers. His grey eyes were like cold slate. 'Your rotten husband should never have set foot inside it and he should never have been buried in hallowed ground. You and the rest of the villagers might think he was God's gift to Kilgarthen just because he threw his money around. I knew him for the callous bastard he really was. You never cared a damn for the place in the past so what are you doing here now?'

Laura physically recoiled, as if he had punched her in the face. Her heart thudded painfully and her breath locked in her lungs. She paled and looked as if she was about to faint. Daisy rushed to her and grabbed her arm.

'Spencer, how could you?' she exclaimed. 'Take Vicki out of the churchyard before she realises what's been going on. Ada Prisk was close by, she might have heard every word.'

'What she needs to hear is the truth,' Spencer scowled. He strode away and gathered Vicki up in his arms from an embarrassed-looking Bunty.

'Aunty Daisy,' Laura pleaded, her voice weak and shaken. 'For goodness sake tell me what Bill did to that man.'

Chapter 8

Andrew Macarthur stopped walking, put his suitcase and briefcase down cautiously at his feet, and anxiously scanned the fog-laden atmosphere for signs of dawn. Aided only by the inadequate light of a small torch, he had been tramping the lanes for what seemed like hours, trying to discover the whereabouts of Kilgarthen.

No taxi was available so early in the morning at Liskeard Station, and he thought he'd been fortunate when the strange old Cornish man he'd shared a railway carriage with had offered him a lift on the horse and cart his equally strange old wife had waiting for him. Andrew thought he'd been offered a lift to Kilgarthen, but the old couple had taken him as far as the village of North Hill where they lived and insisted Kilgarthen was 'just a few minutes away on foot, 'bout two mile or so, boy'.

Although he'd listened attentively to the old man's directions, Andrew had hardly understood his broad accent. He had 'turned right at the shop, walked down the hill and on past the Methodist chapel, then turned left and followed the lane for 'bout a mile'. By then, with not even a solitary cottage to be seen, he was sure he was lost. Eventually he'd found a bridge he was sure the old man had mentioned, then racking his brains for the rest of the directions he'd turned two rights, a left and another right and followed the twisting and turning of a lane. He seemed to be going nowhere.

He was cold from the raw dank air and in a very bad mood. His shoes were muddied, his feet were aching, his trousers were snagged on foliage sticking out indiscriminately from the hedges. His scarf had been torn from his neck by dead brambles and he'd had to fight to get it back.

'Only one thing for it,' he exhaled a long, impatient breath, 'I'll have to find someone to ask the way again. It's like being at the end of the world!' He wished he had a detailed map with him.

Hoping the battery in the torch would last, he strode on and took the next turning to the left. Before long he realised he'd made a mistake. He had turned off onto a rutted track with a low hedge running either side of it and his feet were sinking into deep mud. Cursing under his breath, he turned sharply to retrace his steps and fell over, his cases skidding away from him.

'Damn! Damn! Damn!' He pulled his hand out of four inches of thick, squelchy mud.

Hauling himself to his feet, Andrew peered all around. He couldn't see the road through the fog, and over the hedges on either side of him all he could make out was a small expanse of rugged moorland. The fog obscured the view up ahead. Resisting the urge to swear in fury he picked up the torch and shone it on the ground to find his cases. He used his handkerchief to wipe the mud off his briefcase; there were some important papers inside it. Then he started off carefully back to the lane.

So measured were his steps that he didn't realise someone was walking towards him until they nearly collided. His first thought was that he'd met up with a short, chubby man but a closer look under his raised torch made him realise it was a young woman dressed in baggy men's clothing and Wellington boots that looked too big for her. He hadn't passed her on the short trip up the track so she must have come off the moor.

She looked about twenty years old, ten years younger than he was, with a cascade of brownish hair tied back with a blue and white spotted scarf. She glared back at him from the darkest and liveliest of eyes. Although he seemed to tower over her, Andrew was at a disadvantage and he found he couldn't stop staring at her. She pulled in her cheeks with an air of impatience, waiting for him to speak.

He came to his senses, feeling a fool. 'Hello. I'm hoping you can help me.'

'Lost, are you?'

There was a touch of accusation in her soft lilting voice. 'Um, yes, I must have taken the wrong turning. I didn't realise I had gone off the road. I was looking for the village of Kilgarthen.'

'You should have taken the next left,' she said and made a snaking movement with her hand. 'The lane turns a bit but it would have taken you right into it.'

'Oh, really,' he laughed and was embarrassed at how stupid it sounded. 'I'm afraid I fell over. Is there anywhere I could clean up before I go on to Kilgarthen?'

'I'm on my way home for breakfast,' she said, looking up unblinkingly at him from her great dark eyes.

Andrew could see he was a nuisance to her. 'I'm sorry,' he said anxiously. His hand was hurting and the back of his coat was wet and muddy. 'But I don't want to go on in this condition.'

'I wasn't going to suggest you did. You'll have to come with me.' She walked onwards and left him on the spot, striding confidently over the slippery, uneven ground.

Andrew turned on his heel but had to yank his shoes out of the ground where they had stuck in the mud. The girl walked without a sound but each step he took made a loud sucking noise. He wouldn't have been able to keep up with her if he hadn't had long legs.

'I'm very grateful to you. My name's Andrew Macarthur. I've come down from London and I'm on my way to see Mrs Laura Jennings. Have you met her?'

'No.'

The girl didn't look at him but straight ahead. Despite her outsize shapeless clothes and overlarge boots she moved quickly and gracefully. Andrew fell slightly behind her and studied her back. She obviously didn't care about her appearance, her hair needed attention, having grown long into several lengths down her back.

'What's your name?' he ventured, hoping she'd slow down so he could walk comfortably beside her.

She kept her back to him and muttered, 'Davey.'

He would have said it was an unusual name for a girl but decided the remark wouldn't be appreciated.

After a few minutes' walk they reached a small shabby-looking farmhouse standing in the middle of a muddy yard with a few ramshackle granite outhouses behind it and a high peat stack beside it. Andrew stumbled over the large irregular granite cobblestones. A large brown mongrel dog which had been sniffing around the well came bounding up to them and the girl patted its broad head. Andrew felt himself shrinking inside. The dog was filthy, as if it had rolled over in the farmyard muck, and he prayed it wouldn't be curious about him. His hopes were in vain. The dog left the girl and before Andrew had time to get out of its way it reared up on its hind legs and put its huge front paws on his chest. Andrew had the dog's face close to his, its wide mouth open, long pink tongue hanging out and panting. The dog smelled awful.

Andrew looked helplessly at the girl but she stood and watched, her face expressionless. He tried pushing the dog away. 'Get down!'

The dog walked forward on its hind legs and pushed Andrew backwards. It was strong and Andrew had difficulty keeping his balance. He was about to demand that the girl call her animal off when she ordered quietly, 'Get down, Meg.'

Meg obeyed immediately and sat down beside her mistress. Andrew was furious, mainly because he was horribly embarrassed. He looked down in disgust at the muddy paw prints on his coat. When he looked up again, the girl had moved away and was taking off her boots round the side of the farmhouse.

He marched up to her with as much dignity as he could muster. She stepped inside a door which had black paint flaking off it and he made to follow her.

'Take they shoes off. We like to keep a clean kitchen floor.'

'I... I'm sorry,' he blustered, flushing crimson to the roots of his hair. He gulped and swallowed. The girl opened another door and closed it behind her, leaving him alone in what looked like a sort of shed. He shone the torch round his surroundings. There was a long work bench with a rusty vice attached to it and a row of clumsy-looking tools. Haphazard shelves were built into the walls and were hopelessly cluttered. Many household items, various shaped baskets, a brush and pan, dusters, boot polish and brushes vied for space with old shoes and boots. Farm tools, old pots of paint, a large tin of something called Jeyes Fluid, and a cobbler's last were mixed up with lots of unidentifiable rusty bits and pieces. Vegetables and jars of pickled onions and jams had a space to themselves. Long bunches of small onions were strung up overhead. There was a musty smell.

Andrew put his cases down and sitting on the doorstep he tried to untie his wet muddy laces. They were tight and unyielding and he had to tug with all his might. When that was accomplished he gingerly pulled off his shoes and was dismayed to see that his socks were soaked through up to his ankles. Mud was caked on the hems of his trousers. Glancing round the shelves, he saw a pile of rags and taking one he wiped off the worst of the mud, then cleaned his hands as best he could, grimacing at the pain from the hurt one. He shone the torch on it, expecting to see a gash, but there was only a little scratch. Retrieving his briefcase, he went up to the door the girl had passed through, tidied his short sandy hair with a hand, and taking a deep breath knocked once and turned the wobbly round handle.

'Come in, come in,' came a female voice and he found himself in a warm kitchen in the company of a middle-aged woman who shared some of the girl's features.

'Good morning,' Andrew said, extending his hand. 'I'm Andrew Macarthur. I'm sorry to be such a nuisance. I'm afraid I turned off from the lane by mistake. I met your daughter, Davey, and she said I might be able to clean myself up a bit.'

'Davey's our surname,' the woman said, shaking his hand. She was dressed in a well-worn wrap-around apron, her grey hair was curled over at the ends and secured with hairpins and covered with a black hairnet; she looked friendly but ill at ease. 'And that was Tressa, my niece, you met. Come over to the sink, Mr Macarthur. I've put out a clean towel for you. Then you must have a cup of tea. Tressa's gone to fetch her father, that's my brother, Jacka. He owns the farm. I'm Joan Davey. I've lived here all my life.'

The room was lit by two oil lamps but was dark and dreary and as cluttered as the other room. The windows were made of tiny thick panes and were hung with faded curtains. The floor consisted of cold flagstones, covered here and there with rush mats. None of the furniture matched and much of it looked as if it had been knocked together from scraps of wood. It smelled better than the other room, a pungent smoky odour came from the peat fire but was masked by the delicious smell of fried bacon.

Andrew washed his hands at the wide cloam sink and dried them on a rough towel that looked little better than a rag. He replaced it on the hook beside the threadbare piece of cloth hanging from the draining board. He couldn't do anything about the mud on his clothes, he'd have to wait for it to dry then brush it off.

Joan shyly pointed to a chair at the table which was covered with a faded chequered oil cloth.

Andrew sat down gratefully. A little rest and a hot drink would be very welcome before he went on his way. 'It's good to be out of the wet and cold.'

'The fog will stay down all day,' Joan said, making for the huge brown teapot sitting on a black wrought-iron range that looked to Andrew like something out of the ark. A little door was open and he could see a fire burning behind a grill. 'We're high up, here on the moor.'

'I understand I'm not far from Kilgarthen,' Andrew said, smiling for the first time that morning.

Joan dashed some creamy-looking milk into a tin mug, poured strong tea on top of it and placed it in front of him. 'No, you're not. Shame you came a cropper.'

A door on the other side of the kitchen was opened and Tressa Davey came in. Andrew stood up.

'Dad's finished the milking,' she said, ignoring Andrew and not looking at her aunt as she spoke.

Andrew felt extremely uncomfortable. His display of manners had been lost on the girl. He knew his presence was embarrassing Joan and he wondered if her niece was being deliberately unpleasant to embarrass him.

Tressa took off her coat and hung it up on a hook behind the door with some other outdoor clothing and aprons. She picked at the knot in the piece of string that was tied round her waist over a pair of baggy bib and brace overalls. Andrew kept his slanting blue eyes on her. She put the string in a pocket, pulled the straps of the overalls down and stepped out of them. Next she pulled off a holey thick grey jumper. As she took it off, she looked as if she had discarded over three stones in weight. She was left in an old flannel checked shirt and a pair of rough black trousers obviously cut down and stitched clumsily to her size and held up with an old faded tie.

Andrew was amazed. What was left was a scrap of a girl. She was so tiny he reckoned he could put both his hands round her waist and still touch his fingertips. She was a woman yet a child. And she was pretty. He saw that now. She was very pretty and he couldn't tear his eyes away from her face. Her complexion was clear and pale with slightly pink patches on her cheeks. Her nose was pert and, like her brow, mouth and jawline, perfectly shaped.

She moved about silently, helping her aunt get things ready for breakfast. She passed Joan a pudding bowl. She lifted the oil cloth at one end of the table, pulled out a drawer and took out a handful of knives and forks, none of which matched. She laid four places, putting the last one in front of Andrew. She put a battered square tin tray in the middle of the table then put a large white jug of milk and three assorted mugs on it. She went to the crooked homemade dresser and taking salt and pepper pots off a shelf put them next to the tray. She didn't look at Andrew once. He watched her, absentmindedly drinking his tea, not noticing it was bitterly strong.

Jacka Davey came into the kitchen and put his floppy hat on the dresser. Andrew stood up and the two men shook hands. The hugely built farmer wore equally shabby clothes and looked as ill at ease as his sister did and Andrew guessed the family weren't used to unexpected visitors, or strangers in distress, suddenly turning up. Not that Tressa seemed to care one jot about his arrival.

'Dad,' she said, slicing a long homemade loaf. 'This is that Mr Carthur I was telling you about.'

'It's Macarthur actually,' he corrected her then looked at her father. 'Andrew Macarthur. I'm pleased to meet you, Mr Davey, although I must apologise for the inconvenience I'm causing. I'm on my way to Kilgarthen to see Mrs Laura Jennings.'

'Nice to meet you,' Jacka said amiably, then he looked down shyly. 'I'll walk with 'ee down the lane and make sure you're facing the right direction for the village, but would 'ee care t'share a bit of breakfast with us first? The food's cooked 'n' ready. Now, you will join us, won't you? There's plenty t'go round. You're more than welcome.'

'Well, I… thank you very much. The bacon smells delicious and I haven't eaten for hours. I travelled down from London through the night.'

''Tis nearly seven-thirty. Folk will only just be getting up in the village. Sit down where you were,' Jacka said.

Andrew obeyed. Tressa actually looked at him, pausing in buttering the bread. He smiled but her expression didn't alter and she carried on with her task. She walked round him and sat down at the table.

Joan lifted two plates out of the oven and put them on the table. She next took an enamelled dish out of the oven and served out thinly cut rashers of bacon and fried eggs. Jacka was handed a plate piled high with food. He took three slices of bread and put them on the table beside his meal. A plate with two rashers of bacon and one egg was placed in front of Andrew.

'Help yourself to bread, Mr Macarthur,' Joan said pleasantly. She dished out a bowl of porridge from a saucepan on the range and handed it to Tressa then did the same for herself.

Joan put the teapot on the table and Tressa poured tea into the three mugs on the tray. She put the largest mug beside her father's plate.

'Thank you, my handsome,' he said, patting her arm fondly.

She smiled widely at Jacka and her small face shone like a beacon in the bleak surroundings.

Andrew was captivated and was staring at her when she turned to him. 'Do you want some bread?' she asked tonelessly.

'What? Um… yes, please.'

She pushed the plate of bread closer to him and he took a slice. 'Homemade bread,' he said. 'Delicious.' It sounded superfluous.

'So you're on your way to see Mrs Jennings then?' Jacka asked, after washing down a mouthful of food with a gulp of tea.

'Yes, I'm her solicitor and also her friend. As she's decided to live here for the time being she asked me to send down some of her things. I had some papers for her to sign so I thought I'd bring them myself. I've left them for collection at the railway station.' Andrew wouldn't normally have given away so much information but Tressa's coolness was unsettling him.

'A solicitor, eh?' Joan said. 'You must be some clever.'

'I met Mrs Jennings in the pub the other night,' Jacka said. He was feeling more at ease now and his natural chatty nature was breaking through. 'She was with her late husband's aunty. 'Twas terrible, her losing her husband like that so young. A terrible waste. I lost my two sons in the war and now there's only Tressa left. Tressa means third in Cornish and she was my third child. The Daveys always had sons to carry on the farm, now there's no one left to carry on the name. Mind you, Tressa's a good little worker. She'd work the fields and look after the cattle as good as any man. I'm lucky to have she.'

'I'm sure you are,' Andrew replied, gazing at Tressa's profile. She had finished eating and was looking over the rim of her mug, staring into space.

'I'm glad to hear that Mrs Jennings is getting out and about in the village,' Andrew said, adding pointedly, 'Tressa told me she hasn't met her yet.' He thought the use of her Christian name would stir her to look at him. He wanted to meet her beautiful eyes and see an interest in him reflected back. She got up and put more hot water in the teapot.

'You want some more?' she asked, standing close to him.

She smelled clean and fresh, of the raw tangy odour of the moor. 'Yes, please,' he answered. He didn't move his mug within easy reach of her and she had to lean across him. Her hair touched his face and he had an overwhelming desire to touch it. He put his hands between his knees until she'd moved away. No one offered so he helped himself to milk.

'Thank you very much for the meal,' he said to all three Daveys. 'It was delicious.'

'Bacon came from our own pig, milk from our cows,' Jacka said, digging between his teeth with a dirty fingernail.

'Do you farm mainly in cattle, Mr Davey?'

'Aye. Been Daveys cattle farming here for generations. There's sheep farming round here too.'

'I'm down here for a couple of days. I'd be interested to look over one of the local farms,' Andrew said, eyeing Tressa for her reaction. She was at her father's side, refilling his mug.

'Come up here then,' Jacka said, putting his thickly muscled arm affectionately round Tressa's tiny waist. 'If you're an outdoors man, spend some time with me and the maid. You won't be welcome on Rosemerryn Farm. He that owns it don't welcome strangers.'

'Really?' Andrew replied, his eyes boring into the side of Tressa's face. 'I might take you up on that, Mr Davey.'

As Joan cleared the table and carried the dishes to the draining board, Jacka lit his pipe and took the cigarette Andrew offered him. 'I'll save un fur later, thank 'ee. The women don't smoke.'

Tressa had disappeared outside with a few leftover scraps and came back empty-handed; presumably she had fed them to Meg. She began dressing in her outdoor clothes again. Andrew watched her. Joan gave her an old army khaki bag.

'I'll go ahead with the crib, Dad. You can catch me up later.'

'All right, me handsome. I won't be long.'

'Thanks for your help, Tressa,' Andrew said loudly. He was determined to provoke a response from her.

She looked at him for the briefest moment, cool and detached. She nodded, then was gone.

Andrew looked down at his stockinged feet with a feeling akin to dismay. He was considered good-looking in his own circle. Women were usually attracted to him, he was never short of dates. Tressa Davey had seemed almost oblivious to his existence.

Chapter 9

'Andrew!'

Laura rushed down the stairs of Little Cot, out of the front door and straight into Andrew's arms. 'What are you doing here? I couldn't believe my eyes when I looked out of my bedroom window and saw you walking down the hill. It's wonderful to see you.'

Andrew kissed both of her cheeks tenderly and studied her face. 'You look well, Laura. I must say I was really surprised at you staying on here. Are you sure you're doing the right thing? You could always stay at my flat or with some of your friends.'

Laura wriggled out of his arms. 'What on earth has happened to you? You're covered from head to foot in mud.'

'It's a long story. I've just met this extraordinary girl.'

'A girl? Where? What happened? Come inside and tell me over breakfast. I've just got up. It's a good thing I'm dressed or we'd have the neighbours talking.'

Andrew was impressed at what he saw inside the cottage. 'This is very nice. I was expecting to see something terribly old fashioned and basic, like the place I've just left. I don't want any breakfast, Laura. I've already eaten.'

He took off his coat and Laura made a face at the mud on it. 'What a state you're in. You're like a mucky child. Whatever you've been doing, it sounds very mysterious. Where have you been?'

'To a quaint little place called Tregorlan Farm. I turned off up their track by mistake and fell over in the mud. I met the Davey family, Tressa, her father Jacka, and her aunt Joan.'

'Did you meet anyone else? A son or a labourer? I saw a small man on the property the other day.'

'Oh, that must have been Tressa,' Andrew replied knowledgeably. 'For some reason she wears men's clothing. She's very pretty and very quiet.'

'Is she?' Laura smiled. 'Well, I've only seen her from a distance. Tell me about it in the kitchen while I make myself some breakfast. I'm ravenously hungry this morning.' As soon as they were in the other room, Laura demanded worriedly, 'Why have you come down to Cornwall, Andrew? There's nothing wrong, is there?'

'No more than you know already. I was concerned for you. I wanted to see for myself exactly how you are and I thought it was a good opportunity to bring down some of your personal things, they need to be collected from the railway station by the way, and get you to sign some papers at the same time. I've had all your things removed from the house to my flat. I'm afraid the house will have to be sold to help pay off the creditors you've inherited.'

'Thanks for all you're doing, Andrew.' Laura hung her head. 'I don't care about the house. Bill chose it, it was fussy and too big for our needs, especially as he didn't want a family. I don't think I could have faced going into it again. It means nothing to me but bad memories. It's lovely now being able to do what I please, when I please.'

Andrew held her tightly for a moment then he lifted her face. 'Neither of us will miss him, Laura. Go on, get your breakfast. Don't waste your time on memories of Bill Jennings.'

She shoved a poker through the grill of the range and pushed down the ashes of the fire before putting a log through the opening at the top of the range. It crackled merrily as it burned. 'Who'd have thought I'd be using one of these. Apparently most Cornish homes have these cooking ranges. This one has a back boiler and heats the water too. You're welcome to have a bath if you like. It's through that door there. Imagine, a bathroom downstairs.'

'I see you burn logs. They burn peat at Tregorlan Farm. I met up with Tressa after I fell over. She's not very friendly but she took me up to the farmhouse. She allowed her dog to jump up at me.'

Laura was amused. 'You mean she just let the dog jump up at you and did nothing about it?'

'Yes. Well, she called it off in the end. Then she shouted at me to take my shoes off before I went indoors.'

'She sounds awful,' Laura said sympathetically, putting a small saucepan of water on the range to heat for a boiled egg. 'The man who owns Rosemerryn Farm is absolutely beastly. Think yourself lucky you didn't end up there.'

'Oh, Tressa was lovely.'

'Lovely? In what way? You said she wasn't friendly.'

'I don't know, she just is. I don't think she means to be vindictive or anything. She's just not used to having visitors. When she took off all her outdoor clothes she was so tiny, like some mythical creature you could well imagine living on the moor.'

Laura arched her brows but said nothing. Andrew wasn't usually given to waxing lyrical over a female. The last place she'd expect him to take an interest in one was down here in Cornwall, and a lowly farmer's daughter at that. He'd always been rather scathing abut Bill's origins and made fun of his accent. Tressa Davey must be worth meeting.

'Jacka insisted I share their breakfast,' Andrew went on. 'Like Joan he was a bit shy at first but after a while they both opened up. I think they've fallen on hard times. The place was in a terrible mess and their clothes were old and shabby. Jacka told me his two sons were killed in the war. Now he only has Tressa to help with the farming but she certainly looks tough enough for anything despite being so small. He's invited me to look over the farm.'

'Are you going to?' Laura looked pleased. 'Does that mean you're staying down here for a while?'

He shrugged his wide shoulders. 'I thought I'd stay down here for a couple of days to reassure myself that you're okay. I don't know about tramping over some silly moorland farm though.' Andrew blushed because he knew he was lying. 'I could end up at the bottom of a swamp.'

'You probably will if Tressa Davey has anything to do with it. It'll be lovely having you around for a while.'

'I'll have to see about lodgings. Do you know of anyone who could put me up?'

'You could stay here but it wouldn't be right in a small village,' Laura said, carrying her breakfast to the table. 'We could go up to the shop and ask Aunty Daisy later.'

'Aunty Daisy! Who's that? Don't tell me you've discovered a long lost relative in this village or is it the name of some old Cornish character?' He screwed up his face and pretended to ram a pipe between his lips. 'Aw, ais, me 'an'some.'

Laura smiled wryly. 'She's Daisy Tamblyn and she owns the village shop and runs the sub-post office. She's Bill's aunt and she's been very good to me. It seemed natural for me to call her Aunty Daisy.'

As if on cue, Daisy opened the front door and called out, 'Laura, dear, are you there?'

'I'm in the kitchen, Aunty.'

'I've come down early to see if you had a good night,' Daisy bustled in. 'I was worried you – Oh!'

'Good morning, Aunty Daisy,' Laura said, amused that Daisy had jumped to the wrong conclusion about Andrew's presence. 'I've had an even earlier visitor than you are. This is Andrew Macarthur. He's just arrived from London. You've spoken to him on the telephone, remember?'

'P-pleased to meet you, Mr Macarthur,' Daisy struggled to say. 'I was surprised to see someone else here.'

Andrew shook Daisy's hand and piled on the charm. 'I've come down to see how Laura is and it's a comfort to find she has made friends here.'

'Sit down and have a cup of coffee, Aunty,' Laura said. 'Andrew can pour it.'

'I came down to see if you were all right and to tell you about Johnny Prouse,' Daisy said when she was sitting down with a cup of coffee in front of her. 'I rang the hospital before I came out and they said he can be discharged, tomorrow. I've got a spare key to his cottage and I'm going down to air it out later. Bunty's going to look after the shop. Now, did you have a good night, dear? You weren't frightened by the winds last night or waking up to see the fog?'

'I'm fine, Aunty, you needn't worry. I didn't even realise there were stronger winds than usual last night. I must be getting used to the sounds. That's good news about Johnny. Let me know if there's anything I can do for him. Andrew's going to stay for a couple of days. Is there anyone who could put him up? And he's brought down some of my things and they need collecting at the railway station. Do you know of anyone who would collect them for me?'

Daisy gazed at Andrew as he poured the coffee. Despite his muddy appearance she saw him as a slick city type, more suited to Laura than Billy had been. Just how close a friend to her was he? Was he down here hoping to stake a claim on the beautiful young widow? She shuffled her shoulders primly. 'I'll phone one of the delivery vans who call at the shop regularly, they'll gladly pick up your things for two bob. The pub takes in people all year round. Mr Macarthur can ask there.'

'Of course, the pub. You'll like it there, Andrew. It's called the Tremewan Arms and it's only just across the road and up the hill a bit. The landlord and landlady, Mike and Pat Penhaligon, are lovely people.'

'You have been busy making friends,' Andrew spoke to Laura but he was looking at Daisy. He grinned ruefully. So 'Aunty Daisy' was suspicious of him. That was funny seeing as he'd been captivated by a very different sort of woman a short time ago.

Laura shot Daisy a stern look. 'Not everyone in the village is nice and kind,' she said coolly. She was still smarting that Daisy had refused to tell her yesterday why Spencer Jeffries had hated Bill so much, saying it wasn't her place to say anything and she wasn't sure if she knew the whole story anyway. Laura had made up her mind to find out the truth from Spencer Jeffries himself.

Daisy looked away, rather shamefaced, but Andrew didn't notice. 'The Daveys are a nice lot,' he said.

'You've met them?' Daisy asked, eager to latch on to something else. 'How come?'

Andrew related the story of how he had ended up at Tregorlan Farm. 'She's got a heavenly little face,' he stated enthusiastically, referring to Tressa. 'But it's difficult to get a word out of her.'

'Aye, she's a nice little thing,' Daisy agreed, frowning. Surely this man's interests weren't directed in that unlikely quarter? 'She takes no notice of men, is happy to live in a world of her own. The Davey women don't tend to marry. It's the men who take a bride home to start off the next generation, but now there's no one left to carry on the name after Jacka. Tressa's a hard worker, has to be to help her father make ends meet. A few years ago Jacka lost most of his cattle from some sort of disease and he's never got back on his feet since. He had to take out a second mortgage on the farm. Most of the farmers keep ponies but Jacka had to sell off his which means them tramping over the moor to herd in their cattle. Sometimes he and Tressa take on work on the other farms, hay lifting, tattie picking, even a bit of gardening.'

'Gosh, that's bad luck.' Andrew returned to what was rapidly becoming his favourite subject. 'Tressa's so small. Probably because she doesn't eat very much.'

'What!' Daisy scoffed. 'That maid could eat a horse. She's tiny but she can't half pack her food away. She don't come into the village often but the few times I've seen her at a village social she ate platefuls of food. We don't see any of the Daveys much except for church and then Jacka comes in the same suit, shirt and tie he got married in. They haven't got money to spend on clothes, you see.'

Andrew was looking horrified. 'You mean I ate part of her breakfast this morning and left her to go about her work hungry? She only had porridge. No wonder she was reluctant to have me there. And is being poor the reason why she dresses in men's clothes? They must belong to her dead brothers. Poor Tressa. I must do something to make it up to her.'

'Why?' Laura challenged him. Not that she was against helping the girl but she was curious about Andrew's motives.

The eyes of the two women were upon him. Andrew shrugged his shoulders and said quietly, 'I just have to, that's all.'

–

When Daisy went back to the shop, Laura took Andrew across the road to the Tremewan Arms. Mike and Pat Penhaligon greeted Andrew in their customary warm and exuberant manner.

'We'll be happy to have you stay, Mr Macarthur,' Mike bellowed and Pat told him to speak more quietly. 'Strange thing is, that'll make three Londoners we'll have in the village. Are 'ee all emigrating down here?'

'Well, I can't speak for Mrs Jennings or your other guest,' Andrew said, signing his name in a small leather-bound register. 'But I'll be staying here for two nights and leaving on Wednesday morning. Do you do evening meals as well?'

'Aye, we can do all your meals for you,' Pat replied. 'Just let us know the ones you'll be in for. If you want to go out I can pack you up some sandwiches.'

'That will be lovely,' Andrew said appreciatively. 'You live in a beautiful county although it's very windy. I hope to explore it a little bit.'

'Particularly Tregorlan Farm,' Laura said drily.

Andrew shot her a scathing look.

'Eh?' said Mike, scratching the bush on his face.

'He's made friends with Jacka Davey,' Laura explained mischievously.

'Well, you'll probably have the opportunity to buy him a pint,' Mike grinned. 'He comes in once or twice a week.'

They were in the wide hallway of the pub and all eyes turned to watch a man coming down the stairs. He took each step slowly, as if he was afraid one of his knees was going to give out or he was going to lose his balance. He was about five feet, six inches tall, fortyish in age and dressed in fight shoes, an open neck shirt and a sports jacket.

'You're not going out dressed in just that, are you, Mr Beatty?' Pat fussed like a ducky hen. ''Tis much too cold for that. 'Tis damp and foggy and won't be no good for your chest.'

Mr Beatty stopped on the bottom step and looked bemusedly at his audience. 'I'm just going to the lounge to read the morning papers, Pat. I went back upstairs to fetch my glasses.' He alighted on the red carpet and held out his hand to Andrew. 'Sam Beatty. Did I hear you are to be a guest here, too?'

'Yes, until Wednesday,' Andrew replied in polite solicitor tones. He turned to Laura. 'I'm down to visit this lady. May I introduce Laura Jennings.'

Sam Beatty turned to her. 'Delighted to meet you, Mrs Jennings. I must confess I already know a little about you.' Laura frowned and instinctively took a step closer to Andrew. This was the man who had been watching her two days ago. 'On the village grapevine, you understand,' Sam Beatty added quickly. 'You can't help but pick up information when you drink in a public bar. I understand you live across the road and have recently buried your husband in the church-yard. Please accept my condolences.'

'Thank you, Mr Beatty,' Laura said tartly. She didn't like this man with his long horsy face and thin mousey moustache.

'If you are in the pub tonight perhaps I could buy everyone a drink,' Sam Beatty said brightly, putting his hands behind his back. That made Laura think he had something to hide.

'Mr Macarthur will be dining with me tonight,' Laura said before anyone else could speak. 'Perhaps some other time, Mr Beatty.'

'As you please.' Sam Beatty dropped his head, stepped backwards and withdrew.

'He's down here for his health,' Pat whispered confidentially, tapping her chest. 'Convalescing after an operation.'

'Surely he won't be walking the moor?' Andrew said.

'No. He said he chose a quiet spot where his well-meaning friends can't find him. He said they would smother him with kindness and help kill rather than cure him,' Pat explained.

'I didn't like the look of that man, Beatty,' Laura said when they were walking back down the hill to fetch Andrew's suitcase. 'I caught him staring at me a couple of days ago.'

'Well, you are a beautiful woman, Laura,' Andrew said. 'You shouldn't—'

'Be surprised if men stare at me? Well, I don't want any man staring at me, thank you!'

'Don't get so prickly. I'm glad I've come down here. You need moral support and you aren't going to get all you need in this village, no matter how well meaning some of the natives are.'

Laura put her arm through Andrew's and for a moment snuggled her head against his shoulder. 'I'll cook us something tasty for lunch then we'll get down to the business you need to talk to me about. I'm so glad you're here, Andrew.'

They didn't notice Ada Prisk drawing water at the pump.

Chapter 10

When Daisy got back to the shop, Bunty gave her a quick résumé of who had been in and what they had bought. 'And Joy Miller's coming back for stamps because of course I can't serve in the post office. She didn't look at all well. If you ask me she's coming down with a cold. I'm just cutting this ham carefully for Mrs Roach. You know how Cecil likes it just so. If he was my husband he'd eat what I put in front of him and if he didn't like it, he'd have to lump it. You can pop it in to Barbara when you go down to Johnny Prouse's to make sure everything's fine in his cottage.'

'Thanks ever so much, Bunty,' Daisy said, picking up a tin of biscuits which, among other things, had just been delivered and left in the middle of the shop floor. 'I'll put this in the storeroom. I just had to go down to Little Cot. Laura was so upset over yesterday. When she refused to come for tea with us I was afraid she'd change her mind about staying on here. I'm worried that if she doesn't get things worked out in her mind, her past will haunt her future.'

'She's all right now then, is she?' Bunty asked sympathetically, looking up from the meat slicer on the shop counter.

Daisy shook her head sadly. 'She's still cross with me. But how could I tell her the truth, Daisy? There's only you, me and Ince who really knows what happened between Billy and Spencer. Laura's had enough upsets as it is with her father's death, Billy's death, then learning what state he left her father's company in. What I'm afraid of is she's going to confront Spencer and demand to know what went on.'

'Well, you can't blame her. 'Twas a terrible way Spencer went for her, and in the churchyard, too, of all places. Bound to make the maid angry and curious. It would me.'

'Oh, well, we'll just have to wait and see what happens. She's definitely not going back to London yet anyway.' As Daisy approached the counter, her face broke into a smile. 'You'll never guess who she's got with her now. He's come all the way down from London just to see her. It's that solicitor chap that's been ringing her, Andrew Macarthur. He's going to stay in the pub for a couple of days. He'll turn a few heads in the village, you mark my words, specially the female ones and specially Marianne Roach's. He's ever such a good-looking man.'

'Oh really? So that's who he is. Ada Prisk was in here not long ago. She saw him hugging Laura. Made it sound like he was her lover.'

Daisy was annoyed at that but then began to chuckle. Bunty stopped slicing ham. 'What?'

'Well, first of all I thought he'd come down here after Laura but now I'm not so sure. He lost his way here this morning. Got himself covered in mud. He turned off to Tregorlan Farm and met up with young Tressa. He couldn't stop talking about her. I bet he's never come across anyone like her before, probably couldn't understand why she didn't fall for his charm. If you ask me he's smitten with her.'

Bunty looked astonished. 'Tressa wouldn't notice if every young man on the moor was interested in her. Don't expect she gave him a second thought, except that he was another up-country idiot who couldn't find his way to the village. Fancy that though, a man like he taking a shine to a young village maid.' Bunty shook her head as she returned to the meat slicer and wrapped the two ounces of ham in greaseproof paper. This latest bit of news had little entertainment value as far as she was concerned. 'As soon as he gets back to London he'll forget her. He'd only be interested in those party types.'

Daisy grinned impishly and took a five-pound note out of her pocket. 'Bet you he won't, not that easily. See this? He gave it to me. Do you know what for? To pack up a box of groceries and a bar of chocolate, so he can take them up to Tregorlan Farm.'

Bunty stared at the five-pound note, took off her glasses, polished them on her apron, put them back on and stared again as if she had never seen that much money before. She pursed her wrinkled pale pink lips and her hooded eyes glimmered with suspicion. 'What's he up to, Daisy? He'd better not have designs on Tressa like Harry Lean has, or I'll be straight over to Tregorlan Farm and be putting Jacka on to him. We don't want no funny goings-on aimed at our young women from the likes of he!'

Daisy put the tin of biscuits on the counter, lifted the counter flap and joined her friend on the other side. She put the money under a shopping pad and picked up a pencil. 'Well, I've met Andrew Macarthur and I think he's genuine. Laura says he's been a good friend to her. You see, he shared the Daveys' breakfast, and when I told him Tressa can eat like a hunter, he realised that he probably ate part of hers. Well, you should have seen his face, Bunty. He looked horrified. Said he wanted to make it up to her and that's what this five pounds is all about.'

'Crumbs. You never know what's going to happen next. It'll be a great help to the Daveys. Save them spending on groceries for weeks. But they won't like being offered charity. Jacka will be awful upset.'

'I tried to put Mr Macarthur right, Bunty, but he insisted. As soon as he'd settled himself into the pub he would have been up here and heading straight for Tregorlan Farm, but I managed to put him off until tomorrow. Said the Daveys wouldn't appreciate being disturbed twice in one day, even if it is someone bearing gifts. Perhaps by then he'll have second thoughts.'

'I hope so. If he's staying in the pub he might find out something about that strange bloke who's staying there.'

'What's strange about he?' Daisy ears pricked up. 'Pat said he's convalescing. He looks pale and a bit sickly. He comes in for cigarettes most days. Be better for him if he didn't smoke.'

'Well, I think he's one of them writers. He seems to be taking a very close interest in the village, if you ask me. When I went to see Laura for a contribution to Johnny's collection he was looking at me closely. A man who's convalescing shouldn't be hanging about in the cold staring at people.'

'Mmmm. Oh well, Ada Prisk will soon have his business, whatever it is, out of him. The postwoman brought me a parcel from my cousin Dorothy this morning. I'm hoping there'll be something in it I can pass on to Tressa. Her maid, Susan, is only thirteen but she's a big girl and her castoffs might fit her. It's a good job she's not too proud to let the village folk help her out. But before I take a closer look at it I'd better get on with some work.'

—

Marianne Roach crept round the side of the hay barn and took a furtive look around the stableyard of Hawksmoor House. As she'd hoped, there was no one about. She glanced at her wristwatch. It was two minutes to ten o'clock. She put her hands up to her hair and patted the snood that held it in place. Then she made her way jauntily over the cobbles in a pair of brown leather boots with a deliberate sway of her hips. She found who she was looking for in one of the stalls. Harry Lean was dressed in full riding kit and was saddling a large bay stallion. If he co-operated with her plan, and she was sure he would, a problem that may have been left her by Bill Jennings' sudden death could be solved.

'Hello, Harry,' she purred, walking slinkily towards him. Harry was standing on the other side of the horse. He'd been concentrating on securing the horse's tack and was startled. 'Good heavens, Marianne. What are you doing here?'

Marianne fluttered her heavily mascaraed eyelashes and, poking out her bottom lip provocatively, caressed the stallion's neck. 'He's beautiful. What's he called?'

'I thought everyone in the village knew the names of Hawksmoor's horses,' Harry answered charily, his dark eyes drawn in under a heavy frown. 'This is Charlie Boy. I asked you what you are doing here.'

She ran her red nail-polished fingers slowly over the saddle, tracing the pattern of the fancy stitchwork. 'I heard you were taking a day off work and I thought you'd probably go riding. I know you always leave the stables dead on the dot of ten o'clock and ride the moors before arriving back at the pub for a lunchtime drink. I changed my day off too. I thought we could spend some time together.'

Harry's wide nostrils flared and the corners of his mouth turned white with displeasure. 'What the hell for?'

'Eh?' Marianne's face fell but she rallied quickly, offering a sultry look. 'I thought you'd want to after the other night when you took me for a ride in your car.'

'That was just a pleasant little interlude for both of us, nothing more,' Harry said irritably. He checked the stirrups were in the correct position.

'But surely you want to get to know me better?' Marianne rounded the horse, making the animal toss its magnificent head. Leaning towards Harry, she ran her fingers up his arm. 'I'm sure we'd enjoy an hour or two on the moor together. You only have to lend me one of your mounts. I'm a good rider.'

Harry gathered up the reins and pushed the girl away from him. The pulse in his neck throbbed and stood out against a blue vein. 'I took the day off to enjoy a time of relaxation, not to have a bloody little brat hanging round my neck.'

'You didn't think I was a brat the other night,' Marianne said indignantly. 'Look, I've brought this with me.' She reached inside her jacket and took out a small bottle of brandy.

'Where did you get that?' Harry demanded tersely.

'In Launceston. A man I know bought it in a pub for me. Come on, Harry. Don't tell me you aren't game for a bit of fun. You like women. You've made that plain enough. We could have a really good time in a quiet place together. There won't be anyone about at this time of the year. If you don't fancy the moor we could always go somewhere more comfortable. I'm sure you must know some good places.'

Harry ran a finger round the whorl on his chin. 'Why do you want to have a good time with me?'

Marianne's whole body seemed to sigh with relief. 'Because you're handsome and experienced with women. A girl doesn't want to go with someone who doesn't know what he's doing the first time.'

'You're right about me, Marianne. I do like women. Fully grown, adult women.' Harry laughed unpleasantly. The men in the office would love hearing about this little tart. Some of them would be asking for her name and address. He went on in a sneering tone, 'But you're just a stupid little girl and I'm not interested in you. So clear off and stop bothering me or I'll tell your father what you've just offered me.'

'But what about the other night?' Marianne's chin trembled and she found it hard to keep a grip on herself. 'In your car we—'

'Just kissed and fooled around a bit.'

'I could tell my father it went further,' she spat, the bad temper she'd had from infancy taking over now.

Harry caught hold of her wrist and twisted it until she yelped. 'Now you listen to me, you little bitch! I'm not a man to be fooled with. Although I doubt very much you are a virgin I haven't done anything to you and heaven help you if you say I have. And as for your miserable wretch of a father, I know something about him which would not only ruin his career as a two-bit schoolmaster but would destroy his whole life and your mother's as well. Now, I'm going to let you go and you are going to run along like a good girl and will never ever bother me again. Is that understood?' He turned her wrist cruelly.

'Yes! Yes! All right, I promise. Just let me go!' Marianne begged him, struggling to get free.

Harry pushed her away and she had the added humiliation of landing heavily on her backside. She got up and rubbed at her buttocks. 'I'll get you for this, Harry Lean! Just see if I don't!' With tears flowing down her face and streaking her make-up, Marianne fled from the stall.

Harry led the stallion out in the biting fresh air, a hearty chuckle escaping from his throat. 'There's a couple of women I'd like to have my wicked way with on the moor or anywhere else for that matter, and neither of them is Marianne Roach,' he told Charlie Boy as he mounted him.

—

A short time after Andrew had left to unpack his things at the pub, Laura heard a loud ringing noise and looked out of Little Cot's window to see a butcher's horse and van pulling up beside the pump. Pat Penhaligon came outside with her coat and headscarf on, carrying her purse and a large tin plate. She was soon joined by similarly dressed and armed housewives and a queue formed at the open doors at the back of the van. Laura could hear Pat laughing and joking with the butcher and his other customers and after a few minutes the pub landlady withdrew with her plate of meat.

Laura read the name on the side of the red and grey van: 'Morley Trewin, Master Butcher and Poulterer'. Grabbing her coat and digging about in her handbag for her purse and food coupons, she ran to the kitchen, picked up a dinner plate then went outside to join the queue. A woman was just leaving and Ada Prisk was being served with 'sixpence worth of pasty beef and a piece of lamb, stringed and prepared for a roast, and make sure it's good lean meat!'

'Good morning, Mrs Jennings,' Ada boomed out before the butcher and the two women still in the queue could greet her. ''Tis a brave bit cold today but I dare say you're getting used to it now. I hear there's a gentleman down from London to see you. Friend of yours, is he?'

'That's right, Mrs Prisk,' Laura replied shortly. Smiling pleasantly, she turned to the other women, both ordinary looking and in their late thirties. 'It's Mrs Martin and Mrs Sparnock, isn't it? Your late mother-in-law used to do the church flowers,' she said to Mrs Sparnock. 'I saw you both walk up the hill and you live just along the road from me. I'm getting to know a few people in the village now.'

''Tis a pleasure to speak to you at last, Mrs Jennings,' Mrs Sparnock said. 'Welcome to Kilgarthen. Your husband was a great asset to the village.'

'Aye, he was,' agreed Mrs Martin who then looked shyly down on the ground.

Ada Prisk paid for her meat and nudged Laura as she left the van. 'Staying in the pub, is he? Your friend?'

'Yes, he is,' Laura answered as patiently as she could.

'Here for long, is he?'

'I really don't know, Mrs Prisk. That's his business.' Laura's face closed over and she looked away at the peak of Hawk's Tor.

'Huh! Village is getting full of foreigners, if you ask me,' Ada Prisk sniffed, charging off with her head in the air. Laura was amazed at how fast she could walk for her age.

'You mustn't mind Mrs Prisk,' Mrs Martin said, drawing Laura's attention. 'Meet Mr Trewin. He and his father and grandfather before him have looked after the village for meat for over sixty years.'

'Morley to you, ma'am.' Morley Trewin winked round Mrs Sparnock while playfully brandishing a meat cleaver. 'All the ladies know they can trust me to call three times a week, Monday, Thursday and Saturday mornings, come rain or shine. If you're poorly and can't come to the van then I'll call at your door.'

'Thank you very much,' Laura said, warming to the huge friendly grin that seemed to split the butcher's red face in half.

'He likes a bit of a joke but he's harmless enough,' Mrs Sparnock said. 'And I'll have a nice bit of kidney for the cat.'

'You spoil that ruddy cat,' Morley Trewin said, tossing a scrap of kidney on the scales. 'Wish my missus would treat me the same. Never catch she tickling me tummy while I'm sprawled out in front of the fire.'

Laura laughed with the other two women. 'See what I mean,' Mrs Sparnock chuckled, and Morley gave them another of his winks.

When Laura was looking over the wares in the van, a small boy, swathed in warm clothes, came up behind her. He was carrying an enamelled dish. 'Would you like to go first while I make up my mind what I want?' Laura smiled at him.

The mischievous dark face of the boy, which was covered in treacle toffee, grinned back at her. 'Thank 'ee, missus. Me mother's goin' down with a cold. I'm old enough to come out to the butcher now I'm nearly five,' he ended proudly.

'You're about the same age as Vicki Jeffries,' Laura said thoughtfully, standing aside for him.

'A half pound of pasty meat like me mother usually 'as,' the boy said to the butcher.

'Righty-o, my luvver.' Morley took the dish from the boy and sliced a chunk of skirt off a side of beef. 'This lady is Mrs Jennings, Benjy. Mrs Jennings, this little rascal is Benjy Miller. He lives further down the road from Mrs Sparnock and Mrs Martin and just round the bend. He's a big boy to come up here all by himself.'

Laura looked up and down the road. There was only one vehicle to be seen, the pony and jingle being driven slowly towards them by the fat elderly woman, but some of the rare traffic that passed through the village drove fast. 'Why don't you wait for me and let me walk you back home, Benjy?'

'All right, Mrs Jennings. Me mother's dyin' to meet you. You can come in and 'ave a word with 'er.'

'I'd be glad to. Do you know Vicki Jeffries, Benjy?'

'Only a little bit,' Benjy replied, putting his finger up his nose and twisting it round. Laura pulled his hand gently away. 'Me mother cleans for Mr Jeffries and once she took me with 'er and I played with Vicki. Mother caught us eating a spoonful of sugar. She wouldn't take me again because Mr Jeffries wouldn't like it.'

'I see,' she said. That man doesn't like anything very much, she thought sourly.

The old woman was driving past and she waved briefly to those at the butcher's van. She seemed to study Laura from shrewd green eyes that stood out clearly in her, moon-shaped face. She was as wide as a doorway and filled the seat of the jingle. She was much older than Laura had first thought. Her wide-brimmed bonnet was decorated with ribbons and dried flowers today.

'Who's that woman? Where does she live?' Laura asked Morley.

'That's Ma Noon and she lives right down past the other side of the village in a little place well off the beaten track. She had a smallholding and kept goats but lives only on her pension now. She's a bit strange, some people say she's mad. Your mother won't let you or your brother and sisters go near her, will she, Benjy?' The butcher patted the boy's head and Benjy nodded. 'All the village mothers feel the same way, always have as far back as I can remember. I reckon she's harmless enough. Your husband, Bill, weren't afraid of her. He used to spend hours at her place as a child.'

Laura thought it strange that after all the people he'd talked about, Bill had never mentioned Ma Noon. 'I'd like to meet her,' she said. Ma Noon could tell her something about Bill's childhood.

'Aw, don't you go and call on her, Mrs Jennings,' Morley said in a warning voice. 'She don't like that. She'll only have people on her property that she invites herself.' Benjy was getting impatient to get back to his mother. He took out a purse that was rammed down in his coat pocket and handed it to Morley who took out a half-crown and put in the change. He put the purse back firmly in the boy's pocket.

'I won't be long, Benjy,' Laura said.

She bought two chicken drumsticks for herself and Andrew and some sausages for the next day, then after dropping her meat off in the cottage she walked down the road with Benjy. He insisted on carrying his mother's meat himself and wouldn't let Laura take his hand. They passed the row of cottages below Little Cot and after walking a hundred yards turned off up the lane that led to the school. Benjy preceded Laura up the path of the first house on the corner.

He sprinted round the side of the building and disappeared and Laura assumed he'd entered by a back door. She heard him shouting, 'Mother! I've brung someone back with me.'

By the time she reached the back door, Joy Miller was standing on the doorstep, holding a handkerchief to her nose. 'Oh! Mrs Jennings. Do come in. It was good of you to walk Benjy back. I didn't like sending him up the hill for the meat but I came over all dizzy and I've got to have a meal for my man when he comes home from work. He's a woodsman on the Trebartha plantation and 'tis hard work.'

Inside the kitchen, Joy flopped down on a lumpy armchair which was covered in a brightly covered crocheted blanket. Laura closed the door after her. She recognised the linoleum that had been awaiting collection in the shop.

'Can I get you anything, Mrs Miller?' she said anxiously. 'Shall I call the doctor?'

'I don't need a doctor,' Joy replied, holding her head with her chubby hands. 'My head will clear in a minute. Sounds awful asking when you've been kind enough to visit me but I'd love a cup of tea, if you wouldn't mind. And I'll take a couple aspirins.'

'Not at all,' Laura smiled, glancing around. 'I can see where the tea things are kept. What about Benjy? Would he like a drink?'

Benjy had taken off his coat, hat and scarf and was playing with some toys scattered over one corner of the floor.

'Thank you. He usually has a drop of warm milk at this time of the day. You'll find a saucepan up on the shelf near the sink.'

'Have you any more children at home?' Laura asked as she made the drinks.

'I've got three at school. I had my four one year after the other, that's what you get when your husband's home, invalided out of the army, but thank God Bert survived the fighting.' Joy swallowed the aspirins. She pointed to her sagging stomach. 'That's how I lost my figure, although I was always on the plump side, but that's how my man likes a woman, thank goodness. And look at my hair. With a bunch of children always under your feet you don't get much time for titivating. Haven't had it cut and styled in ages. Mind you, it never was like your lovely blonde locks.'

Laura watched Benjy playing. 'So Benjy is your baby, so to speak. There don't seem to be any babies in the village.'

'No, that's a funny thing. Me and Natalie Jeffries brought things to a standstill. S'pose someone will start a baby boom off again one day soon. You, um, didn't have any children?'

'No,' Laura replied and the bitter regret was evident in her voice. 'I would have loved to have had a baby.' She shook her head to dismiss the bad memories. 'Oh, well. Is there anything else I can do for you? Benjy bought pasty meat. Who's going to make them for you? I would gladly but I wouldn't have a clue where to start. Do you want some dusting or washing done?'

'That's very kind of you but my friend, Sylvia, from Lewannick, will be here this afternoon. She'll make my pasties and there isn't anything else that needs doing. There is one thing though, I can't go to work today at my little cleaning job. I told Bunty Buzza in the shop I thought I'd be all right but when I got home I felt dizzy. I've managed to tell Mrs Sparnock I won't be needing her to look after Benjy for me. Could you tell Mrs Tamblyn I'm too poorly to go to Rosemerryn Farm, then if anyone's going that way they can drop my apologies into the farmhouse.'

Laura's eyes lit up. 'I can do that for you.' This gave her the perfect excuse to go to the farm and hopefully find Spencer Jeffries there and demand to know what had happened between him and Bill. And she would see Vicki too.

Chapter 11

Laura leaned her bike against the side of Rosemerryn farmhouse and looked round warily for Barney, the border collie. She hoped that as she had come on an errand for Joy Miller it would soften Spencer's attitude towards her. She had no doubt that the hatred he harboured against Bill was justified. Perhaps she could apologise in some way to him, say something to make him see she wasn't also the villain of the piece. Most of all she hoped he'd allow her to stay with Vicki while he went about his work.

She went round to the back of the house and rapped smartly on the door. She daren't call out and go inside as the villagers did; Spencer would probably bite her head off. As she waited, her courage began to fail. Every word of the bitter tongue-lashing she'd received in the churchyard was echoing inside her head. Vicki opened the door and Laura smiled at the little girl, then she breathed a sigh of relief as Ince Polkinghorne appeared.

'Hello,' Vicki said cheerfully, hopping on one foot then the other as the two adults stood gazing at each other. Even though she had a good reason for being here, Laura was flushed with embarrassment and Ince looked clearly worried.

'I, um…' Laura began.

'Is everything all right?' Ince asked. 'I'm waiting for Joy Miller to turn up so I can go to work.'

'Yes, I mean no. That's what I've come about. I've brought a message from Joy Miller. She's got a very bad cold. She's feeling dizzy and can't come to work. I said I'd bring the message to the farm.'

'That was very kind of you.' Ince smiled. He had been worried that Laura had come seeking a confrontation with his boss; Spencer had told him he'd had words with Laura but not the content of their quarrel.

'Come in and see my dolly's cot,' Vicki said. She was holding Ince's hand.

'Well...' Laura hesitated. She didn't want Spencer to come home and cause a scene in front of Ince. Now she was here she realised she wouldn't have got the truth out of the stony-hearted farmer anyway with Vicki present. It would have to be when he wasn't with his daughter.

'Come in,' Ince said, moving himself and Vicki back from the door. 'If you've been kind enough to bring us a message the least we can do is offer you a cup of tea before you go.'

Laura still wasn't sure. 'Won't... someone mind?'

'Too bad if he does,' Ince replied as Vicki trotted on before them into the roomy kitchen. 'I don't pander to all Spencer's bad moods. This is my home too. Besides, he's gone into Launceston to the agriculture store and won't be back for ages.'

As Ince reached for the tea caddy, Laura knelt down beside Vicki and admired her wooden rocking doll's cot. It was painted pink and decorated with fairies, elves and pixies. A doll was lying in it covered with knitted blankets.

'It's lovely,' Laura said, unable to resist stroking Vicki's silky hair. Then she straightened the collar on Vicki's dress and pulled her cardigan round her shoulders properly. 'What's your dolly called?'

'Elizabeth, after the princess, but I call her Lizzie. Daddy made the cot and Uncle Ince did the paintings. Clever, aren't they?' Laura pulled back the top cover and Vicki beckoned her to come closer. She said softly in Laura's ear, 'They made a fuss about it. Like a pair of old women.'

'Vicki,' Ince chided gently.

Laura watched fascinated as the little girl made a petulant face at her uncle. 'You fussed about how big it was, what colour to paint it and what pictures to put on it. You wanted the cot to be bigger and Daddy wanted Goldilocks and the three bears on it. Aunty Daisy was here one day and she called you a pair of old women.'

A big smile was spreading over Ince's face and he turned away to fill the teapot with boiling water.

'You did a very good job on the cot, Ince,' Laura said to his lean back, her voice full of laughter.

'Thank you.' He carried the teapot to the table. 'As you can see,' he bent down and kissed the top of Vicki's head, 'this miss is a proper little madam.'

'She's beautiful,' Laura breathed, leaning forward and kissing Vicki's cheek. It felt as soft as feather down.

Vicki blinked and grinned impishly. 'Don't forget to kiss Lizzie too.'

Both Ince and Laura kissed the doll which Vicki lifted from the cot and after this piece of adult indulgence she moved away to an armchair to undress it.

Ince pulled a chair out from under the table and Laura sat down.

'Everybody seems to live in their kitchens in Kilgarthen,' she commented as he pushed a mug of strong tea towards her.

''Tis the most comfortable place to be and the warmest in winter. Most folk only light their sitting room fires over Christmas.'

'I keep forgetting it's nearly Christmas. I wonder if Vicki's father would mind if I bought her a present. I'll get something for Joy Miller's children too, Benjy's very sweet. Do you think it would be appreciated, Ince?'

Ince was looking at her thoughtfully. He smiled in the gentle way that was his, adding an unusual but beguiling masculine attraction to his pleasant face. He looked completely at ease, leaning back in his chair, the sleeves of his checked shirt rolled up, his big hands resting lightly on the table. Laura felt here was a man she could confide in and trust.

'So you're still going to be here at Christmas, Laura. Presents would be appreciated in the Miller household but not so much here perhaps. Still, when a present's wrapped up, labelled and delivered, well... you can't disappoint a child, can you?'

Laura smiled and looked down at the table. 'Joy Miller having a cold gave me the perfect excuse to come here. I fully intended to ask Spencer why he and Bill hated each other so much. Bill must have done something terrible for him to hate me as well. He doesn't even know me. Bill and I didn't have... a good marriage.' She looked up at Ince and met the understanding in his dark eyes. 'You knew, didn't you? That everything wasn't well between us?'

'I had an idea. I felt that some things about him didn't quite add up.'

'What sort of things?'

'Simple things mainly. He'd say something and be smiling with his mouth, but not with his eyes. Most people took the things he did for the village at face value, but, I'm ashamed to say this really, I felt there was an ulterior motive to everything he did.'

'Some of Bill's gestures probably were to show loyalty to the place he was brought up in, but I think most of it was to show off. He had a top position in my father's company and it was an important company, but it was only one among many from where I come from. Bill was only small fry in London. In Kilgarthen he was cock of the walk.'

'He never mentioned you and I can't understand why he never brought you here. I'd have thought he'd be proud to show off his beautiful wife.'

Laura smiled at the compliment. 'I don't think he would have been able to strut around in the same way with me here.' She was also suspicious he'd gone with other women but she kept that to herself. 'What do you know about Bill and Spencer?'

Ince turned his face away and scratched a fingernail down the handle of the teapot. Laura got up and stood in front of him. Disappointment was thick in her throat. 'You aren't going to tell me, are you?'

He shook his head and looked directly into her eyes. 'I'm sorry, Laura.'

'But I have to know, Ince. My mind's been in turmoil since Spencer blasted me in the churchyard. You didn't hear him. To speak to someone like that in a holy place means there's a lot of hatred in his heart. It will be difficult settling down here knowing someone hates me and not knowing why. I'm going to have to ask him.'

'I do understand,' Ince said, rising and standing close to her. 'I'll have a word with Spencer after Vicki's gone to bed tonight. I'll tell him you'll be seeking a word with him and he must answer you truthfully.'

'Thanks, Ince. You're a good man.'

'Why are you talking about my daddy?' Vicki said, her heart-shaped face raised to theirs, cot blankets clutched in her hand.

Laura took the blankets from Vicki. 'We were just discussing why he'd gone into Launceston. Do you want me to cover up Lizzie for you?' she asked, hoping Vicki hadn't heard what she and Ince had said.

'Aunty Daisy and Aunty Bunty knitted the blankets for me,' Vicki said, tapping Laura on the shoulder as she crouched over the doll's cot. 'They do that because I haven't got a mummy,' she added matter-of-factly. 'Have you got some children? They could come and play with me.'

'I haven't got any children, Vicki. But I'd love to play with you.' Laura glanced at Ince. He was watching them uncertainly with his hands stuffed inside the pockets of his brown corduroy trousers. Laura felt a warm glow on her cheeks. 'If you want to get on with some work, I'd be only too happy to stay with Vicki, Ince.'

He looked at the clock on the mantelpiece and glanced out of the window. 'We're going to have some rain pretty soon. There are a few things I wanted to get on with in the yard. Half an hour wouldn't hurt.'

'I'll have to be going then anyway,' Laura told him. 'A friend, well, he's my solicitor also, has come down from London to see me. He's staying at the pub and I'm cooking him lunch. Is there anything I can do while I'm here? What did Joy usually do on a Monday morning?'

'Don't bother with that, you just play with Vicki,' Ince grinned. 'I can see you'll enjoy it. I'll be back soon.' Vicki showed Laura every item of doll's clothes she'd had made for her and Laura made up her mind to ask Daisy to teach her how to knit so she could add to the collection. Slipped in with Daisy's next contribution, Spencer need never know.

'You've got a nice lot of toys, Vicki.'

'Hundreds,' Vicki said proudly. 'Would you like to see my bedroom? I've got lots more up there. A rocking horse, a doll's house...'

As the little girl twittered on, Laura looked at her watch. Fifteen minutes had passed since Ince had gone outside. 'Just for a little while. I have to be going soon.' Taking her hand, Vicki led the way to a door which opened to reveal a narrow flight of stairs. They were covered in the middle with a thick green canvas-type of carpeting, kept in place by shiny brass stays. There were three doors at the top of a short landing, the occupants of Rosemerryn Farm each having their own bedroom.

Vicki stood on tiptoe and pulled down on the latch of the nearest door and they entered a small single bedroom. It was situated above the kitchen and because of that was quite warm. The bedding was pulled back, its top cover a patchwork quilt made in bright colours. The rest of the furniture was made of sturdy golden oak. A small china chamber pot could be seen protruding out from under the bed. As Vicki had said, the room was packed with toys.

'I've never seen so many toys before, Vicki,' Laura said, taking it all in and looking out of the small panes of the window on to the yard below. She could see Ince going into a barn, humping a huge sack on his shoulders. 'You're a lucky little girl.'

'Wish I had someone to play with though,' Vicki retorted in a grumbling voice. 'I'm glad I've got you for a while.' Laura could sense the loneliness in her voice. She felt angry. Although he lavished all the love in the world on her, Spencer Jeffries was unwilling to allow his little girl to grow up and it wasn't good for her.

Vicki took Laura's hand again and pulled her out of the room. 'See in here,' she said, her hand reaching for the latch of the opposite bedroom door. 'I've got a big bride doll in here.'

'I don't think we should go into someone else's room,' Laura protested.

'Daddy won't mind,' Vicki returned, pulling her through the doorway.

There was a big double bed with a brass headboard and foot. The wardrobe, tallboy, marble-topped wash-stand and dressing table were in walnut. The dressing table had an embroidered duchesse set on it, a woman's brush, comb and mirror set, and many cosmetics. The bride doll was on a stand on the tallboy and there were two large silver-framed photographs on either side of it.

Laura followed Vicki who was pointing to the doll which was dressed in a white silk Victorian crinoline, wax floral headdress and long net veil. 'That was my mummy's. She died when I was a baby. Daddy said I can have it in my room when I grow up.'

'It's beautiful. I'm sorry about your mummy.' Laura's eyes were on the photographs. One was of Spencer and Natalie on their wedding day, they were gazing at each other adoringly. The other one was of Natalie on horseback on the moor. She was leaning down from her horse smiling into the camera. Natalie had been exceedingly beautiful. Vicki had the same wonderfully shaped eyes. Laura touched the photograph of Natalie on horseback. 'Is this your mummy?'

'That's right, Mrs Jennings.'

Laura's heart froze so rapidly she thought she'd die on the spot.

'Daddy! You're back early,' Vicki exclaimed, running to Spencer.

'Yes, I am, and it's a good thing too.'

Laura turned round slowly. She dreaded facing the loathing coming her way. Spencer was standing in the doorway, his head slightly bowed because he was taller than the doorframe. His face was the harshest she had seen it, his grey eyes blazing like clear diamonds. She thought the very breath of Spencer Jeffries would turn her to stone.

'I... I... Vicki was showing me some of her toys.'

'Vicki, go to your bedroom and play in there, please,' he said grimly. 'I want to have a few words with Mrs Jennings.'

Vicki looked at them curiously but sensing her father's gravity she tripped along to her own room and closed the door.

'Downstairs, you!' Spencer snapped at Laura.

He waited for her to obey, which she did on shaky legs, then he closed his bedroom door with a bang. He bounded down the stairs after her and closed the door at the bottom.

Laura knew her intrusion was unforgivable. She wanted to speak, to explain about her errand, her reason for being here, but the words stuck in her throat. Suddenly she felt she couldn't breathe. Seized with a feeling of panic, she wanted to get out of the farmhouse and into the cold air. She snatched up her scarf and gloves from the table and shrieked when Spencer leapt forward and swiped them out of her hands.

'You're not going anywhere, woman, until I've had my say,' he snarled. 'How dare you come here and walk all over my house! What are you doing alone with my daughter? Didn't I make it plain enough to you yesterday? You aren't welcome here, nor near my child. I don't want her to have anything to do with you, not ever. What have I got to do to get rid of you? Drown you in a bloody bog on the moor?' He was shaking with rage, his bold fair features twisted out of all recognition.

Laura couldn't bear any more. Forgetting that Vicki was just above them, she lost control. 'How dare you speak to me like that, Spencer Jeffries. If you've got something against me because of Bill then have the decency to tell me what it is because I haven't got a clue! I'm trying to start a new life for myself but I'll get nowhere if every time I see you I get a barrage of hatred.'

Then she lunged at Spencer. 'I didn't come here for this!' she cried, lashing out with her fists. 'I didn't come to cause trouble. I came over here to tell you that Joy Miller is poorly and can't do her work for you today. And I'll have you know, you wretched swine, that whatever Bill did to you he did a thousand things worse to me! He treated me worse than the dirt under his feet. He was cruel and evil and he despised me.' She was trying to scratch his face, and Spencer struggled to fight her off. 'Think yourself lucky that you've got a child because Bill wouldn't let me have a baby, the thing I wanted most in all the world. He was a terrible man and you're no better! I hate you!' Burning tears of despair were flooding down her face. Then she saw a flash of white-gold hair across the room and became still. Spencer gripped her tightly or she would have fallen to the floor. She was horribly aware that Vicki had opened the door at the bottom of the stairs and was standing on the last step, her little face puckered up and about to cry.

'Oh no,' Laura gasped. 'Vicki, I... I...' She wrenched herself away from Spencer and he went to Vicki and picked her up.

'Why are you fighting?' Vicki asked in a trembly whisper. 'You frightened me.'

Spencer looked at Laura. His anger was gone, replaced by distress and shock.

'I-I'm sorry, Vicki,' Laura blurted out, her hands to her face in horror.

She ran out of the room and past Ince on the doorstep as he was coming in to find out what the shouting was about. 'Laura...'

She pushed him aside and ran to her bike. She scrabbled with the handlebars and became nearly hysterical when Barney started barking and jumping at her. She got her feet in the pedals and screamed when she was pulled round.

'It's all right, Laura. It's Ince. I've told the dog to go away.'

'No, get away from me. I want to get out of here.'

'I'm going to help you do that. You're in no fit state to ride home. Let me take you on the cart.'

Laura felt her last bit of strength seep out through her legs and she fell against Ince. Holding her up he walked her to the cart and lifted her up on the seat then got up beside her. Laura stared straight ahead as they bumped down the rough track and Ince put his arm round her to keep her steady. He drove towards Kilgarthen but when they came to a wide gateway he pulled the horse into it. He turned to her.

Laura didn't see the cattle grazing in the field, only the fear and incomprehension on Vicki's face. How could you do that to that little girl? She asked herself viciously.

Ince put his hand under her chin and pulled her face round to him. With his other hand he pressed on her shoulder. 'I'm sorry, Laura.'

Her eyes filled with hot, scalding tears. He pulled her towards him and she flung herself into his arms. She wound her arms round his body under his coat and put her face against his neck so she could feel his warmth. Then she sobbed her heart out. Her emotions spilled out in an ever growing stream. All the bitterness, coldness, numbness, uselessness, all the things Bill had made her feel, all the things he had taken from her. She wept with grief for all the wasted years, for her father's death and the ruin of his company, and the acute feeling of loss at having no children.

She would get over all that. She knew when her tears were ended it wouldn't matter so much any more. But there was a new pain in her heart. She cried over the terrible experience that had caused her to upset the sweet innocence of little Vicki. She'd never forgive herself for that, but somehow she vowed she would make it up to her.

Ince held her close and stroked her back and caressed her hair. He didn't speak, it wasn't necessary. All she needed for now was his closeness.

Chapter 12

Lower down the hill from Little Cot Ada Prisk was knocking on Mrs Sparnock's door. Mrs Sparnock answered it with her hair covered in a scarf wound tightly like a turban and a long-handled cobweb duster in her hand. She held back a sigh.

'I'm sorry, Mrs Prisk, but I'm very busy,' she said, trying to sound determined.

'Oh, I don't want to come in,' Ada said, but narrowed her face coldly. 'I'm just on my way to see Mrs Jennings. I made too much apple crumble for my tea last night. I thought she might like to finish it off. Probably doesn't know how to cook good plain food.'

'I'm sure she'll appreciate that,' Mrs Sparnock replied dubiously.

Ada came to the real reason why she'd called. She moved closer to the other woman and her advantageous height put her thin lips next to Mrs Sparnock's ear. 'I see that solicitor chap's in there again with her.'

'Is he?' Mrs Sparnock bent her head so she could see round the door. 'How do you know?'

'I saw him go in, of course. Didn't give her time to have her breakfast decently. It's as I expected.' Ada raised her nose disapprovingly. 'She's a widow. Got an attractive face and figure. Her father may have squandered his money but I bet Bill left her quite a bit. We'll see all manner of men knocking on her door.' Ada looked all round to make sure they weren't being observed. 'These city people are loose with their morals, you know. Wouldn't know respectability if it jumped up and smacked them in the face.'

'She seems a nice woman though,' Mrs Sparnock returned in hushed, slightly shocked tones.

'We'll see,' Ada said sharply. She straightened herself up and turned to face the home of her quarry. 'Well, I haven't got time to spend chatting to you all day. Good morning, Mrs Sparnock.'

Mrs Sparnock returned the pleasantry and watched the tall figure hastening up the hill. She decided against cleaning away the cobwebs; she would clean the outside of her windows instead.

—

Laura was getting fed up with the sympathetic looks Andrew kept casting in her direction. 'I've told you a dozen times, Andrew, I'll be all right. If you want to go over to Tregorlan Farm, then go. I've got plenty to do and you're under my feet. I've got my housework then I'm going down to see if I can do anything for Joy Miller, then later today old Johnny Prouse is coming out of hospital and I'm going to call on him with Aunty Daisy.'

'But I don't like leaving you alone,' Andrew said stubbornly.

'Andrew!' Laura moved briskly to the broom cupboard and took out a long-handled brush. 'I'll sweep you out of the door.'

Andrew jumped back and the head of the brush narrowly missed his toes. 'But you were so upset yesterday, that chap had to bring you home. Goodness knows how you would have arrived here if it wasn't for him. You looked terrible. I've never seen you like that before. Look, why don't you come to Tregorlan Farm with me? It'll be good for you, meeting new people.'

'No, thank you.' Laura tightened her facial muscles. 'I've had enough of farmers for the time being.'

'Except for the one who brought you home?' Andrew challenged her, standing his ground with his hands on his hips. 'I noticed you and he were rather matey.'

'Ince is different,' Laura retorted, colouring up in his defence. 'Don't read anything wrong into his kindness. He's warm and gentle, he's comforting to be with.'

'But not exactly like a big brother in the way that I am to you?'

'If you don't get over to Tregorlan Farm soon the Daveys will be out on the moor and you won't be able to find them,' Laura said angrily.

'I think they let their cattle graze the common pasture land as well as their fields.'

'How do you know that?' Andrew was amazed.

'I know a lot about what goes on around here already. Village people are very chatty. Well, are you going now or are you going to risk giving me a nervous breakdown from sheer exasperation?'

'All right, I'm going.' He held up his hands in submission. 'I suppose you'll be okay. Your Aunty Daisy is just up the road.'

Reassured that Laura was unlikely to lapse into one of the crying fits she'd suffered frequently since Ince Polkinghorne had helped her into Little Cot the previous morning, Andrew made eagerly for the door. A sharp rat-a-tat-tat on the other side startled him.

'Oh, who's that?' Laura said, vexed. She was even more vexed when Andrew opened the door and she saw who it was. Seizing her chance, Ada Prisk pushed past Andrew into the room and held out the dish in her hands to Laura.

'It's half of an apple crumble, Mrs Jennings,' she said in a sugary voice. 'I thought you might like it.' She lifted off the tea towel it was covered with. 'Apple crumble is something of a speciality of mine. You only need to put it into the oven and warm it up for about half an hour.'

The old woman was only here to slake her curiosity, Laura was sure and she took the offering with a curt, 'Thank you, Mrs Prisk.'

Ada's shrewish eyes were peering into every corner of the room. They washed over Andrew and seemed to sum him up in one penetrating perusal. He stepped back a couple of paces, a look of alarm on his face. It was like being given an intimate examination in full public view.

'So you're Mr Macarthur. Must be nice for Mrs Jennings to have a familiar face around. So these are electric lamps. Pretty shades. I've heard that electricity is dangerous. Wouldn't have it myself. Lovely silver, but then you must be used to having valuables of every kind. Are you going to decorate for Christmas? S'pose you don't feel up to it with Bill just laid in his grave, and it wouldn't be proper anyway. Still, never mind, there's always next year. Or won't you be here next year? Lovely photograph of Bill. None of you, I see. I bet Bill would have loved to have photographs of children on the mantelpiece. Didn't you want any children? Thought they'd tie you down, I expect.'

'How could you possibly know anything about me?' Laura snapped, angrily bringing the old woman's monologue to an end.

'Well, I—'

A sudden cold draught of air made Ada whirl round. Andrew was holding the door open. 'If you don't mind,' he said in his coolest professional voice, 'Mrs Jennings and I are very busy.'

The flesh on Ada's hawk-like face rose upwards as she bristled with indignation. 'Well, I'll be going now,' she said acidly.

'You might as well take your dish with you,' Laura said. 'I don't like sweet food.' With an insincere smile she added after a deliberate pause, 'But thank you for the thought.'

Ada wanted to say a great many things but the couple had been polite and she had breached many points of etiquette. Her comments would be best left said to others. With head down like a charging bull, she swept out of the room.

Andrew closed the door quickly and leaned his back against it. 'What a dreadful woman. I hope there aren't too many like her.' On a sudden thought, he opened the door and looked up and down the hill. He saw Ada Prisk talking to another woman who was cleaning her windows. 'She's already spreading her gossip.'

'Ohhhh, I could do something wicked to that woman,' Laura uttered with great feeling, clenching her fists.

'I'll make you a cup of tea,' Andrew said.

'You will not,' Laura asserted herself. 'The old dear's given me back some fighting spirit. Off you go to Tregorlan Farm now!'

-

The two gossiping women had disappeared when Andrew tied the box of groceries onto the back of Bill's bicycle, which he was going to use to ride to Tregorlan Farm. He was annoyed when Sam Beatty came up to him.

'Good morning, Mr Beatty,' he said politely, but coolly. He hoped the other man wasn't angling for an invitation to come with him.

'Good morning, Mr Macarthur,' Sam Beatty replied, smiling broadly and rubbing his woollen-gloved hands together. 'I'm sorry I missed you at breakfast. I don't get up very early. Are you off for the day?'

'I thought I'd take the opportunity to roam across the moor.' That should do the trick, Andrew thought gleefully. A convalescent wouldn't be able to undertake anything arduous.

'I bid you good luck with it,' Sam Beatty said. 'I only wish I was up to it myself but I find a slow walk along the lanes beneficial, although of course I have to be careful in damp atmospheres. But we have the sun out this morning, should be a lovely day. Perhaps you'd like to tell me about your excursion over a drink tonight. I trust Mrs Jennings is quite well?'

'Why shouldn't she be?' Andrew asked suspiciously. After what Laura had said of her doubts about this man, Andrew also distrusted him.

'Oh, no reason,' Sam Beatty said lightly, but his thick eyebrows rose up to his hairline. 'Just exchanging pleasantries. I'll let you get on, Mr Macarthur. Goodbye.'

Andrew rode off, unsure whether he ought to regret his moment of rudeness. The man was probably only trying to be friendly.

He had been worried he'd have difficulty finding Tregorlan Farm again but when he saw its signpost in the hedge he shouted, 'Yes!' excitedly.

In the clear daylight he saw that there was a way over the track which would give passage to a wide vehicle without too much difficulty, but he walked the bicycle up to the farmhouse so the groceries wouldn't be jolted about. Daisy had packed up the box for him but had begged him not to risk upsetting the Daveys with what she had finally called an insensitive gesture, but Andrew had a cover story worked out.

He tramped up to the side door of the farmhouse. He had come prepared for farm conditions today. He had already intended to walk the moor while he was here and he had brought old clothes and his hiking boots from his university days when he and some friends had walked the Pennines. Even so, he looked smarter than the average Cornish labourer.

He knocked loudly on the door and Joan Davey answered him almost at once.

'Mr Macarthur,' she said nervously. 'Fancy seeing you again so soon. Would you like to come in?'

'Good morning, Miss Davey,' Andrew said, putting the box down and pulling off his boots.

Joan peered down into the box as she went on, 'You'll have to excuse the state of the kitchen. I've just started some ironing. I'd come out to the back-house to fetch the washing basket.'

They went into the kitchen carrying their burdens. Joan had spread sheets over one half of the table to do the ironing on and Andrew put his box down on the other half. Joan put the washing basket down on the floor, her nose still over the contents of the box.

'Can I get 'ee a cup of tea, Mr Macarthur?' She picked up a cloth and her hand hovered over a black flat iron heating up on the range.

'No, thank you,' Andrew replied, eager to get on. 'I thought I'd take Jacka up on his offer and go out in the fields with him. Looks like I've missed him. If you point me in the right direction, perhaps I can catch up with him.'

'Jacka went out over an hour ago but Tressa should still be about the place. She'll take you to Jacka.'

'Right, I'll go and find her then, before I miss her too. I wanted to drop this off first.' He pointed to the box and went on unashamedly, 'Where I come from it's the custom to repay the hospitality shown to distressed travellers. It's only a little something. I hope you'll except it with my good wishes. You were all very kind to me yesterday morning. I was very appreciative of your help in finally getting me to Kilgarthen.'

Joan dropped the cloth and rubbed her rough hands down her apron. She smiled shyly. 'Well, I... I'm sure it's very kind of you. There was no need for you to do this. Jacka won't know what to say.' She lifted up a packet of tea and Andrew watched the childish delight spreading across her rugged face; he was reminded of his young nephews on Christmas Day.

'Tinned peaches,' she said, lifting the items out and putting them on the table. 'Cracker biscuits and, good heavens, a bar of chocolate! Tressa loves chocolate. I don't know what to say, Mr Macarthur.'

'You don't need to say anything. Just enjoy it. Now I'll be off to find Tressa.'

To save Joan any more embarrassment, and because he was desperate not to miss Tressa leaving the farmyard, Andrew rushed to the door. He put his boots back on rapidly, then went to track down his real reason for being here.

He rounded the house and saw Tressa, with Meg, several hundred yards away as she headed off for the fields. She was wearing the same chunky clothes, the same spotted scarf tied back her hair at the nape of her neck.

'Hey! Tressa!'

She turned round and waited for him. As he got closer, half running, she seemed to be staring right through him. When her eyes alighted on his smiling face, her wide full mouth stayed clamped in a straight line. The smile drained from Andrew's face and he felt a fool; he couldn't think of one single word to say to her. Meg ignored him.

'Lost again, are you?' Tressa asked in a wary tone.

'No! No, I... I've come to take up your father's offer, to look over the farm.' Now he was talking, his words were coming out thick and fast. 'I've just been speaking to your aunt. She told me you're heading his way. Can I walk with you?'

'I suppose so.'

She made Andrew feel he was a major irritation to her but he didn't care. This country girl would soon fall for his charm. He'd only have to get her talking. She turned round and walked on. He kept beside her, his hands casually inside his coat pockets.

'It's a lovely day,' he said.

There was a short silence before she replied, 'Yes, it is.'

'I suppose you're so used to the weather you can always tell what mood it's going to be in.'

Again, a pause. 'Not always.'

'Meg is quiet today. She didn't jump all over me.'

There was that hesitation again before she spoke. 'She does what I tell her.'

Andrew became quiet. Her remark had sounded something like a warning. Had she commanded the dog to jump up at him with its big muddy paws the day before?

They tramped on through two hayfields then through a field where the herbage had been eaten down to the roots and liberally manured. In the next field were four cows in calf, feeding on a supplement of hay.

'They're fine-looking animals,' Andrew said, hoping some flattery about the livestock would bring the girl to a friendlier frame of mind. 'What breed are they?'

Tressa took her time looking them over. Andrew had to ask his question again. Eventually she answered, 'Moor cross-breeds. A bit of South Devons with Ayrshire.'

'Are all the moorland cattle that breed?'

'Mostly.' They left the field by an easy climb over the stone wall and were on open moor. Andrew felt the cross-winds tugging at his coat and buffeting his face. His eyes watered and he screwed them up. He knew from Laura that the mountainous hill up ahead was called Hawk's Tor. He hoped they wouldn't have to climb it. In this wind it would make talking rather difficult. He glanced at Tressa. The wind didn't seem to have any effect on her. She wore the same inscrutable expression.

'Is Jacka far from here?' Andrew had to raise his voice to be heard above the whistling of the wind.

'Yes, but I know where he is. I can follow his tracks.'

'Can you?' he asked incredulously. He couldn't see any sign of anyone having walked over the moor. 'How?'

Tressa turned her head to look at him. Andrew's heart fell, the expression on her lovely face told him she thought him stupid. She answered in one biting word. 'Practice.'

Andrew strode on beside her in silence. Trying to get to know this girl was harder than trying to crack walnuts with no teeth. After a while she stopped and spoke in the longest sentences he'd had from her yet. She pointed to the summit of the tor.

'See up there? 'Tis said the ghost of a lost eighteenth-century traveller haunts the top of the tor. If you get the sun behind the tor at the right angle, like it is today, some of the rocks shine and form the image of the lost soul on horseback. He rode up there to try to see his way off the moor, fell off his horse and broke his neck. Keep looking and you'll see him.'

Feeling he was getting somewhere at last, Andrew shaded his eyes with one hand and peered up at the summit. He stayed motionless for several moments. 'Whereabouts is the horse and rider supposed to be? I can't see anything.'

He received no answer. He looked at Tressa but she had gone on many yards ahead with Meg. She beckoned to him. Andrew walked forward eagerly but after only three steps he felt his feet sinking in thick mud. He carried bravely onwards, reasoning it must be safe as Tressa and Meg were standing on firm ground up ahead, then he cried out in fright as his legs sank down to the knees into a wet oozing bog.

'Help! Help! I'm sinking.'

Tressa stood and watched him, her face a straight mask.

'Don't just stand there, Tressa. Help me!' Then the horror that he would sink down and disappear in a boggy part of the moor was replaced by a greater horror. Tressa and her dog had obviously skirted round what was only a small patch of bog marked by a growth of reeds, and she had deliberately let him walk into the bog to make a fool of him. She had probably made up the story about the lost traveller too.

He dragged one foot to the side of the slimy sucking mud and followed it with the other. In four side steps he reached the edge and after a humiliating struggle he hauled himself out onto firm ground. Tressa had not moved. She and Meg were like two statues blending into the bleak background behind them. Only Tressa's hair moved, lifting on the wind. She was still watching him.

Sucking in a deep angry breath, he strode up to her. 'Very well, Miss Davey, I get the message loud and clear! But it's more usual when a woman is not interested in a man simply to tell him!'

She didn't reply and she didn't change that same stone-cold expression. Andrew was completely at a loss with her. He shook his head. 'You're... you're not human.'

There was nothing he could do to pull even a few shreds of dignity together. He headed back the way they had come. When he got to the stone wall of the field, he turned to see if Tressa and her dog were still standing on the same spot. They were nowhere to be seen. He sat down on the wall and put his head in his hands.

—

'Come and look at all this.' Joan danced about excitedly as her brother and niece came into the kitchen for their evening meal.

Jacka laughed. 'What's up with you then? You won something on a raffle?'

'Look! Both of you.' Joan had laid out the contents of the box Andrew had left with her along the widest part of the dresser.

'Where did all this come from?' Jacka exclaimed, scratching his head and making a rasping sound on his thick coarse hair.

'From Mr Macarthur. He said it's the custom where he'd come from to return hospitality to travellers in distress. He said he was ever so grateful to us for helping him yesterday. Kind of him, wasn't it? There's more than what you can see there. I've put half a pound of butter in the cold cupboard. We haven't had this much food in the house for years.'

'He was here today?' Jackie pushed out his lower lip and picked up a packet of sugar and a bag of plain flour, one in each hand.

'Aye, didn't you see him? He said he was going to look round the farm with you, like you said he could. He left here to find Tressa.' Joan looked at her niece who was hovering behind the table. 'Didn't you see him either, Tressa? Oh, no! Don't say he got lost on the moor!'

Jacka turned to inquire and saw the defensive expression on his daughter's face. 'Well?' Jacka demanded.

Tressa tilted her chin and her dark eyes burned with defiance. 'I saw him briefly. He didn't like getting his feet wet so he changed his mind and went back to the village.'

Jacka and Joan exchanged puzzled looks. 'What do you mean he didn't like getting his feet wet?' Jacka asked severely.

'Yes, what do you mean, maid?' Joan repeated suspiciously. 'He had proper walking boots on.'

'Were you offhand with him?' Jacka roared, beating a hasty path round the table. He clutched Tressa's arm, gently but firmly. 'Tell us what happened.'

Tressa blinked, something she rarely did. 'He walked through a boggy patch, that's all.'

'He what? He wouldn't have walked through it if you'd pointed it out to un. Why didn't you do that?' Then as the truth dawned on him, Jacka's face drooped to his chest. 'You never made him walk through it on purpose?' he wailed. 'What on earth did you do that for? Are you bleddy mazed, girl? What's he ever done to you? And him coming here and being so kind to us too! Well, I'll tell you what you're going to do. You won't taste a thing out of his kindness to we until you get down to the pub where he's staying and apologise to un.'

Tressa tried to wriggle away from her father. 'But Dad—'

'But Dad nothing. There'll be no supper for you until you get back. Now you get up those stairs this instant and wash and put on a dress and off to the village with you. You're not to take Meg with you and don't you dare come back until you've put things right with Mr Macarthur. Go on, before I really lose my temper with you and smack you one.'

Tressa rushed from the room and ran up the stairs. Jacka followed her to the foot of the stairs and shouted after her, 'I should never have spoiled you the way I did! Just cus you're the only child I've got left! That man's got as much right to walk over the moor as we have! It all belongs to the Lord! And comb your bleddy hair!'

'Jacka! Calm down,' Joan implored him, pulling on his arm. She was worried when her brother got so angry he swore. 'You'll bring on one of your turns. She's doing as you said, now leave her be. Come back to the kitchen and have a mug of tea. I'll dish up the supper.'

At his place at the table, Jacka kept up a barrage of grumbles. 'She isn't like no other young maid. Spends too much time on her own, she does. If she's not working, she's out on the moor alone or else she's in her room reading, reading, reading those damned books she gets off the travelling library. Not romantic stuff but adventure and war stories. Where's that going t'get her? You know, Joan, I wish she'd meet some nice young man and get married and give me some grandchildren.'

–

Lighting the candle in her room, Tressa pulled off her clothes and stood in her underwear, a long flannel vest and a most unbecoming pair of white cotton knickers. She poured out the hot water from the pitcher her aunt had carried upstairs for her into the bowl on the washstand. She shivered with the cold but she was more concerned with the way her father had shouted at her. Jacka seldom got angry with anyone, especially her, but at the moment he was furious with her. Things had happened today to rock her private little world.

'Blast Andrew Macarthur,' she muttered, moving to the alcove where the few clothes she owned hung from rough wooden hangers on a rope. She took down a plain grey dress with contrasting white collar and sleeve cuffs, a dress that had once belonged to Daisy Tamblyn's niece and was too young in style for her. She contorted her slight form to get the zip up at the back then impatiently fastened a row of tiny pearl buttons down the front. The dress was a reasonably good fit but Tressa wouldn't have liked it if it had been made to measure and suited her. She preferred to wear her brothers' clothes.

Her brothers had been several years older than she was and had doted on her. She missed them desperately. From the moment they had marched off to war she had retreated into the world of boys' adventures they had shared with her from comics and storybooks. She didn't want a life outside that fantasy world or a life outside the farm. She objected to strangers coming into her life, whatever the reason. She couldn't understand what interest the stranger with the hoity-toity voice who'd stumbled on to her father's land yesterday could have in her or her family. She'd given him short shrift, but instead of getting rid of him for good, it had led to her having no choice but to see him again.

Next she took a cardigan out of her chest of drawers. Joan couldn't sew well but she was a good knitter. She had saved up the money to buy the wool and had made the cardigan from a pretty pattern for Tressa's birthday two years ago. Tressa hardly wore it and it smelled musty. She wrinkled up her nose but she wasn't really worried; she didn't care what Andrew Macarthur thought of her. He had called her 'not human'; she didn't know what he'd meant by that, but she hoped he wouldn't be happy to see her when she turned up at the pub. With a bit of luck he might have returned to London and her apology wouldn't be necessary.

Her legs were cold and she pulled a pair of thick black stockings out of her underwear drawer. This would mean she'd have to wear a suspender belt and she detested the very thought of it. In a fit of temper she threw the contents of the drawer onto the floor.

The face that looked back at her in the small square mirror on the wall showed a sulky young woman with a pale face who looked much younger than her twenty years. She was narked that she looked so feminine. She wished the weather would wrinkle up her face and make her look rough and masculine. She yanked the scarf out of her hair and grudgingly obeyed her father by combing her hair until all the tangles were out. The longest length of the earthy-coloured mass that she shook down her back nearly reached her waist and as she retied the scarf she vowed that if she had her way she'd cut it all off in a short back and sides. Her father called a woman's hair 'her crowning glory' and he had forbidden her to have it cut short; he only allowed her to trim the ends but she rarely bothered.

Tressa hated upsetting her father and didn't want to face him again until she'd come back from the Tremewan Arms. She crept down the stairs, put on her straight unflattering camel coat and her only pair of shoes, flat brown lace-ups, and reluctantly left the warmth of her home.

Chapter 13

'Oh, damn!' Spencer was struggling to sew a button on one of Vicki's dresses. When he tugged on a knot which had formed in the thread it snapped. He threw the dress aside.

Ince got up from his chair across the hearth and picked it up. 'You're making a mess of this. She's supposed to be wearing this in the concert, remember?'

Spencer got up and paced the kitchen floor. 'I can't think why I let you talk me into letting her take part in it,' he said moodily. He picked up one of Vicki's toys discarded on the floor and dropped it in her doll's cot.

'It'll do her good,' Ince said bluntly. He was beginning to find it harder to stay patient with Spencer's insistence on keeping Vicki wrapped up in cotton wool. 'She's got a sweet little voice and it will give her the chance to show what she's been doing in her dancing lessons. It'll help build up her confidence.'

'Can't think why I let you talk me into letting her take them.'

'It's what Natalie would have wanted for her,' Ince pointed out gently. 'She would have wanted Vicki to enjoy herself. Can't you see that, Spencer?'

'I suppose so,' Spencer admitted reluctantly.

He went to the window over the sink, pulled the curtains aside and moodily stared out. The sky was cloud free and an illuminated indigo, sparkling with a myriad stars and a bright full moon but he didn't notice them. He was thinking about what had happened in his house yesterday.

He'd felt a little ashamed of his spiteful behaviour towards Laura after the Sunday morning service and it had been pricking his conscience as he'd driven back from Launceston. He'd asked himself why he was so hostile towards her. She was a reminder of her late husband and the way he had once hurt him and Natalie, but why did it matter so much? He didn't mix much in the village; apart from church he just had the occasional drink in the pub so he wasn't going to see much of her.

Laura Jennings was a beautiful woman. Natalie had been beautiful. Did he resent the fact that the Jennings woman was alive while Natalie was dead? That was unreasonable. Was he that unreasonable? He hadn't felt the least bit concerned when he'd heard Bill Jennings had died. He had upset Ince by refusing to attend the funeral and hadn't given the dead man's widow a single thought. It was suddenly seeing her outside his house, talking to Vicki and touching her that had made him behave in such an unreasonable way ever since.

As he'd turned off Rosemerryn Lane for the farm he'd told himself to watch his attitude in the future; it wasn't good for Vicki to see him sniping at people. Then he'd seen Laura's borrowed bike and felt dismayed. Why was she so pushy? If she had come to ask questions about him and Bill Jennings then here with his child around wasn't the time and place. He'd try to be friendly but tell her firmly the past was in the past and it would have to stay there. But when he'd found her in his bedroom, looking at the photographs of Natalie, something inside him had exploded. His bedroom was his sacred place. It was where he had first made love with Natalie and where Vicki had been conceived. It was where he had spent every bitter night without her since she'd died. How dare this woman invade his sanctuary? Only after he had blown his top and she had become hysterical had he seen how unfair he'd been. And Vicki had been badly frightened.

The cold air seeping through the window chilled Spencer's raised arm and he finally noticed the sky. 'There'll be a hard frost tonight,' he muttered aloud. He began pacing the floor again.

Ince had sat down with the dress and rethreaded the needle. Without looking up from his work, he said, 'You'll feel better if you take the courage to go and apologise to her.'

'What are you talking about?' Spencer returned guardedly, turning round and leaning his back against the sink. 'You know very well what I'm talking about.'

'Don't you start preaching at me, Ince!'

'I don't need to,' Ince replied patiently. 'Your conscience is telling you what to do. Hate and unforgiveness is a terrible burden for any man to carry for five years. Add guilt to it and it could crush him.'

'Who do you think you are? A damned oracle or something?' Spencer felt cornered and fought his way out of it by making excuses. 'How was I to know the woman didn't have a happy marriage? I thought she was one of those women who spent their lives happily manipulating their husband's career. Holding dinner parties for company directors and judges and hoping one day her husband will get a knighthood. I didn't know that bastard had been cruel to her. You thought he was,' Spencer asserted accusingly, pointing his finger. 'Why didn't you tell me?'

'Would it have made any difference? You found Laura guilty of a crime she didn't commit merely by association. You would still have treated her coldly.'

'I wouldn't have gone for her so wildly!' Spencer hurled across the room, grinding his foot in the corner of a rug and curling up its edge.

'So, it's my fault now, is it?'

Spencer made a gesture of hopelessness. 'Of course it isn't. I just didn't expect her to turn up at the house. I... I don't know what to do now, what to say to her.'

'Saying sorry would make a good start. And if you want Vicki to settle again you've got to show her that things between you and Laura are all right. She was really upset and you can't blame Laura for that. You treated her disgustingly.'

'You're a good friend, Ince,' Spencer said wryly, prodding the rug back into place. 'You're making me feel worse by the moment.'

'That's what friends are for, aren't they? To put us right on our faults. Why don't you go over to see Laura now? The sooner you say you're sorry, the sooner you'll feel better. You could invite her to tea tomorrow.'

Spencer's face had begun to show acquiescence but Ince's last statement brought the anger back. 'Invite her to tea! What the hell for?'

'For Vicki's sake,' Ince stressed, remaining in command of the situation. 'I'm sure Laura would come for Vicki's sake if you put it to her in that way. The sooner Vicki sees the pair of you on good terms, the less time she'll have to think about your quarrel and get things distorted in her little mind. She likes Laura. She can't understand why, in her words,' Ince pointed a finger, 'you were being beastly to her, what you could have said to make Laura become hysterical. You did a lot of damage to them both yesterday. Laura you may not care about, but I do, and you've always said you'd do anything for Vicki.'

Running his hands roughly through his fair hair, Spencer trod about on the spot then walked over to the armchair Ince was sitting in. He crouched down before his friend and put on his most appealing face. 'You go and see her for me, just at first. Tell her I'm going to apologise. She seems to trust you.'

Ince shook his head firmly. 'No, it would be better coming from you.'

'But she's got one of her friends here with her. You said he threatened to punch the lights out of me. I'm not afraid of some soft-bodied city slicker but another quarrel might make things worse.'

'That's a risk you'll have to take. To send me first would seem insulting and cowardly.'

Spencer could see he wasn't going to succeed in bribing or persuading Ince. 'All right, I'll go,' he uttered as if he was the injured party in the dispute and being expected to put it right was unjust. 'I hate doing this sort of thing. I'll go to the pub first for a good stiff drink.

'Spencer, I think you ought to tell her what she came here for,' Ince said quietly when Spencer had reached the door.

Tears were not far away from Spencer's eyes. 'I can't. Some things are too painful.'

'What is the matter with you two tonight?' Daisy said in exasperation, looking from Laura's glum face to Andrew's. They were sitting round a table in the Tremewan Arms with Bunty. 'Have you got some terrible business problems? What long faces. You both look more miserable than Cecil Roach and that takes some doing.' Andrew had gone back to Little Cot licking his wounded pride and confided in Laura about the trick Tressa had played on him. She had commiserated with him, agreeing that were some horrible people in Kilgarthen. They had spent the rest of the day together, going over the necessary papers she had to sign to help wind up her father's company, and then they had drifted into a melancholy silence. A visit to the pub with the two middle-aged women who had turned up on the doorstep and suggested they all go for a drink had not cheered them up.

'Everything's fine, Aunty Daisy,' Laura said, finishing her drink. She had been thinking about her dinner invitation with Felicity Lean for the following night and wondering if she would find out something about William Lean being Bill's father.

'Do you want another drink, Laura?' Andrew asked, trying to sound hearty, before Daisy could badger them again. 'What about you two ladies? Same again?' Andrew went to the bar and found, much to his chagrin, that he was standing beside Sam Beatty. His bruised feelings left him in no mood to exchange small talk with this character. But Sam Beatty seemed just as disinclined to speak. They said 'Good evening' and that was all.

'I feel awful,' Andrew told the group when he came back with the tray of drinks. 'Sam Beatty seems really down tonight. I haven't been very friendly towards him. I keep forgetting he's a sick man. Shall I invite him over?'

'Yes, go on,' Bunty said promptly. 'Poor fellow. Don't want him to think we're an unfriendly lot round here.'

'And you'd like to get to know something more about him,' Laura commented wryly.

Daisy laughed. 'Well, it's something to do.'

'Would you like to join us, Mr Beatty?' Andrew asked the other Londoner when he took the empty tray back.

Sam Beatty seemed pleasantly surprised. 'Oh, yes. Thank you. For a little while, then I think I'll have an early night.'

Sam pulled up a stool and joined Laura's table. Andrew passed round his packet of Senior Service. The bar door opened and Spencer came in. His eyes zoomed in on Laura and he went crimson. He nodded curtly to her and after exchanging greetings with Daisy and Bunty he went to the bar.

Andrew saw Laura's reaction. She paled considerably. Sam Beatty was watching her too.

'Is that the vile-mouthed Spencer Jeffries?' Andrew whispered, putting his mouth to Laura's ear.

She nodded, turning slightly so the man in question wasn't in her line of vision.

'Do you want to leave?' Andrew asked.

'No,' she replied resolutely. 'I'm not going to let him spoil my evening.'

'Is something wrong?' Sam Beatty asked. There was a hint of authority in his voice and Laura felt obliged to answer.

'No, Mr Beatty. The man who just came in is a troublesome local farmer. I've had some words with him, that's all.'

'Has Spencer upset you again?' Daisy and Bunty asked in unison, their eyes boring into Spencer's broad back.

'I don't want to talk about it,' Laura replied, emphasising each word. She felt foolish under Sam Beatty's eagle eyes.

'It's about time I had a word with he!' Daisy said indignantly. She was halfway out of her seat but plonked herself down again. Spencer was making his way over to them.

Ignoring everyone but Laura, he stood stiffly behind her shoulder. 'Can I have a word with you, Mrs Jennings, please?'

Laura refused to turn round and look at him. Clutching her glass of white wine she said, as if she had difficulty getting the words out between her teeth, 'I think we've said all there is to say to each other, Mr Jeffries.'

'Go away now or I'll throw you out of the pub myself,' Andrew threatened, rising to his feet. Sam Beatty followed suit.

'Keep out of this, you!' Spencer snarled, clenching his fists. He might be ready to eat humble pie but he wasn't going to be ordered about by this upstart. 'It's none of your business. I was speaking to Mrs Jennings.'

'Spencer!' Daisy protested.

'Stop it, all of you,' Laura pleaded.

'It'll only take a few minutes,' Spencer persisted.

'She's told you she's not interested!' Andrew shouted. 'Don't you understand plain English!'

'Now then!' A booming voice interrupted the raised voices round the table. A darts match and a euchre game were brought to an untimely halt. The pub became silent, all attention was rooted on them. 'We'll be having no more of this, will we, gents?' Mike Penhaligon said fiercely, as he approached the table.

He pushed Spencer in the chest and he was forced to take a couple of steps backwards. 'Back to the bar with you, young man, and you other two sit down. I won't have the ladies' pleasure spoiled.'

Laura had turned round. She couldn't read the cluster of expressions that vied for supremacy on Spencer's face but suddenly he looked just like Vicki had when she'd started to cry yesterday. She found herself saying, 'What did you want to say to me?'

Spencer was furious at being embarrassed and wanted to take a smack at Andrew Macarthur's sassy face. He wanted to shout at Laura to forget it but he couldn't let Vicki down. There was no way, however, that he'd say what he wanted to in front of all these flapping ears.

Coughing to clear his throat, he said, 'I'd just like a few minutes alone with you.'

'Well?' Mike, the self-appointed referee of the proceedings, turned to Laura. 'Do you want to speak to him, m'dear?'

'Yes, but only for a few minutes.'

'You can go into the residents' lounge. But I'm warning you, Spencer. Watch your tongue where this lady is concerned.'

'But Mike,' chipped in Pat, who had entered the bar. 'I've just shown someone in there. There's a visitor for Mr Macarthur.'

'What?' exclaimed Andrew, and Sam Beatty's ears pricked up. 'Who on earth is visiting me here?'

'It's Tressa Davey,' Pat told him.

'Tressa?' Andrew became animated. 'I'll see her at once,' he said eagerly.

'Tell she t'come in here,' Mike roared at Pat.

'You know that maid won't set foot in the bar, Mike,' Pat reminded him.

Mike stroked his beard. All the customers in the pub were hanging on his next word. 'Then Spencer and Laura had better go into our sitting room. You show Mr Macarthur into the residents' lounge, m'dear.'

Laura had never felt so silly or self-conscious before. But before she followed Mike and the overbearing farmer she whispered at Andrew accusingly, 'I thought you said you never wanted to see that girl again. When I've got rid of Jeffries, I'm going to come and meet her. I can't wait to see what she's like.'

'No! I... I'll see if I can persuade her to come in here after I find out what she wants.' Andrew knew Tressa would hate people looking her over.

When Laura, Spencer and Andrew were being shown to their respective rooms, Sam Beatty resumed his seat. He raised his glass to Daisy and Bunty who were too amazed by all that had happened to speak. 'Never a dull moment round here, eh, ladies? Tell me about the village.'

Andrew closed the lounge door after him. Tressa was standing stiffly in the middle of the room with her hands stuffed in her coat pockets. Her face looked as if it was carved from stone. She was engulfed in an old-fashioned coat but it didn't conceal her slender grace and loveliness.

Andrew had a good idea why she was here and felt on safe ground. He moved towards her, stopping just inches away. He could smell a musty odour on her clothes but it did not mask the natural sweetness that was hers.

She said nothing. Andrew wasn't going to ask her why she was here. He raised an inquiring eyebrow.

134

She opened her mouth a little. He waited patiently for what she had to say.

'I… I came to say I'm sorry.' Then she moved back from him.

He advanced on her. 'Sorry for what?' He sounded puzzled deliberately.

Tressa glared at him. To her mind he had a stupid grin on his face. She knew he was playing games with her. 'For making you walk through that patch of bog.'

'What about ordering your brute to jump up at me with muddy paws the first time we met?'

'That too,' she muttered ungraciously.

Andrew was enjoying himself. He could have gazed at her pretty pale face all night. He knew her cheeks would be cold and he wanted to warm them with his hands. The fire had burned low in the room and he guessed she had endured a long cold walk. He wanted to hold her in his arms and make her warm. 'Want me to forgive you, do you?'

She let out a frustrated sigh. 'Yes.'

He put his head cockily on the side. 'Okay, I will, but only if you have a drink with me.' He had a great desire to show her off in the public bar as his guest.

The cheek of this man! Tressa flounced round a chair and headed for the door. 'I'm not that sorry. My father made me apologise to you and it's up to you to take it or leave it.'

'Tressa!' Andrew's heart thumped down to his shoes. 'Look, I didn't mean to be flippant. I'm sorry.' How had she managed to turn the tables on him so quickly? He rushed to the door and got there first. 'It was good of you to come. You've had a long walk. You look cold. Let me ask Mike if I can borrow his car to drive you home.'

'That short distance?' she said scornfully. 'I'll be home in a trice.'

'But Tressa!'

'But what?'

'Well, I, um…' He had to think of something to keep her here. 'Was that the only reason you came to see me?'

'Oh, thank you for the things you gave my aunty, if that's what you want, my gratitude.'

'No, I didn't mean that. You're more than welcome to it.' He was at a loss now. 'Do you have to go? Have a drink first, to warm yourself for the walk back.'

'No, thank you.' She put her hand on the doorknob. 'Excuse me.'

Andrew wanted to see more of her, he wanted to ask her out to dinner or to the cinema. There must be a cinema somewhere round here. But he felt she wouldn't understand what his invitation meant. She'd certainly refuse. He moved aside and she left him without another word.

Tressa walked down the passageway that led to the outer doors. Harry Lean was coming towards her,

'Hello, darling. I've never seen you in here before. Seen the light at last, have you? Found a social life is appealing after all?'

Tressa ignored him and tried to walk by. She'd just extracted herself from one wretched man's company only to have this lecherous swine loom up on her. Harry shot an arm out to stop her. 'Now don't be like that. You don't want to go home yet. The night's still young.' He moved in close and put a hand under her chin and moved the other to her waist. 'And so are you. Young and lovely and you're letting yourself go to waste keeping yourself cooped up on that little farm. I could show you how to live life to the full.'

Tressa pushed his hands away from her. 'Get out of my way, Harry Lean!'

Andrew had stayed where he was, feeling crestfallen. When he heard Tressa's angry voice, he came flying out of the room.

'Come on, darling,' Harry said, putting his hand on Tressa's shoulder and pulling her to him. 'Don't be so unfriendly.'

'Back off!' Andrew shouted. He rushed down the few feet of the passageway and yanked Tressa away from Harry.

Tressa shook Andrew away from her. 'I can handle him,' she scowled. 'He was about to get my knee in a painful place.'

Harry was highly amused. 'You must be Andrew Macarthur. Taken up being guardian angel of the village maidens, have you?'

'And you must be that heel, Harry Lean,' Andrew, snarled back. 'If you ever lay a finger on this girl again you'll have me to answer to!'

Harry laughed. He looked at Tressa. 'Aren't you the lucky one, darling? Two suitors after you, and you can bet that neither of us has honourable intentions.'

'Speak for yourself!' Andrew seethed. 'Now get away from us.'

'Isn't that Tressa's decision? Well, darling, what do you say? Which one of us knights in shining armour would you like to have escort you home tonight?'

'I just want to leave here,' Tressa hissed angrily, elbowing her way past both men.

'Looks like we've both lost for the night, Macarthur. How about a drink? I've never come across a woman yet who's worth fighting over.'

'Go to hell,' Andrew scratched out. Pushing Harry aside, he ran after Tressa.

She was outside the door, taking in deep lungfuls of fresh cold air.

'Does he often make a pass at you like that?' Andrew asked her.

'He's done it once or twice,' she replied, looking up at the sky. 'He doesn't worry me.'

'Well, he should. One day he might go too far. I really think you should let me drive you home.'

Tressa gave a low whistle. Meg came bounding up to her. 'I'm well protected.' Jacka had forbidden her to take Meg with her but she couldn't help it if the dog *followed* her. She walked off up the hill.

'Good night, Tressa!' Andrew called after her.

She didn't call back. Andrew spun round and thumped his fist against the pub wall.

–

The Penhaligons' sitting room was spacious; Spencer was standing in front of the piano and Laura kept the width of the room between them by staying just inside the door.

'I'd be grateful if you'd say whatever it is you have on your mind quickly so I can get back to my friends,' Laura said in her unfriendliest tone.

Spencer folded his arms. He was willing to apologise but he wasn't going to grovel. 'It's about yesterday. I was out of order and

I want to apologise for the way I upset you. I had no idea how things were between you and your husband. I take full blame for all the unpleasantness that's happened between us since your arrival in the village.'

Laura wouldn't have believed she'd ever hear these words coming from the mouth of this man. She summed up the new situation rapidly. She was sure she knew what had brought this on. 'Has Ince been speaking to you?'

'He only repeated what you told me. He's anxious that we get on better terms.'

'I see. And are you?'

'To be truthful, not particularly. You're still a stranger to me. I'm not much interested in others and what they do.'

'That's what I thought,' Laura said coolly. 'I'm not in the least bit concerned about you but I am about Vicki. I'll never forgive myself for lashing out at you and upsetting her. She didn't deserve that. Is she badly affected?'

'She's upset. It's the first time anything like that has happened in our home.'

This tore at Laura's heart. 'I feel guilty about that. I went to your house yesterday to ask you what Bill had said or done to you to make you hate me so much, but I should have realised it was unwise with Vicki there. Now we're bringing things out into the open, I'd like to know what it was.'

Spencer closed his eyes tightly for an instant. 'It would serve no purpose to tell you now. I don't want to talk about it.' The old familiar contempt was back in his voice. 'I'm only concerned with Vicki. Ince has come up with a suggestion for us to put things right with her. I hope you'll seriously consider it. If you would come to tea and if we could show Vicki that we don't hate one another it will help to settle her mind. Will you think about it?'

Laura turned away. She couldn't stand his cold grey eyes boring into her another moment. The thought of going to Rosemerryn Farm again made her feel physically sick, but how could she say no to putting things right with little Vicki? Her father might have big enough shoulders to accept all the blame, but she couldn't make any excuses for her part in upsetting Vicki.

'I would like to have the opportunity of saying sorry to Vicki. When would you like me to come?'

Spencer sighed. Part of him had been hoping she'd refuse. 'Ince suggested tomorrow, the sooner the better for Vicki's sake.'

'Yes, of course.' Laura looked at him again. He seemed tired, slightly dejected. 'What time shall I come?'

'About four o'clock. Ince will be there. You don't have to worry. I'll keep a low profile.'

'Will it be all right if I bring something for Vicki?'

A spark of resistance lit up Spencer's eyes. 'What sort of something?'

Laura realised how possessive he was of his daughter. She would always be on uncertain ground with him. The tea tomorrow was going to be an ordeal; it would be difficult acting pleasantly to Spencer when she'd rather see him tumble off the top of Hawk's Tor and take his wretched pride and animosity with him, but she would enjoy seeing Vicki and Ince.

'I was only thinking of a few sweets or something,' she replied curtly. 'But if you think—'

'That'll be fine,' he interrupted. 'Tomorrow at four then.' He walked towards the door. 'I must be getting back.'

Laura moved out of his way. Neither of them offered the courtesy of saying goodnight. When she heard the outer doors of the pub bang as he left the building she wished she didn't have to go back to the bar and face the curiosity of the others. She had lost interest in meeting Tressa Davey. Andrew would probably rail against her going to Rosemerryn Farm the next day. For all this she blamed Bill; what was happening was the consequence of something he had done. Would she ever stop hating him?

Chapter 14

Cecil Roach was sitting in his ten-year-old Morris Eight, the pride of his life, which he had driven carefully along the lanes to keep as much moorland mud and debris off it as possible. He had arrived ten minutes ago at a designated quiet spot where he had arranged to meet someone. Here, in the shelter of Bostonodan Wood, he was reasonably sure that no one from the village would come across him. Except for the front windscreen of the car, the windows were steamed up. He didn't wipe them dry.

Cecil drummed his fingers, clad in new leather driving gloves, impatiently on the steering wheel. He was taking a rehearsal of the school choir in half an hour and had a lot of paperwork to get through this morning. If the person he was meeting was late he would have little or no time to peruse the merchandise he was going to buy. He took off his gloves and ran his hot sticky hands down his trousers in anticipation. He undid his coat buttons and loosened his tie. This was not only because he was beginning to feel hot but to look the part if he was seen by someone he knew. He would say he'd been feeling under a lot of pressure lately and had taken a drive to calm himself, and that he had been forced to stop after becoming breathless. The sweat that broke out on his neck and forehead was real, but for a different reason.

Five minutes passed and a fish delivery van pulled up and stopped in front of Cecil's car. A young man in white overalls and pulled-down cap got out and walked to the Morris Eight. He had a brown paper package in his hand. Cecil wound down his window. The fishman looked all around then passed him the package. Cecil gave him a five-pound note.

'Same time next month?' Cecil asked urgently, keeping his head down. His breathing was getting heavier.

'See you then, sir,' the fishman said, eyeing Cecil slyly. Then he got back into his van and drove off.

Cecil untied the string round the package and opened it with trembling hands. He pushed the paper aside and found a bundle of magazines. Before he feasted his eyes on their contents, he stuck his head out of the window and looked behind to make sure no one was about. He could see no one, man or beast, and he could hear no vehicles approaching. He wound up the window.

The cover picture of the first magazine showed a voluptuously built blonde bending forward in scanty underwear. She was revealing a lot of flesh but not enough for Cecil. He turned to the inside pages. As the pictures progressed, the woman discarded the top and then the bottom of her underwear, striking many different poses. There were three magazines in the package and Cecil rummaged between them and came up with a set of ten foreign postcards. They all depicted a different woman, some no more than girls, in various poses and states of undress. An uncontrollable feeling swept through Cecil's loins and his hand, hidden under the brown paper, went down to his trousers.

There was a knock on the car window. Cecil almost leapt out of his skin and he hastily wrapped the brown paper round his illegal merchandise. His heart was thumping unbearably. He prayed it wasn't the local policeman out cycling on his rounds. Thrusting the package on the floor at his feet, he wound down the window with a trembling hand.

A man he had seen recently about Kilgarthen lowered his hunter-hatted head and looked in at Cecil. 'Good morning to you. I hope I am not intruding, but is everything all right?'

'Yes, yes,' Cecil gasped out, running a sweaty hand through his sparse hair. 'I... I'm just t-taking a breather, that's all.'

'Haven't I seen you in Kilgarthen?' the stranger went on, his sharp pale eyes searching Cecil's stricken face. 'My name's Sam Beatty. I'm presently staying at the Tremewan Arms, convalescing from an operation.' He stuck his hand in the car and Cecil had no option but to shake it.

He forced a smile. 'P-pleased to meet you, Mr Beatty. I'm Mr Roach, headmaster of the school.' Cecil racked his brains for something credible to say. There was something persistent and interfering about this man. If he said he was ill, Sam Beatty might insist on getting a doctor for him. 'The village C-Christmas concert is coming up and, and I'm eager the school should perform well in it.' If only his heart would stop pounding. It was making lucid speech very difficult. 'I s-sometimes take a little drive somewhere alone, to think about what the choir is singing and if I have the best possible lines for our sketch.'

'I see. That's a good idea,' Sam Beatty said, flicking his eyes round the inside of the car. 'It's a fairly mild morning and the surroundings anywhere on the moor are good for thinking things over, aren't they? I managed to get a lift out here from the greengrocer delivering to the village shop. I was dropped off a few yards up the lane. I'm going to take a gentle walk back to the pub.'

'I hope you are recovering well, Mr Beatty,' Cecil said, trying to sound sincere. He was desperately wishing the man away from him. 'I'm sure the air is doing you good.'

'I'm feeling better every day, thank you, Mr Roach. Well, must get on, leave you to your,' he paused for an instant, 'thinking. Good morning.'

'Good morning,' Cecil mumbled, winding up the window the moment Sam Beatty took his nose out of it.

Cecil watched Sam Beatty walk away in his wing mirror. When he was out of sight, he gathered up his package. He looked at some of the pictures again. It was no good. The wonderful intense feelings he could not get from the occasional lovemaking he performed on Barbara had abated in the sheer terror Sam Beatty had made him feel. It would take ages to work them up again. He made a mental note not to look at his merchandise here in future but to force himself to wait until he was safely in the little study he'd had converted in the attic of School House.

He retied the string around the package and started up the engine of the car. He couldn't bring himself to turn round and drive past Sam Beatty. It would mean a long detour round the lanes to get back to

Kilgarthen. Damn and blast! And woe betide those miserable children if they didn't sing like songbirds when he got back!

–

'You can't really be serious about going to tea with that mean-mouthed farmer,' Andrew stated angrily, giving Laura a disparaging look then throwing his suitcase heavily into the boot of the Penhaligons' Hillman Minx. After the threat he'd received from Spencer Jeffries and the encounter he'd had with Harry Lean last night he was feeling more than disgruntled with the men of Kilgarthen. 'Are you a glutton for punishment or something? I thought you would have had enough of that kind of loutish behaviour from Bill.'

Laura squirmed in her shoes. She glanced hastily around the pub car park; these days she half expected Ada Prisk to be listening in or observing everything she did. 'I've explained over and over to you that I'm doing it for his little girl, Andrew. I behaved badly too and upset her.'

'You could put that right without going to the farm,' Andrew protested stubbornly, opening the door of the passenger seat. His face was pale, set like granite and drawn from a sleepless night.

Laura put a restraining hand on his arm. 'Tressa Davey must be a remarkable young woman. I've never known anyone have this effect on you before. I shall make a point of meeting her.'

'You won't if she sees you coming first,' Andrew muttered ruefully. 'She's not at all sociable. If you do speak to her, though, tell her I'm not a bad sort. The main thing about Tressa is that she doesn't see me or any other man as a possible romantic partner. We don't exist for her in that way.' A look of pain passed over his face. 'Oh well, never mind,' he gave an unconvincing laugh. 'I'll probably never see her again.'

As Mike came towards the car, Andrew pressed a hand on Laura's shoulder. 'I don't like leaving you here, Laura.'

'I'll be fine. It's what I want.' She smiled as convincingly as she could. 'You will take care of yourself?'

'Never mind me, just you be sure to take care of yourself. You'll be feeling vulnerable for a very long time.'

'I know but I'm not alone here,' she tried to reassure him. 'I have Aunty Daisy and Bunty, and Johnny Prouse to help look after to keep me busy, and Ince.'

–

Just after lunch Laura tapped on Johnny Prouse's little cottage door and walked in just as Daisy had told her to do. She stopped on the long-faded hall rug and paused for a few moments to study the array of old photographs on the white-painted walls. Each one was labelled with a name, date of birth and date of death. From the names and dates, Laura reckoned that all of Johnny's relatives were probably dead. There was a magnificent photograph of Johnny as a straight-backed young man with a humourous smile playing round the corners of his mouth, his dark eyes twinkling merrily, the hat on his head displaying the name of his ship, the *Sir Harry*.

Lifting the latch of the nearest door, she gingerly put her head round it and found Johnny in his front room. He was sleeping in a winged armchair, covered up to the neck in a coarse grey blanket, his slippered feet peeping out the other end on a square tapestry-covered stool. He was snoring lightly, the soft puttering lifting the wisp of white hair that had strayed from the striped woolly hat he wore. He had sustained cracked ribs and cuts in the accident and black and blue bruises shadowed his eyes and the tip of his chin.

'Johnny,' Laura whispered. 'Johnny.' If he stayed asleep she intended to call back a little later.

The old man murmured and smacked his thin ragged lips, Laura started to retreat and close the door but at the last moment Johnny lifted one eyelid and rumbling like a traction engine woke up. 'Eh? What? Who's there?'

Afraid she had frightened him, Laura spoke up quickly. 'It's me, Johnny, Laura Jennings. I'm sorry I woke you. Shall I come back another time?'

After a short struggle, he managed to sit up straight. He pushed the blanket down to his waist and rubbed the drowsiness from his bleary eyes. 'No, don't go away. Come on in, m'dear. 'Tis nice of you to come and see me. 'Tis a bit boring all this resting I have to do but the doctors insist. I keep falling off to sleep when I've got no one to talk to.'

Laura closed the door and sat down on a piano stool which was the closest seat to Johnny. 'I'm very sorry about Admiral, Johnny. He was a sweet little dog.'

'Aye,' Johnny said softly, immediately becoming misty-eyed. 'He was getting on a bit. Wouldn't have had him for many more years but he didn't deserve to go that way. All the time I had him I'd never known him to run off like that before. Good job it was quick 'n' over with. He wouldn't have felt a thing. Someone buried him in my back garden so he's close by.' Johnny took off his woolly hat. 'That's better. Ridiculous thing. Daisy made me wear this. Anyone would think I was a littl'un.'

He grinned boyishly but Laura had detected a wobble in his voice. 'Is everything all right, Johnny? You're not worrying about anything?'

'To be honest I'm worried about that lorry driver. He could sue me for damages and I've got no money to pay for that sort of thing.'

Laura took his brown speckled hand. 'I'm sure he won't do that. It was an accident and he would have had insurance for just such a happening.'

'Well, he did send me a friendly letter.' Johnny cheered up a little. He pointed to the top of the piano. ''Tis up there. He's got a broken ankle and banged his head. He came out of hospital the same day as me.'

Laura glanced round the room. The furniture was made of good solid wood and had been given the benefit of Daisy's duster. A huge chest with carvings of sea scenes on every side stood under the window. There was a battered companion set by the hearth and a wireless on a shelf. A small table covered with a gold-coloured crushed-velvet cloth was loaded with vases of flowers. While he'd been in hospital Daisy, Bunty and Roslyn Farrow had decorated the room for Christmas to cheer Johnny up. 'You've had a lot of cards, Johnny, and so many bunches of flowers too. You must have a lot of friends.'

'I have. Things are gradually getting back to normal here since the war. We lost four young men, a man in his forties and a maid in the

WAAF altogether. But I've still got some good neighbours, m'dear. You're my newest one and here you are.'

Laura stood up and took off her coat. 'I haven't come just to talk. I want to pitch in with the others and help. I think that fire could do with some more logs, then I'm sure you'd like a nice cup of tea.'

'Rather have a drop of rum.' Johnny winked and looked like an impish boy.

Laura smiled then gave him a mock no-nonsense look. 'It's tea or nothing. You'll have the district nurse after me.'

'Ahhh,' Johnny laughed cheekily. 'A drop of rum would have set me up proper. How're you settling into Little Cot then?'

'Everything's going very well, thank you.' She paused with a log in her hand. Johnny enjoyed a chat and it was good for him not to dwell on the accident. This was the perfect time to ask about Bill. 'I suppose you miss Bill.'

Johnny nodded his head mournfully. ''Tis been awful, two deaths in such a short time. We have something in common, m'dear, both being bereaved.'

'I feel closer living in the place where Bill was born and grew up.' Laura told a lie then the truth: 'He used to talk a lot about his childhood. He talked about you sometimes, Johnny.'

'Did he?' Johnny looked pleased. 'Did he tell you about the time I threatened to smack his backside for scrumping apples off my tree? I would have done it too but he was too fast for me. Could be a right little so and so at times. I can hear his mother now shouting at un t'come in and stop making mischief.'

'Was he very mischievous then?'

'More than most boys of his age, I reckon, but he was clever, and bright. He had a bit of a temper on un and was very rebellious as a youth. I always thought the village wasn't big enough for un. 'Twas no wonder to me when he left to make something of himself. Needed a challenge, I suppose.'

Laura had attended to the fire and she lingered to talk before making for the kitchen. 'I never knew his parents. What were they like?'

146

'Ron and Faith Jennings? Quiet mostly, hard working. Nice couple, I liked 'em.'

'It's just struck me that they only had the one child – Bill.' Laura made her voice sound extra thoughtful. 'I wonder if they wanted any more.'

'Couldn't say about that. Wouldn't know nothing about their private life. P'raps they found Bill handful enough, eh?' Johnny chuckled.

'Yes, perhaps.' So Johnny didn't know of the rumours about Bill being William Lean's son, or he didn't choose to mention them. 'Bill's cottage was once owned by the Leans. I'm told Felicity is a good woman but I don't care for her son.' Andrew had told her about Harry's sexual overtures to Tressa Davey and Laura was outraged. 'The village hasn't really got a big house now, I understand, with Felicity's husband long dead and Harry selling their property.'

'Oh, William Lean was selling off their property long before he died. He weren't a pleasant character, I can tell 'ee. Think yourself lucky that if you don't like Harry you won't have to meet his father. He never passed a civil word to no one that man. Was nothing but a stuck-up snob, if I should say the words,' Johnny ended indignantly.

'Bill said he was a tyrant.'

'He wouldn't have Harry or his late daughter mixing with the village children. William Lean used t'ride his horse through the village with his head up in the air. Bill, being a bit of a young devil, used to shout cheeky things at un. Well, one day Lean took a real exception t'something he said and he got off his horse and strammed Bill's legs with his riding crop. Bill's father was home that day and there was a terrible row. Ron shouted at him that he had no right to behave like he was lord of the manor. Now, m'dear, where's that cup of tea? My mouth is parched from all this talking. A bit later on, if you like, you can walk me to the doctor's surgery.'

Laura was distracted for a moment, chewing over what Johnny had told her. She hadn't learned much. Then she looked at the old man. 'What did you say? Walk you to the doctor's surgery? You're much too weak to go anywhere yet.'

The nearest doctor's surgery was stationed in Launceston but one of the three doctors in the practice held a surgery for Kilgarthen's residents at Bunty Buzza's house on Wednesday afternoons, between two and four o'clock. After providing hot water and towels for the doctor in her sitting room, Bunty would hand over her spotless kitchen for use as a waiting room, then she would disappear discreetly upstairs until the doctor called up to her that all his patients had gone and she could come down and make them both a cup of tea.

Three people arrived at the surgery at two o'clock on the dot. Joy Miller had come about her cold and had brought Benjy with her. The other patient was Marianne Roach.

Joy Miller mopped her streaming red nose. She looked anxiously at Benjy who was looking longingly at a bowl of fruit in the middle of the table. 'You can't have any, Benjy,' she sniffed noisily. 'They belonged to Miss Buzza.'

'I'm only looking, Mum,' he replied shyly. He was feeling shy because Marianne Roach was staring at him fiercely. He went to his mother and held on to her hand.

Marianne noticed Joy looking at her. She coughed and put on a hoarse voice. 'These colds are a killer, aren't they? I don't suppose the doctor can do anything but you feel you ought to come along and see him.'

'Had yours long?' Joy inquired.

'It's been building up over a couple of days. I was aching all over when I woke up this morning and felt too awful to go to work.'

'I know what you mean. I hope they're managing all right on Rosemerryn Farm without me. My Bert was coughing this morning. I hope he doesn't go down with it too. We can't afford for him to be off work. I suppose my children will get it one by one.'

'Yes,' Marianne agreed weakly. 'I hope it doesn't go through the school. My father won't be pleased if half the children are unable to perform in the concert.'

'Aw, that would be a shame. Two of mine are in the choir and have been practising their carol singing every night. My eldest boy is in the sketch. He's going to be the shoemaker. Mr Roach wrote it, didn't he? You must be very proud of your father, Marianne.'

'Yes,' Marianne replied, looking away impatiently.

The doctor put his head round the door. He was middle aged and portly with round glasses perched on his humourous face and wearing a crumpled grey suit, his colourful bow tie awry. 'Ah,' he said in a high-spirited fashion. 'I see I have some customers.' He rubbed his long hands together. 'Who's first?'

Marianne had arrived first but she paled and felt rooted to the chair. 'You go first, Mrs Miller. It'll be less time hanging around for Benjy and you look in worse condition than me.'

Joy got up gratefully. 'Oh, you are a dear. I won't be long.' She joked with the doctor as she went through the door, 'It's not for my usual reason, Dr Palmer. I stopped at Benjy and there I'll stay.'

Marianne moved to the seat closest to the door to show she was next in case someone else came in. She hoped no one would be there while she saw the doctor, but at once Laura led Johnny Prouse in on her arm. A feeling akin to fierce hatred filled Marianne's heart for Bill Jennings' beautiful young widow. She tossed her head as Laura settled Johnny in a high-backed chair from which he could eject himself with the minimum of effort.

'Are you comfortable, Johnny?' Laura asked like a mother fussing over a newborn baby. 'I should have insisted you let the doctor come to your cottage. I don't know what he's going to say about you coming out like this.'

'I told you the hospital said I could take a breath of fresh air. Don't 'ee go worryin' now. You're a good maid to help me. I hate being stuck indoors. P'raps after—'

'Certainly not!' Laura exclaimed. 'I'm taking you straight home. You've only been out of hospital a day. You mustn't do too much too soon. Do you want to end up in there again?' She sat down beside him and said, 'hello' to Marianne. Marianne turned her head and glared at her.

Johnny was peering at Marianne, making her feel grossly uncom-fortable, but his accident had left his mind befuddled and he was having trouble recognising people. Eventually, he said, "Tis young Marianne Roach, isn't it? The schoolmaster's daughter?'

'That's right, Mr Prouse,' Marianne replied. 'I was sorry to hear about your accident and about your dog.'

'Thank you,' Johnny said, his tears threatening to appear again. 'He's gone on to greater glory now. How are you then, m'dear? Have 'ee met Mrs Jennings? She'm only a newcomer to the village but she's been some good to me.'

'I've only seen Mrs Jennings at her husband's funeral,' Marianne said, flinching when the scraping of a chair leg in the sitting room spoke of Joy Miller preparing to leave.

'I'm sorry we haven't had the chance to speak before, Marianne,' Laura said, wondering if the girl had inherited her tart character from her father.

Joy and Benjy Miller came out of the sitting room and stopped to speak to Johnny and Laura. Dr Palmer raised his eyebrows to see Johnny, but as he was accompanied and was obviously being well looked after, he beckoned to Marianne. A moment later she was sitting meekly facing him over the dining table.

Dr Palmer had served Kilgarthen for many years and he knew all of its residents. 'Now what can I do for you, Marianne?' he said kindly. 'I don't see you very often.'

She blushed to the roots of her hair and her breath felt tight in her chest. She couldn't believe this was happening to her. How could she have been so stupid? How could Bill Jennings have been so irresponsible? 'It... it's rather delicate.'

'Don't be embarrassed. I've been a doctor for over thirty years. If it's a woman's problem, don't forget I've heard it all before.'

If it was possible for her to go redder in the face, Marianne would have. 'I... I saw Dr Sedgewick last week...' She crossed her fingers and prayed hard.

'Yes,' Dr Palmer said, searching for her notes among the pile he had on the table. 'And what was that for?'

'I had to have a test,' she said in a very small voice, bowing her head and looking at her hands twisted in her lap.

Dr Palmer glanced at her then opened a piece of paper he took from her file. He read it, his face becoming grave. 'I have the result here.'

She couldn't look up. Tears pricked her eyes. She had no hope left. 'Wh-what is it?'

'I'm afraid it's positive, Marianne.'

'You mean I'm…'

'Yes, it means you're pregnant.'

'Oh, no! What am I going to do?' Marianne crumpled in the chair and burst into tears. Dr Palmer rose and poured a glass of water from the jug Bunty had left for him. He rounded the table and put it into her trembling hands, holding it for safety. 'Take a sip. Go on. Then take a couple of deep breaths.'

Marianne obeyed. He put the glass down and held her hands firmly. 'What am I going to do, Doctor?' she repeated despairingly. 'My father will kill me.'

'Well, first things first. What about the baby's father? Will he support you? Is there any chance of you getting married?'

'N-no,' she sobbed. 'He wouldn't be interested. Anyway, he was married.'

'Nonetheless, he must be made to take on his responsibility.'

'He wouldn't have anything to do with it,' Marianne bleated, getting panicky. She wasn't going to tell the doctor who the father was and she had come to realise that even if Bill Jennings hadn't died, he wouldn't have helped her. 'He'd only get angry and deny it.'

Dr Palmer patted her hands. 'Then the only thing you can do is to tell your mother. Of course she'll be very upset but in my experience most mothers come shining through in cases like this. Your mother is a particularly nice woman, Marianne. I'm sure she'll stand by you.'

'But she's terrified of my father!' Marianne exclaimed. 'I've told you, if he finds out he'll kill me.'

'Things are never as bad as they seem. You're in an emotional state now, my dear. I'm afraid you can't keep pregnancy a secret. Tell your mother. She'll be the best one to tell your father, she'll know when to pick the best moment.'

'But… but can't I…'

'Can't you what?'

'Have an operation or something to get rid of it?' she implored him, tears dripping off her chin. 'I've heard it can be done. No one need ever know.'

Dr Palmer shook his head. 'You're young and healthy, Marianne. Nothing could justify that. Take a day or two to get used to the idea. Tell your mother, then when you're ready come together to see me at the main surgery. Now, have you got a hanky?'

'Yeh-yes.' She fumbled in her coat pocket and produced one.

'Dry your eyes and drink the rest of the water. Take a couple of deep breaths and when you go out people will only think you've got a bad cold.'

Marianne knew she could do nothing more to ease her predicament today. She followed the doctor's instructions and went into the waiting room. She pretended to have a fit of coughing and rubbed at her nose and eyes, hoping that those waiting – there were four more people here now – would be fooled. When she saw Laura, she had an idea.

She stood in front of her. 'Mrs Jennings. Could I possibly call on you later today?'

Laura disappointed her. 'I'm sorry, Marianne, but after I've taken Mr Prouse home I have to get ready for an invitation to tea and then I've got a dinner appointment. We'll have to make it some other time.'

Before she burst into tears again, Marianne blurted out, 'Oh, never mind.'

She fled the house and ran down the hill and into the churchyard. She wove her way through the graves and stopped at the newest one, the mound of earth where the body of Bill Jennings lay under a heap of rotting wreaths.

'You bastard!' Marianne shouted despairingly, kicking at the earth.

Chapter 15

It was only because Ince would be there that Laura managed to pluck up the courage to knock on the front door of Rosemerryn Farm. It was answered by Spencer and he awkwardly showed her inside and took her coat and scarf.

'Have you told Vicki I'm coming?' Laura asked rigidly, watching his face for signs of rancour.

'Yes, she's quite excited. We've had no one but Daisy and Bunty over for a meal before.' He looked unsure of himself. 'Thank you for coming. Before we go in,' he expelled a long breath through his nose, 'Ince has come up with another idea. He thinks it's best if we call each other by our first names, to sound friendlier for Vicki's sake. I hope you don't mind.' Laura thought he probably did.

'No, not for Vicki's sake,' she said tight-lipped, clutching a bag of gingerbread men that she'd baked herself, hoping Spencer would find something that could be put on the table more acceptable than sweets. The hallway of Rosemerryn Farm seemed very small with the two of them in it.

He swept back his hair, something he did often when nervous. 'Right then, we're in the kitchen. We always eat in here, it's bigger and cosier.'

Vicki was wearing a pretty pink and white dress and ran to the door to greet Laura. 'Thanks for coming, Mrs Jennings,' she chirped, holding out the corners of her dress. She had obviously been well rehearsed and Laura wondered if it was Spencer or Ince's doing.

'Thank you for inviting me, Vicki,' Laura said, putting on her best smile, which for Vicki was genuine. 'I've brought you some gingerbread men, to put on the tea table. I remembered that it was your favourite story.'

Vicki clapped her hands. 'Ooh, lovely.'

Ince took the bag of biscuits from Laura. He welcomed her warmly but said nothing more for now, he was going to let Spencer do the honours at this meal. The two men were dressed smartly in white shirts and ties but their trousers were casual. Laura was glad she had not overdressed and had put on a simple straight skirt and a matching jumper and cardigan.

'Come and sit down, Laura,' Spencer said, hesitating slightly over her name. He escorted her to his chair at the fireside. Vicki immediately dropped her doll on Laura's lap.

'See, I've dressed Lizzie up in her best outfit for you.' Laura admired the doll then gazed at the shining face of the little girl. She was astonished that anyone could look so innocent, be so perfect. Her skin glowed honey-gold, her cheeks had a healthy rosy hue. Her deep-set blue eyes were like sparkling gems, her hair was tamed at the top of her head with a large sugar-pink ribbon, a few tiny curls lay on her forehead.

Spencer put his hands on Vicki's shoulders and she gazed up at him. The breath caught in Laura's throat as she saw the love between them. He turned his attention to Laura. 'I've explained to Vicki that we're both very sorry about the row we had the other day. I've told her that adults can behave very silly at times, but that we've made it up and are friends now.'

'That's right, Vicki,' Laura said. 'I'm very sorry I shouted and frightened you.'

'That's okay,' Vicki said, happy with the explanations. 'Will you read me a story after tea, please?'

'I'd be delighted to,' Laura replied, feeling she'd received the highest honour in the world.

'Well, then,' Spencer said in a slightly more relaxed voice. 'Ince has made the tea. Shall we eat?'

Ince had put Laura's gingerbread men on a plate with a lace doily on it, in a place of honour on the table. It joined ham and cheese sandwiches, oat biscuits, sausage rolls and a caraway seed cake.

'This all looks delicious,' Laura said, allowing Spencer to show her to a chair. 'Specially the cake.'

'Daddy nearly dropped it,' Vicki said brightly, wriggling about on the big cushion on her chair, her face showing she was eager to tuck in. 'And he said a bad word.'

As Ince looked down at his plate smiling, Laura deliberately heightened Spencer's increasing embarrassment by staring at him. She felt elated. He was finding this more trying than she was. 'Did he?' she said sweetly.

Spencer put his elbow on the table and chewed his thumbnail. 'Will you say the grace, Ince?' he growled.

After the blessing, Ince passed the plate of ham sandwiches to Laura. She took one and put it on her plate. Spencer poured out the tea and his hand was shaking a little as he put a cup beside Laura.

'Is that how you like it?' he asked as if something was constricting his throat.

Laura wondered if she was seeing a shyer, more sensitive Spencer or whether he was hating every moment of her being there and was gritting his teeth. She looked in the cup. The tea was stronger than she preferred but she said, 'Yes, thank you,' and turned her attention to Vicki. 'Your dress is very pretty, Vicki. You look lovely in it.'

'Thanks, Mrs Jennings. Lots of people think you're lovely. I heard them saying it in church.'

'Really?' Laura said self-consciously, trying to get down a bite of ham sandwich and praying she didn't choke on it. She knew both men were looking at her. What were they thinking? Did they agree with the church members? For the first time she became aware of just how good-looking Spencer was. He was powerfully built, his fair hair was thick and shiny, his face was rugged, weather-scarred but somehow beautifully worn like the moor, his eyes were a clear crystal grey and penetrating under a strong brow. Ince was also an attractive man. His body was similarly built from hard work, his face was kinder, gentler, totally appealing, and she had felt the warmth of his capable arms round her. What a thing to strike you when you're sharing a tea table with a child, Laura thought, feeling nervous. She strove to think of something to change the subject.

'Your dog doesn't come inside?'

'Barney never comes inside,' Spencer said, finally helping himself to some food, a sandwich which he broke apart with brute force. 'He's wild by nature.'

I've gathered that, ran through Laura's mind.

'Are you going to be in the concert?' Vicki asked her as she took a gingerbread man for herself and began picking off its candy peel and currant buttons and facial features.

'I've promised Mrs Farrow, the vicar's wife, that I'll help with painting the scenery.' She smiled at the little girl, grateful to her for claiming her attention. It would have been an enjoyable meal if Spencer hadn't been there.

'I'm going to sing and dance. I go to Bodmin for dancing lessons.'

'I'll look forward to seeing you sing and dance. I'm sure you'll be the best act in the concert.'

'Daddy and Uncle Ince can't sew a button on my concert dress prop'ly. Can you do it for me, please?'

Laura glanced at Spencer for his reaction. 'I'd be pleased to have a try.'

'Thank you,' Spencer said in a neutral tone.

Laura would have given anything to know what he was thinking. He ate little of the meal and she declined a second cup of tea to get it over with as quickly as possible. They left the table, and after a short private discussion between the two men, Ince removed the dishes from the table and began washing up. He refused to let Laura help him. Vicki fetched a storybook and climbed up on her knee. This was the best part of the afternoon.

'Perhaps when you've read the story you'd be kind enough to sew this button on this dress,' Spencer said, holding up the dress, a frilly blue silk concoction, and a glass button.

'I'd be glad to,' Laura replied with a smile. She felt more confident now the meal was over and she was enjoying having Vicki close to her.

'I'll get the sewing box then,' he said, turning on his heel. He put all three items on the table.

156

When the story was read – it was *Cinderella* this time – Vicki climbed down off Laura's lap and fetched the sewing things. Laura took only a few moments to sew the button on the dress.

'That's a relief,' Ince said gratefully as he dried his hands. 'Our hands get rough and clumsy on the farm.' He held out his hands to show the calluses. 'It'll save one of us taking it over to Daisy's.'

'I was glad I could help,' Laura told him. 'Will you be doing anything in the concert, Ince? How about you, Spencer?'

'I'm singing the "Old Rugged Cross",' Ince said, beaming with pride. 'I'm told I've got a good tenor voice. I belong to the village male voice choir. I'll be performing in their spot too.'

'I shall look forward to that. And you, Spencer?'

'I'm playing the piano for Vicki,' he told her, and she knew he'd imparted the information grudgingly.

'Sounds like the whole village is getting involved. What about your neighbours the Daveys? I'm thinking about Tressa in particular. I haven't met her yet but my friend has and he was quite taken with her.'

'Tressa's very sweet but rather shy,' Ince said. 'She'll probably just come and watch. Joan and Jacka might do something. One year they sang a medley of American minstrel songs. He has to be careful with his chest now.'

Spencer was looking at Laura darkly. 'And just what sort of interest has your friend got in Tressa Davey?'

Laura looked back at him primly and answered in the same cool manner. 'Nothing untoward, I can assure you.'

'It had better not be,' Spencer mumbled. He headed for the door. 'If you'll excuse me, I must feed Barney.' He didn't wait for her permission and left the room.

Vicki tugged on Laura's arm. 'Do you want to see me dance?'

'I'd love to,' Laura replied delightedly. The atmosphere was much lighter now that Spencer had gone. Ince rolled back a mat so Vicki could dance on the lino. Laura stood beside him and watched Vicki, enchanted by her graceful movements.

'How am I doing?' she whispered to Ince.

'Fine,' he whispered back. 'Spencer's not very comfortable but Vicki's perfectly happy and that's all that matters.'

'Do you think we'll get on better after this?'

Ince took his eyes off Vicki for a moment. He grinned boyishly. 'Well, it won't ever be as bad as before. Listen, I've got a few hours free on Saturday afternoon. If the weather's dry and clear, would you like to climb to the top of Hawk's Tor with me?'

'I'd like nothing more,' Laura replied enthusiastically. 'I've been wanting to climb up there but I'm too nervous to attempt it on my own.'

'Very wise. That's settled then.'

Laura stayed another half-hour then said she would have to leave to prepare for her dinner appointment with Felicity Lean. She thought it was a reasonable excuse but Spencer scowled. How unpredictable he was. Could she ever do anything right for him? Did he want her to go or to stay? Or was it because he thought Harry would be there and he was someone else Spencer hated?

She was comforted by the knowledge that Vicki was disappointed she had to go and she would soon be seeing Ince for the walk to the top of the tor.

—

Laura was shown into the drawing room of Hawksmoor House by a local woman who introduced herself as Mrs Biddley and explained that she was Mrs Lean's daily help and was doing the catering tonight. Laura was dismayed to find Harry was at home and alone in the room. She was still angry with him for passing on gossip about her financial position. He had better not make a pass at her.

She accepted a sherry from him, sat down as far away from him as she could, then looked round the room, studying the paintings hanging from a high dado rail. There were similar touches in the room to ones she had noticed at Rosemerryn Farm. Striped curtains, silver-plated photographs, lace runners, the same sort of blue and white porcelain ornaments.

Harry watched her from a Chinese watered-silk sofa, looking altogether too handsome in a dark suit and smoking a cigar. He was a dangerous man in more ways than one where women were concerned, he must have broken many hearts.

'Mother will be down in a minute,' he drawled. 'I'm afraid she's hopeless with the time. Can I get you another sherry?'

'No, thank you,' Laura held up her nearly full glass. 'I'm fine with this one.'

'I must say you look very beautiful tonight.' He leaned forward, resting his arms on his legs. 'But then you're the sort of woman who would look beautiful in rags.'

She wished she had worn rags, instead of a tucked and fitted long black dinner dress. She had pinned up her hair and wound black and white beads round her neck. She hadn't wanted to seem drab next to the sophisticated Felicity Lean. She didn't bother to thank Harry for his compliment.

'How have you enjoyed your first week in Kilgarthen?' Harry lifted his sensuously curved brows. 'I was most surprised when you decided to stay among us.'

'I like the village very much and most of the people are friendly. I'm not at all pleased with you though, Harry Lean. It's all round the village about my father's company going bankrupt.'

He smiled smugly and wrinkled his nose. 'Think of it as a favour. The news would have come out eventually, better now than later. It will mean they won't expect you to splash money that you haven't got round the village. From what I've heard, the villagers feel sorry for you. Because of the pride they had in Bill they're feeling honoured that you've stayed. You should fit in here nicely. I understand you've made yourself something of a guardian angel, helping to nurse Johnny Prouse.' The sardonic amusement that seemed a constant feature of his conversation was very much in evidence. 'I think I can make a guess at one person in particular who hasn't welcomed you, though.'

He was waiting for her to respond but Laura wasn't about to discuss Spencer Jeffries; Harry probably knew about the scene in the churchyard. 'I understand you keep several horses here,' she said. 'Do you think your mother would let me ride one?'

'The horses belong to me, actually, and you are welcome to ride at any time. I'll inform the stable hand. We must ride together. I could show you some lovely and interesting places on the moor, some are ancient. When are you free?'

Laura was sure the places he would take her to would be very lonely and he wouldn't be interested in anything historic. 'I've got quite a lot on at the moment. I'm helping out with the Christmas concert.'

'How quaint,' he said, smiling disarmingly.

'Will you be going, Mr Lean?'

'Oh, Harry, please. I can't stand all this Mr and Mrs nonsense. No, I will not be going to the concert, Laura. Not my scene at all. Mother will probably go, as a guest of honour or something.'

Without you there it will be an all the more enjoyable evening, Laura thought. She doubted if the villagers would miss his presence.

A few minutes later Felicity Lean entered the room with a cat-like walk, bringing with her a cloud of heavy exotic perfume. She wore an exquisite French-styled evening gown, her hair and make-up were skilfully done. She held out long red-nailed fingers. 'Mrs Jennings. How sweet of you to come. Do forgive me for being a little late. I expect Harry has told you I'm absolutely hopeless with the time. Have you got a drink? Ah, good. Pour me a large vermouth, will you, darling,' she purred at Harry.

As she said the last word, her body gave a tiny lurch and Laura realised that Felicity was slightly drunk. Laura felt her heart sinking. Was this meal going to be another ordeal?

They ate an excellent meal of asparagus soup, crown roast of lamb and sherry trifle, served in a dining room furnished throughout in solid Victorian pieces, a complete contrast to the more modern lines of the drawing room. The house wasn't as big as Laura had imagined it would be, roughly the same size as Daisy's and Bunty's put together. It probably had no more than five bedrooms, but the Leans' style and taste gave it a colonial aura.

'You must come again, in the daytime, Laura,' Felicity said from the head of the large rectangular table after she'd drunk two glasses of wine in quick succession. 'See the house in the daylight.'

'That would be nice,' Laura replied, uncomfortably aware that she was still under Harry's persistent gaze.

'After the village concert, Laura's going to ride with me, Mother,' Harry said, leaning back in his chair and loosening his bow tie.

'Oh, good,' and Felicity gave a little hiccup.

'Do you ride, Felicity?' Laura asked. Her eyes flicked to Harry. If he was aware that drink was getting the better of his mother, he seemed unperturbed.

'Not these days,' Felicity replied, pouring the last drop from a bottle of red wine into her glass. 'Now, it would be silly for you, Harry, to stay here alone with a bottle of port. Bring it into the drawing room, darling, where Mrs B-Bidd— will serve us coffee.'

'Mrs Biddley, Mother,' Harry said hastily, rising and offering both women his arms.

Laura refused the port and because Felicity's hands were shaking, she took it upon herself to pour the coffee after Mrs Biddley had served it. She looked at a photograph on the wine table beside her and gave a start. The beautiful woman in the photograph was Natalie Jeffries.

'My late sister,' Harry said in a low voice.

Laura turned to Felicity. She was beside the gramophone looking over the selection of records, a glass of port in her hand. 'Yes, she was my d-darling daughter,' the older woman affirmed, her eyes misting over. 'She died just after Vicki, my granddaughter, was born.'

Vicki had not mentioned she had a grandmother and only Daisy and Bunty had been allowed to look after the little girl. Why not her grandmother? Because of her drinking problem? And why hadn't Daisy told her Felicity Lean was Vicki's grandmother? Because she thought she'd ask painful questions? Did this secret have anything to do with Spencer and Bill's quarrel?

'I'm very sorry, Felicity,' Laura said softly. 'Vicki is a dear little girl.'

'I haven't had the chance to find out for myself,' Felicity blurted out, the drink loosening her tongue. 'Natalie had a kidney problem. She was born with it and should never have had a baby. But when she became pregnant she was determined to go through with it. I pleaded with her to tell Spencer, to tell him that there could be danger to her life during her labour, but she refused. She didn't want Spencer to worry.' Tears were running down Felicity's rouged cheeks.

'She was booked to have a Caesarean operation and he would never have known she had a health problem. She was going to be sterilised to make sure she only had the one child. But Vicki arrived early and Natalie's kidneys weren't able to take the strain of a normal labour. When the hospital told Spencer the reason for Natalie's death, he was beside himself with grief and guilt. When he found out that I'd known about it all along he went out of his mind. He swore he'd never forgive me and that he'd never allow me to have anything to do with Vicki.' Felicity was sobbing, and Laura went to her. 'My own granddaughter, my own little girl's baby.'

Harry joined them and put his arms round his mother, hugging her close. 'Come along now, Mother. You've had enough for one night. Let me and Laura help you to bed.'

After a few moments, Felicity collected herself and pushed her son firmly away from her. She wiped her eyes on a silk handkerchief 'I – I'm all right. Please forgive me, Laura. I don't usually drink so much and get like this. It's because you've been recently widowed, you see. It's brought back all the agony. It's hit me harder than ever that Spencer will never forgive me, that I'll never see Vicki grow up. I don't think she's even aware that I'm her grandmother and Harry is her uncle.'

'I'm terribly sorry, Felicity,' Laura said gently. Her mind could hardly cope with the strength of her anger towards Spencer Jeffries. How could he be so cruel?

Harry helped Felicity to her feet and to the door. She bid Laura 'Goodnight' and Mrs Biddley helped her up the stairs.

'Only I and Mrs Biddley know how Mother gets when she's heart-broken,' Harry said, helping himself to a large brandy. 'I think I know you well enough to trust you to be discreet, Laura, or I would never have given you Mother's invitation.'

'That makes me feel humble,' Laura said, accepting a glass of brandy. She understood now why Harry stayed at home to live with his mother and she admired him for that. 'What a terrible situation. I can't believe someone could be so unforgiving, although perhaps I can as far as Spencer Jeffries is concerned.'

'Spencer adored Natalie. He probably loved her too much, that's why he can't forgive Mother.' Harry shook his head sadly. 'He said if he'd known about Natalie's kidneys he would have insisted she stay in bed and rest. He would never have left her side. He was denied that opportunity and said there's no excuse for Mother not telling him. I often think that if it wasn't for Vicki, Spencer would have shot himself.'

Laura gasped. 'Well, he certainly seems to have strong feelings if his hatred for Bill is anything to go by.'

Harry's voice dropped to a soft, caring tone. 'I'm glad you came tonight, Laura. Mother will feel terribly embarrassed in the morning but it's helped her to bring her feelings out in the open. I'll explain that you were sympathetic.'

'If there's anything I can do to help, Harry, I'll be glad to.'

'If you could befriend Mother, that might be a great help to her and I would be very grateful to you. She was telling the truth, about her drinking. She's not an alcoholic. She just has a drop too much when the pain gets unbearable, like on the anniversary of Natalie's death.'

'That can't be far away,' Laura said thoughtfully. 'Vicki told me she'll soon be five and will be going to school.'

'January the tenth. Vicki was born on the seventh. She could have started school last term but Spencer insisted on keeping her at home as long as possible. My worry is that he'll smother her and not let her grow up to develop her own character.'

Laura smiled at Harry. He had many ways she couldn't tolerate but he was not without a saving grace and she was warming to him. 'You would like to be a proper uncle to Vicki, wouldn't you?'

'I would, very much.' He looked at her deeply. 'I don't care much about anyone other than Mother and Vicki. I was very close to Natalie. I hate Spencer for what he's done to Mother.'

Laura felt herself shifting away from Harry. He was a frank man. She felt that if he knew Bill had been his half-brother he would say so, but a few questions wouldn't hurt.

'How did your father die, Harry?'

Harry raised a puzzled face over the second glass of brandy he was pouring for himself 'Why do you want to know that?'

'Oh, you know how people in a small community gossip. Someone mentioned that he had a tragic end. I was just curious.'

He brought the brandy bottle over to her and she knew he wouldn't tell her anything unless she accepted another drink. She dutifully held out her glass. She watched the fiery liquid trickle into the bowl warm in her hand. He put the bottle down and sat on the arm of her chair, close to her.

'He shot himself.'

Laura flushed guiltily. 'Oh, I'm sorry. I wouldn't have asked if I'd known it was anything like that.'

Harry slid his eyes from hers to her lips. 'I don't mind talking about it, there was no love lost between us. It happened thirteen years ago. He'd made some bad speculation on the stock exchange. He was forced to sell off a lot of property to bail us out. He was a very proud man. He couldn't take the disgrace. One day he went off on the moor with his handgun and blew out his brains.'

Laura shuddered. 'How terrible.'

'Dead and gone. My father. Your husband.' Harry stroked a tendril of hair near her ear. 'Why don't we forget the dead and think about the pleasures of living?'

Laura stood up and handed him her glass. 'I think it's time I was leaving.'

Harry held up the two glasses of brandy and spread his arms in an innocent gesture. 'I'm not stopping you.' When Laura had left the room and Mrs Biddley was fetching her coat, Harry downed the contents of both glasses and added to himself, 'This time...'

Chapter 16

'It's beautiful up here!' Laura exclaimed excitedly, turning round in a circle. 'I didn't think I'd be able to see so far.'

'I thought you'd like it,' Ince said simply. 'We're lucky to have a clear day, you can see to the limit of each horizon.'

'Like it? It's breathtaking.'

They were standing on the square, flat-topped granite rock that was the summit of Hawk's Tor. The sky was pale blue with a few isolated grey-tinged clouds drifting on the wind. A thousand feet below was Hawkstor Downs and the scattering of local farms, their average size about one hundred and eighty acres. They were linked by winding lanes, not all giving access to motorised vehicles. All the colours were faded, the bushes laid bare, surfaces bleached. Here and there the gorse had been swaled, burnt as a management technique to create new growth for grazing the following year.

'Thanks for bringing me up here, Ince. It's a climb I wouldn't have attempted alone in winter, the weather can change so suddenly.'

'It's a fairly easy climb, apart from the last twenty feet over the boulders, and the path is well worn by sheep and holidaymakers and locals.'

'Maybe, but I'm glad to be in your company.'

Ince smiled gently. He pointed out the green and grey contours of Dartmoor on the northern horizon, many, many miles away. To the south they could see the blue stretches of Plymouth Sound winding its way to the sea. He named the other tors which sheltered the Trebartha valley and had enabled this part of the moor to become one of the earliest settlements of Cornwall. To the south-west rose Trewortha Tor and then the tor named King Arthur's Bed; Ince explained that there was no reliable evidence that the mythical king had ever slept on it. On Twelve Men's Moor was the highest tor, Kilmar, an awesome and majestic sight on the eastern flank of the moor, the half-mile ridge of granite at its summit resembling the serrated edge of a saw, and on East Moor where wild ponies roamed they could see Fox Tor.

Also sheltering the Trebartha valley was the four-mile stretch of the many woods that made up the Trebartha plantation, where fir and spruce grew with natural woodland of ash, beech, and oak. More coniferous trees were planted on the slopes of Smallacombe Downs. In the middle distance rose the tower of North Hill's church which stood on a low hill right in the centre of the village. As the wind blew in every direction, the landscape seemed to change its shape and colour every time Laura lifted her eyes.

She looked for signs of Spencer and Tressa and Jacka Davey on their farms but saw only livestock browsing on the open moor and in fields that were divided by low stone walls flanked by fern banks. She was thrilled when she saw a buzzard hawk take wing and glide majestically on the chilled air as it sought prey. Ince told her sparrow hawks and kestrels could often be seen out hunting.

Beyond the Trebartha Woods she traced the River Lynher, following its course east to west where it merged with the Withey Brook and continued on to Kilgarthen. From up here the village looked more than familiar, it seemed to beckon a friendly hand to her and she felt she'd known it all her life.

'I'd never have been able to pick out all the places on my own, even after what Bill had told me,' she said to Ince with a childlike sense of awe.

'I come up here often,' Ince said. 'I'm fortunate to have always had the peace and quiet.'

'So you've lived in the village all your life?'

'That's right.' Ince went quiet for a moment. 'I did my bit for the country working the land but I felt guilty about not fighting.'

They scrambled down to a spot sheltered by small trees and a tumble of rocks. Despite being well clad, the cold penetrated Laura's coat and she gave an involuntary shiver. Ince unwound the faded woollen scarf from round his neck and put it over her shoulders like a shawl, then he pulled her silk headscarf out from the top of her coat, put it over her head and tied a neat bow under her chin.

Laura was surprised with herself for allowing him to do it. It was the first time in years she'd let a man touch her this closely. 'Thank you,' she smiled, partly at Ince, partly because she was pleased with herself for losing some of her reticence. 'I suppose you're used to doing this sort of thing for Vicki.'

'I don't think of you in the same way as I do Vicki,' he said, looking directly into her eyes for a moment. 'Shall we sit down and huddle out of the wind? I've brought a flask of tea with me.'

He took a blanket out of the crib bag he had brought with him and laid it on the ground. They sat down closely side by side and Ince put a flask cup of steaming strong tea in her hand.

As he poured one for himself, she remarked, 'I know you farmers have rights of common here but I'd have thought the cattle would have been brought in nearer the farms in winter, put in barns or something.'

'We house the cows in milk and young stock at night. We have heavy rainfall on the moor and the herd would soon trample an enclosed field out of existence. Actually cattle do well on the open downs, they're stronger and healthier. In stormy weather they find a fold or hollow, or a hedge or the lee of a wall to shelter in.'

'You make it sound easy,' Laura said, 'but I know it's a tough life, working out in all weathers.' Reminded of where Ince was living, and thinking that there were no other Polkinghornes in the village, she asked, 'Haven't you got any family, Ince?'

'No. My parents died years ago. The Sparnocks took over their cottage. I lodged with Johnny Prouse until Natalie died then I moved into the farm. Sometimes I think I could never leave and give up my role of helping to bring up Vicki, but part of me wants a wife and family of my own.'

'That's understandable, everyone wants to make their own way in life.' She had herself, before Bill had stifled her hopes and aspirations. Laura felt warmed through that Ince had confided his feelings to her. He was a comfortable man to be with. 'It's unusual, two men bringing up one little girl alone.'

He hadn't missed the slight frown on her face. 'You look as if you don't approve.'

'I don't approve of Spencer's over-possessiveness,' she replied staunchly. 'I think Vicki needs the gentler touch of a woman. I think it's a terrible shame he won't let Felicity Lean be a grandmother to her. I get so angry when I think how it's breaking her heart. After all, she lost her daughter. Loving Vicki the way he does, you'd think Spencer would be more understanding.'

'I see you're catching up on all the local gossip,' Ince said wryly. 'You've only been here just over a week but you're already fitting into the village.'

'I've had a lovely time over the past two days helping with the scenery for the concert,' she said enthusiastically. 'The hall has an excellent stage. Bill didn't stint with the money he spent in the village.'

'And how do you feel about that?'

Laura shrugged her shoulders and drank the last drop of her tea. 'I'm glad the villagers have a fine hall.' She moved a bit closer to Ince. Here was a man she knew she could trust with anything. 'Ince?'

'Yes?' he said, hesitating as he pushed in the flask cork. 'Would you mind if I confided in you?'

'No, not at all. You have my word it won't go any further.'

'There's something I want to ask you about Bill. I've heard that his real father was William Lean. Do you know if it's true? You're not much older than he was but you must know all the village gossip.'

'There were rumblings to that effect. But I can tell you one thing, Laura. Whether he was or not, Bill believed he was William Lean's son. He went up to Hawksmoor House and confronted him with the rumours. He was about fourteen years old, not long before Lean died. Lean threw him out. He made trouble for Bill until he died. If anything went missing in the village, Lean informed the police and suggested Bill had taken it. He was a very cruel man.'

'Being the son of a rich man would have appealed to the Bill I knew. Feeling he was rejected by his real father and having to live as the son of a poor stable groom instead of having a life like Harry's could account for some of Bill's failings. Bill was christened William, makes you wonder why.'

'I can see why he strove to better himself,' Ince said, always one to look for the good in others or make excuses for their bad behaviour.

'He ended up as cruel as the man he thought was his father.' Before she said something else that sounded bitter, Laura ended cheerily, 'Well, at least I have the chance to start over again. You must have heard the rumours about my father's company going bankrupt. It was Bill's fault. He was good at his job on the board of directors but he used some shady characters to finance his schemes. When he died they demanded their money back, they had everything tied up legally. All I've got left is the cottage, some money in the bank and some jewellery. When I've decided where my future lies, I'll either get a job round here or sell up and move back to London.'

Ince put his hand over hers. She felt his warmth and strength through her glove. 'I hope you decide to stay.'

–

When Laura arrived home she found someone waiting for her. The dark, brooding look on Marianne Roach's pretty face made her forget the pleasant two and a half hours she'd just spent with Ince.

'Can I speak to you, Mrs Jennings?' Marianne said in a decidedly aggressive manner.

Laura considered her for a few moments, then said, 'You'd better come inside.'

Marianne refused to take off her coat and sit down. As Laura discarded hers, she realised she still had Ince's scarf; it smelled comfortingly of him. She built up the log fire then faced the sulky girl.

'What can I do for you, Marianne?'

For a moment Marianne dropped her aggression and Laura thought she was going to burst into tears, but she pushed out her chin and clenched her fists. 'I… I'll come straight to the point, Mrs Jennings. I've been plucking up the courage for days to say this but Bill owes me some money.'

'Bill borrowed money from you?' Laura asked incredulously. With the way Bill spent money in the village and showed off, it seemed unthinkable that he'd borrow from a young working girl.

'Are you accusing me of being a liar?' Marianne snapped back.

'No, of course not. It seems so unlike Bill, that's all. Please sit down, Marianne, and let's talk this over.' Laura pointed to an armchair by the fire. Marianne's expression changed and she seemed unsure of herself as she sat down. Laura remained standing. 'Now what's this all about? But first let me assure you that if Bill borrowed from you I will pay you back in full.'

'B-Bill borrowed from me to buy a present. I work in Launceston and I met him there one day. It was on his last visit down here. He was about to go back to London and he wanted to take a present back for you. We were in this shop and it was about to close. He'd run out of money and he had his heart set on... on an ornament. I'd just got paid and I offered to lend him the money. He said he'd pay me back when he was here next, but then he... he died, and I...'

'Would like your money back?' Laura was looking at the girl with her lips tightly pursed. 'How much was it?' Marianne's head was bent over and she was looking down at the floor but Laura could see her turning crimson. 'It... it was a special present. It cost one hundred pounds.'

'One hundred pounds?' Laura blurted out. 'I doubt that you'd have that much money in your purse. I thought you were lying and now I'm sure. Bill never brought me presents back from Cornwall and he certainly never gave me anything the last time.'

Marianne sprang up. Tears of rage were in her eyes and her mascara started to run. 'Well, maybe it was for someone else!' she wailed. 'Or perhaps he bought it for you for Christmas.'

'Bill was a show-off,' Laura said acidly. She had a good idea exactly what Bill's relationship had been with this girl and she wasn't about to be conned by her now she'd lost her sugar-daddy. 'When he bought me presents they usually came from Harrods.'

'Ohh!' Marianne moaned, putting her hands up to her face. Then she looked at Laura with a venomous expression. 'I should have known better to come to you for help, you bitch!'

Laura would normally have been stung to fury by the girl's insult but there was something desperate about her. She had said the word 'help'. Laura moved smartly to stop her making a hasty escape. 'Why don't you tell me the real reason behind your coming here, Marianne?'

Marianne was crying. She felt so ashamed. She had made up the story hoping Laura Jennings would fall for it and give her the money. It had been her only hope. A girl friend of hers had said she knew someone who would perform an abortion but it would cost one hundred pounds. If she had thought it through clearly she would have realised her plan was hopeless.

She took a handkerchief out of her jumper sleeve and wiped her nose. 'I'm sorry. I shouldn't have come here. You don't deserve this. I know you didn't have a happy marriage with Bill. He used to say horrible things about you. I hated you when I first saw you but after what you've done in the village I can see he was lying. Please let me past. I must go.'

'Were you in love with Bill? Is that what this is all about?'

'I don't know about love,' Marianne snorted, making her nose run. 'I guess I was mesmerised by him.'

'I'm sorry, Marianne. At least you're well out of it now, before you got in too deeply with him. Bill would have rejected you eventually, quite ruthlessly, too. I hope we can be friends. Look, don't be offended, but if you're short of money, perhaps I can help...'

'N-no. I'll be all right. I was just... I really do have to go, please, Mrs Jennings.'

Laura was puzzled and wanted to try to get more out of the girl but her look of acute shame touched Laura's heartstrings. She moved away from the door. 'Call in any time, Marianne.'

When she had gone, Laura regretted the lameness of her last words to her. Any woman left heartbroken by Bill Jennings needed comfort and she had been unable to give it. A rush of rage shot through her. She wanted to run across the road to the graveyard and stamp all over Bill's grave.

–

Daisy closed the shop on Saturday afternoons and today she was spending the time stocktaking. Laura had offered to help her. They were still working hard as teatime approached. Laura's thoughts were on Marianne's distress as she wrote down figures in a ledger for Daisy.

'That's a box of twelve Carnation evaporated milk,' Daisy said. She glanced at Laura who was gazing absent-mindedly across the little storeroom. 'You still with me, dear?' Daisy laughed, raising her voice.

'What? Oh, I'm sorry. What did you say?'

'That's three thousand boxes of Carnation evaporated milk.'

'Three thousand – oh, Aunty Daisy, I nearly wrote that down.'

Daisy's wrinkly face was mobile with speculation. 'You like him, don't you? Ince. He's a good man. You must have got on very well this afternoon, by the look of it. You could do a lot worse and very little better.'

'Aunty Daisy, what are you suggesting?' Laura said in mock outrage. 'Bill's only been dead two weeks and he was your nephew. I'd have thought you wouldn't have approved of me going out with another man so soon, and it wasn't like that anyway. Ince and I are only friends.'

'For now,' Daisy said knowingly. 'I know what Bill was to me but don't forget I know your circumstances. Anyway, I wasn't expecting anything serious to happen yet. Ince isn't the sort of man to rush things.'

'I'm fond of Ince, but no more,' Laura said emphatically. 'What would the villagers say if they thought I was looking for a new husband so soon? They'd be shocked and outraged – quite rightly, too.'

Daisy was unshakable. 'I was thinking of this time next year. They'd like to see Billy's widow stay in the village and married to another local. We'll see.'

Laura rolled her eyes and shook her head. '*How* many boxes of that milk?'

A loud banging on the shop door disturbed them. 'I'll go,' said Daisy. 'Someone's forgotten something for their Sunday roast, I'll be bound.'

Laura heard Daisy talking to someone with an unfamiliar voice and curious to see who it was, she went into the shop. One look at the shopper's baggy clothes and big Wellington boots and she knew it was Tressa Davey.

'A heaped teaspoon of bicarbonate of soda in warm water will do the trick,' Daisy was saying to Tressa. 'He'll be right as rain in no time.'

The old ill-fitting men's clothes she wore detracted nothing at all from Tressa's natural loveliness and Laura understood why Andrew had become so quickly smitten by her. There was something spellbinding about her and it was enhanced by the fact that she probably never saw people in terms of attractiveness herself and couldn't understand how other people, especially men, saw her. No wonder Harry Lean sought to make her a conquest.

'Ah, Laura, you haven't met Tressa Davey, have you?' Daisy said.

'No. I'm pleased to meet you at last, Tressa,' Laura said and held out her hand. She sensed Tressa's reluctance to shake it but she kept it there, giving the other young woman no choice. She felt the warm roughness of Tressa's long-fingered hand but it was snatched back after a moment. 'Someone poorly in your house, is there?' she asked.

'My father,' Tressa muttered, tossing her head like a restless moor pony. 'He's got bad indigestion.'

'Oh, dear. What a shame. My friend, Andrew Macarthur, met your father and your Aunt Joan.' Laura paused for effect. 'He found them extremely welcoming and friendly.'

Laura was thrilled when Tressa flushed guiltily and she knew from Daisy's look of fervent curiosity that she was on the scent. 'Andrew's a kind and honest man, you know, Tressa.'

Tressa gulped and Laura knew she'd hit a raw spot. 'Gone back to London, has he?' Tressa asked gruffly.

'Yes, but we keep in touch. He might phone me tonight.' Laura raised an impertinent eyebrow. 'Pass on a message to him from you, can I?'

Tressa's lively dark eyes burned in her skull. 'I've got nothing to say to he. How much is the bicarb, Mrs Tamblyn?'

Daisy took the money and handed Tressa her purchase in a paper bag. Tressa looked as if she couldn't get out of the shop quickly enough, but Laura had one parting shot. 'Next time I speak to Andrew, I'll pass on your regards, shall I, Tressa?'

Tressa swung round at the door with her mouth wide open. She let out a loud 'Umph!' and left, slamming the door.

Daisy grabbed Laura by the arm. 'What was that all about? And don't go round all the houses telling me.'

Laura told Daisy about Andrew's attraction to the quiet farm girl. She felt she had got even for the way Tressa had treated him.

'I thought he was interested in her but I didn't know he'd made such a strong play for the maid. She came to see him in the pub that night. I never could make out why. What happened then?'

'Her father sent her there to apologise for making Andrew walk through a bog. He tried to get her to have a drink with him but she spurned him again. He was so forlorn about it. I've never seen him so upset. Before he left he asked me to put in a good word for him if I met her. Well, I've done that, though it was obviously a waste of time.'

'You're telling me. You ended by putting her back up. Well, well, you never know what's going to happen next. I can't wait to tell Bunty how she treated him. A solicitor all the way from London falling head over heels for that dear little maid. I can't think of a more unlikely couple in the world than they two.'

Laura was still chuckling as they returned to the storeroom. 'Unless it's me and Spencer Jeffries.'

Chapter 17

Two weeks went by in which Laura saw plenty of the heavy rainfall Ince had told her about on Hawk's Tor; at one stage water ran like a stream down the village hill. On a trip into Launceston to buy wool so she could knit some doll's clothes for Vicki she had been frightened by the sudden whoosh of rain water bombarding the sides of the bus as it had splashed up from dips and ditches. But it was wonderful to snuggle up in front of her fire while the elements lashed against the walls and windows of Little Cot.

Very little happened in the village but she saw that even the smallest events had a pattern to them, like the petals of a flower slowly unfolding in the summer sunshine. Most noticeably, Johnny Prouse steadily recovered, and one fine afternoon he went for a short stroll on Laura's arm.

Laura had gone twice for morning coffee with Felicity at Hawksmoor House, each time making sure Harry wouldn't be there. She had invited Felicity back to Little Cot but Felicity explained that she disliked going down into the village. She had talked fondly of Natalie's childhood and how proud she was of Harry who was enjoying an excellent career. She hadn't mentioned her husband. Laura felt increasingly sorry for the lonely woman.

The scenery for the Christmas concert had been finished and rehearsals were taking place. Cecil's regimented drilling of the school's contribution had taken effect and the children themselves were confident of the quality of the final performance they would give. The sketch Cecil had written was based on the fairytale of the Elves and the Shoemaker, the elves in this case being piskies. Laura was learning about Cornish folklore; piskies were mischievous 'small people', much given to pranks, about eighteen inches in height who dressed in 'sugar-loaf' hats and little red cloaks. She couldn't wait to see the children in their costumes which Daisy and Bunty were industriously making out of old curtains. Laura tried to talk to Marianne when she turned up at the hall one afternoon with a message for her father, but the girl ignored her. Marianne hadn't looked well. Spencer brought Vicki so she could see the stage she'd sing and dance on and she had a wonderful time playing with the other children, but Spencer seemed aloof and grumpy.

The occasion that caused the biggest stir was the sudden departure of Sam Beatty. As the days had gone by he had kept a low profile and Laura had almost forgotten his existence until he'd knocked on her door and bid her goodbye two days ago. His recuperation was complete and he left looking healthy and energetic. Daisy was certain he would show his face in Kilgarthen again.

Laura realised that every dwelling in Kilgarthen was decorated for Christmas and, rebelling against Ada Prisk's comments that as a widow she shouldn't decorate the cottage, she asked Daisy to order a fir tree for her. It was delivered that afternoon and she bought holly, ivy and mistletoe from children selling it at the door. Bill had spent time here over Christmas so she reckoned he'd have some decorations somewhere. She fetched a stepladder and lifted the hatch to the attic in one of the spare rooms. Using a torch, she saw various boxes just inside the hatch and right in front of her eyes was one labelled Christmas decorations. She decorated the front room lavishly, using all the pretty sparkly things Bill had bought, then looked for some more drawing pins to hang up strings for cards. Bill had pushed a lot of odds and ends in a drawer of the wardrobe in the main bedroom and Laura tried there.

At the back of the drawer she came across a cloth bag and tipped out its contents. It contained a set of diaries dating back over several years. She looked inside the front cover of some of them and there was Bill's handwriting, the older the diary, the more childish the writing. She froze. She'd been trying to glean information about Bill from the villagers in an effort to understand his cruel behaviour towards her, and

176

here in her hands was what could well tell her everything she wanted to know and more. She stared at the diaries. Suddenly she dropped them as if they were burning her hands. She couldn't bring herself to look at them now. She was feeling happy. She might learn things that would upset her terribly. She wanted to enjoy every moment of the festive season. Perhaps in the new year... She gathered up the diaries and took them to the spare room. She tossed them on top of the wardrobe. Up there she wouldn't be tempted to read them.

Laura slept uneasily that night. In her dreams she read evidence in Bill's diaries that suggested he was everything from Attila the Hun to Adolf Hitler.

Ince had invited her to Rosemerryn Farm the next day to help put up the Christmas decorations there and she was glad to get out of the cottage. She proudly took a cake tin of yeast buns which she had learned to bake herself. Ince let her in and she was instantly disappointed.

'Where's Vicki? I've brought some sugar-candy canes for her to put on the tree.'

'Spencer's taken her shopping in Bodmin,' Ince said, automatically making a pot of tea. The people of Kilgarthen drank gallons of it.

'That's further away than Callington or Launceston.' Laura was most annoyed. 'Contrived to stay out until I've gone, presumably.'

'No,' Ince said, carrying a box of decorations to the table. 'It's something of a tradition for Spencer and Vicki to go shopping together just before Christmas. You don't mind, do you? About being here with me?'

'No,' Laura replied truthfully. She trusted Ince.

'Right then.' Ince rubbed his big hands together, his dark eyes twinkling. 'Let's get started. I'll climb the stepladder, you can pass me the decorations and put up the lower ones. We must make sure we leave some things for Spencer and Vicki to put up, including putting the crib together.'

Laura passed drawing pins to Ince as he hung paper streamers from beam to beam across the low ceiling. They put some tinsel and baubles on the gigantic fir tree Spencer had bought from the Trebartha plantation, leaving a few more and the crowning star for Vicki and Spencer.

'We'll let them drape the pictures and mantelpiece with tinsel,' Laura said as she made a table display with holly, ivy and a tall red candle. 'I wouldn't want to upset his lordship.'

'Eh?' Ince said, twisting his head round from the spot by the stairs door where he was securing a huge spray of holly. His face was red with the effort and Laura laughed.

'I think you need a break. It's my turn to make the tea. You are going to try one of my yeast buns, aren't you?'

'Of course.' Ince got down from the stepladder and pushed it aside. He moved to Laura and glanced up at the sprig of mistletoe over their heads. Not entirely on impulse, he bent his head and kissed her cheek.

He hadn't touched her or tried to hold her but Laura backed away, her eyes blinking rapidly with shock.

'I'm sorry,' Ince said, his voice low and grave. 'I didn't mean to offend you.'

Only then did Laura realise they had been standing under the mistletoe. Her heart sank that she had shrunk away from such an innocent gesture. Ince wouldn't do anything to hurt her. 'You didn't offend me, Ince,' she said, 'you just took me by surprise.'

The hurt in his dark eyes faded and he smiled, that gentle understanding smile, and Laura felt so reassured and comfortable she moved up close to him and placed her head on his chest. Ince sighed with relief and put his arms round her and held her closely against him.

Laura raised her face and looked into his eyes. 'You are a most considerate man, Ince.' She thought, if only Bill had been more like you. Then she kissed his cheek.

Ince kissed her forehead and they separated, feeling content to be in each other's company alone.

They were sitting at the table eating and drinking when there was a terrific crash outside in the yard.

'What was that?' Laura said anxiously.

Ince was already on his feet. 'Sounds like the wind's blown something down. You stay here in the warm. I'll try not to be long.'

178

'Come back if I can do anything to help.'

Moments later the kitchen door was opened but it wasn't Ince coming back. Spencer came in carrying Vicki and two bulging shopping bags.

'Ince invited me here,' Laura explained hastily. She was disturbed by how easily this man could unsettle her and make her feel guilty.

'Fine,' Spencer said. He didn't look vexed to see her there. 'We came back early. Vicki's got a headache and she's feeling hot. I think she's getting a cold.'

'Oh, are you feeling poorly, darling?' Laura said, going to them and taking off Vicki's hat and stroking her hair.

Vicki lifted her head off her father's shoulder and nodded mournfully.

'Could you take these?' Spencer said, referring to the shopping bags. 'They're heavy and cutting into my hands.'

Laura took the bags which were filled with Christmas food and items that were obviously presents. She watched as Spencer put Vicki down on her feet and took off her gloves, scarf and coat. He kissed her and felt her forehead. He looked worried.

'What do you think?' he asked Laura. 'Do you think I ought to get the doctor for her?'

Laura looked critically at Vicki and felt her forehead too. She looked sleepy and her cheeks were a pretty pink. Laura frowned as she thought about it. 'Well, she's not burning hot and her cheeks aren't a bright red. Perhaps if she was given half an aspirin crushed with a little sugar and put to bed with a hot water bottle… It's what my mother used to do for me.'

'I think that's a good idea,' Spencer said, lifting Vicki up. 'Where's Ince?'

'He's out in the yard. Something blew down and he's gone to investigate,' Laura said, keeping her eyes rooted on Vicki, she felt an overwhelming longing to take care of the little girl. 'Can I help you with Vicki? Whatever fell down, it sounded serious.'

Spencer looked from Laura to his daughter as if he was in two minds about what to do.

179

'I can manage,' Laura reassured him. 'If you just tell me where to find the aspirin and hot water bottle.'

A fierce gust of wind rattled down the chimney and helped Laura's cause.

'Well, if you're sure you can manage. You'll find everything you need in the cupboard next to the fireplace.' Somewhat hesitantly, Spencer relinquished Vicki into Laura's care and went upstairs to change his clothes.

Laura sat Vicki in her father's armchair and gave her the aspirin and sugar, then quickly filled a hot water bottle covered in a knitted case in the shape of a smiling clown. She carried Vicki upstairs, undressed her and put on her nightie which she found under her pillows. Vicki was nearly asleep. Laura sat on the bed and stroked her forehead and softly sang a nursery rhyme until the little girl closed her eyes. When she was fast asleep, Laura caressed the golden hair that was splayed on the pillow.

Half an hour later she heard a heavy step on the stairs and Spencer came into the room. 'How is she?' he whispered.

'She went to sleep almost at once,' Laura whispered back.

'Thank you for staying with her,' he said, stroking Vicki's face and bending to plant a tender kiss on her cheek. 'She's quite cool now. Will probably be bursting with energy again tomorrow. Come down and have a cup of tea with me and Ince.'

They left the bedroom door open in case Vicki became restless or called out. Down in the kitchen Ince was washing his hands at the huge cloam sink.

'Did you manage to repair the damage outside, Ince?' Laura asked.

He turned and smiled at her and Spencer did not miss the special warmth in their communication. 'It was a large sheet of galvanised roofing that had fallen off the old trap house,' Spencer said from behind her. 'We nailed it back in place.'

'That's good,' Laura said, and without thinking she made the tea and was surprised at how natural it felt. Before today she would have been worried about upsetting Spencer.

'These are nice,' Spencer said, biting into a yeast bun. 'One of Daisy's?'

'Laura's,' Ince told him.

Spencer raised his fair brows. 'Really?'

'Only three days until the concert,' Laura said conversationally. 'I'm really looking forward to it and my first Christmas in Kilgarthen.'

'You must have a meal with us over Christmas, mustn't she, Spencer?' Ince said, looking at his friend as if he was daring him to say no.

Spencer's clear grey eyes were narrowed as he looked from Ince to Laura. She waited with bated breath for his answer. 'Of course,' he said, and he actually smiled at her.

It took her by surprise, not just that he gave it but, once again, how handsome he was. Bill was dead and here she was, a few weeks later, in the company of two very good-looking, available men. Only their characters, although very different, prevented the local unmarried females beating a determined path to their door. Laura thought herself fortunate; one man had a gentle, pleasing disposition which had stopped her from sinking into a lonely bitterness, the other man had a beautiful daughter whom she loved being with.

—

Andrew Macarthur was at home listening to similar weather to that beating against Kilgarthen's dwellings, but only momentarily. He cast aside the book he was reading. He crossed the lounge of his flat and poured himself a Scotch but didn't drink it. He wished he'd gone out with the friends who had asked him to a party, then he was glad he didn't. He had been restless and like a bear with a sore head since he'd got back to London. His two partners had started to raise disapproving eyebrows at him; today he had turned down the second lucrative case he'd been asked to represent that week. He was junior partner in the office and Mr Walmesley and Mr Britton would soon be having words with him.

He had brought some work home with him and he went to the table where he had tossed it. He sat down, picked up his fountain pen but shut the first file the instant he opened it. He wasn't interested in its contents. It wasn't a challenging case and he hated this sort of thing anyway, a divorce petition by a pampered, rich woman who was bitterly intent on stinging her adulterous husband for every penny she could get out of him. A lot of these cases were coming his way; since the war had ended, the divorce rate had increased fivefold. One of the juniors in the office could just as easily deal with this one before it got to court. His other work was important but not vital. He could leave instructions for it and nothing would need his attention or signature for a few weeks. He had looked carefully into Laura's situation and he had a few papers for her to sign, then nothing was likely to happen for several months while the bureaucratic wheels slowly turned.

He threw his pen down on the table. He was bored. None of his girl friends, either career women or social butterflies, provided interesting company these days. Nothing in his life was challenging any more. Nothing seemed worthwhile. What on earth was the matter with him? Before he'd taken that trip down to Cornwall, his lifestyle had been to his total satisfaction.

The doodles he'd been making on a notepad on top of the files caught his weary eye. Tressa. TRESSA. *Tressa*. Tressa Davey. He knew she was the reason for his discontent. He could hardly believe the effect she'd had on him. He drew a large heart round one of her names and put an arrow through it. But the arrow that he felt in his own heart was not Cupid's. Tressa Davey had mercilessly driven a hundred barbs through it and he'd been suffering ever since.

Was Tressa merciless? No, she wasn't deliberately merciless – well, just a little. She was immature. She was what one could call a child of nature. She was innocent, ordinary and absolutely beautiful. She had misunderstood his intentions. He wasn't another Harry Lean. But did she really understand what he was like anyway?

Just before he left the office his secretary had asked him if he wanted to put a personal letter in with the papers for Laura. He'd said he would and brought it home with him. He would write to her now. Perhaps that would take his mind off his misery for a while.

'Or you could deliver the papers personally,' he mumbled. It took a few moments for his brain to catch up with his voice. Then he jumped to his feet and shouted at the top of his voice, 'Why don't I go down to Cornwall and deliver the papers personally?' It wasn't Laura he was picturing in his mind, however, it was Tressa Davey. 'I'm not going to let you get away from me, you gorgeous creature. I'm going to fight to get you until the bitter end.'

—

On the day of the concert Laura spent the morning with Roslyn Farrow going over the arrangements and putting chairs in the hall. When Laura left, she took a quick bath and washed her hair. She was heating up some soup for lunch when there was a knock at the door.

'Oh damn,' she breathed in extreme annoyance. She was in her dressing gown, a towel was wrapped round her hair. She'd have to dash upstairs and get dressed.

The knocking became more insistent, and fearing that Johnny Prouse had become ill, she gingerly opened her front door. She was shocked to see Spencer on the other side.

'Spencer! What's the matter? Is Vicki ill?'

'No,' he replied, 'but it's Vicki I've come to see you about.'

Laura knew the gossips would have a field day if they knew she'd let a man into the cottage while wearing next to nothing, but she was afraid that if she asked Spencer to wait while she got dressed he'd take umbrage and go away. Holding the silk dressing gown tightly round herself, she let him in.

Spencer swept his eyes over her as he took off his hat. 'Sorry if I've come at an awkward moment.'

'I won't have much time to get ready tonight,' Laura explained self-consciously. 'There's nothing wrong, is there?'

'No, no, not at all.' He took his time answering her. He was admiring her tall figure, its distinctly feminine curves accentuated in the most interesting places where she was clutching the silk gown to her. It was a long time since he'd set his eyes on a near naked female form and he took a great deal of pleasure in doing so now. 'I've come to ask you a favour.'

'About Vicki?' Laura felt hope rising inside her. She'd do anything to get closer to Vicki Jeffries.

'Yes, it's about the concert tonight.' It was Spencer's turn to become self-conscious and now he looked all round the room rather than at her. He turned his hat in his fingers. 'Well, I… The thing is, when I took Vicki to the rehearsal, all the other children had their mothers there. They'll be there tonight behind the scenes getting their children ready, putting on their costumes and so on. Vicki will be the only one with her father. I'd feel silly and I'm afraid she'll feel different from the others. Daisy will be busy with her act and she's old enough to be Vicki's grandmother. I, um, was hoping that you wouldn't mind getting Vicki ready for her act.'

'I'd be delighted to, Spencer.' Laura meant it with her all heart. There was nothing she'd like more.

'You would? Oh, good. We'll see you there then.' Now that bit of business was out of the way he looked at her again, the colour of his eyes turning warm and smoky.

He made no move to go but Laura felt she couldn't invite him to stay and have a cup of coffee while she was wearing only her dressing gown. And then she realised he was looking at her closely, appreciatively, in precisely the same way she would expect from Harry Lean. The hat became still in his hands. His eyes were lingering on her most intimate places.

'Spencer, do you mind?' The words came out thickly.

He misread her, and even then took several moments before he tore his eyes away. 'Oh, I'm sorry, you want to get on. I'll see you tonight.'

He left, leaving Laura with the uneasy and indignant feeling that he had seen all she had to show.

Chapter 18

Barbara Roach called anxiously up the stairs to her daughter. 'Marianne! Will you please come down now. Your father and I are waiting to go to the hall.'

'I'm not going!' Marianne shouted back in a rage. 'How many times have I got to tell you?'

'Please,' Barbara pleaded. 'You're making him very angry.'

'He can go to hell and so can you!'

Barbara sighed. Chewing on her bottom lip, she went to the kitchen. What was the matter with the girl these days? She had refused to come out of her room all day. She'd seen the doctor and he'd said it was only a bad cold. The symptoms seemed to have cleared up. Marianne wasn't coughing or sneezing, she didn't sound congested and she didn't look hot and flushed. Just pale and very sulky. Perhaps the cold had left her feeling depressed. It wasn't like Marianne. She usually bounced back quickly after an illness. Last night when a group of her young friends had turned up in a car asking if she wanted to go to the pictures, she had turned the offer down. Oh well, Barbara thought wearily. If she's not better soon I'll talk to Dr Palmer myself. She gulped and swallowed painfully and a recent bruise in the small of her back began to throb. Now she had to face her husband with the news of their daughter's obstinacy.

Having taken Barbara into Launceston that day to do the last of their Christmas shopping, Cecil had been putting his car into the garage. He came back indoors and combed and Brylcreemed his hair in front of the hall mirror. He was wearing his most determined look; determined that the schoolchildren would perform their very best for him tonight.

Barbara joined him, ready to leave. She was carrying her contribution to the refreshment tables wrapped in tea towels.

'Where's Marianne?' Cecil demanded, his brow furrowing like a ploughed field as he slicked the few strands of hair that had the hopeless task of covering the top of his shiny head.

'She says she's not coming,' Barbara told him in a timid voice, her face twitching in anxiety, the dark bags under her eyes deepening in colour. She had been dreading this moment; she knew she would be blamed.

'What? Why not?' Cecil's huge Adam's apple moved up and down menacingly. 'What's got into that girl these days? She's always rude and sulky. She hardly goes to work, she's always grumbling there's something wrong with her. She'll lose her job if she doesn't buck up her ideas, and it's a damned good job!' He prodded Barbara painfully in the chest. 'Why didn't you insist on her coming with us? You're her mother. You're no more bloody good as a wife and mother than a cow with a blasted crutch!'

'It's best to let her stay home, dear,' Barbara said, trembling, the food on the plate in her hands at risk of tumbling off. 'She hasn't got over her cold yet. It's left her feeling weak and down in the dumps. There's several people poorly with one at the moment. Besides, if we force her to go in the mood she's in, she might say something to show us up. You know what she can be like.'

'Bah! I wanted all my family to be there tonight. I wanted your support. Is that too much to ask?'

Barbara had walked past Cecil and reached the door. He pushed her hard between the shoulder blades and her nose hit a square of frosted glass. It hurt her and she knew it would stay red and swollen all night. She'd have to say there were two members of the Roach household who had colds.

—

Laura put a plate of egg and pickle sandwiches, a plate of sausage rolls and a large chocolate gateau she had made on one of the long trestle tables in the village hall. Then she unloaded the box of table decorations she had made from slim layers of wood, pine cones gathered at the edge of the Trebartha woods, tinsel, holly and gold-painted ivy.

'You are clever, Laura,' Roslyn Farrow said in admiration, squeezing her arm. 'As Kinsley keeps saying, we may have lost Bill but we're blessed to have gained you. What a pity I couldn't rope you in to do an act. I'm sure you can sing or dance or recite a poem.'

'I'm happy helping out behind the scenes, Roslyn,' Laura replied, surveying the tables with a critical eye. The snowy white cloths were barely visible beneath various shaped platters of food of every description. 'Looks like we're going to have enough food for tonight.'

'Don't you bet on it. It's amazing what the villagers can come up with despite the shortages but my lot can shift mountains of the stuff.'

'It must be lovely having a family,' Laura said longingly.

Roslyn eyed her thoughtfully. 'Well, you're young enough to marry again one day, Laura, and have a large brood of children.'

'And it won't be difficult for you to find someone to father them,' attested Ada Prisk, letting a plate of ginger biscuits hit the table with a thud. She stood very straight, her hands gripped tightly in front of her, a withering look on her sour face. 'They're queuing up for the job already.'

Roslyn sighed and pulled on Laura's arm to lead her away but Laura wasn't going to let the old woman get away with that. 'And what exactly does that mean?'

Ada smoothed unnecessarily at the table cloth. 'You're an attractive, rich young woman. I'm sure you must have some money of your own and Bill would have been heavily insured. You've had your solicitor friend sniffing round you already and Ince Polkinghorne took you to the top of the tor. There was that other strange London fellow, he was interested in you, and Harry Lean, but then he of course goes after anything in a skirt so he wouldn't leave you out. You've even had Spencer Jeffries calling at your house and the only woman he's ever shown interest in before was his poor dead wife.'

Laura put her hands on her hips, her blue eyes ice-cold and spitting fury. Roslyn feared the evening was going to be spoiled by a heated quarrel before it had even begun.

'Don't forget Johnny Prouse, Mrs Prisk.' Laura hurled each word with venom at the old blabber-mouth. 'I spend a lot of time alone with him and I even spoke to the milkman this morning! You should mind your own business, you nosy old shrew!'

'Well, really!' Ada retorted indignantly, shaking her tall thin body like a bird ruffling its feathers. 'You should watch your mouth, young woman.'

'Me?'

Before Laura could say anything else, Roslyn stepped between them. 'I think Mrs Jennings has a point, Mrs Prisk. Your remarks were untoward to a recently widowed woman.'

The last thing Ada Prisk wanted was to go down in the estimation of the highly respected vicar's wife. 'Well, I, um, didn't mean any harm. I was only referring to Mrs Jennings' beauty. It's something she can't easily hide. Gentlemen are bound to notice it.'

The audience had started to arrive and, not wishing to ruin the concert, Laura retreated to sell programmes. She tried to take her mind off Ada Prisk by thinking over what Roslyn had said about there being time for her to have a family. The last thing she wanted was another husband, but more than anything else in the world she wanted a family. To achieve that she'd have to marry again. At least tonight she would have the opportunity to act as a mother.

The seats were nearly filled when Ince, Spencer and Vicki arrived. Roslyn took over the programme table while Laura led Vicki backstage to change into her dress. Make what you will of this, Ada Prisk, Laura thought defiantly. Ince, who was the third act on, came backstage with them.

'Would you like to meet me in the pub for a drink afterwards?' he whispered to her.

'Yes, I would, thank you,' she replied. She was going to start the tongues wagging tonight.

Vicki chattered excitedly as Laura helped her out of her jumper and trousers and sturdy shoes and into her pretty blue dress. As Laura tied on her dancing shoes, her attitude towards Spencer softened at his thoughtfulness in wanting Vicki to feel the same as the other children.

Backstage, in a little side room, there was a noisy squash of women and children struggling into costumes and applying make-up and Vicki was just part of the commotion. Spencer would have been out of his depth here.

Leaving the crush, Laura led Vicki by the hand and took a peep round the curtains to see who was in the audience. Johnny Prouse was sitting importantly in the front row beside Pat Penhaligon who had left Mike to a quiet night on duty at the pub. Felicity Lean was also in the front row, studying the programme and occasionally looking around and smiling at various members of the gathering. When Felicity saw Spencer, she looked sad and hurt and when she caught his eye he looked away. Laura wanted to challenge Spencer about the way he was shutting Felicity out of Vicki's life, but it was none of her business and she would do nothing to risk the relationship Spencer was allowing her to establish with Vicki.

Laura was surprised to see Harry sitting beside his mother. He had turned round and was talking to Jacka Davey but his eyes were on Tressa who was talking to her Aunty Joan. Tressa was wearing a pretty dress but it was old fashioned and didn't suit her. Laura thought it a pity she didn't do something with her hair. She felt guilty for teasing the girl in Daisy's shop and wondered if she could make it up by offering to do her hair sometime. She was good at that. Roslyn had roped her in to help with the hair and make-up behind the scenes tonight.

Someone else came in, a solitary male. Laura gasped as he paid the threepence for his programme and sat down on the end of the last row of chairs. He caused a mild stir and some folk brought him to the attention of others.

'What is it?' Vicki asked, squeezing in front of Laura.

'It's my friend Andrew Macarthur. I wonder what's he doing here.'

'Perhaps he's come to watch me sing and dance,' Vicki said innocently.

'That must be it,' Laura said, dropping the curtain and ushering Vicki to her place in line. She hoped it wasn't something serious, but Andrew had looked happy and relaxed, and surely he would have telephoned her if there were problems with the settlement of Bill's estate.

Cecil Roach was master of ceremonies and after an eloquent but lengthy speech the school choir started the proceedings with a carol. The next act was a twelve-year-old-boy with a small white poodle who jumped through a hoop. Laura clapped loudly after Ince had finished his hymn. She congratulated him on his superb tenor voice and promised to attend the Methodist chapel one Sunday to hear him sing again. Mr Maker, the elderly man who'd spoken kindly to Laura after her first Sunday in church, recited a long poignant poem about the two world wars, which he'd written himself. Daisy and Bunty's comedy act as a pair of big-bosomed gossips getting their news mixed up made Laura ache with laughter. Ada Prisk left in the middle of their turn, presumably to go to the toilet.

Halfway through the show, there was a short interval of ten minutes to allow the audience to stretch their legs. The village male voice choir started off the second half with a wide selection of songs and Ince performed again, looking most handsome in his maroon blazer and tie. Bert Miller, Joy's husband, played a medley of popular songs on a mouth organ, comb and paper, the spoons and a piano accordion. The sketch named the Shoemaker and the Piskies that Cecil had written was almost professionally acted and very well received. He was pleased with the children and told them so when they herded off the stage. Laura saw some of them visibly sigh with relief; they could enjoy their Christmas holiday now.

Vicki was on next and tears of emotion filled Laura's eyes at her clear tinkling voice as she sang and danced a Judy Garland number. Laura sought Felicity's face and saw her wiping her eyes with a handkerchief. When Vicki came off to thunderous applause, Cecil waylaid her and told her he was looking forward to seeing her at school next term, that she was likely to be the star of the school. Filled with pride, as though she was the little girl's real mother, Laura hugged and kissed her as she changed her clothes.

'Did you hear Daddy playing for me?' Vicki asked proudly. 'He's very clever.'

'Yes,' Laura lied. 'He did a wonderful job.' She had been so wrapped up in Vicki's performance she hadn't heard a note of Spencer's rendering on the piano. Laura was thrilled that he didn't come back-stage to reclaim his daughter, allowing Vicki to stay with her until the concert finished, even through the community singing at the end.

Laura was terribly embarrassed at the final curtain when Roslyn took over from Cecil and thanked her publicly for all she had done for the village. Laura had to leave Vicki with Ince and go on to the stage and receive a bouquet of flowers which was presented to her by Roslyn's daughter, Rachael.

A loud murmur of voices went up and there was a scraping of chair legs as the centre of the hall was cleared and the chairs put round the sides. The eating and tea drinking began but Laura found herself still the centre of attention. She had yet to talk to Andrew and find out why he was here. He had waved cheerily to her and was now chatting to Jacka and Joan Davey; Tressa was nowhere to be seen. Laura was worried that Spencer would take Vicki straight home before she could extricate herself from those gathered round her but when the last well-wisher headed for the food tables, he came up to her with Vicki who was eating a slice of the chocolate gateau.

'Thank you, Laura,' he said sincerely. 'You made the evening go well for Vicki. She won't feel so nervous about starting school next term now.'

Laura thought this was the ideal opportunity to suggest something that would help Vicki fit even more easily into school. Vicki had listened politely to Cecil Roach on the stage but the look on her face had showed she'd been daunted by him.

'You could always let Vicki play with some of the other children, Spencer. I'd be happy to bring them to the farm and supervise their play or take Vicki to their homes – the vicarage, for instance.'

Spencer looked almost helpless. 'Yes, I suppose…'

'Can I, Daddy?' Vicki piped up now she had swallowed a mouthful of cake. 'Can I have someone to play with me? I liked it when Benjy played with me that time.'

'All right, pipkin.' Spencer ruffled her hair, dislodging her ribbon which Laura instantly put right. He'd do almost anything to make her happy. 'We'll see about it after Christmas before school begins.'

'It must be hard seeing them grow up,' Laura said sympathetically. She saw Felicity standing by the doorway, evidently about to go, looking wistfully at her granddaughter. 'What a pity you haven't got any relatives.'

She saw Spencer's jaw tighten and heard his sharp intake of breath. 'You'd better get yourself something to eat while there's still some food left. If you'll excuse me, I think Ince wants a word with you.' Taking Vicki by the hand, he led her backstage to collect her dress and dancing shoes.

–

Tressa had been to the toilet and was alone in the outer hallway making her way back to the hall. Her mind was on the food she'd left on a plate on one of the tables. Aunty Joan was only a plain cook and made nothing like the delicious-looking chocolate cake. Tressa had a big slice waiting for her. She hoped no one would eat it before she got back. She was dismayed to see Harry Lean approaching her.

'Don't you try to stop me getting past,' she threatened him, balling her fists.

'I've just seen my mother to her car and was coming back for my coat. No law against that, is there?' Harry smiled like a cat about to devour a saucer of cream. 'But now we're here like this, Tressa, my dear, why don't we have a little chat?'

Tressa backed away. 'What about?'

'No need to be suspicious, darling. I know about your father's financial difficulties. I have thought of a way to help him. Interested?'

As Harry Lean was an intelligent man who dealt with finance, Tressa dropped her guard. Her sweet young face brightened. If her father's worries could be lifted this Christmas could be one of the happiest he'd ever had. 'You have a way to help Dad?'

'Yes.' Harry moved closer to her. 'I know a way he can get hold of one hundred pounds. A sum of money like that would see the end of all his money worries. You'd like that, wouldn't you?'

'What does he have to do?'

'Not him, sweetheart. You.'

'Me?' Tressa was puzzled. 'What's it got to do with me?'

'Well, it's like this, Tressa. I'll let your father have one hundred pounds, which he wouldn't have to pay back, if you do something for me.'

Harry was walking towards her and Tressa was moving backwards. Her back was brought up against the wall holding the rows of pegs the villagers' coats were hanging from.

'You mean you're offering me a job at Hawksmoor, with the horses? You'll pay my wages in advance?'

'I wasn't thinking of anything like that at all, darling,' Harry said huskily, a heat unrecognisable to Tressa shining out of his dark eyes. His arms were about her in an instant. 'Let me show what I do mean.'

Too late Tressa realised what he was up to and she began to struggle. Harry had hold of her tightly. He was pushing her back into the coats and her arms were pinned against her sides as he brought his mouth down over hers. Tressa couldn't scream and the only movements she could make were with her feet, but he was standing with his legs astride, out of harm's way. Tressa was horrified. She felt sick to the core of her being. She felt she was being smothered. When he pushed his tongue into her mouth she became frantic.

Harry took his mouth away and pulled her head back by her hair. He had enjoyed that long kiss. Tressa's struggles meant nothing to him. 'You get the picture, darling?'

'You rotten bastard!'

She screamed as loudly as it would come out of her throat. 'Let go of me!' He had loosened his grip and she wrenched herself free then immediately launched herself in a violent attack upon him.

Harry howled as one of her fists hit his brow bone and the other was plunged into his guts. Tressa lashed out with all her might, shouting and screaming, gouging at him with clawed fingers, kicking his shins and yanking on his hair.

'You little hellcat!' Harry yelled. 'Surely you aren't going to turn down all that money?' He grabbed her wrist and turned it round in a vice-like grip, his thumb digging into her flesh.

'Get away from me!' Tressa screamed.

Hearing the commotion, people began coming through the hall's double doors towards them.

'Help! Help! Someone's being killed!' shrieked Ada Prisk.

'I'll see your family driven off the land for this,' Harry hissed at Tressa, letting her go and moving away from her.

Andrew shoved his way through the crowd to get to them first. Tressa's distress was plain to see. Her eyes were twice their usual size, her face was an ashen globe in the brown mass of her tangled hair and her whole body was shaking.

'You filthy bastard, Harry Lean! You've gone too far this time. Outside! Get outside! I'm going to beat the living daylights out of you.' He snatched a handful of Harry's shirt and started pulling him towards him.

'Let him go,' Kinsley Farrow ordered harshly, trying to thrust himself between the two men.

'Not on your life!' Andrew bawled, glaring at the angry vicar. 'You can see what he was trying to do.'

Harry turned this to his advantage and punched Andrew in the soft flesh of his stomach. Andrew cried out in pain and rage and aimed a punch at Harry's jaw. Harry ducked but too late; the iron fist hit his face and then both men were pitching in for a full-blooded fight. People were forced to scatter out of their way while Tressa pulled herself in tight to the coats. The shock and horror on her face turned to despair.

Andrew had been middle-weight boxing champion in the army and Harry was strong and trained in self-defence. They both got in many hard blows and within minutes their shirts were ripped, ties yanked off and faces bruised and running with blood. It took the combined effort of a group of burly farmers to prise them apart.

'That's enough!' stormed Kinsley Farrow, backed up by the equally furious Reverend Brian Endean. 'How dare you brawl in here like a couple of hooligans. In front of women and children too. Get out, the pair of you. Get out!'

'Don't worry,' Harry scowled, spitting blood out of his mouth. 'I'll never set foot inside this crummy little hall again.'

He made Tressa squeal when he reached up beside her and pulled his coat off a peg. He glowered at her for a moment then strode out of the hall, making the animated onlookers fan out before him, and banging the outer door behind him.

'You too, Mr Macarthur,' the vicar said sternly.

'But I—'

'If you wish I'll have your explanation tomorrow before the morning service, but you will leave now.'

Andrew shot Tressa a pained look then left in an angry mood. He couldn't see why he should be thrown out like the scurrilous Harry Lean. Laura made to follow him, glad that Spencer had left with Vicki and she had not heard or witnessed the fight, but she stopped when Jacka Davey suddenly assailed his daughter.

'What is the matter with you, maid? Have you gone completely mazed? Fighting with a man in public, using vile language, disgracing me like that.' Jacka put a hand on his chest and his breathing came quick and heavy. 'Look at the state of you. You're not like a woman at all.'

'But Dad,' Tressa pleaded, moving towards him.

'I don't want to hear it,' Jacka said, turning away. 'I don't want to set eyes on your face again tonight.'

Joan Davey didn't know whether to go to her brother or her niece, but as Jacka was turning a sickly shade of puce, she followed him, hoping a cup of tea would calm him down.

Kinsley Farrow and Brian Endean were urging the spectators back into the main body of the hall and after a few awkward moments a reluctant trickle turned into a steady flow. The people of Kilgarthen would look forward to the sermons in church and chapel the following morning.

Only Laura and Ince were left with Tressa. They exchanged looks, the girl had not deserved Jacka's outburst. Laura went to her. She would have put an arm round her but Tressa looked fierce and unyielding, like a small animal caught in a trap, who would bite anyone who came to help it.

'I'll take Tressa to my cottage, Ince, and then I'll take her home. We'll have to forget about the drink. I'll see you over Christmas.'

Ince nodded understanding. He felt sick. Even in the darkest part of his soul he couldn't understand how a man could try to force his attentions on a woman. 'Can I do anything for her, Laura?' he said gently.

Laura shook her head and spoke softly. 'Right now Tressa needs to be with another woman.'

Chapter 19

Laura ushered Tressa into Little Cot and took her coat from her. The girl looked at her blankly and Laura didn't know what to say so she offered the usual comfort. 'I'll make us a cup of tea. I know I could do with one. Can I get you something to eat, Tressa?'

'No, thank you. I think I would be sick.' Tressa gave an involuntary shiver.

'Are you cold?' Laura put a motherly arm round the girl's slim shoulders.

'No. It's the shock, that's all.'

Laura felt a slight tensing of Tressa's body and she let her go. Either Tressa didn't like being touched at all or she wasn't ready to be comforted so soon after being forced into Harry Lean's arms.

'Sit down by the fire and make yourself comfortable. I won't be long in the kitchen.'

Despite her recent ordeal, Tressa took an interest in her surroundings. She had never sat down in a new armchair before. She had never seen electric lights except in the second-hand magazines Daisy passed on to her aunty. She had never seen luxury things like silver candlesticks or oil paintings. The decorations on the Christmas tree were shiny and new, not like the old tarnished and home-made ones displayed on the bush of holly at Tregorlan Farm. There was a chess set sitting with its players in their positions on the sideboard and she wondered what it was.

'This is a lovely cottage,' she said when Laura came back with a tea tray. 'You have some lovely things.'

'Bill did all the work and chose the things in it, but I've grown to like them.' Laura poured a strong cup for Tressa. 'Sugar? It will help you feel better after the shock.'

'Two, please.'

Laura put two spoonfuls of sugar into Tressa's cup and stirred it for her. She poured her own tea and pushed a plate of biscuits towards Tressa. 'Help yourself'

'I like your gramophone,' Tressa said. 'My brothers often said they'd like to have one.'

'You're welcome to play it any time you like.'

Tressa looked at Laura with the innocent childlike quality that Andrew had fallen for and Harry Lean had so ruthlessly sought to take and spoil. 'Can I? That's kind of you. I thought you didn't like me. I thought you were teasing me in the shop.'

'I was a little,' Laura admitted guiltily. 'I'm sorry. It was childish of me. You upset Andrew, you see, and I was hitting back at you.'

Tressa nodded. She had wondered herself about Andrew's sudden reappearance but was too private a person to mention him. 'My brothers, Matty and Jimmy, were killed in the war.' Tressa's sadness turned to anger. 'They would have half killed Harry Lean for what he did to me.'

'What exactly did he do, Tressa? You don't have to tell me but it might help to confide in someone.'

'He said he would give my father one hundred pounds if I had sex with him,' Tressa said bluntly. 'Then he,' and she shuddered, 'grabbed me and kissed me.'

'The rotten swine! That man wants locking up.'

'People think I'm naive where men are concerned,' Tressa went on. 'In some ways I am but I know all about that sort of thing; after all, I am a farmer's daughter. I misunderstood him at first. I thought he wanted me to work for him, with his horses. Then he showed me what he meant. I feel very foolish.'

'There's no need for you to feel foolish.' Laura raised her voice in indignation. 'He must have frightened you badly. The police ought to be informed. Shall we drink our tea and go up to the shop and use the telephone? Harry Lean mustn't be allowed to get away with it.'

'There's no need for that,' Tressa said adamantly. 'I hurt him and Andrew Macarthur hurt him. Harry Lean made a big fool of himself tonight and he won't be able to show his face in the village for months.'

'It's up to you but I think it's a shame to let him get away with it. Poor Felicity.' Laura shook her head sadly. 'As if that woman hasn't had enough bad things happen in her life.'

Tressa suddenly succumbed to emotion and her eyes filled with tears. Her hands shook and Laura took her cup and saucer from her and this time Tressa let her hold her.

'It's my father I'm worried about,' the girl sobbed. 'He said I'd disgraced him, that I'm not like a woman. Just lately he's been saying I ought to do myself up and look for a husband. He says he won't be around for much longer to give me a home. I'm afraid he might throw me out.'

Laura stroked Tressa's hair as she would Vicki's. 'Your father wouldn't do anything like that, Tressa. He's a good and caring man. I'm sure he loves you. The incident with Harry Lean, unsettled him, that's all, and he blew his top. I expect someone in the hall has already told him what really happened and he'll say sorry to you when you get home.'

'Do you think so?' Tressa stopped crying and looked up at Laura hopefully. Laura was struck at how childlike her face was.

Before Laura could answer, there was a loud knocking on the door. Tressa wiped her face hastily with her hands.

'Whoever it is, I'll get rid of them,' Laura said.

She opened the door to Andrew. He had his hands rammed in his pockets and was shivering with cold. His face was bruised and puffy. He peered round the door.

'Is Tressa all right?' he asked with his teeth chattering. 'I saw you bring her in here. I've waited a while so you could talk to her. Can I come in?'

Laura felt she could hardly deny Andrew entrance to her home. She hadn't had the chance to speak to him yet and he had gone to Tressa's aid. 'It's Andrew,' she told Tressa. 'Would you mind if he came in?'

'No, of course not.' Tressa looked quite composed and was drinking her tea with her head lowered over the cup.

Without bothering to take off his coat, Andrew went straight to her. For the second time that night she had her cup and saucer taken out of her hands. Andrew held on to them tightly. 'Are you all right, Tressa? Are you sure?' He pushed up the sleeve of her dress and exposed her bruised flesh. 'He hurt you, that savage! I saw the marks on your arm in the hall.'

Tressa pulled her hands away and covered her wrist. 'I'm fine now, really I am. You shouldn't have fought with him, he hurt you too.'

'I don't care about that,' Andrew said impatiently, looking deeply into her eyes in such a tender way that Laura was left in no doubt why he was back in Kilgarthen again so soon. She retreated to the kitchen to get him a cup; she would take her time.

'I'll break his bloody neck if he ever lays a hand on you again,' Andrew vowed. 'In fact I could break his neck anyway.'

'I don't think I'll have any more trouble with him,' Tressa said, moving back in her chair, away from his vehemence.

'But he tried to rape you.'

'No, he didn't.' Tressa was desperately searching for a way to still his indignant protests. She was afraid he really would go after Harry Lean. 'He only kissed me. If he wanted to do anything else he could have ridden to my father's farm any time I was there alone. He has been punished. I hurt him and you hurt him. And I was telling Mrs Jennings, he will be too ashamed to show his face in the village for ages, and then knowing him, he will act as though nothing has happened. I just want to forget all about it, for my father's sake.'

'All right,' Andrew said uncertainly. He wouldn't do anything that would risk upsetting her. 'If that's what you want.'

Laura was hovering by the door and she could see how eager Andrew was to please Tressa. She hoped he wouldn't leave Kilgarthen with a broken heart; she had seen Tressa shy away from him. She dismally remembered Daisy's words about them being an unlikely couple. Andrew was looking rather lost now and she came to his rescue.

'Take your coat off Andrew, and have a cup of tea,' she said, putting on a cheerful voice as she came fully into the room.

'I'd rather have something stronger,' he said.

'Sit down. There's some brandy in the sideboard. Then I'll fetch something to bathe your hands and face. You're going to have a black eye in the morning. The villagers aren't going to forget your fight quickly with that as a constant reminder.'

Andrew wasn't listening. Tressa was making a third attempt at drinking her tea and was gazing into the fire. He was gazing at her.

—

Before dawn the next morning Andrew was knocking on the door of Tregorlan Farm. Jacka answered him in his vest with his braces hanging down over his baggy trousers.

'Good heavens! Mr Macarthur. Didn't expect to see you here like this.'

'Please don't turn me away, Jacka. I've come to apologise to you and Joan for my part in the disturbance last night. I was hoping you'd let me explain what happened and allow me to put in some work on the farm by way of recompense.'

It was too early in the morning for Jacka to fathom out why the gentleman solicitor should be interested in his family affairs. He shook his head as if trying to clear away a blockage. 'You'd better come in then, boy.'

Andrew was heartened by the dropping of 'Mr Macarthur'. Laura had told him of her conversation with Tressa. If Jacka Davey was hoping his lovely daughter would consider finding herself a husband, he was hoping that Jacka would consider he fitted the bill.

Last night, after a bit of persuasion, Tressa had allowed him to drive her home in the Penhaligons' car. Laura had come with them, the two women sitting in the back seat. He'd glanced at Tressa often in the rearview mirror but she had hung her head, probably worried about what her father would say to her. She hadn't said a word until she'd got out of the car and greeted a barking Meg. Then looking back in the car she'd said, 'Thank you both very much. Goodnight,' in the saddest

201

of voices. At that moment Andrew had wanted to hold her. Just hold her. To comfort her. She'd gone inside without a backward glance and left him with a loneliness so deep and strange he'd felt something alien had reached out from the murmuring moor and stolen his heart.

But now he was back. And he wasn't going to give up his quest easily.

Laura had warned him he must go slowly. That Tressa would find anything in the slightest way blatant unforgivable after her ordeal with Harry Lean. Andrew knew that unpeeling the layers of solitude Tressa kept herself shrouded in wasn't going to be a simple task. But deep down he was certain she was a woman who wanted and needed to be loved and could love back. He was going to try to unfold the petals of that precious flower.

Joan Davey was greatly embarrassed to be found in the kitchen in her hairnet and without her false teeth in. She hurried away to 'see to herself' and left the two men to consume the contents of the big brown teapot.

'I want to thank 'ee for thinking of Tressa like that last night,' Jacka said, tucking in his shirt and doing up the buttons. 'I don't approve of fighting, mind. 'Twas shameful of 'ee both. Never, was the Lord's way.'

'Do you know the full story, Jacka?'

'Aye. The vicar told me. If I was younger I'd be over Hawksmoor meself and sorting that rotten young fellow out, but things went far enough last night, and I don't want Mrs Lean upset. She's a good woman, had a lot of tragedy in her life. 'Tis best if it's all forgotten.'

'That's what Tressa said,' Andrew commented.

Jacka stopped buttoning his shirt. 'Oh, you saw her after, did you?'

'Yes, in Laura Jennings' cottage. She was very upset.'

'She'll be down to breakfast in a minute.' Jacka smiled fondly. 'I'll put things right with her then. You going to church later?'

'I never go to church, Jacka. I thought that perhaps if you gave me a few jobs it would be less work for you to do when you come back. You'll be able to put your feet up this afternoon.' Andrew next turned to the matter he hoped would earn him Jacka's trust and respect, but he wanted to help the Daveys anyway. 'I thought that while I'm here we could talk about grants and subsidies for farmers. I've dealt with the legal side of that sort of thing.' That was a lie. 'I hope you won't think I'm interfering but I was wondering if you're claiming everything you're entitled to. I could find out for you, if you like. Save you the time and trouble and I could plough through the red tape much quicker than you.'

Jacka scratched his head. He didn't seem to have understood a word of what Andrew had said after offering to do some work for him. 'That's very kind of you, I'm sure. I don't suppose Tressa will want to go to church either, but then she usually talks to God when she's out on the moor. You must stay on and have dinner with us.'

Mindful of the Daveys' delicate financial circumstances, Andrew said hastily, 'I'm afraid Mrs Penhaligon has taken it for granted that I'll be having dinner with her and Mike at the pub.'

'Then come back for tea. Joan always puts on a good table. Jam and cream on homemade splits, her home-cured ham.'

'Thanks. I'd like to.' Andrew was mentally knocking up Daisy to buy some cake from the shop.

Tressa came into the kitchen dressed for work. She looked at Andrew in utter surprise. 'Hello.'

'Good morning, Tressa. How are you?'

She looked guiltily at her father. Jacka opened his arms wide and matched the gesture with a beam on his ruddy face. Tressa ran to him and he cuddled her in close and kissed the top of her head.

''Tis all right, me handsome. I know what happened last night and I'm sorry I blamed you and shouted at you. Do you forgive your silly old dad?'

'Of course I do, Dad,' she said happily, her voice muffled against his shirt.

Andrew felt quite jealous of Jacka, holding the girl he'd fallen in love with.

He refused breakfast, explaining that Pat Penhaligon had made some porridge for him last night and he'd only had to heat it up. He was disappointed when Jacka gave instructions for the jobs. Tressa was to go to the fields and check on the stock while he would work with Andrew in the yard until it was time to go to church.

–

Andrew opened the lid of the well and hooked it back. The water halfway down in its depths lay opaque and still, dark as night, and somehow secretive, like Tressa's eyes. He stared down, mesmerised. If he made a wish and threw a penny down there to break the round and glassy surface, would it come true? To gain Tressa's affections, he had better make it half a crown – in fact all the loose change he could find in his pockets.

'Can't you figure out how to work the pump?'

The question was asked tonelessly but he turned to meet what looked like disbelief on Tressa's face. Andrew yanked his hands out of his pockets. 'Pump? Oh, the well, you mean? Of course I do. I was just thinking.'

He quickly lowered the pail. The winch creaked, the chain rattled, the noises seemed to echo in protest round the yard and he felt even more foolish. As if she didn't think him capable of doing the job, Tressa stood and watched. He was glad Jacka had left for church after they had attended to the two snuffling pigs.

'Have you finished your work, Tressa?'

'I've come back for more hay.'

'That must be hard work. When I've finished here I'll help you.' He was hoping for a more amiable walk over the moor with her.

She disappointed him. 'No need,' she said. 'I've got a sleigh to pull it on. Anyway, if you've only just started drawing water for the house and yard, at the rate you're going, you'll take all day.'

He looked down in the well. He had stopped turning the handle and the pail was floundering on top of the water like an upturned boat, only a little water filling it. 'Oh,' he muttered, embarrassed. He let the pail down until its rim disappeared below the surface then winched up a full pailful as fast as he could. He hauled it up, lifted it over the edge of the granite side then put it down on the ground without slopping much water over the cobblestones.

He looked at Tressa with a smile on his face, but she'd gone. In her place was Meg with her long pink tongue hanging out, waiting for a drink. Andrew shrugged resignedly. He poured most of the water carefully into a huge pitcher then carried the rest to Meg's drinking bowl.

While she greedily lapped it up, she allowed him to pat her scruffy back and fondle her ears. 'Well, I've made some headway with you, Meg. Now all I've got to do is somehow get your mistress to like me.'

Chapter 20

On Christmas Eve Laura put a holly wreath on Bill's grave. She stood in the ice-cold wind and drizzle and viewed his mound of rich moorland earth dispassionately. The earth was beginning to level out and in a few months the headstone she had ordered would be erected. 'In Loving Memory' – not Laura's love but the villagers' love. She wouldn't destroy the myth they'd built up round Bill. There was no point, Bill's dead fingers were losing their grip on her.

She still wasn't sure whether Bill had harboured a genuine affection for the people of Kilgarthen or had simply wanted to show off his good fortune in front of them; it probably lay somewhere between the two. One day, when she felt able, she would read his diaries and see what they revealed.

Looking down at his grave she was glad now she'd had no children with Bill. She'd have hated having to lie to them about their father's true character. Hopefully the memories of his cruelty would soon fade from her mind. She wasn't concerned that his body lay just across the road from his home – her home, she thought of it now. Bill was in his place.

A child's voice drifted across to her from the other side of the stone wall. Then another. It was Benjy Miller and his brother and sisters on their way to the church for the children's nativity service. Then she heard Vicki's excited chatter as she met up with Benjy. With no more thoughts of the late, great Bill Jennings, Laura walked away.

At the church door Laura was amazed to see Andrew heading towards her. His hat was pulled down tight and he was beating his arms to ward off the cold.

'Andrew! Are you going into the church?'

'Yes. Why ask me in that tone?' he retorted defensively.

'Oh, no reason… It must be the magic of Christmas, wonders will never cease.'

'Well, I'm allowed to go in there, aren't I?' he bellowed, then realising this wasn't the place to display ill humour, continued in a husky whisper, 'The place won't go up in a blaze of fire and brimstone, will it?' His face was as red as cranberry sauce.

'You tell me, Andrew,' Laura said patiently, looking above the heads of the children and adults gathering for the service until she saw the person she was now expecting. 'Ahhh.'

'Ahhh what?'

'It's Tressa Davey. What a surprise. But then I do remember Roslyn Farrow telling me within your hearing that the children's nativity service was a particular favourite of Tressa's.'

'Oh, shut up!' Andrew growled in a low voice.

Jacka and Joan reached them, walking either side of Tressa. 'Nice to see you here, boy,' Jacka said heartily. 'You'd better come in with us. We without young 'uns sit at the back.'

Laura entered the church after them and made a beeline for Vicki and managed to get a seat next to Ince. He squeezed her hand furtively.

Andrew had rarely held a hymn book since his school days and Tressa was forced to help him out of his fumblings to find the first carol. He used this to get attention from her for the next three carols. After the service, which he agreed was enchanting, he managed to engage Tressa in a half-decent conversation outside the church. He was going to extend an invitation to her, craftily, via Jacka, whom he was counting on would insist she go, to join him for a pre-Christmas drink in the pub. He nearly swore with fury when Daisy grabbed his arm and told him there was an urgent telephone call for him at the shop.

—

Andrew had bad news for Laura and he sought her out among those enjoying mulled wine in the pub. He drew her aside for a private talk.

'John Walmseley, one of my partners, has just got in touch with me, Laura. The Morrisons have made a new demand. I'm afraid there won't be enough money left over to pay them off in full.'

'What sort of sum are we talking about?' she asked fearfully. 'Will I have to sell the cottage?'

'It wouldn't be enough.' He rested a hand on her arm. 'They're asking for another five thousand pounds.'

Laura felt her insides shrinking. Her world was falling apart again. Selling Little Cot would be bad enough but she'd have to leave Kilgarthen and Vicki behind and once more face an uncertain future. 'What can I do, Andrew?'

'Don't worry about it now. John is going to look into it after Christmas and if there are any problems I'll go back to London and sort it out myself. First we'll make sure Bill actually owed the Morrisons that amount of money. Nothing pointed to that fact before, they might be trying to pull a fast one. I'm sorry to tell you now but I thought you had the right to know. Let's try to enjoy ourselves, eh? Is Tressa here?'

Andrew's unshakable calm made the problem sound less serious than it had at first seemed. It was Christmas, a time for happiness, peace and goodwill. Laura filed the Morrison brothers and their demand into a little corner of her mind to be dealt with in the new year.

'No,' she said, answering Andrew's question. 'She went back to the farm to do the evening milking.' Laura looked at him artfully. 'I'm going to join Ince. He's over there, with Jacka and Joan.'

Andrew smiled contentedly. 'That means Tressa's all alone.'

–

Barbara Roach was convinced this was going to be the worst Christmas of her life. Marianne was still suffering from the mystery virus and was continually bad tempered. A few minutes ago Barbara had asked her to help prepare the vegetables for Christmas dinner tomorrow and she had run out of the house in a flaming temper without stopping to put her coat on.

Although worried about Marianne, Barbara was relieved to have the house to herself; Cecil had gone out somewhere in his car. As she stood at the sink peeling potatoes, tears fell silently down her face. She was dreading tonight. Since the school's resounding success at the concert, Cecil had been in a jubilant mood and had wanted to be intimate every night. With each succeeding night he'd wanted to do it earlier in the evening and had started to demand that they do some disgusting things. Barbara had been repulsed by her husband for some years. Now his demands made her feel physically sick.

Soon after the attic had been converted into a study for Cecil, Barbara had heard him making strange noises when he'd been up there alone. As he was a man who took much care with his appearance, she had assumed he'd been doing keep fit exercises, specially as he'd come down in a somewhat exhausted state. But now he was making those awful noises with her in the bedroom and he insisted that the bedroom light stay on and she had glimpsed his distorted face. She had a different idea of what he was doing up in his study now and she felt sick to her bowels; he made her feel used and dirty.

The back door slammed and she nearly jumped out of her skin. With fear burning in the pit of her stomach, she waited for Cecil to come in to her and realise they were alone. Oh, why did he have to have a job that gave him such long holidays? Why couldn't he spend more time on his other hobby, bee-keeping?

After several moments he had not come in and she crept nervously to the door. There was no one there. Marianne must have left it open when she'd stormed out and it must have slammed shut. Barbara locked and bolted the door with trembling hands. She went back to the kitchen, sat down at the table and cried her heart out.

-

Marianne trudged through the village with her arms folded in front of her. She hated her mother at that moment. Hated her for not having the courage to stand up to her bullying father, hated her for being so nice. It was perfectly reasonable to ask for your daughter's help with the long and tiring Christmas preparations, but Barbara's pale and drawn face had infuriated Marianne and she hadn't been able to stop herself from throwing another tantrum. Now she felt guilty for hurting her kind mother's feelings. Damn you, Mother, if only you were stronger I could tell you.

She heard the throaty roar of Harry Lean's sports car racing up behind her. She turned round and flagged him down. He was forced to stop or he would have run her over.

'What the hell do you want?' he snapped when he wound his window down.

'Please, Harry, I need your help,' she begged, leaning into the car. 'I'll do anything you ask if you'll just do me a favour.'

'If you're offering me a roll in the hay again I'm not interested.'

'I'm in terrible trouble, Harry. If you would just—'

'I can guess what sort of trouble you're in,' Harry snarled, pushing her away from his car. 'Get lost, Marianne. Sort it out yourself.'

It was the final straw. Harry Lean had been her last hope. She'd tried everything else on the advice gathered from one of her girl friends: thumping herself in the stomach, drinking two bottles of gin one after the other, sitting for ages over a potty of hot steaming water. They hadn't worked and were probably quite dangerous. She couldn't tell her mother she was pregnant and when her father found out he would throw her out, homeless and penniless. There was no way out.

She started to run. As fast as her legs would carry her, she ran through the churchyard, scrambled over the wall ripping her nylons and scratching her hands and legs. She was on the moor and she started to run again. She slipped, feeling the coarse growth stinging her knees, but picked herself up and resumed her crazy flight. Her heart was thumping in her brain, she was out of breath, but she didn't care.

She'd just keep going. And going. She'd run and run and when she couldn't run any more she'd fling herself down and stay there. Stay there all night and die on the moor.

–

Meg was getting used to Andrew and didn't make much fuss when he entered Tregorlan's yard on foot. She followed him about as he looked for Tressa. There was no sign of her in the shippen with the five milking cows. She wasn't by the pigsty or in any of the outhouses. Andrew let himself into the house and Meg ran off. Tressa wasn't in the kitchen. He opened the door on the other side of the room and was about to call her name when he heard her voice. She was in the other downstairs room, the sitting room. He opened the door slowly and silently and saw her kneeling at the foot of a holly Christmas tree where a few presents lay wrapped in plain brown paper. A soft light from the peat fire gave her brown hair a golden hue and Andrew thought her an angel.

She was talking softly. He watched and listened and his heart went out to her. She was talking to her dead brothers.

'It wouldn't have been very much this year, money's tight as usual. But I would have bought you a lovely warm scarf, Jimmy, and a whole new jar of Brylcreem for you, Matty. I'm hoping Dad and Aunty Joan have got me a nightie. Mine's so worn out you can see through it now and it doesn't keep me warm any more: Dad's awful worried about money. He's worrying me and Aunty Joan because he gets awful indigestion. He says things could be even worse next year but we've met this man from London. He's a friend of Bill Jennings' widow and he's her solicitor. He talks posh but is very clever. He's going to see if we can get something called grants and subsidies off the government.'

Tressa started to talk about more personal family things and Andrew closed the door. It didn't seem right to listen in on everything she was saying. He wished he could have got more clues to how she felt about him. He hadn't realised that his voice must seem 'posh' to her. He hoped it wouldn't spoil his chances with her. Dear, sweet, Tressa, he thought, talking like that as if her brothers could hear her; it must bring her comfort. He hoped that one day soon she would let him have a share in her private little world.

He waited until the low drone of her voice had stopped then he opened the kitchen door, made lots of noise and called, 'Hello! Tressa!'

She opened the sitting room after a few moments and her face was dark with suspicion. 'What are you doing here?'

Andrew felt as young and foolish as he had on his first date. 'I missed you leaving the pub and I wanted to give you something.' To counteract her stern look he looked over her head. 'What a pretty Christmas tree. Pat's decorated a huge spray of holly in the pub. Is it a Cornish tradition?'

Tressa turned to look at the holly bush and Andrew took the opportunity to move past her in the doorway. He wasn't going to leave yet. He went up to the Christmas tree. The decorations were mainly made of twisted shapes of silver paper and wads of cotton wool. A battered tinsel star sat on the prickly top. 'Your decorations are lovely.'

'My brothers made most of them,' Tressa said defensively, staying in the doorway.

Andrew took a parcel wrapped in brightly coloured Christmas paper out of his coat pocket. This was an open declaration to Jacka of his intentions towards his daughter as much as a present for Tressa. 'Shall I put this under the tree with the other presents?'

'What is it?' Tressa asked bluntly.

'It's just a little something for you.'

'What for?'

'No special reason. People usually give their friends presents at this time of the year.' Andrew bent over, intending to put the present with the others.

'Whatever it is, I can't take it. I haven't got anything for you.'

'I don't give presents in the hope of receiving something back, Tressa.'

'Nevertheless, I won't accept it.'

Andrew straightened up. He was terribly disappointed. He hadn't thought it would be this difficult just to give the girl a small gift. She had very little in life but she wasn't the least bit interested in what his gift to her was. In desperation, he tore the paper off it. 'It's only some toiletries, Tressa. It's nothing special.'

He held out the inner package to her. There was a naked silence. For an agonising moment he thought he was going to have to leave totally defeated. Then she took it from him and he had to disguise his relief with a rumbling cough.

Tressa turned the package over and over. It contained a tin of talcum powder, four bath cubes and a bar of soap. She could see what the soap was but she had no idea what the rest was meant for. 'What are these?'

Andrew pointed to the bath cubes. 'You put these in your bath to soften the water and make it smell nice. This is talcum powder. You sprinkle it on to help dry yourself.'

She looked at him uncertainly. He lifted off the pretty cardboard lid and took out the tin of talcum powder. Turning the top, he sprinkled some powder on the back of her hand and wrist and rubbed it in. 'Smell it,' he said. 'As you can see from the label, the fragrance is called jasmine. Jasmine is a tropical flower.'

Tressa put her nose almost on her hand. 'It's lovely. But I can't take it, it must have cost a lot of money.'

'You might as well take it, Tressa,' he begged. 'I've got no use for it.'

'You can give it to someone else.' She looked down at his other hand. 'I'd liked to have that though, if you don't mind.'

'What?' He sounded incredulous. 'The wrapping paper?'

He handed it over to her and she gave him back the toiletries. She took off the tinsel rosette the shop assistant had put on the parcel and meticulously folded up the paper. Then after taking her time deciding what would be the best place, she carefully put the rosette on the holly bush.

Andrew stroked the back of his neck and shook his head. He didn't understand Tressa's reasoning but felt he had made a little progress with her. He was hoping he'd be offered a cup of tea now but was met again with brutal frankness.

'You'll have to go now. I've got work to do.'

'Oh,' he sighed. 'Well, in that case I'll wish you a very happy Christmas, Tressa.'

He had no choice but to leave, but on the way through the kitchen he left the toiletries on the table. Tressa could either throw them away or let her aunty have them.

Tressa came through to the kitchen to get herself something to eat before she took a long walk with Meg; she had no work to do. As she washed her hands at the sink, she wrinkled her nose at the strong chemical smell of the soap on her skin then sniffed the pleasant exotic odour of the talcum powder on her wrist. When she dried her hands, she saw the present on the table where Andrew had left it. She threw down the worn rough towel, and before her father or aunt could come home and ask her about the toiletries, she picked them up and ran upstairs to hide them in a drawer in her bedroom.

–

Ince was thinking about Laura as he walked back along the lanes to Rosemerryn Farm. How beautiful she was, what a good woman she was, how she hadn't been left bitter and twisted by her tormented years as Bill Jennings' wife. He was remembering how wonderful it had felt to kiss her cheek and then hold her under the mistletoe. He was calculating what would be a decent length of time to wait before he could ask her as a widow out to dinner with him. He thought he stood a chance with her; he knew he didn't have a great deal in common with her but nor did the other men in Kilgarthen.

He was walking past a stretch of open moorland when he heard a sound that chilled him to the marrow. Loud and shrill, it sounded like a soul in eternal agony.

He spun round in all directions, peering through the starlit darkness, trying to locate the source of the terrible wailings. His heart almost stopped when the figure of a woman flew across the moor several yards away from him. The woman fell, uttering a scream of rage and swearing foully. She crawled forward on hands and knees, crying and cursing.

Coming to his senses, Ince plunged after her, his shoes sinking into the soggy growth. 'Stop! You're heading for the stream. It's deep in there!'

The woman ignored him and kept to her perilous course. The narrow stream that ran through this part of the moor was swollen with the rain and was deep enough for someone to drown in. The woman didn't stop but plunged straight into the freezing water and threw her head down under the rushing torrent.

Ince was at the stream in a couple of minutes and jumped in beside the woman. He grabbed her long hair and pulled her head out of the water. She shrieked and tried to wrench herself away, raking her long nails down his hands and beating on his chest, muttering wildly in the foulest of language.

Ince dragged her up onto the bank of the stream, then forcing her arms behind her back he gathered her to his chest. She kept up a desperate struggle. 'Stop it! I'm trying to help you.'

'You should have left me,' she wailed. 'I wanted to die.'

He recognised her voice. 'Marianne! How on earth did you end up like this?'

She collapsed against him and he lifted her up in his arms.

'You should have let me die, Ince Polkinghorne,' she cried.

Holding her as best he could, Ince wriggled out of his coat and wrapped it round her. He had to get her warm and dry as quickly as possible. The village was nearer than Rosemerryn Farm. Marianne was a light weight; he picked her up and headed for School House.

There was no one about as he went down the hill through the village with his burden hiding her face in his chest. His steps slowed as he neared Little Cot. He'd been wondering why a young woman who was blessed with as many privileges in life as Marianne Roach would want to take her own life. He knew her timid mother would be distraught to see them turn up on her doorstep like this and her father so furious that neither would be any help to the poor girl. Ince stopped outside Laura's home. He would ask her for help.

'I'll get some towels and blankets and something for her to wear,' Laura said, pushing Ince, who was still holding the dripping wet girl, towards the fire. 'We must get her out of those wet clothes as quickly as possible.'

'Thank God you were home, Laura,' Ince said. 'I couldn't let her parents see her like this.'

Ince retreated to the kitchen to make the inevitable tea while Laura helped the limp and now docile Marianne out of her wet clothes. A cursory look showed a couple of light bruises on her stomach which she could have received in a fall but no signs of a beating on her body; Laura was convinced Cecil Roach was a cruel man. She got Marianne into dry clothes then wrapped a towel round her head. Pulling an armchair up to the fire, Laura wrapped her in blankets.

'Marianne,' Laura said firmly, lifting the girl's chin and making her look at her. 'Have you fallen foul of Harry Lean? I had another girl not many days ago sitting in the same chair who very nearly did.'

'No, not him,' croaked Marianne.

'It is a man then?'

'What else?' Marianne shrieked bitterly, showering Laura with spittle. 'Can't you guess what's wrong with me? Why I felt that it would be best if I put an end to it all?'

Hiding her shock at the sudden display of venom, Laura said gently, 'Are you pregnant?'

'Yes,' Marianne spat at her. 'Guess who by.'

Laura didn't need to guess. The spite on the girl's face told her. She felt all her new-found confidence and happiness that even new financial worries hadn't spoiled evaporating, leaving acute emptiness in its place. Bill had found another, more lasting way, to get back at her.

Ashen-faced, Laura slumped down in a chair and Ince rushed to her, forgetting Marianne. 'What is it, Laura? Are you ill?'

'It's my fault,' Marianne admitted, her voice trembling, as Laura clutched Ince's hand. They were both looking at her for an explanation. 'I told her I'm pregnant but I was cruel in telling her that it's Bill's baby. I'm really sorry, Mrs Jennings.'

'I didn't think Bill brought girls here,' Laura gasped helplessly.

'He didn't,' Marianne said. 'We met... in other places.'

'How long did it go on for?' Laura demanded.

'Ever since my sixteenth birthday.'

'What? For two years?'

'Yes, I'm sorry.'

Laura gulped at the thought of Bill seducing the girl when she had been little more than a child, but she still felt bitter. 'I suppose I can hardly blame you. You were only a child when it started. I suppose you were dazzled by Bill's bigshot reputation.'

Marianne started to cry but Laura couldn't bring herself to comfort her.

'He… he said you were going to divorce him… and he'd marry me, and we'd have a blessing in the church and then he'd take me to London.'

'It was all lies,' Laura said harshly.

'Yes,' Marianne squeaked. 'What am I going to do?'

'First you're going to get dried out thoroughly and then we'll both take you home,' Ince said, taking charge of the situation. 'We'll make up some story about you getting wet through and having to borrow some of Laura's clothes. You'll have to tell your parents about the baby, you can't keep it a secret much longer. Bill was last down here over three months ago, you'll be showing soon. Perhaps you should wait until after Christmas, when things are quieter.'

Marianne looked at Ince goggle-eyed then shifted her gaze to Laura. 'I… I know I've got a cheek asking, Mrs Jennings, but… but would you come to the house when I tell my mother? I'm not brave enough to tell her on my own.'

The thought of Bill's baby conceived and growing inside Marianne's belly when he had always denied her a child of her own was unbearable to Laura. She could hardly bring herself to speak. 'Why don't we wait until after Christmas. Come and ask me again then.'

Chapter 21

Laura was invited to tea and supper at Rosemerryn Farm the day after Boxing Day. Vicki rushed to her the moment she was inside the door.

'Laura, come and see my presents. Did you have a nice Christmas? I wish you'd been here on Christmas Day so I could see you opening your presents. Did you have lots of things? Will you read me a story from my new fairytale book?' Vicki was jumping up and down and helped Laura to take off her coat and put down a shopping bag she had brought with her.

Laura hugged and kissed her and delightedly answered all her questions, taking her hand and exclaiming at all her many gifts.

'You're a lucky little girl. I received a bottle of perfume from my friend, Mr Macarthur, and a lovely headscarf from Aunt Daisy. Bunty Buzza gave me a box of hankies and your Uncle Ince gave me a pair of gloves. I'll read you a story after tea, shall I?'

Spencer raised his eyebrows at Ince from his chair by the fire where he was enjoying a quiet drink.

Ince kept his head down over a thank you letter he was writing at the table. He wasn't sure where he stood with Laura. She had been rather aloof since Marianne Roach's revelation about her pregnancy.

'Now I've seen your presents,' Laura said to Vicki, 'I've got a little something for you in the bag I brought with me. Would you like to see it?' Laura had waited until now to give Vicki her Christmas present because she'd wanted to see her open it herself.

'Yes, please.'

'Would you run and fetch the bag?'

'All right.'

Vicki carried the bag to Laura who took out a fat parcel wrapped in Christmas paper with Father Christmases all over it. Watched by the two men in her life, Vicki unwrapped the parcel in great excitement. It contained two complete outfits for her baby doll.

'I hope you like them. Aunty Daisy taught me how to knit.'

'Oh, thank you, Laura,' Vicki squealed, wrapping her arms round Laura's neck and hugging her so tightly she was nearly choked. 'It's the best present I've ever had. Lizzie can wear the nightdress, bonnet and bootees tonight and I'll put the pram suit on tomorrow. Can I come to your house tomorrow? I'll bring the pram Father Christmas brought down the chimbley for me. We can push Lizzie round the village and show everyone how pretty she looks.'

Laura felt her gut tighten with excitement at the thought of having Vicki to herself for the day. 'Of course you can come to my house, if it's all right with your daddy. I'll cook us something special for lunch and bring you home in time for tea. We could ask Benjy to come and play as well.'

Laura and Vicki looked at Spencer for permission. He and Ince had been feeling forgotten. By the determined look on Vicki's face, there was no doubt that if Spencer said no she would throw a rare tantrum. Laura was hopeful, he had agreed that Vicki could mix with other children.

'You can go, pipkin,' Spencer said a dry voice. He knew he had agreed that Vicki could leave the farm and play with other children but he wasn't pleased with the notion. 'Thank, you for the present, Laura. It was very good of you.'

'Good, I'll come and fetch you at ten o'clock,' Laura told Vicki. 'We'll have a lovely day together.'

'I like you, Laura. I wish you lived here all the time.' Vicki picked up Lizzie and rocked the doll in her arms. 'What I really want is a mummy. When can I have a new mummy, Daddy?'

Spencer gagged on his drink and looked as if the foundations of his soul had been shaken. He looked at Ince in desperation for help. 'It's time to get tea, isn't it?'

Ince got up from the table and made a fuss of clearing away his writing materials.

Realising that somehow she'd upset her father, Vicki became quiet and put her doll glumly back in its cot, but she soon started chattering again as they ate. Then Laura offered to do the washing up.

'You are a grown-up little girl,' Laura smiled down on Vicki as she passed her the dried dishes to put away on the dresser. 'You can help me bake a cake tomorrow.' Then she looked purposefully at Spencer. 'It's for Mrs Lean. She's poorly. I'm hoping it will cheer her up.'

'You're not taking Vicki to Hawksmoor House!' Spencer snapped, springing up from his chair.

Ignoring Ince's warning look, Laura played the innocent. 'I wouldn't dream of taking Vicki anywhere without your permission, Spencer.'

'I'd rather you just stayed in the village,' Spencer said gruffly.

Vicki took Laura's hand and they went back to her Christmas toys. 'Story time now.'

When the story was over, Vicki wanted Laura to play Snakes and Ladders with her, and she wouldn't allow her father or Ince to join in with them. She insisted Laura play with her until she was almost sleeping on her feet.

'Come on, pipkin,' Spencer said firmly. 'It's time for bed.'

'I want Laura to put me to bed,' Vicki murmured sleepily, rubbing her eyes.

Spencer swept Vicki up in his arms. 'Laura's done enough for you since she's been here. You've almost worn her out.'

'No, no.' Vicki struggled and pushed on her father's broad shoulders. She was tired and fretful. 'I want Laura to put me to bed. I want Laura!'

'Vicki!' Spencer was extremely annoyed.

'Why don't you let me put her to bed, Spencer?' Laura asked, holding out her arms towards Vicki. 'Then you can come up and kiss her goodnight.'

Spencer let Vicki go reluctantly.

'It won't hurt for one night,' Ince said, after Laura had carried Vicki upstairs.

'I'm not jealous,' Spencer said edgily. 'It's just strange that she prefers someone else doing something for her than me or you.'

'I suppose Vicki will need a woman's influence as she grows up,' Ince remarked thoughtfully, more to himself than to Spencer.

'Not if I can help it,' muttered Spencer. 'When I've been up to say goodnight to Vicki, I'm going out for a breath of fresh air. I'm feeling claustrophobic in my own house. That woman had better not start interfering in my life.'

'Where's Spencer?' Laura asked when she finally came downstairs. Vicki had insisted she stay a while longer after Spencer had kissed her goodnight.

'Gone outside for a walk. He likes the occasional cigarette but doesn't smoke in the house for Vicki's sake. Can I get you a glass of sherry before supper, Laura?'

'Sherry would be nice but I don't think I could eat another bite. I've eaten far too much over this Christmas period.'

'Have you missed the things you usually did in London?'

'Only the things I did with my parents. I've some family but no one close. My friends will be busy socialising and I'm not in the mood for parties.'

'Can I ask you something, Laura?' Ince passed her the sherry and stood close. 'What is your friend Andrew Macarthur doing down here? The whole village is agog with speculation. Those who don't think too deeply reckon he's after you.'

'If Andrew gets his wish, hopefully it will soon become apparent. What do you think?'

'I think from the way he went for Harry Lean on the night of the concert he's after Tressa Davey.'

'You're right, Ince, but you won't tell anyone, will you? She's not the easiest girl in the world for a man to catch and it would only complicate things if she found out people were talking about her.'

'I was interested in her once,' Ince said, smiling at the memories of his failure. 'But I didn't get anywhere at all. I might as well have been a bulrush growing in a bog. Her idea of going out for a drink is supping crystal clear water from a moorland stream. She is lovely, though. Andrew Macarthur seems a decent sort of man. I hope he's successful, although I can't see how it would work out. There's no way she'd go and live a domesticated life up in London.'

Laura sipped her sherry and watched the light from the fire dancing through the glass. 'If Andrew is successful, I'm sure he'll think of something.'

Ince asked his next question carefully. 'Have you made up your mind about Marianne Roach yet? Whether you'll be there when she breaks the news to her mother?'

'No, and I'd rather not think about that when I'm enjoying myself.'

'Are you enjoying yourself in my company?'

She looked at him fully. 'Yes.'

Less sure of himself than when he'd last been alone with her here, Ince put a gentle arm round her shoulders. Laura rested her head against his chest and closed her eyes. It was comforting to be close to him.

He wanted to kiss her but was afraid she'd object and end their slowly forming relationship. Laura was content to stay like this. Being with Vicki had made her forget some of the emptiness Marianne Roach had scored inside her. Ince filled in some more of the spaces.

'We'd better sit down and have our drinks,' Ince said, his voice low and husky. 'I don't want Spencer to come in and see us like this.'

—

Laura had a wonderful time with Vicki the next day. Vicki brought her doll's pram and a bagful of toys and they drew pictures and coloured them in, read through the whole fairytale book and made the cake for Vicki's rejected grandmother. Laura laughed as she showed Vicki over the cottage and the little girl sat at her dressing table and made a mess of her face putting on her lipstick. When her face was washed, they had a lunch of chicken pie and ice cream then roasted a few chestnuts over the open fire in the front room.

Laura supervised the play when Benjy joined them for the afternoon and then they walked him, with the doll's pram, back home. Laura had packed a paper bag with more gingerbread men for Vicki and was buttoning up her coat to take her home when Spencer turned up.

'Ohhh, I wanted to walk back with Laura,' Vicki said grumpily, stamping her foot.

'I had to get some things in the shop,' Spencer said in a no-nonsense voice. 'Aunty Daisy is wondering why you haven't been there to show her your doll's pram. I'll take you up the hill now.'

Spencer took Vicki away with him and came back a few minutes later. Laura was wrapping the cake she and Vicki had made in grease-proof paper. She knew she was going to get a reprimand for some reason and was in no mood for it.

'I'm busy in the kitchen. If you want to talk to me it'll have to be in there.'

'You know that I have something to say to you then?' he said tightly, following her through.

'You never bother to hide your feelings, Spencer Jeffries. What have I done wrong this time?'

He stood beside her, squaring his shoulders. 'I just want to say that I don't want Vicki coming here to become a regular thing. She's my daughter. I have the right.'

Laura bustled him out of her way as she reached for a cake tin. 'I agree with you. You have the right to do what you think is best for Vicki, but have you thought everything through clearly?'

'What the hell does that mean?'

'There's no need to be aggressive.' Laura put her hands on her hips. 'Why do you always have to take that line? It's a great pity you're not more like Ince.'

'Would you mind getting straight to the point?' Spencer interjected, leaning towards her.

'Very well. I was thinking about her grandmother, Felicity Lean.'

'That's none of your bloody business! If you think you can live in this village for five minutes and play the lady and interfere in my affairs then you're very much mistaken.'

Spencer made to hurtle out of the kitchen but Laura grabbed his arm and pulled him back. 'Spencer, will you listen for a moment instead of getting all fired up. Stop and think about the future, man! Everybody in the village knows Felicity is Vicki's grandmother. She starts school in a few days' time, one of the children might tell her. Have you ever stopped long enough to consider that? Don't you realise that the vice-like grip you keep on Vicki isn't good for her? How is she going to feel when she learns you've been keeping secrets from her?'

'I'll tell her the truth! That Felicity Lean's a dreadful woman and I've only been protecting her.'

'That's not true and you know it,' Laura shouted back angrily. 'Felicity only kept from you what Natalie asked her to. It's not Felicity's fault that Natalie died. It's nobody's fault. Natalie had a serious health problem. You have no more right to deny that poor woman her granddaughter than you have to deny Vicki the love and attention of her grandmother. It's not what Natalie would have wanted you to do. It's you that's dreadful!'

Laura ended on a gulp. She knew she had gone too far. Spencer pushed her away from him so forcefully she hit the table behind her. For one terrible moment she thought he was going to come after her and unleash some of the rage that was making him shake from head to foot. His face was a cold mask, his grey eyes shone queerly. Laura shuddered. It was as if something dead was glaring at her.

He pointed a finger at her and strained his words out between clenched teeth. 'How dare you involve yourself in my family life. You've got no right. I know you've got something going with Ince but he'll just have to meet you here instead. If I ever catch you on my land, if I ever learn that you've spoken a single word to my daughter again, I won't be responsible...'

When he had gone, Laura fell down on a chair. She felt cold right through, as if she'd been out on the moor for hours with hardly any clothes on. She had tried to help Vicki and Felicity and had failed alarmingly. Now the one thing in her life she wanted and enjoyed the most, to spend time with Vicki, to be part of her life, she had just lost for ever. It was ironic, she would never have shouted back at Bill in that way, but now she had sown a wind and reaped a storm.

There was a knock at the door. Like someone in a stupor, she answered it. It was Marianne Roach. Laura said nothing, she stood aside to let the girl in.

'Thanks for seeing me, Mrs Jennings,' Marianne said, twisting her hands together in front of her body self consciously. 'I... I was wondering if you'd thought about coming to see my mother with me yet? I've thought of nothing else over Christmas. I know how unfair it is to ask you to do this for me when it's Bill's baby I'm carrying, but you've been so kind to some of the other villagers.'

'Sit down, Marianne,' Laura said numbly.

Marianne suddenly became aware that she wasn't the only one who might have problems. 'Are you all right, Mrs Jennings? You look as white as a ghost. Can I get you anything?'

'Yes, you can,' Laura said, flopping down on the settee. 'You'll find a bottle of brandy in the sideboard. You can pour me a large glassful. There's some lemonade in there too if you want some.'

Marianne poured a large brandy for Laura, all the while glancing at her anxiously. She had never seen anyone looking so shaken. She sat down with a glass of lemonade. 'Have you had a shock, Mrs Jennings?'

Laura raised her glass. She looked and spoke as if she was drunk. 'Call me Laura. No, I haven't had a shock. I've just had something reaffirmed for me, something I've always known, that nearly all the men in the world are callous bastards. And you know that too, don't you, you poor girl? You've been seduced and left pregnant by the worst, or perhaps the second worst, one in the world. Of course I'll come with you to tell your mother that you're pregnant. And if your damned father kicks you out or threatens to hurt you, you can come and live with me.'

Chapter 22

Harry Lean was meeting an acquaintance in the historic fourteen-century Bell Inn public house in Launceston. Harry bought the other man, a heftily built, middle-aged, balding individual, a double Scotch.

'I take it you have some information for me then, Hugh?' Harry rubbed his soft hands together and grinned like the Cheshire Cat.

'Had a little look through the files for you this morning, old boy,' Hugh said, gulping at his whisky and wiping his fat lips with the palm of his hand. 'I think you'll find it most interesting.'

'Go on.' Harry moved his bar stool closer to Hugh and lit a cigarette.

'As you thought, Harry, Jacka Davey bought his farm from your father on a mortgage from the bank I work for. He's now behind on three repayments. He had a letter warning him that the bank will take steps to repossess the property if he doesn't pay half the amount due by January the first.'

'And has he?'

'Oh, yes. We received his letter and postal order this morning.'

'Damn!' Harry growled. 'I wanted to get that dirt farmer off the property. I was going to make the bank an offer it couldn't refuse.' Harry could, too; since the mismanagement of the family affairs by his father, Harry had been astute in his career moves and business management and had built up a healthy bank balance to ensure that he and his mother would never want for anything. It hadn't worried him before, the selling off of the Leans' property around Kilgarthen; he didn't want the bother of collecting the rents and selling Little Cot to Bill Jennings had broken ties with a man he despised. If he had secured Tregorlan Farm, he would have promptly sold it again.

'You want to get back the farm your father sold off, is that it, Harry?'

'No, I want to pay back the farmer's daughter for showing me up in public and refusing me the pleasure of her body.'

Hugh laughed uproariously. 'Tell me about the daughter, Harry. I shall be most interested to hear about her.'

Harry shook his head ruefully and a lecherous smile marred his handsome face. 'She would have been delicious. A virgin of course. Rather strange in her ways, talks to herself a lot, but as pretty as a picture. A tiny little thing. Twenty years old and has no more idea what to do with her body than a nun. I love the very smell of her, so young, fresh and untried. I don't think a man could ever take her beyond the experience of it being the first time. Think of it, Hugh. Bliss, bliss and more bliss, over and over again.'

'Mmmm…' Hugh licked his fleshy lips. 'And she refused you?'

'Damned near tore my face off! I swore revenge on her then and I meant it.'

'Were you hoping she'd turn to you if she became homeless?'

Harry slapped Hugh playfully on the shoulder. 'Do you know, I never thought of that. You've cheered me up. She'd rather live in the gutter than succumb to me, but she might be willing to reconsider my proposition if it meant keeping the roof over her father and aunt's head.'

'Well, in that case, I might just be able to help you.' Hugh took an envelope out of the inside breast pocket of his flamboyantly styled suit. 'This just happens to be the letter and postal order from Jacka Davey Esquire. I could delay paying it into his account for a few more days, for a small consideration of, say, fifty pounds? Then you can put your bid into the bank. What do you say to that, Harry?'

Harry pushed back his shoulders and stretched his entwined fingers out in front of him. With face abeam, he said, 'Excellent, it's cheap at the price, Hugh, old boy.'

While her son was engaged in underhand dealings, Felicity Lean was thanking Laura for the cake she'd baked for her. 'You are kind. I was afraid you wouldn't come again after what Harry did to that poor girl and I have come to value your friendship, Laura.' There was emotion in her pale blue eyes and a slight tremble in her voice.

'That had nothing to do with you, Felicity,' Laura said, taking a seat in the drawing room which boasted a floor-to-ceiling Christmas tree complete with dozens of tiny white candles in silver clip-on holders.

'I don't know what came over Harry. He must have had too much to drink before the concert started. He's never done anything like that before. Tressa Davey is very pretty. Dresses like an urchin and has terrible hair, but I can see that she would be appealing to young men. I understand from Mrs Biddley that your solicitor friend is quite taken with her. I hope Tressa wasn't too badly distressed. I've been wondering if I should write and apologise to her on Harry's behalf. What do you think?'

'Tressa's made of stern stuff, Felicity, and she seems confident nothing like that will happen again. I should let it die a natural death.'

The tired, almost defeated look that was beginning to etch deeper fines in Felicity's regal face eased a little, and for a few moments she looked more like the vibrant purposeful woman she had once been. 'Oh, you're such a comfort to me. I think you understand how I feel about little Vicki more than anyone else.'

Laura looked down guiltily at the carpet. 'I think I probably do but I fear I might have made things worse yesterday.' In a flat, apologetic voice she told Felicity of her latest altercation with Spencer.

Felicity sighed heavily then shrugged her graceful shoulders. 'Even if Vicki learns I am her grandmother, Spencer will still continue to deny me access to her. How could things be worse? At least someone had the guts to say something to him on my behalf at long last. I thank you for trying to make him see things from my point of view.'

Mrs Biddley brought in a tray of coffee and tiny mince pies and because Felicity was distracted, staring at Natalie's photograph, Laura did the honours. 'Was he a beast when he married Natalie? Were you worried at all about her?'

'No,' Felicity said emphatically, gathering her wits together. 'Spencer was always quiet and intense but he adored Natalie. I can't ever remember him raising his voice to her.'

'Well, he has to me,' Laura said bitterly. 'More than once.'

'It was the shock of Natalie's death that changed him, Laura. It was so unexpected, he's never been able to get to grips with it. He threw himself into fathering Vicki and never allowed himself to grieve over Natalie. He puts flowers on her grave, but he's shut his mind to the fact that she's dead. He just feels bereft at not having her with him, that she'll never come back to him. He's all lost and mixed up inside.'

'You're very understanding towards him, Felicity. I can't forgive his behaviour towards me. I had a cruel husband and I ended up hating him. I hate his memory. I won't tolerate another man abusing me.'

'I'm sorry,' Felicity murmured and turned her head away. She was running out of energy, she didn't want the little she had left used up by listening to another's troubles; she had enough sorrows of her own and they made her rather selfish.

The two women lapsed into a mournful silence. They both needed a comforting hand but they weren't close enough to make any such intimate gestures to each other.

'Could I take a look around the stables?' Laura said to change the subject. 'I haven't got time to ride today but I think it's a good idea to get to know the mount I'll use.' Laura knew from a piece of barking gossip from Ada Prisk that Harry was going up to London for a few days after doing a bit of business in Launceston today.

'Yes, of course.' Felicity rose to her feet. 'I'll come with you. I could do with a walk in the fresh air. After all the rain and drizzle we've had, it's such a lovely day. I hope you'll be careful when you go riding, Laura. You aren't used to the moor.'

'I'll be fine. I bought a detailed map of the moor when I was last in Launceston.'

'Yes, dear, but it's not the same as having local knowledge. When you arrived you said you were busy today. Does that mean I can't persuade you to stay for lunch?'

'No, I'm sorry. I'm afraid I have to meet someone,' Laura said grimly, thinking of the reason that forbade the ride today. 'I'm helping someone to sort out a problem.'

–

Barbara Roach looked anxiously from her daughter's taut pale face to the beautiful young woman she had unexpectedly brought home with her. Barbara knew there was something ominous brewing; until yesterday Marianne had not had a good word for Laura Jennings, in fact each word had been edged with spite and seamed in hatred. Trouble, trouble, there was always trouble. Why had Marianne suddenly made friends with someone she had so recently hated? The two of them appeared not only friendly, there seemed to be a bond between them. Barbara resented it. There had never been a bond of any sort between her and her surly, wayward daughter.

Barbara told Marianne to show Laura into the sitting room. She stayed in the kitchen to make a pot of tea and delay the inevitable bad news. Or was it bad news? The most likely reason for this unexpected visit was the announcement that Marianne was leaving home, that Laura Jennings knew of a friend in London who would put her daughter up and help find her a job. It would be one source of tension out of the house. And without Marianne here, she might be able to pluck up the courage to leave her vile, despicable husband.

Barbara didn't have the courage to ask Marianne or Laura outright what was this was all about. She poured the tea and passed round the plate of dainty fairy cakes, then sat and waited for one of them to speak.

'You're probably wondering what I'm doing here, Mrs Roach,' Laura ventured, daunted by the other woman's demeanour of suffering and misery which sat on her shoulders like a heavy black cloud. Laura was more than suspicious about Cecil Roach being a cruel husband; the last time she had gone to the butcher's van she had listened in on a piece of gossip about the Roaches. Ada Prisk had 'just happened to be passing by School House the other day' and said she had heard Cecil bawling at 'the poor unfortunate woman, he went on for ages, he did, and then there was this terrible smacking sound and I heard Barbara scream'. It was easy to draw conclusions from what Ada Prisk had said, even the wrong ones, but there was a suspicious-looking bruise on Barbara's cheekbone. When Cecil learned that Marianne was pregnant, Laura was afraid he would take his anger out on his wife.

Barbara forced a wan smile. 'I knew you would have called here eventually. I would have invited you myself, but things were hectic before Christmas with the concert and everything and, and...' She ran out of excuses and sipped her tea.

Laura looked meaningfully at Marianne who was hanging her head in shame. She knew her father would take the news of her pregnancy out on her mother. 'I think you should tell your mother without any beating about the bush, Marianne. It would be simpler and kinder.'

Barbara dropped her cup into its saucer, making a loud chinking noise. A chill rose round her heart and squeezed it tightly. 'What is it, Marianne? Are you really ill? Has the doctor said it's more serious than you've told us?'

Marianne's tears weren't far away. She had rehearsed a hundred different ways how to tell her mother about her baby and each time she had nearly cried. She had felt like the little girl she had been for only a short time of her childhood, having forced herself to grow up all too quickly to block out the feelings of unhappiness her overbearing, constantly critical father caused the family. She couldn't stand seeing her kind and loving mother being shouted at and brutalised. She had come to think only of herself and her needs, to seek adventure outside her dismal home environment, to shut out any thoughts about her mother's sufferings.

She had found some of that excitement with Bill Jennings, the local hero. He had secretly showered her with little gifts from the day of her sixteenth birthday. He had asked her to meet him clandestinely. Soon he had taken her to the moor and given her her first lesson in love. Marianne had believed it was love, now she knew better. She had overlooked Bill's bad temper and impatience, the times when he'd snapped and sworn at her. It hadn't been the pressure of work, an unhappy marriage with a proud, arrogant wife who looked down on him that had made him harsh. It was his natural character. Then there had been the times when he hadn't wanted to see her; he had probably gone with other women. Marianne had begun to admit this after she'd seen what Bill's widow was really like. How ironic that because of her sulky behaviour she had alienated everyone in the village and could only ask Laura Jennings to be her comforter. If Laura had not come with her she would have deliberately caused a row with her mother so she could have blurted it out and blamed her, but when Laura had agreed to come with her it had humbled her. She couldn't let her gentle, loyal mother suffer another moment of agonised waiting.

'I'm in trouble, Mother,' she whispered, and scalding tears coursed down her face.

Barbara looked stunned. 'You mean you've lost your job?' Oh no, what was Cecil going to say?

'N–not that sort of trouble... a b–baby.'

In case there was any doubt in Barbara's mind about what her daughter was trying to tell her, Laura said softly, 'I'm afraid it's true, Mrs Roach. Marianne is pregnant.'

Marianne collapsed in a flood of tears. Barbara gagged on the gulp of air her lungs had gasped in and she gripped the table. Laura felt pity deep in her heart for them both. A cruel man had been partly responsible for the trouble that affected them and another cruel man would heap his rage on Marianne's shame.

'Oh, my God.' The words of desperate prayer were trawled from the depths of Barbara's being. 'Oh, dear Lord. What are we going to do? What will he say?'

Suddenly Marianne was on her feet and across the room. She threw herself on her frightened mother. 'Help me, Mother. I'm sorry. I'm so sorry.'

Barbara could hardly believe it. Her daughter needed her after all these years. Marianne, whose presence in the home she had almost grown to fear and despise, was her little girl again. It gave Barbara hope and a little courage. She stroked the sobbing girl's hair. 'Don't worry, darling. We don't have to do anything for a while yet. We'll think of something. I'll think of something.'

Laura got up. She had played her part and it was time to leave. 'I think I'll be going,' she whispered to Barbara.

'Thank you, Mrs Jennings,' Barbara said, her voice firm, her eyes glittering with tears but her face unusually composed. 'I'll let you know what we decide to do.'

—

Laura felt drained as she made her way home; her encounter with Spencer and what she had witnessed in School House were taking their toll. When she saw Ince standing outside Little Cot, her heart lifted and she walked up the hill with renewed vigour. She hoped he would come in and talk to her, stay for dinner. She wanted no one else's company but his right now. He would offer her his gentleness and kindness, without pressure, without worries of any kind.

'Laura!' The moment he saw her he rushed to her side. 'I've been here twice today and not found you home.'

Without a moment's hesitation, she linked her arm through his. 'Well, I'm going home and staying there now, Ince. I hope you can come in and stay with me.'

Ince couldn't have wished for anything more. 'You look all in,' he said, gazing into her eyes. 'What have you been doing all day?'

'Oh, nothing that can't wait until another time to tell you,' she replied as she opened the door of her home and let him step inside first. She had a triumphant look on her face. The comings and goings to Little Cot must be making a stir in the village, and the way she felt at the moment, she couldn't give a damn.

'Are you all right, Laura?' Ince demanded the instant she'd closed the door. 'Spencer came home in an almost murderous mood yesterday and all I can make out is that it must have had something to do with Vicki playing here. I couldn't get a word out of him. He left Vicki with me and went out on the moor and stayed there nearly all night. He still refuses to tell me what happened, except to call you a couple of choice names. Vicki's in a right state. She believes she's done something to upset her father and doesn't know what. When she mentioned your name, he snapped at her and made her cry. For goodness sake, what happened?'

Laura let her coat fall to the floor. She had tried as hard to shut Vicki's darling little face out of her mind as she had Spencer's wrathful words and warning. Now she had to face them again. 'Oh, Ince,' and she felt herself crumpling at the knees. 'I've ruined everything.'

Ince was standing close and as his arms moved to wrap themselves round her she threw herself against him. He led her to the settee and held her tightly. He stroked her hair and the side of her face for some moments, giving her time to calm herself.

'Can you tell me what happened, sweetheart?' he breathed softly after what seemed an age but was only a few minutes.

Laura sighed heavily. She didn't want to, but it was best to get it over with. And Ince had the right to know; he lived with Vicki and Spencer. She nestled in closer to him and put her hand into his, feeling less shaky and more resolved as his strong fingers tightened round hers.

'I think Spencer was jealous of my friendship with Vicki. He came for her, not looking perhaps for a confrontation but he had something to say. He took Vicki up to Daisy then he came back alone. He said he didn't want her playing here to become a regular thing. I know it's not really my business but I've been worried about the excruciatingly tight hold Spencer keeps over her. I pointed out that when she starts school the week after next someone might tell her that Felicity Lean is her grandmother. After all, it's common knowledge. I tried not to sound interfering but he went berserk. I told him that he was a terrible man. He threatened that if I ever talk to Vicki again or go to the farm he won't be responsible for his actions.'

It brought back all the pain and humiliation and she was forced to wipe away stinging tears. 'I realise that it's all my fault, Ince. What right do I have to tell him how to run his life? He doesn't like me and he never will. I spoke out of turn and too soon. Spencer hadn't come to say Vicki couldn't come here again. I should have let things move at his pace. It's nothing to do with me if someone tells Vicki about her grandmother. I should just have let things happen. I've ruined the only thing that's brought me real happiness in years, being part of Vicki's life.'

Ince was quiet, more quiet than someone not talking. Laura looked up at his face. He was staring into space, as if he could see through the wall into the kitchen and was picturing yesterday's scene of fury. She willed him to say something. His silence was nearly as unbearable as Spencer's bad temper.

'You've opened up some terrible wounds,' he said at last.

'Wounds that will never heal?'

'Yes,' he replied grimly.

'And there's nothing I can do to heal the rift this time,' she murmured, more to herself than him.

'It's not entirely your fault, Laura. Spencer's not what can be called a reasonable man.' Ince put his hand under her chin and raised her face to his. 'I know what Vicki has come to mean to you. Does this mean you will leave the village?'

'I don't know, Ince. I haven't really thought about it.'

'You still have friends here. Isn't there anyone else who means something to you in Kilgarthen?'

She knew he was referring to himself and she realised that he was hoping for something more from her than friendship. She looked into his gentle dark eyes and saw the warmth and tenderness that came from deep inside him reflected there. He was a man who would never abuse a woman and treat her like the dirt beneath his feet, stifle her hopes and ambitions, make her feel less than human. He was strong and masculine and, she suddenly saw, very desirable.

She stroked his face. 'You mean something to me, Ince.'

He gathered her in and kissed her lips. His mouth was warm and tender as it moved over hers. She pressed her mouth to his, opening her lips and releasing a feeling of slowly stirring passion in both of them.

His hands caressed her tenderly, down her arms, up over her shoulders, running up and down her back. He slid his lips down her neck and behind her ears, pressing and searching. Delicious tingly sensations were growing steadily inside her, not bursting out and frightening her and filling her with shame, but warm, heady, natural feelings, enriching her, making her murmur in his arms. Laura had not been made love to in this way before. She wanted more.

Ince's need was becoming too strong; he stilled his hands before they caressed her somewhere that would offend her.

Disentangling her arms from him, Laura stood up. She pulled Ince to his feet. She moved towards the door.

'Do you want me to go?' he asked in a pained voice. He had very little experience with women and felt awkward and uncertain.

For an answer she locked the door then returned to him. She took his hand. 'We can't stay here, someone might look in through the window.'

They went upstairs and Laura opened the door to one of the spare bedrooms. She wasn't going to take this gentle wonderful man to Bill Jennings' bed. Inside the room she felt shy. They both felt shy. She wanted this though. She had been a widow for only a few weeks but hadn't been a wife for years. She wanted to make love with this understanding man. He would make her feel like a woman. He wanted her for herself alone and would fulfil a need in her that had never been cherished or satisfied. It would be a time of love and total giving.

Chapter 23

'Let me push the wheelbarrow, I'm stronger than you.'

'You are not stronger than I am,' Andrew declared as Tressa bounded on just in front of him. It was difficult pushing the old rusty wheelbarrow up the incline of rough narrow track over the moor. The ground under their feet was shifting and soggy and tufts of grass and gorse tugged at their boots. Tressa had seen him almost stumble and had used the same irritating superior tone she had treated him with since Jacka had welcomed his offer of working on the farm. 'Tell me again where we're going.'

'To Reddacoombe Farm. 'Tis been deserted for nigh on forty year. We need moor stone to repair a wall and as the ground's too wet for collecting on the moor we're going to take some from Reddacoombe. It's not needed there any more and it's just the right size and shape for what we want.'

'I see.'

'That'll make a change.'

His sigh came out like a growl and he wished she'd slow down and not stay in front of him where he couldn't see her face. He didn't like this sort of banter. Last night after supper at Tregorlan Farm Jacka had invited him to stay and join the family in the sitting room and 'help finish off the Christmas drink'. Andrew had jumped at the chance, hoping Jacka and Joan would withdraw after a while and leave him alone with Tressa. Still in their working clothes, the three Daveys had settled down cosily and he'd soon realised he wouldn't be granted his wish. He was pleased when Tressa produced a battered rectangular cardboard box and asked, 'Want a game of draughts?' Putting his glass of beer down on the floor he eagerly helped lay out the pieces on the much–used board. 'You can be white,' Tressa said. 'I'm always black.' Then she'd looked at him in a way that Andrew could only describe as slyly.

Five games later, all of which she had won quickly, he became aware of the reason behind that sly look. He noticed Jacka grinning behind his pipe and beer as he warmed his toes in front of the fire, and Joan chuckling behind her knitting and drop of sherry. He glared at his smug opponent and began the next game with determination creasing his brow. As Tressa jumped the last of his men in a noisy zigzag, he let out a cry of indignation.

'Are you getting windy?' She put her head cockily on the side and instead of wanting to hold her to him, he wanted to shake her until her teeth rattled.

'Don't be silly,' he retorted ungraciously.

'I always used to beat Jimmy and Matty at draughts,' she told him through perkily pursed lips as she set up the board again. 'And they always got windy.'

'I am not windy,' he growled, 'whatever that stupid expression means.' He'd never thought he'd be rude to her but his male pride had taken a hard blow; he rarely lost at chess which was a much superior game to draughts. 'So you don't want to risk another thrashing?'

'I'm not a poor loser if that's what you're suggesting.'

'Is that a yes or a no?'

'Yes, yes, of course.'

'Try thinking your moves out a little more.'

'What?'

Jacka laughed, a loud rumbling sound that began in his fat stomach. He pointed his pipe at his equally amused sister. 'Hear that, Joan? 'Twas just the same 'tween she and the boys.'

'I remember, Jacka,' she chortled. 'They loved that maid but never liked it when she beat 'em, and she were only a child back then.'

That had made Andrew feel even more embarrassed but worse than that was being compared to Tressa's brothers. He prayed she didn't see him like that.

The wheelbarrow hit a tussock of reedy grasses and the handles were torn out of his hands.

238

Tressa turned round and again there was that smugness on her face. She gave a little shake of her head to toss away a wispy strand of brown hair from her eyes and raised an eyebrow. 'Want to take a rest?'

No, I want to take you in my arms and kiss you and crush you to me and run my hands through your wonderfully messy hair and touch you and make love to you and I want to tell you how much I love you and I want you to tell me that you love me.

When words like that ran through his mind with a raw intensity, his blue eyes blazed in his taut face, he clenched his fists, his body shook and he didn't appear to be breathing.

Tressa met his piercing eyes without flinching. Although these moments puzzled her and made her tingle strangely from head to toe, she was not one to be beaten down. Again she wondered why he had come back to Kilgarthen and seemed to be in no hurry to leave; it was two weeks since he had suddenly turned up at the concert. Early one morning when she'd been carrying the milk churns to the stand for collection she'd seen Mrs Sparnock bicycling down Rosemerryn Lane. Mrs Sparnock had repeated Mrs Prisk's gossip that Andrew Macarthur was 'down here after Mrs Jennings, in indecent haste if you ask me'. If that was true, why did he spend more time at Tregorlan Farm than in the village? So he wouldn't appear to be an obvious suitor in 'indecent haste'? Today he had brought Laura with him. She, however, had chosen to stay with Aunty Joan rather than traipse the moor with them and he hadn't seemed in the least concerned, in fact he had advised against her joining them with the weather being inclement. As he had promised, he had obtained some application forms for a government subsidy for her father and helped him to fill them in. Was he hanging about to see the outcome of that? Did he care that much for her father's rights and livelihood? Whatever his reason for staying in Kilgarthen, she found him a rather strange man.

'Why haven't you gone back to London?' she challenged him.

Andrew's heart sank and the glitter went out of his eyes, but he replied mildly, 'Why? Can't you wait to get rid of me?' He hoped he wasn't about to receive a blistering 'yes'. There had been no need to return to London to look into the Morrison brothers' demand for a further five thousand pounds. His partner John Walmesley had informed him he was confident that no such debt was owed. But Andrew's romantic endeavours had not progressed at all. His hope that Jacka would see him as a suitable husband for Tressa and join in his campaign had not been realised. Neither Jacka nor Joan seemed to have noticed his feelings for Tressa any more than the girl herself had. He was fearful now that if the older couple did come to realise why he spent so much time among them, they would think him unsuitable because of his career and his middle-class background.

Tressa shrugged her slim shoulders, making the oversized coat rise up to her neat ears. 'It's all the same to me what you do. We'd better get on. 'Tis building up for a shower. 'Tis cold enough for hail.'

The wind was whipping up to a frenzy and the clouds were lowering in the darkening sky. He hoped the old farm wasn't far away. As they made the top of the incline he saw the deserted low buildings sheltered in a rolling valley below them.

Tressa tapped on his arm. 'If we hurry we can make the farmhouse before the hail comes.'

He needed no more encouragement and with the squeaky wheelbarrow easier to push downhill than uphill they reached the remains of Reddacoombe Farm in a few minutes. Nettles, docks and thistles, decaying and gone to seed, stood dejectedly against the walls. Tressa told him to push the wheelbarrow into what had been the outdoor closet. Andrew noticed it was similarly furnished to the basic convenience at Tregorlan Farm. A very small building with a slanted slate roof, at one end it had a wall-to-wall wooden board with a hole over a bucket, except this one was larger and boasted two holes. Its twin buckets had been removed but the nails and pieces of string where sheets of old newspaper had hung were still there. Communal toileting – Andrew had not expected that. He ran across the yard into the farmhouse.

'Close the door,' Tressa ordered. 'Keep out the cold.' She was sitting on one of a pair of abandoned low stools, pouring tea from a flask. 'We might as well have an early crib.'

The door was hanging on its top hinge and he had to lift it up and push hard to close it. It blocked out much of the light and as the small square window panes were coated in dust he could hardly see Tressa in the gloom. To reach her he picked his way carefully over pools of water, bits of fallen debris and rubbish discarded by careless picnickers. As she handed him a flask cup of tea, hail suddenly beat down fiercely on the building and he was momentarily startled.

'It won't last long,' Tressa declared.

Andrew got the impression she was trying to comfort him and he realised she saw him as an inferior on the farm and moor. Knowing how hard the work was and how dangerous the moor could be, he admitted he was.

'Then we can fill the wheelbarrow with stones and take them back to the farm before the next shower,' he said.

'You're learning. Want a sandwich?'

'Yes, please. I'm always ravenously hungry when I'm out like this.' Now he knew why she ate so much and stayed so tiny.

They listened to the hail thundering on the roof and striking the window panes as they ate spam sandwiches. Draughts from the numerous holes in the walls lifted the dust on the floor.

'Why did the last owners leave here?'

'They died of old age, first the husband then the woman. Dad said Mrs Trethewey was a devil of a woman. Milked her cows and fed her pigs and chickens up to the day she died with her boots on. Nobody inherited it and nobody moved in. The stock was taken away and the place fell into disrepair, as we see it today.'

'Sad really. Makes you wonder about their lives.'

'I'll show you something of what their ancestors were like,' Tressa said in an excited voice after she'd repacked the army bag.

She went a few steps into the next room which had once served as the parlour. Andrew followed her and she put out a hand to stop him going in any further than where she stood. Ragged curtains were drawn at the single window and it was dark and dreary but he could just make out a wide deep hole dug out in the middle of the stone-flagged floor.

Tressa pointed to the hole. 'That was a "hide". Where smugglers used to hide their contraband.'

'Like in the book *Jamaica Inn*? That's amazing.' Suddenly afraid he was being made a fool of again, he tapped her shoulder. 'You're not telling me a story yourself, are you?'

'No, honest.' She shook her head. 'Dad told me. Me, Matty and Jimmy used to come here and make up adventure stories.'

Andrew was about to ask her if she thought of him in the same light as her brothers; he might as well know, but she exclaimed, 'That's odd.'

'What's odd?' He followed her line of vision and saw a cigarette packet lying on the floor about a yard away from their feet. 'Perhaps a hiker took a rest in here.'

'There wouldn't be any hikers in the weather we've had lately. I was here only two days ago with Meg and the packet wasn't here then. Harper's Bazaar. I've not seen that brand before.'

Andrew frowned. He had. It was an expensive brand favoured greatly in the clubs of the capital city.

'The hail's stopping. We'd better get ready to start work,' Tressa said tightly. She was greatly annoyed that a stranger had come to one of her special private places. Looking moodily at Andrew, she muttered, 'Have you brought gloves with you?'

'For heaven's sake, Tressa, I'm not a complete idiot,' he returned. Sometimes he wondered if she saw him as a man at all let alone a romantic partner.

–

Carrying a packet of soap flakes, Laura followed Joan who was humping a huge basket of dirty laundry, into one of Tregorlan's outhouses. As they pushed through the galvanised iron door, the wonderful smell of stored apples hit Laura's nostrils; she felt like a small child allowed to see inside an Aladdin's cave. The high windows let in very little light in the ramshackle building and Joan lit two lanterns and hung them up on hooks. The roof was made partly of rusty iron and curved timbers and it was rather like being inside a cave. Laura watched amazed when Joan lit a strange contraption that looked something like a large primus stove and put a huge pot of water on its top to boil.

'Jacka knocked this together years ago,' Joan said proudly, referring to the stove. 'It heats the water up quickly and has never let me down.' She took the packet of soap flakes and sprinkled some into the water.

'Can I do something to help?' Laura asked. She had hardly spoken to Joan Davey before arriving at the farm with Andrew just after breakfast but they were getting along well, and although rather shy, Joan seemed glad to have another woman to chat to.

Because Johnny Prouse was so much better and wanted to be his usual independent self, and to take her mind off missing Vicki, Laura had asked Andrew if she could come to the farm with him today. She also wanted to witness for herself how Andrew was getting on in his attempted courtship of the elusive Tressa.

Joan handed her a long narrow piece of bleached wood. 'You can stir the flakes into the water if you like while I sort out the washing.'

Laura stood at a safe distance and stirred the water, likening it to a witch stirring up her potions over a cauldron. A good witch, of course; she wished she could whip up a love potion that would work on the other woman's niece. Joan tipped the laundry onto the stone floor and sorted it out into piles of whites, coloureds and handwash. She dragged an ancient creaking mangle out from its resting place in a corner, and a washtub and board. Laura felt she'd stepped back into another era. She forgot her troubles for a time.

She was greatly relieved that the Morrison brothers' fresh claim for money had been discounted, but the repercussions of the quarrel with Spencer marred the happiness she'd found at feeling she was accepted and belonged in Kilgarthen. She was also apprehensively waiting for all hell to break loose when Cecil Roach was informed of his daughter's pregnancy. Barbara had told her they were waiting for term to begin when he would have to spend most of his time in the school building.

Laura had something special that was balm to her soul – Ince. She'd had no regrets as she lay in his arms after they had made love. It had been Ince who had suggested they take their new feelings one step at a time. He'd kissed and caressed her with gentle affection as they'd agreed they wouldn't make love again unless something permanent came out of their association. He didn't want to compromise his faith and Laura didn't want to be rushed into something she'd later regret. She had moved out of the master bedroom tainted with Bill's presence and now slept in the bed she and Ince had used and the memories were a warming comfort to her.

'When the flakes have dissolved, I'll put the sheets, pillowcases and smalls in to boil first,' Joan said. 'Every now and again I pound on 'em with the stick to help get the dirt out.'

Laura watched wide-eyed as Jacka's longjohns were put in with the bed linen and then some knee-length drawers. The other pairs of knickers, big and ugly, must be Tressa's and she felt sorry for the girl not having any feminine underwear. She would never feel womanly and attractive if those were the only things she wore. A small cotton nightdress was tossed in next, a garment so thin that Laura saw through it before it hit the bubbling water. Andrew had told her of Tressa's Christmas wish for a new nightie; apparently it hadn't materialised.

It took two hours to complete the washing, the women taking it in turns to go out to the well and draw more water. When the laundry had been washed, scrubbed, rinsed and mangled, they hung it up on lines in the outhouse because there was no chance of it drying outside today. They tipped out the dirty soapy water, packed away the mangle and washtub then carried the towels and tea towels into the kitchen to dry over the range.

They found Tressa and Andrew there, back from Reddacoombe Farm and refilling their flask before they went off to the fields to repair the damaged wall.

Laura raised her eyebrows at him in question. Andrew shrugged his shoulders wearily and put on a dismal face. Tressa was going about her task of filling the flask wearing her usual faraway expression. He needed help and while Laura had worked in the outhouse she had formed a plan that might turn things round a bit. There was a dance in the village on Saturday night, ideal circumstances for romance to blossom.

Chapter 24

Tressa lazed back in the warm fragrant water. It was pure luxury. The white enamelled bath was in a room all of its own. There was space to stretch out in it rather than having to sit cramped with knees up to her chest like she did in the oval-shaped tin bath in the kitchen at home. The water actually came out of two taps, one hot and one cold, doing away with the need to heat water on the range and cool it down with buckets of cold water from the pump. Here Tressa had the chance to use the jasmine bath cubes and soap Andrew had left for her and its lovely perfume filled the air. She'd washed her hair using the little sachet of shampoo Laura had given her. It was much better than using soap. Now she was lying back and relaxing in the warm sweet-smelling water like some grand lady.

When Laura had asked her if she'd like her to do her hair for the dance, Tressa's instinctive reaction had been to decline the offer. She'd intended to go to the dance, her father had insisted on it, rabbiting on again about her needing to meet some nice young man and thinking about her future, but people like Laura usually wanted to form friendships and Tressa had never felt the need for any kind of friendship. Then Laura had said she could play the gramophone if she came to Little Cot to get ready for the dance. That had been an irresistible pull. She'd be able to tell Matty and Jimmy about that later.

She'd arrived at Little Cot half an hour ago with her shoes and the dress she was going to wear in a bag. Laura had shown her over the cottage and after seeing her delight at the bathroom had told her she could use it if she wished; she'd have to wash her hair anyway. Then Laura had tactfully asked her if she'd care to have some underwear given to her as a Christmas present, explaining that her

'Aunty Maureen' always got her size wrong and it was too small for her. Now the small pink cotton bra and matching French knickers were lying on the bathroom chair with Laura's bathrobe, waiting to be put on.

When the water got cold, Tressa climbed out of the bath and pulled out the plug. She wrapped a fluffy white towel under her armpits then bent over the bath and swirled the water round and round as it emptied away; it certainly beat having to carry the tin bath outside with Aunty Joan and tipping the water away in the yard. As she straightened up, her elbow touched a jar of bath crystals on the shelf and knocked it over. The strong smell of roses wafted upwards and masked the smell of the jasmine. The little accident startled her. Fortunately the jar hadn't broken and Tressa picked it up and put it back in its place, then she crouched down and began sweeping the crystals into a pile using the sides of her hands.

Suddenly the bathroom door was swung open and she gave a little cry of alarm.

Andrew was standing there and he looked as if he had been given the shock of his life. 'Tressa!'

'Laura said I could take a bath here,' Tressa explained in a tone that was almost a wail, like a child pleading that it wasn't being naughty, 'I knocked a jar over.'

Her startled expression made his heart turn over. 'It's all right, darling. I just popped in to see Laura but she doesn't seem to be in and I was making sure she wasn't being robbed.' Neither of them noticed that he'd called her darling. His eyes were rooted on her.

Tressa had never felt so embarrassed in all her life, she straightened up and gazed back at him, her pretty pale face covered in a bright pink blush, her hands grasping the towel protectively round her, her long wet hair dripping over her slender bare shoulders.

She looked so young and vulnerable, deliciously innocent, her soft female form moulded under the towel, that he longed to hold her. His feelings were so intense he was afraid she'd read his feverish mind. He knew he must go before he frightened or offended her.

'I—I'll leave you to it then. Don't worry about the crystals, they'll brush up easily.' As he turned to go, he saw the box of toiletries he'd

246

tried to give her for Christmas and his heart soared. He hastened from the room and closed the door before his face gave his elation away. So she'd accepted them after all; she must think something of him, like him a little bit.

He had wanted to ask Laura what he should wear to the dance tonight. He didn't want to overdo it, and he knew the villagers expected things to be just so. She must have popped out for something. He hoped she wouldn't come back for ages.

He worked fast. He made coffee, searched in the cupboards for some cake – he'd noticed Tressa was very partial to cake – and found a chocolate swiss roll. He put cups and saucers and a jug of hot milk on the tray and carried it into the front room.

He pranced about the room excitedly. Moving an occasional table nearer the settee, he put the tray on it. He tossed his coat and other things on the chairs so there was no room to sit on them. He flopped down on the settee and tried to look casual. He pressed his fingertips to his face to stop it twitching. He took several deep breaths and rubbed his chest over his hammering heart. When the bathroom door opened, he lurched to his feet, his eyes set on the doorway where Tressa would appear.

She was surprised to see him there and stood self-consciously in Laura's bathrobe, her towelled hair tumbling arrestingly over her shoulders. 'You're still here?'

'I thought you'd appreciate a hot drink on such a cold day and something to eat. Come and sit down.' He patted the space beside him.

She looked back uncertainly into the kitchen. 'I need to find a brush and clear up the mess I made.'

'I'll do that in a minute, come and sit down.'

Tressa thought that in the circumstances, with her wearing very little, she ought to ask him to leave. But she hardly had the right to turn one of Laura's friends out of her home. And the food and drink looked and smelled good. It never crossed her mind that he could have something dishonourable on his mind; she couldn't make up her mind about Andrew but she knew he was no Harry Lean.

She padded over to him in bare feet. She didn't sit close and he resisted the impulse to edge nearer to her; he was ever mindful of Laura's advice not to rush her, knowing she would bolt like a wild pony. He breathed in the intoxicating aroma of her and jasmine talcum powder; he would always adore that heady combination.

'Have some cake.' He lifted the silver coffee pot. 'Black or white?'

She looked at him as if he'd gone mad. 'Black or white what?'

'Coffee. Do you take milk?'

'I don't know. I've never drunk it before, we can't afford it.'

Andrew's heart ached. He wanted to give her everything in the world. 'Try it with milk. I'll make sure it's not too strong.' He watched her take the first tentative sip.

'It's nice,' she said, glancing at him.

'Good.'

After that she ate and drank without talking, and all the while he gazed at her. She gave no indication that she was aware he was doing it. A droplet of water fell off the tip of her hair and his heart burned with the desire to stroke the spot on the bathrobe where it fell on her arm.

Remembering her promised treat, Tressa got up suddenly.

'You're not going?' he asked anxiously.

'Laura said I could play the gramophone. She said I only have to wind it up.' She turned the handle cautiously, as if she was afraid she would break it off, then moved the needle across. Instead of 'Chattanooga Choo Choo' there came a loud scratching noise. 'Ohhh! I've broken it!'

'Don't worry.' Andrew sprang to her side. 'These things are tricky but I think I can put it right for you.' He made a great show of lifting off the needle arm and hummed and hawed like an aged scientist deliberating over something of great national importance. He placed the needle in the correct place on the disc. 'There we are.'

When she heard the music, Tressa clapped her hands with glee. 'Thank you, Andrew.' It was one of the few times she had called him by name.

She sat on the settee and listened to the song with a childlike delight. When it had finished, Andrew put on 'White Christmas' and the room was filled with the crooning of Bing Crosby.

'This song is wonderful,' Tressa said dreamily. 'He's got a wonderful voice.'

'It's the theme tune of a film called *Holiday Inn*,' Andrew said, thinking she probably didn't know the fact. 'It's an excellent film. I've seen it many times.' He was looking through the records. 'Bill had a good collection. I'll find some big band music to put us in the mood for tonight. Do you like dancing, Tressa?'

She made no comment and he looked at her. She was paying no mind to the music but was looking at him intently. He smiled at her, intending to ask her to spare him a dance tonight; it would be heaven to hold her in his arms at last. He never got the chance. Laura came back and ordered him out.

'Thank you for making the coffee for Tressa but you have to leave now, Andrew,' she insisted. 'Tressa and I have to get ready.'

'Oh, very well,' he muttered grudgingly, putting on his coat.

'What did you want to see me for anyway?' Laura asked as she showed him to the door, forbidding him one last look at Tressa as she pushed him gently off the doorstep.

He'd completely forgotten. 'Nothing important. See you both tonight.'

–

Ince put a final polish on his shoes then smoothed at his curly hair in the mirror on the kitchen wall.

'Why can't I come to the dance with you, Uncle Ince?' Vicki asked him for the umpteenth time, her fists rammed in appealingly under her chin as she watched him from the table.

'I've told you, princess, you're too young. It'll be your turn in a few years when you're a beautiful grown-up lady.'

'Are you going to dance with Laura?'

'I expect so,' Ince replied uncomfortably, seeing the reflection of Spencer's stern face in the mirror.

'Bet she'll look beautiful,' Vicki said wistfully. 'I wish I could see her.'

Vicki knew better than to talk about Laura to her father but he didn't stop her mentioning her to Ince. Spencer viewed his closest friend and daughter from a stony-faced distance. Vicki missed Laura and was hurt and puzzled about why there had been a sudden unexplained break in their friendship. Spencer knew he wasn't being fair to Vicki but Laura's remarks about Felicity, his mother-in-law, had hurt too much. He couldn't forgive Laura, even though he'd come to admit that what she had said was true. Felicity had only been following Natalie's wishes about keeping quiet over her poor health. It wasn't Felicity's fault Natalie had died. It wasn't anybody's fault, except perhaps the snow's for not letting the ambulance through so Natalie could have the Caesarian operation. It was his fault that Felicity had suffered for nothing for nearly five years and that Vicki had never known the love and care her grandmother would have lavished on her. He couldn't do anything about that now, no matter how unfair and wicked it was. His feelings were too raw.

'I'll see you later then,' Ince said to him after he'd hugged and kissed Vicki goodnight. He knew he wouldn't. Spencer would be closeted in his room when he got back. He wouldn't be sleeping. He'd be remembering his loss and if it cut to the roots of his soul like it often did, he would be softly crying.

—

Andrew asked Mike Penhaligon's advice about what he should wear for the dance and Mike told him that most of the men would wear their suits. Andrew changed into his, a Mayfair creation, far superior in cloth and style to those he would mingle with tonight. He put on a plain grey tie to tone it down.

He joined Mike in the bar for a drink. 'Phew, you smell like some foreign sheik, boy,' Mike exclaimed heartily at his expensive aftershave, pushing a small Scotch at him. The landlord winked and rubbed furiously at the thatch on his chin. 'After the maids tonight, are 'ee? If so, you'd better cheer up a bit. You look ruddy miserable.'

'Not miserable, Mike,' Andrew corrected him. 'Serious. I'm seriously trying to work out a plan so that one maid in particular will finally take notice of me and fall head over heels in love with me.'

Mike bashed him playfully on the arm. 'One maid in particular, eh? Let me see now. You turn up here again out of the blue five minutes after leaving for London. You can't wait to get out your bed every morning and are off and out. You're hardly here at all, in fact. Your hands are getting grimed up and tough from hard outdoor work.'

Andrew grinned. Mike was going to wring every drop he could out of the situation.

'You always head off in one direction and come back from the same way. Jacka Davey's got no complaints about all the extra unpaid help he's been receiving and Joan is delighted her cream teas are so well appreciated. Let me see. Someone else lives on that farm, I b'lieve. A dear little maid, as pretty as a primrose. Couldn't be she, could it? It couldn't be young Tressa Davey who's caught your fancy, eh?'

Andrew lifted the Scotch towards his lips to disguise his growing discomfort but Mike clutched his shoulder, half dragged him over the bar top and whispered in his ear, 'How're you getting on with her?'

'Not very well,' Andrew admitted, feeling foolish. He related the tale of the jasmine toiletries and how Tressa had been looking at him rather than listening to Laura's gramophone not so long ago. 'I think I might be getting somewhere at last, Mike, but it's very slow work.'

Mike looked around the bar as if the two men were conspirators in some crime they were about to commit. Pat was wiping a glass and looking at them curiously but he ignored her. 'Too eager,' he told Andrew like a deliberating judge. 'That's your trouble, boy. You've been showing that maid just how eager you are. Now, take my advice, and ignore her a bit. When you get to the dance tonight, don't throw yourself all over her, just stand back and ignore her. Get her guessing. She knows you're interested in her all right. She's playing hard to get. Sometimes at the dances we get one or two pretty young maids from outside the village. Dance with they. Dance with anyone, but don't fall over yourself to dance with her. She won't like that. She must be used to being the centre of your attention by now. I can guarantee she'll come running to you like a dog after a rabbit if she thinks you've got fed up and are looking elsewhere.'

Andrew shook his head. His heart was full of doubt. 'I don't know, Mike. It's too risky. She might not give me another chance.'

'I didn't say ignore her like she don't exist, just play hard to get for a while. Get her puzzled. Get her thinking. I reckon Laura's hard at work for you anyway. If she's got the maid over her place getting her all dolled up, well, it isn't for my benefit, is it, boy?' Mike tapped his large nose. 'Tactics, boy, tactics. 'Tis what gets things done in the end.'

—

Laura was looking forward to the dance. Although she still felt sore from Spencer's rage, at least her preoccupation with their violent quarrel as she'd gone over every word time and time again had made her forget all about Bill and her life with him. She felt she could rise above this too. And there was always the hope she would see Vicki again. Spencer still took her to visit Daisy and she would probably see her in the shop one day soon.

She walked down to the village hall with Tressa beside her, proud of the way she had helped turn the girl out. She had cut Tressa's hair to one straight length and persuaded her to let a pretty mother-of-pearl encrusted slide sweep it back from her face. A belt with a diamanté buckle from one of Laura's evening dresses had made her blue dress look more fashionable and enhanced her enviable slim figure. Laura had been worried about her shoes, those horrible brown clumpy things Tressa usually wore would have spoiled the whole effect. She had nothing that would fit the girl's feet and was delightfully surprised when Tressa took a pair of strappy high-heeled shoes out of her bag.

'These belong to Aunty Joan,' she explained. 'She used to dance a lot in her younger days and luckily we're the same size.'

'Can you dance, Tressa?'

'Yes,' the girl answered. 'I didn't want to learn but Aunty Joan was so keen on teaching me I didn't have the heart to refuse.'

'Jacka and Joan not coming tonight?'

'No, they usually do but they said they were too tired. Dad isn't very well these days. He gets a lot of indigestion.'

'What a shame,' Laura said. Were the older Daveys making a deliberate withdrawal tonight in the hope Tressa would meet a nice young man? Joan had told her of Jacka's wishes for his daughter. Laura could only marvel that they couldn't see what Andrew's motives were for being so often at the farm. The match was unlikely in many ways and she supposed they could see no further than the ends of their noses. She hoped they wouldn't object if the day ever came when Tressa returned Andrew's love.

The camel coat doesn't matter, Laura thought, looking Tressa up and down one last time as they entered the communal building that was already buzzing with voices and echoing to the strains of 'In The Mood' from the local band. Tressa would be taking the dowdy thing off. There was no doubt that Andrew would notice just how lovely the girl he adored was looking tonight. Laura hoped that the difference in her appearance would make Tressa feel grown-up and feminine and would lead to a change in her feelings towards him. She hoped there wouldn't be any Harry Leans here tonight to spoil things.

The two women were surprised to find Andrew wasn't there waiting for them. Laura expected him to rush forward and press a soft drink into their hands and ask Tressa to dance with him. She didn't have time to ponder on it, Ince claimed her immediately for the next dance and she left Tressa with Roslyn Farrow.

'You look lovely, Tressa,' Roslyn said with a glint in her mischievous eyes. 'Your father might regret staying at home and not keeping an eye on the admirers you'll draw tonight.'

Tressa smiled ruefully as she held Andrew's cigarette lighter – he'd left it in Little Cot. She was searching through the faces in the crowd. 'There's quite a few people here already.'

'Yes, we should raise a goodly sum towards the church and school funds. There are a few faces missing. Only Mr Roach has come tonight. I'm afraid both Marianne and Mrs Roach are poorly with colds. It's lovely to have Johnny Prouse with us although I'll have to watch that he doesn't dance too much and tire himself out.'

'Who's this young lady you're talking to, my dear?' Kinsley Farrow enthused jovially as he drew near to them. 'Good Lord! Tressa! You look a real treat, doesn't she, dear?'

'She does, my love, I was just telling her,' Roslyn smiled, scanning the people and looking for the same man she hoped Tressa was looking for. Thanks to Mike Penhaligon, it was all round Kilgarthen that Andrew Macarthur, that quite nice up-country bloke, was chasing after the almost unapproachable Tressa Davey. Was Tressa all dressed up tonight for him? She had never taken any trouble with her appearance before and she was certainly looking for someone.

It was an hour later when Andrew turned up laughing uproariously with Mike Penhaligon. 'Where have you been?' Laura hissed, tugging on his arm and trying to disengage him from the noisy landlord. 'There's plenty of young men here, some have come from North Hill, Lewannick and all over, and Tressa has been dancing with every one of them.'

Andrew groaned and made to go to Tressa who was being ardently chatted to by a tall good-looking youth in army uniform next to the stage, but Mike yanked him back. 'Leave her guessing, boy. Don't show you're too eager, remember?'

'Mind your own business, Mike,' Laura snapped scornfully, pulling Andrew away from him.

She was outraged the next moment when Mike lifted her hand off Andrew's arm. 'Leave this to us men, m'dear,' he said, winking slyly. 'We know what we're doing.'

'Well, of all the...' Her protests were lost in the hubbub as Ince whisked her away for another dance.

'Just a few minutes,' Andrew insisted to his unasked-for love counsellor. 'The opposition looks too good to risk more than that.'

'That'll be enough to show her, I reckon,' Mike laughed. They were soon joined by a group of men eager to listen to Mike's side-splitting jokes.

Tressa wasn't much interested in the soldier and this time when she looked round the room she spotted Andrew. Their eyes met but instead of leaving the other men and coming over to her, he simply nodded and looked away. She was puzzled and disappointed. This was strange. He was usually so attentive. She had taken his presence on the farm for granted since Christmas and it hadn't been until earlier this evening in Little Cot that she had considered how she felt about having him around her. She didn't find him strange any more. She realised she enjoyed his company. This feeling of disappointment was completely new to her.

She'd been silent for so long, trying to sort out her thoughts, that the soldier got the message and left her standing there alone.

Andrew was heartened to see Tressa was still looking at him. He'd had enough of this 'ignore her' nonsense. He'd go over to her and ask her to dance with him. A sudden surge towards the entrance of the hall by the men around him carried him along with them and the moment was lost. Someone had entered and they were all eager to greet the newcomer. Andrew found himself shaking hands with Sam Beatty.

'I see we're both back in this neck of the woods, Mr Macarthur,' Beatty said, his grin seeming to stretch his horsy face to twice its length. Beatty scanned the gathering. 'I see the charming Mrs Jennings is here. I trust you are both keeping well?'

'We are, thank you, Mr Beatty,' Andrew said a trifle impatiently. 'Would you please excuse me? I've promised this dance to someone special.' Escaping from the group of men and the women now pressing round Sam Beatty, Andrew dodged Ada Prisk who, because she couldn't get close enough to the newcomer, was about to ask him why the other Londoner was back among them.

He was finally at Tressa's side. He didn't care about Mike's advice and blurted out. 'You look absolutely beautiful, Tressa. Would you like to dance with me? I promise you that I dance better than I can push a wheelbarrow.'

—

Andrew drove back to Kilgarthen from Tregorlan Farm thinking the evening could not have worked out better. He wasn't sure if Mike's ploy had worked but Tressa had agreed to dance with him and she had felt soft, warm and pliable in his arms. She had even looked into his eyes for a moment and made a mild compliment on how he looked in his suit. He was grateful to Joan for teaching her to dance but he was surprised she could also jitterbug. If the villagers thought he was a show-off as he gyrated round the floor with her, he couldn't have cared less.

It had been arranged that Ince Polkinghorne would drive Tressa home, but knowing he would probably want to spend more time with Laura, Andrew had artfully offered to do the job for him; Mike had said he could use his car. When he fetched Tressa's coat, Mike had grinned broadly and given him the 'thumbs up'.

Tressa didn't talk much on the drive home and insisted he did not get out of the car to see her to the door. How he would love to have kissed her goodnight. 'Would you like to come to the pictures with me one evening next week, Tressa?' he asked boldly.

She made him wait for an answer as she picked up the bag containing her other clothes and a pair of shoes which were lying at her feet. 'What's on?'

'I don't know. I'll find out and let you know tomorrow. Does that mean you'll come?'

She looked straight ahead out of the car windscreen rather than at him. 'If it's all right with Dad.'

'Oh good.' He hadn't felt so boyishly excited since his school days. As soon as he got back to the pub he'd dig out a local newspaper and see what was being shown at the nearest cinemas. He wouldn't be able to sleep. He'd be back at Tregorlan Farm at the crack of dawn. He'd help with the work then he'd go to church with the family to make a good impression on Jacka.

He turned off the Tregorlan track into the lane and almost immediately was dazzled by a flashing fight. He slowed down. He saw a man holding a torch, standing astride in the middle of the road flagging him down. 'What's going on here?' Bringing the car to a halt he wound his window down and stuck his head out. 'Are you in trouble?' he called as the man closed in on him.

'Fanks fer stopping, mate,' the man said in a deep throaty voice. Andrew recognised a Cockney accent. 'Me van's skidded into the ditch. Would'ya mind helping me push it out?'

Andrew was mindful of his suit and good shoes but in the mood he was in, he would have walked to the moon for anyone. 'I'd be glad to,' he said, getting out of the car.

'Good on yer, mate. Blimey, yer all togged up. Been out fer a fancy meal, have yer?'

'No, a village dance,' Andrew said, his memories still keeping him warm despite the biting cold night air.

'This won't take long. Me mate's behind the wheel. Wiv a bit of extra muscle, we'll have the van back on the road in a jiffy.'

Andrew strode up to the back of the van and put his hands on the door on the side furthest away from the ditch.

'That's the ticket, Mr Macarfur. Hold it right there.'

How did the man know his name? The next moment Andrew felt something hard being pushed into his back. He turned round and found a gun being shoved into his gut. 'What the...?'

'Nice 'n easy now, Mr Macarfur,' the man said, his voice now taunting and crisped with a menacing edge. 'Be a good bloke and get into the back of the van.'

Andrew was frightened but peered through the darkness to get a good look at his assailant. He was large-framed and wearing a long dark overcoat and a woollen hat pulled down over his ears and forehead. It was difficult to get a good view of his face in the shadows, all he could see were two black slitted eyes and a big nose, but Andrew had a good idea who he was. 'Why?' he forced his voice to sound calm. 'What are you going to do with me?'

'That's my business,' the Cockney rasped, lifting the gun higher until it was level with Andrew's eyes. 'Now don't get me angry. Just do as yer told.'

His aggressor opened the van doors and Andrew was bundled inside.

Chapter 25

Spencer stood on the shore of Polzeath beach on the north coast with his hands rammed in his pockets, staring across the hostile grey surge of the raging Atlantic Ocean. Out in the waters lay the dreaded Doom Bar, the graveyard of many a sailing ship as it had entered the Camel Estuary for Padstow. The harsh east wind and salty air stung his face and he was forced to screw up his eyes to be able to see. He didn't feel the cold which reddened his nose, his tight mouth and the tips of his ears.

He hadn't been here for over five years; in the fifth month of Natalie's pregnancy, they had stood on this spot together, warmed by the hot sun, happily thinking of names for their baby. They had made plans for all their futures together. Natalie had loved this beach, she'd loved the wild rugged coastline with its striking headlands that had withstood the worst of the elements for centuries. She had enjoyed their day out, the last time she'd ever come here.

He could still hardly bring himself to believe that Natalie was dead, gone for ever. Oh, why hadn't she told him the pregnancy could put her life in danger? Why had she left him? Moisture seeped from Spencer's eyes but it had nothing to do with the fierceness of the elements he was facing.

He'd never intended to come here again, but today he'd felt he had to get away from the farm and had ended up here. Was he searching for that long-lost happiness? He'd wanted to get away from Ince's obvious happiness at having a close and growing relationship with the beautiful widow. The beautiful widow, that was how he referred to Laura Jennings in his mind. He couldn't say her last name, it belonged to the repugnant man who had once hurt his beloved wife so much.

Worst of all, he'd had to get away from the little girl who was the only reason he kept going. He couldn't face the questions on her sweet face, knowing he couldn't answer them. Why was he so grumpy with her? Why was he being horrible at times to Uncle Ince? Why couldn't she see Laura and Benjy? He'd asked Ince to look after Vicki for the day and take her to the Methodist chapel with him then go on to Daisy's for dinner. Being the good friend he was, Ince had complied without asking questions and Spencer had told him he had no idea when he'd be back.

He hadn't invited Barney to come with him but the dog had leaped into the car and he couldn't be bothered to order him out. Barney liked it here. He was racing hither and thither across the beach, enjoying the different environment, stopping every now and again to sniff at a piece of driftwood or seaweed or the remains of a gull. As if he sensed his master's melancholy, every now and then he glanced anxiously at him. Spencer found his devotion and carefree spirit a comfort.

The tide was rolling in, surging forward on long gigantic breakers, thundering and tossing up white lacy spray, getting closer and closer to his feet. He watched the sea without feeling, and for one terrible moment he wanted to stay here and let it wash over him, to let the waves get higher and deeper and sweep him out to sea. He wanted to end it all. Blot out the pain, blot out his terrible aching loss.

But he couldn't do that to Vicki. He couldn't do that to Ince. He knew what it meant to live with your heart breaking; they didn't deserve that. He knew he had to pull himself together. If he truly loved Vicki in the way he should, he must let her mother rest in peace, and for Vicki's sake seek peace for his own soul. He must care for his beautiful innocent daughter like other people did. She was dependent on him. Ince loved her as if she was his own child. Daisy and Bunty loved her as if they were grandmothers to her, and her real grandmother loved her from afar and had suffered needlessly because of him.

And Laura cared for her. He could say her first name now he had admitted that. She had cared enough to tell him what he was doing to Vicki and Felicity, to point out what he was cruelly denying them. He was shot through with painful guilt when he pictured how Laura had recoiled from him when he'd hurled abuse at her in her own home, he could feel her shock and distress. He had a lot to put right. He must find the strength from somewhere to do it.

With the roar of the ocean pounding in his ears, he didn't hear a warning bark from Barney and he found his feet in two inches of cold water. He moved backwards quickly then walked on, heading for the lichen-covered, purple and grey rocks at the foot of the cliff. The wind had risen and Spencer had not realised that it was sweeping off the top layers of sand all the way back to the road. He was covered in a film of fine yellow grains. He rubbed a hand down over his face to loosen the stiffness his grief and the cold had made. Barney trotted loyally at his side.

You've been useless, Spencer chided himself, weak-willed and spineless, taking out your grief and bad temper on your daughter, friend and two innocent women. You've caused them all a lot of pain.

That's half the battle in life, Natalie's voice echoed inside his head, *realising your faults. The hard part is doing something about them, and only you can do that.* She had always been a sensible woman.

I will do something, Spencer promised her memory. The best I can for Vicki in the future, and I'll apologise to Ince and some day I'll put things right with the others. He was glad he had come to Polzeath. He should have done it years ago, instead of shutting himself away and brooding on the farm. He sat down on the rocks. He'd stay here for a while, alone with Natalie one last time. Then he'd leave and with the love of those who cared for him he'd stop looking back.

–

Laura hadn't gone to the Sunday morning service so she slipped across the road for evensong. Afterwards she collared Jacka in the porch before he rushed home like the few other worshippers who had turned out on the bitterly cold evening. She was fishing for news of how Andrew and Tressa might be getting on and whether Jacka had realised himself yet that anything romantic was afoot.

'Andrew must have been keen to work for you today, Jacka. Mike told me he must have slept at the farm last night and forgot to tell him of the arrangement.'

'Eh?' Jacka said, scratching his head before putting on his hat. 'We haven't seen un today. Tressa's a bit puzzled. He said t'she last night he'd be over in the morning as usual.'

'Where on earth is he then?' A niggle of worry chewed at Laura's insides. 'He'd only be at the pub or on the farm. He wouldn't have suddenly gone back to London without telling me, and besides, his things are still at pub. He took Tressa home in Mike's car last night, did you see any sign of it on the road?'

'No,' Jacka replied, his face suddenly twisting up. He tapped his chest as a spasm of pain caught him there. 'Strange, isn't it?'

'What's strange?' Kinsley Farrow, always quick to hone in on problems and worries, asked from behind them, nudging Laura's arm. 'Nothing wrong, is there?'

'It's unlikely to be anything to worry about, Vicar,' she answered, but her worry was growing into the first prickling sensations of real fear. What was Andrew playing at? This was so unlike him. 'It's just that Andrew Macarthur seems to have disappeared overnight. He was supposed to go to Tregorlan Farm this morning but didn't turn up and the Penhaligons said he didn't return to the pub last night.'

'So no one's seen him since he took Tressa home after the dance? He's frightfully keen on her, of course. Do you think she could have told him she's not interested or something and he's gone off somewhere to lick his wounds?'

'What are 'ee talking about? Are you two saying that Andrew's been after my maid?' The astonished farmer glared at the red-faced vicar then confronted Laura for an explanation.

'He hasn't done anything he shouldn't have, Jacka,' she reassured him hastily. 'He's fallen in love with Tressa and has been very honourable about it. He's been working on the farm hoping that she'll notice him as more than a casual labourer and one day soon will return his feelings.'

''Pon my soul!' Jacka exclaimed, looking as if he needed to sit down. 'That's been happening under my very nose and I never realised it!'

'You don't mind, do you?' asked Laura anxiously, taking him by the arm because he looked rather faint.

'Well, I… I don't know. Flipping heck – sorry, Vicar.'

'Perhaps we could think about that a little later,' Kinsley said seriously. 'For now we ought to find out where Mr Macarthur has got to. I'll dive into the vestry and get rid of my vestments then I'll go to the pub and ask the Penhaligons if he's come back. Laura, I suggest you ring someone in London and find out if he's been in touch there.'

'What shall I do?' Jacka said, his concern for Andrew's disappearance resurfacing.

'You go home and see if he's there. If he is, then tell him to let us know he's safe and well,' Laura said. 'I'll ring London from Aunty Daisy's and talk to her. You never know, Andrew might have said something to her. I'll come to you in the pub, Vicar.'

Daisy was as concerned as Laura when John Walmesley told them over the telephone from London that Andrew had not been in touch with him or their other partner and that they had agreed to him having indefinite leave in Cornwall 'until he had sorted something out that was on his mind'. Trying not to feel panicky and dramatise something that probably had a simple explanation, the two women rushed down the hill to the Tremewan Arms.

'He's not been back here,' Pat said, meeting them in the hall. 'His room's been left exactly how it was when he got ready for the dance.'

'So he must still be wearing his suit,' Laura said, her stomach knotting up with worry. 'Did he take his overcoat?'

'No,' Mike said, holding up the garment in his huge paw. ''Tis here.'

'But I don't understand,' Laura murmured, trying to keep a grip on herself. 'Surely when he left Tressa he would have driven straight back here? He wouldn't have just gone off somewhere else.'

'Well, he might have had a reason for going somewhere else,' Kinsley said. 'We could get in touch with PC Geach and ring the hospital just in case he's had an accident. Then all we can do is sit tight and wait until he turns up.'

'I could ask Mr Beatty if he's seen him or if Andrew said anything to him, but he's out at the moment. He didn't say where he was going. We'll just have to wait till he gets back,' Pat said.

'If we learn nothing from the phone calls, I'm going over to Tregorlan Farm to talk to Tressa,' Laura said, turning to Daisy and holding her hand for support. 'She was the last one to see him, apparently. Perhaps she can throw some light on what might have happened.'

–

The moment Jacka got home he called Tressa down from her room where she was half-heartedly reading a cowboy book. She was in a bad mood. She had been disappointed when Andrew had failed to turn up this morning, then angry, then she had got moody and retreated back into her own private little world where nothing could disturb her. She had been looking forward to going to the pictures; she had only been twice in her life before. She had got used to Andrew's company, used to the way he kept looking at her. Having lost the brothers she'd idolised, it was good to have a friend after all these years. She tossed the book aside and got off her bed. What did her father want? He sounded vexed. Had she done something to upset Andrew and was to be torn off another strip? She had done nothing wrong as far as she could see. She would refuse to trip off to the village tonight and make another apology.

'What's up, Dad?' she said, going into the kitchen. She was concerned at the awful grey colour of his face and went to him in his chair by the fire. Kissing his cheek, she crouched before him. 'You don't look well. Are you feeling poorly again?'

'That's only the cold air,' Jacka shrugged off the concern for his health. He included Joan in his next sentence. 'Have either of 'ee seen Andrew Macarthur since I've been t'church?'

'No,' Joan answered, pausing over the mug of tea she was pouring out for her brother. 'Nothing wrong, is there?'

'Well, seems he didn't go back to the pub to sleep last night and then he didn't turn up here this morning. Laura Jennings is worried about un. Did he say anything to you when he dropped you off last night, Tressa?'

'Like what?' the girl frowned.

'Like whether he had plans to spend the night somewhere else.'

'No. He asked me if I'd like to go to the pictures with him and said he'd tell me tomorrow, meaning today, what films were being shown.'

Jacka clasped Tressa's hands tightly in his and looked searchingly into her dark eyes. 'And what did you say t'he?'

Tressa's heart gave a queer leap. Her father had never looked at her in this way before, coolly serious and somehow accusing. Feeling very embarrassed, she replied, 'I said I'd like to go, if it was all right with you, of course.'

'Well, it isn't!' Jacka growled, tightening the grip on her hands so she couldn't wriggle free. 'I reckon I know where he's gone. After some tart somewhere to get what he can't from a decent girl. Men like he who live in the big cities and've got fancy jobs are always up to that sort of thing.' His eyes narrowed. 'Has he ever tried to touch you or kiss you?'

'No! Not ever,' Tressa raised her voice and managed to wrench her hands away. She beat a hasty retreat to the other side of the room. 'What a horrible thing to say about someone who's been so kind and helpful to us. Andrew's not like that. He's a decent man, I know it!'

'How could you know anything about men?' Jacka scoffed, getting angry. 'You're either working or got your head stuck in a bleddy book! I can see what he's up to now. He's out to seduce you. That's what all his help was for. To get inside your drawers!'

'Jacka!' Joan cried.

'You're disgusting, Dad,' Tressa shouted, hurling her arms about in the air. 'I may not know much about men but I know the difference between one like Harry Lean and Andrew!' Bursting into tears, she ran from the room, the first time she had done so in her life.

A short time later she was called down from her room again and had to relate her last few words with Andrew to an extremely anxious Laura who had arrived with Daisy, Mike and Kinsley Farrow.

'So as far as you can see there was no reason why Andrew wouldn't have gone back to the pub?' Laura repeated again, trying to get the facts as clear as possible in her mind.

'No, I've told you. I'm sure he intended on going straight there,' Tressa said tetchily, giving her father an unfriendly glance as her own worry for Andrew rose.

'And he was in a good frame of mind?' Kinsley asked.

Laura sighed impatiently. As Tressa had agreed to go out with him, he must have been deliriously happy. She sensed the friction between Tressa and Jacka. If it had anything to do with Andrew, she wanted to know. 'Is everything all right here?' she asked.

'Just my old trouble, a spot of indigestion,' Jacka explained.

''Tis about time you saw the doctor about that,' Mike said, recalling the many times he had seen Jacka massaging his chest in the pub.

'It would help if I didn't have so much worry,' Jacka said under his breath, but everyone heard it. Tressa tossed her head impatiently; all except she and Joan thought he was referring to his financial worries.

'Why don't you call down to the surgery on Wednesday?' Daisy said, smiling to lift the mantle of gloom that had settled in the room. 'Just to be on the safe side. Well, we'd better get back, leave you to the rest of the evening.'

'You'll let us know if he turns up?' Joan said as the visitors shuffled towards the door. 'Just to stop us worrying.'

'Aye, we'd like to know that,' Jacka said, his face grim.

In the last of the lantern light before the door was closed on them, Laura shot Kinsley a hostile look and he turned his head away guiltily. Thanks to him blabbing about Andrew's feelings about Tressa, Jacka's attitude towards Andrew had changed. He probably thought that only a local man was suitable as a husband for Tressa. Wherever Andrew was, if the girl of his dreams returned his love, he now had another hurdle to breach.

Laura couldn't bring herself to go to bed and after assuring the others that she'd be all right on her own, she sat by the fire. At midnight there was a knock on Little Cot's door. She rushed to open it. 'Andrew?' She was disturbed to see two burly men in dark overcoats standing there. 'Have... have you come about Andrew Macarthur?'

'That's right, Mrs Jennings,' one of the men said. 'Can we come in?'

She stepped back. 'Yes, of course.' With her heart thumping in fear, she asked timidly, 'Are you from the police?'

'No,' the man who had spoken before replied. He stretched out a thick hand marbled with prominent veins on which the word HATE was tattooed in capital letters.

Laura was about to shake his hand but snatched hers back. She regretted allowing these two men into her home. There was something terribly wrong here.

Her heart sank and she began to tremble when she heard the words, 'I'm Vic Morrison and my friend and I are here on behalf of myself and my brother Archie.'

'What have you done with Andrew?' Laura squeaked. She was terrified. Even before Andrew had mentioned the Morrison brothers in connection with Bill, she'd known they were vicious criminals, both having been in prison more than once.

'I'm glad you're quick on the uptake, Mrs Jennings. He'll be quite safe as long as we can successfully complete a little bit of business with you.' Vic Morrison took off his hat and revealed an almost bald head. His nose was crooked, having been broken in two places, and a dark stubble adorned his wide jaw. Although the other man had been introduced as a friend, he shared similar features. They both looked hard, determined and deadly serious. Their broad shoulders were held back, their fists curled into balls. The coats on their backs were expensive cashmere, their shoes snakeskin, and the cigarette lighter Vic Morrison took out of an inside pocket was solid gold.

'I-I'll do anything you say, just don't hurt Andrew,' Laura gasped, her eyes filling with tears.

The other man took her arm and led her to a chair at the table. Vic Morrison slowly lit a cigarette then bent forward and put his brutal face a breath away from hers. He reeked of an intoxicating aftershave. 'I'll tell you why we're here and put you out of your misery. Your late hubby owes us some money. Five thousand notes, to be exact.'

'B-but my solicitors looked into your claim and they said he didn't owe you that sum of money.'

266

Vic Morrison put a heavy hand on her shoulder, making Laura cringe away from him. 'It had nothing to do with his dealings with your father's company, this was borrowed as a personal loan. He liked to try his hand at the dogs. Now Billy-boy promised us he would pay back every penny. That's why we're here, Mrs Jennings. We've come to collect it off you.'

Laura couldn't think straight. She was nearly out of her mind with fear. 'B-but Bill bankrupted the company. I've only got a little money in the bank. You can have that. Take anything you want but please don't hurt Andrew and let him go.'

'You've got more than that.' Vic Morrison put his hand over her chin and squeezed tightly, making her lips purse. He blew smoke into her eyes. 'You've got this cottage. It's all done up nice and modern. The sale should bring in two or three thousand, then you'll just have to come up with the rest somehow. You see, we have a policy of collecting every penny we're owed.'

'I-I haven't got that sort of money,' she wailed. 'What will you do with Andrew?' Vic Morrison took his hand away and drew a line across his throat and gave a horrible laugh. He brought the hand back to clutch Laura's throat but she grabbed at it. She had remembered something that could be Andrew's salvation. 'Wait! I have some jewellery. It was my grandmother's. I know it's worth a lot of money, over five thousand pounds, my father told me that years ago. It must be worth a lot more now. You can have it, all of it. It's kept in a bank vault in London. I have the code word needed for access to it. I'll phone Andrew's partner and authorise him to collect it and hand it over to your brother. Now please will you let Andrew go?'

'That's better,' Vic Morrison said in a sugary-sweet voice, patting her cheek and making her blink and his friend guffaw like an idiot. 'You can write me out a nice little official document saying you're willingly handing over the full value of the jewellery as repayment of your husband's loan. We don't want any trouble with the cops now, do we? Accusing us of making you do something under threat, if you get my meaning.'

Laura wrote the letter on Bill's headed stationery. Her hands were shaking and it took three attempts before Vic Morrison was satisfied.

After she'd addressed the envelope to the Morrisons' legal representatives, he sealed it and made Laura jump out of her skin by tapping it on her shoulder. 'Thank you for a nice little piece of business, Mrs Jennings. Do you know, looking at you makes me wonder why old Billy-boy ever played away.' He signalled to his crony and they made for the door.

'Wait!' Laura flew after them. 'What about Andrew?'

'Don't worry, you'll see him again, after we've got the jewellery.' Vic Morrison winked a hooded eye. 'You understand we have to be sure it actually exists. Now you be a good girl and go to bed and have a good night's sleep. If you want to see your friend again, don't be foolish enough to contact the Old Bill. You can't prove anything anyway. And if at any other time you ever think about reporting what's happened, we can always get Macarthur, you or someone else you care about later. Think about it, Mrs Jennings. Goodnight.'

When they had gone, Laura locked the door then crept back to the armchair by the fireplace and curled herself up in it. She prayed fervently for Andrew's safety. It chilled her to the marrow to think that those dangerous villains must have been in the village last night, watching Andrew's movements and waiting for the opportunity to abduct him. Where was he now? Where were they keeping him prisoner? Had they hurt him? She didn't dwell on the possibility that they might already have killed him; she didn't doubt that they would if their orders weren't followed to the letter.

She couldn't go to the police but should she tell someone? Perhaps Mike Penhaligon. He was a noisy, jolly individual but strong-minded and sensible and could be trusted not to do anything that would risk Andrew's life. How would Tressa react if she knew Andrew was being kept prisoner by one of the most brutal firm of villains in South London? Had she allowed Andrew to kiss her last night? Had she been disappointed when he hadn't turned up on the farm as expected? They were small details in comparison to the danger Andrew was in but it helped her to feel less shocked and afraid as she drifted over them.

A few minutes passed while she tried to make up her mind what to do when there was another knock at the door. Her flesh leapt and her eyes opened wide with alarm. Had Vic Morrison and his crony come back? If so, why? Clutching her arms about herself, she went to the door and called out feebly, 'Who's there?'

'It's us, me and Pat,' returned Mike Penhaligon in a hissing whisper. 'We've got Sam Beatty with us. Let us in, Laura, it could be important.'

What on earth could Sam Beatty want with her? Could he throw some light on when and where Andrew had been forcibly taken? She let them in and at once the trio could see there was something wrong.

'What's happened, Mrs Jennings? Has it got something to do with the Morrison brothers? Have you have an unwelcome visit since you last saw Mike and Pat?'

Laura looked in amazement at Sam Beatty who had spoken. 'Why?' she asked. 'Did you have something to do with it? If you've hurt Andrew I'll… I'll…' She was shaking from head to foot.

'Hush now,' Pat said, moving to her and rubbing her back as if she was a small child needing comfort. 'Mr Beatty is a policeman, come down all the way from London. He's here to help.'

'Detective Sergeant Sam Beatty,' he said, showing Laura his badge. 'I suggest you sit down and tell me what's happened.'

Laura felt frightened and relieved. Frightened that a policeman was involved now but relieved that he didn't seem to be about to call in the local police and cause a fuss in the village. She related what had occurred between her and the two villains. 'How do you fit into this?' she asked Beatty at the end. 'I take it this has something to do with the reason why you're in Kilgarthen at all and seemingly snooping around. I thought you were taking a rather close interest in me.'

'We've known a long time in the force that your late husband was involved up to his neck with Vic and Archie Morrison. You probably don't need me to tell you what a nasty pair the Morrisons are. We're eager to get them out of circulation. It was a long shot but I was sent down here to see if they had something on Bill Jennings and made any illegal approaches to you. If you will stand up in court and testify they threatened you and admitted kidnapping Andrew Macarthur, it could mean a long stretch for Vic at least.'

'I'll do nothing of the sort!' Laura snapped vehemently. 'It'll put Andrew or perhaps someone else I care for in danger.' She was thinking of Vicki in particular and hoped the Morrisons had no idea how she felt about the little girl. 'All I want is for Andrew to be safe. And don't you dare call in any more police! I shall deny that Vic Morrison and the other man were ever here.'

'There's no need to get more alarmed, Mrs Jennings,' Sam Beatty said soothingly. 'It's only courtesy to let the local police know when you're working on their patch. I'll have to inform them but I'll think they'll agree with me that they can't do anything more than keep an eye open for possible places where Macarthur is being hidden. I shall inform my superiors that you'll be phoning Macarthur's partner tomorrow morning and that they mustn't stop the Morrisons from being handed the jewellery. Of course you are at liberty to give your property to whom you wish. We may be able to get that back for you somehow at a later date. But I shall have to insist on being with you when you make that call.'

'If nothing goes wrong, when do you think they'll let Andrew go?' Laura asked fearfully.

'I'm afraid your guess is as good as mine, but I must warn you that they've done this sort of thing before and the victim hasn't survived. They're very careful not to leave witnesses to their kidnappings. It's difficult to prove anything against them these days. They've learned a lot from the times they were caught and jailed.'

'Oh, dear God, no! Oh, Andrew.' Laura collapsed in tears.

Pat held her as she sobbed. She was fighting back tears herself. 'We'll take her to the pub. It wouldn't do if anyone called on her tomorrow and sees her like this.' Her coat was put over her shoulders and Laura allowed herself to be bundled across the road.

Chapter 26

Laura sat up in the pub's sitting room all night with Pat, hoping and praying that Andrew would turn the key to the outer door and walk in. It seemed ages ago that she had come into this room with Spencer and he'd asked her to tea at Rosemerryn Farm for Vicki's sake. She had thought about Ince, but when Pat tactfully asked her if she wanted him there, Laura had shaken her head, saying that the fewer people who knew of Andrew's predicament the better. She didn't need Ince to be with her. It would have been good to see his comforting face but nothing more.

Knowing that John Walmesley got into the office early, Laura rang him on the pub telephone at eight thirty sharp. He was astounded to find himself in the company of two of Sam Beatty's colleagues and listened amazed as he took down her instructions as to what he was to do with her grandmother's jewellery; Laura told him he had full authority to act on her behalf in London in her absence. Before she rang off, she pleaded with him to follow her instructions to the letter. Hopefully soon, and please God the London police did nothing to intervene, her grandmother's jewellery would be in the Morrisons' possession and word would be sent to Cornwall to release Andrew unharmed.

It was decided that if there was no sign of Andrew by midday, word would be put about the village that he had disappeared, suspected of being lost on the moor. The locals would be encouraged to join in a search for him in case he hadn't been taken far away, or had been released and was trying to walk back to Kilgarthen. Laura went home to wait until then. To her growing horror, it began to snow.

Tressa banged on her door just before midday when Laura and Sam Beatty were about to walk through the village and ask the neighbours to search for Andrew. Before the snow could settle, Mike Penhaligon had already cycled to Rosemerryn Farm to ask Spencer to go round all the other outlying farms on his horse which was used to hard weather conditions. Tressa had trudged through the snow which was now thickly covering the ground.

'Is there any word?' she asked, lifting off the large woolly hat she had pulled down over her ears.

'Afraid not,' Laura said mournfully. 'Not even of Mike's car.' She invited Tressa inside for a few minutes, and because of the way Andrew loved her, his reason for being in Kilgarthen, Laura told her the truth behind the mystery of his disappearance.

Tressa was shattered. She went as white as the snow. 'I don't believe it. Things like that don't happen round here.'

'I'm afraid I brought the trouble with me,' Laura said. 'Are you going to help in the search, Tressa? The wretched snow has limited the places where we can go,' she added in despair.

'Don't worry,' Tressa said firmly.

'Ask people if they've seen anyone or anything unfamiliar or strange lately,' Sam Beatty said to Tressa as they stood on the doorstep. 'Even the most insignificant thing might help.'

The situation seemed incredible to Tressa and she wished things were as they normally were. What had happened was not like some adventure in her imagination or the boys' comics and library books she read. Life was showing it had an impossibly cruel and terrifying side to it. 'There's lots of abandoned places on the moor. I'll check them out. Thank goodness the wind hasn't blown the snow into drifts. We could really be in trouble otherwise.'

'I want to go with you,' Laura said earnestly. It had been harrowing just waiting and hoping. She badly needed to do something positive to find Andrew.

'You're not used to the moor, Mrs Jennings,' Sam Beatty pointed out, and she had to admit he was right. 'It will help more if we go round the village. If the road's passable, we'll try to drive to Tregorlan

Farm later.' He turned to Tressa who was tucking her hair in under her hat and looked anxious to get on. 'Miss Davey, I beg you to be very careful. The men who kidnapped Andrew Macarthur are vicious brutes. I'd feel better if you had someone with you.'

Realising good sense was important in this situation, Tressa nodded. 'I'll get my father to come with me.'

Tressa trudged back to Tregorlan Farm as fast as she could. She was almost at the door when she remembered the cigarette packet she had seen at Reddacoombe Farm with Andrew. She ran into the kitchen without taking off her boots, shouting as she went, making Meg bark and jump about in excitement. 'Aunty Joan! I need to get Dad! It's very important!'

There was no one in the kitchen and she was dismayed to find a scribbled note left on the table: 'Tressa. Helping Jacka with a cow that's fallen in the snow. We're in the top field.' The top field was the one nearest to the moor and although it wouldn't have taken her long to get there, she couldn't ask her father to abandon the welfare of the animal. She felt guilty about not going to help him and Joan but they had brought most of the stock next to the farmyard and laid out plenty of straw for fodder. Andrew could be in mortal danger and might need her more than the cattle.

She turned the scrap of paper over and wrote a note of her own: 'Andrew *kidnapped*. Could be at Reddacoombe. Gone to look. Tressa.' She jotted down the time: 12.45. If she was away for an unusually long time, Joan or Jacka would come looking for her. There was hot water in the kettle and she speedily poured some into a flask, adding lots of sugar from their precious supply. She stuffed one of her brothers' scarves, a hat and a pair of gloves into the army bag, took the tin tray off the dresser and tucked it in under her coat, then ordering Meg to stay put, she set off across the moor.

The going over the uneven ground was extremely tough. There wasn't so much snow on the open moor; the wind which made her eyes sting and water and reddened her nose had swept it clean in parts like a giant broom and the surface was ribbed and streaked. But where the snow was thick, it had disguised well-known landmarks, transforming each familiar patch of heather and boulder, packing into the pits and depressions. Strange shapes were wrought by the skirling wind, making her unsure where it was safe to place her feet. Her progress was slow.

Her breath produced clouds of vapour in front of her. Her lips felt as if they were cracking. From time to time, her feet sank deeply into the snow and she had to put both hands on the top of her boots to pull them out. The force of the elements and her struggles took all her effort. Halfway up the incline, she was painfully out of breath. Her chest hurt, her lungs heaved. She was forced to stop and breathe in through her nose and regain some strength.

She clawed the last few feet to the top of the hill and Reddacoombe Farm was visible, apparently deserted, in the valley below. The buildings were layered in sparkling white snow and there was no sign of anyone there. It was here that the tin tray came in useful. Tressa sat on it, intending to sleigh down the hill on it in the same way she had done with her brothers. She had a bumpy ride until she was about halfway down, then the tray slewed sideways out from under her hands and bottom, skidding away from her while she was sent into a crazy tumble. She came to a halt flat on her face, the breath knocked out of her. She was angry with herself for the delay and clambered to her feet, panting and coughing. Shaking the snow off her face and clothes, she ignored it where it filled the top of her boots and wet her legs. She started off again, plodding carefully all the way down to the bottom so as not to risk another fall and waste more time.

Remembering Sam Beatty's warning, she stood quietly on the outskirts of the farm and gazed all around. It looked empty, devoid of all life. As she got nearer to the buildings, she saw no footprints or anything else that would suggest anyone was here or had been here. She looked cautiously into all the outhouses but found nothing. There was only the farmhouse left.

The door rocked on its one remaining hinge as she pushed her way in. It looked the same as it always did. She was afraid, afraid Andrew wouldn't be here and afraid his body was.

She called out softly, 'Andrew.' She listened but there were no sounds except for the ominous shrieking of the wind which was steadily picking up in strength and volume. She crept through the room, her flesh prickling, filled with a horrible sensation that someone would suddenly leap out on her.

Moving into the other room, her heart missed a beat and her breath quickened. Her eyes were drawn immediately to the old smuggler's hide dug out of the floor. Something was down there which hadn't been there a few days ago. Something bulky and still, covered with a piece of dark cloth. Tressa tore the curtains off the window to let in more light. She looked again. The shape was large enough to be a man lying curled up. With fear growing inside her, she moved to the edge of the broken floor and carefully lowered herself down beside the shape.

Her heart hammered as she reached out and took a handful of the black cloth. She could draw on none of the bravado of her storybook heroes, this was real and terrifying, and she was facing it alone.

With one sharp movement she yanked the cloth away from the shape and screamed at the top of her voice. 'Andrew!'

She fell on her knees beside him. He was lying on his side, his knees drawn up, his chin lowered towards his knees. His hands were tied behind him. There was blood on his sandy hair and a gag round his mouth. 'Please don't be dead,' she cried, shaking uncontrollably. 'Please don't let me be too late.'

Gently she pushed her hand in under his head and turned it so she could see his face. He felt cold. His eyes were closed and there were bruises on his cheeks and brow. She shook him. 'Andrew!' There was no response. She pulled at the knot at the back of his head, undid the gag and pulled it away. Then putting her arms round the top of his body, she heaved him into a sitting position. He half slid back to the floor. Gritting her teeth, she tugged him up straight again and pulled his body forward and rested his head against her chest. He felt horribly limp. She felt for a pulse in his neck but could feel only cold skin. She pushed her hand down the back of his shirt but he was cold there too.

'Andrew, move.' She shook him and his head flopped about. 'For goodness sake, move!'

Lying him down again, she undid his suit buttons, her hands clumsy with trembling nerves, then laid her head on his chest. She listened for a heartbeat. Before she could settle her head to concentrate, his body twitched. She cried in joy. 'Andrew, don't give up. I'm here, it's Tressa.'

She set to work rapidly to release his hands; the string was knotted so tightly she had to use her penknife to cut through it. She pulled him to a sitting position again and holding him against her, she rubbed his back. The piece of cloth that had been covering him was thin crepe but it was better than nothing. She wrapped it round his shoulders. Then she started rubbing at his icy hands. His head was resting on her shoulder and he lifted it a tiny bit.

'Andrew, Andrew,' she called loudly to try to break into the recesses of his semi-conscious mind. 'Come round, Andrew. Open your eyes. Say something. Come on, Andrew, you can do it. Try, Try.'

She held his face between her hands and rubbed his cheeks over the bruises. His eyes twitched and blinked and for a moment he opened them. 'Come on, Andrew, wake up. It's Tressa. I've come for you. Wake up, Andrew, wake up.'

'Tr-tress…'

'That's right, Andrew,' she encouraged in his ear, her heart surging with hope. He began to shiver and she knew that was a good sign. 'Try again. It's Tressa. Say my name again.'

His face contorted and he opened his eyes. She stared into their blueness. His chin trembled. 'Tressa… you really here?'

'Yes, Andrew, I'm really here. You have to try to move. Get your circulation going again. I've got to get you away from here.' It was a very real fear. Despite the weather, there was a possibility the villains would come back and this time they might kill them both; and the snow and wind were getting fiercer. 'Keep talking to me.'

She rubbed at his limbs, desperate to get some feeling back into them for him. As she worked he spoke to her in short broken sentences. 'Afraid… I wouldn't see… you again.' Resting him against herself, she opened the army bag. She took out the scarf and wound it round his neck then pulled the woolly hat down over his head. 'Tressa… so cold.'

His hands were like blocks of ice. Opening her coat, she pulled the layers of top clothes out of her trousers. 'I'm going to try to warm your hands, Andrew. I want you to try to rub them over my back.'

Despite his plight, he seemed horrified. 'Make you c-cold.'

'Don't worry about that. Your hands have been tied up, probably for hours, you don't want to lose them for good.' Holding his wrists, she pushed his hands inside her clothes and round her body and encouraged him to hug her close.

He had longed for this and through the mists slowly fading from his brain, he obeyed her command happily, but he couldn't feel where he was touching her and he was unaware of her flinching at his icy contact with her skin. After a while she pulled his hands out and rubbed them vigorously between hers. 'You're going to be all right, Andrew.'

'Of course... couldn't leave without telling... I love you.'

She stopped her ministrations for a moment. She stared at him wide-eyed. Could it be true? Or was his mind rambling? No time to think about that now. She had to get him out of this pit and somehow back to the farm and warmth and safety. She put the spare pair of gloves on his hands and then held a flask cup of sweet hot water to his lips and managed to get him to take a few sips. Then she drank some herself; she needed all the strength she could get.

Andrew was quite lucid now and he was aware of the dangers they were both in. He couldn't control his shivering and although it was extremely unpleasant, like Tressa he knew it meant he had some life flowing through his frozen body. He knew he must have been very close to death when she'd found him. Before that he'd known only the terrible coldness and darkness and he had been drifting into the first throes of hypothermia. Her courage and determination gave him the strength to fight for his life and not to risk hers.

She got him to his knees and he made a supreme effort not to crumple back to the floor. It was agony, it tore and burnt at every nerve in his body but he wouldn't give up with Tressa here helping him.

Keeping a grip on him, Tressa scrambled out of the smuggler's hide and laid the top part of his body over the edge of the stone floor. She knew every tiny movement was painful for him but it had to be done if he was going to come out of this alive. She lay on the floor and reaching down took hold of his trouser waistband with both hands. Then she pulled with all her might. He could do nothing to help her. She tugged and strained and her lungs felt they were bursting and her back about to break, but bit by bit she hauled him out of the hide until he was lying in a heap beside her.

She gasped in much-needed air, praying she hadn't damaged herself and would be unable to carry on with the rescue. She had lost track of time and hoped her father or aunt would soon find her note and come to her aid.

With a tremendous effort, Andrew moved his arm and laid it over her. 'Tressa... you all right?'

She turned to lie on her side and face him. She was able to smile although she felt as if her whole body had been racked. 'Yes. We'll carry on in a minute.'

She took a few more deep breaths and got up on her knees, then she lifted him up so she could put her arms round his chest from behind. A few inches at a time, she dragged him along the floor until he was in the main room of the farmhouse. She propped him up against the wall and wrapped the black cloth round him. She went to fetch the threadbare curtains from the other room to help keep him warm and spotted the mysterious cigarette packet on the floor. She picked it up and put it into her pocket.

'You c-can't drag me... back to the farm,' he got out through chattering teeth. 'Too much for you... n-never make it.'

She knew he was right. She crouched down in front of him and held his hands. They were the most important parts of his body to keep warm. 'But we have to leave here. Those men might come back.'

'No,' Andrew couldn't shake his head but he thought he did. 'Got what they wanted. Gone back to London... left me to die.'

'Oh, Andrew,' she murmured, stroking his cheek. She looked hopelessly round the farmhouse. 'There's some bits of stick and some rubbish lying about. I could burn my bag but I've got nothing to light a fire with.'

'My lighter,' he said, feeling glad that he could at last help in their desperate situation.

Taking the cigarette lighter from the inside breast pocket of his suit, she dragged him over to the open fireplace. She hastily gathered up the sticks and discarded picnickers' rubbish and managed to light a small fire. Taking out the flask, she put the strings of the canvas bag into the flames. When they were burning she pushed the bag into the body of the fire and it made a good blaze.

'More cheerful,' Andrew muttered gratefully, feeling optimistic and content to be here alone with the woman he loved so much.

'Help will come soon,' Tressa said, huddling in as close to him as possible. 'I left a note for Dad. People are out looking for you but only a few of us know the full story.'

'Is Laura all right? Is she worrying about me?'

'Those men frightened her but didn't hurt her. She's very worried about you.'

'Were you?'

She began rubbing his hands again and lifted his legs to keep his circulation going. 'Of course.'

'Tressa. In case I don't get out of this. Will you do something for me?'

'You're going to be all right. Don't talk like that,' she muttered rather crossly. 'What do you want me to do?'

'Kiss me.'

She looked away and did not reply. It was totally unexpected and made her feel foolish. She was out of her depth where this sort of thing was concerned.

'Just a small kiss will do. Please, Tressa. A small one won't hurt you.'

He was pleading with her and she was acutely embarrassed. But it didn't seem reasonable to refuse his request in the light of his ordeal.

'Oh, very well,' she said tetchily, making an impatient face at him. She put a peck on his cheek but Andrew moved his head before she could move hers away and pressed his lips against hers.

'Thanks,' he smiled happily. 'If I do die then I'll die a contented man.'

'You're not going to die!' she snapped angrily. 'Don't say anything like that again.'

He had the strength to raise his arm and putting it round her, he hugged her closer to him. 'I adore you, Tressa.' This was as good as any place to tell her.

'Don't say things like that.' She felt herself squirming and it was more uncomfortable than feeling so very cold.

'Why not? It's true. You like me a bit, don't you?'

'I–I have to go outside and see if I can find something else to burn, the fire's getting low.'

'Don't make excuses. The fire's fine for a while longer. I love you with all my heart, Tressa. Why do you think I came back? Don't you feel something for me too? Don't I mean anything to you?'

Tressa's face burned and her cold cheeks stung. Andrew raised his hand to her face. What on earth could she say?

How did she feel about him? She wasn't used to examining her innermost feelings. He had spoken of love, the kind of love shared between a man and a woman. She knew nothing of that at all. She had never expected or hoped that she would fall in love and get married like most young women of her age did. She had never had a female friend to talk to about love. Her aunty had never spoken of it. It was never mentioned in the books she read.

'Hello! Tressa!'

The loud voice calling to her from outside made Andrew swear in pure frustration.

'It sounds like Spencer Jeffries,' she said, never feeling more relieved in all her life. She half rose to her feet. 'Hey! Spencer! We're in here!'

She met Spencer at the door. 'Did I hear you say we?' His voice was thick and heavy from the cold. 'Have you found him?'

'Yes, Andrew's alive but very weak. Is there any chance we can get him back to the farm? Could we carry him? It would be very difficult but we could try.'

'No need to carry him,' Spencer said, gazing down at the creaking door. 'We can use my horse to tow him back on that. I called at Tregorlan and saw your note. I didn't wait for Joan or Jacka to come back. I added a postscript to your note and grabbed a blanket to bring with me just in case.'

Moving to Andrew, he placed the blanket round him. 'Don't worry, Macarthur. We'll wrap you up snugly and drag you back like a sick Red Indian.'

Andrew scowled his thanks. He was grateful to be rescued; he and Tressa were in great danger without urgent help, but why couldn't this blasted farmer have arrived just a minute or two later!

Chapter 27

It was almost ten o'clock at night. The snow lay thick on the ground and Kilgarthen was cut off from the rest of the world. Daisy looked down affectionately at Laura's sleeping face. Her strong beauty was marred by hours of tormented thoughts, worry and unbearable strain; fatigue had finally got the better of her. Sam Beatty and Mike had insisted it would be foolhardy to travel to Tregorlan Farm after they'd circulated the news round the village, pointing out they didn't want casualties all over the place, it was best to leave the searching to those experienced on the moor.

The fire was burning low and the log basket almost empty. Piling the last few logs on the embers, Daisy put on her coat, and taking a torch with her, crept outside to fetch some more.

Someone knocked on Little Cot's door and although Laura stirred restlessly in her chair she did not wake up. The door had not been locked, so Andrew could just walk in. The person on the other side waited a few moments then tried the latch. Spencer came straight in and on seeing Laura slumbering by the fire, he went over to her.

He looked down on her face in the same way as Daisy had done, but not with a concerned affection that tore at his heart. He was stunned by how vulnerable she looked, her clear ivory skin pale from her ordeal. She was breathing softly, her shapely body rising and falling gently under a thin blanket. She was gorgeous, with her golden hair falling about her slender shoulders like the fairy princess Vicki compared her to. No wonder Bill Jennings had wanted her as his prize, and Ince was falling in love with her. Spencer was stirred with desire.

He knew she wouldn't be alone and Daisy probably wasn't far away. Not wanting to appear to be a voyeur, although he wanted to carry on feasting his eyes on her, and because it would be cruel to delay the news he had brought with him, he bent over Laura and shook her arm gently.

She woke with a terrible start and sat up straight as a bolt. 'Andrew! Oh, it's you. What do you want?' She was terrified, her blue eyes startled to twice their size. Spencer felt the biggest heel in the world for having hurt her feelings so badly on more than one occasion.

'It's all right,' he said hastily, his hands hovering over her, wanting to touch her in reassurance but knowing it almost certainly wouldn't be welcomed. 'I've come with good news. Macarthur is safe and well and recovering at Tregorlan Farm.'

Laura's body seemed to collapse with relief. Tears sprang to her tired eyes. 'Are you sure he's all right? Is he hurt? Oh, thank God, thank God.' She sobbed with all her heart and Spencer knelt down beside her and held her hands. In her relief she clung to his strength.

'He had been tied up and left for dead at Reddacoombe Farm,' Spencer said quietly. 'Tressa found him. She probably saved his life. When I got there she had lit a fire and got his circulation going. Between the two of us and my horse we dragged him back to Tregorlan on an old door. It was hard work and took a long time but we managed it in the end. It was too dangerous to try to get him to the hospital and the doctor wouldn't have been able to get through the snow. Jacka and I put him in dry clothes, then we wrapped him up warmly and put him to bed in Jacka's sons' room. He's been thumped around a bit and has a nasty bump on his head but I reckon Macarthur's a tough nut, he'll come through. Besides,' he smiled, and passed Laura a hanky from his coat pocket, 'he's got the girl he loves looking after him with all her devotion. Tressa's a strong woman. That's enough to make a man come through any ordeal, eh?'

Laura blew her nose and nodded. 'Th-thank you, Spencer. I've never spent a more miserable time in my life. If anything had happened to him I'd never have forgiven myself because he wouldn't have come to Kilgarthen in the first place if it hadn't been for me.' She looked at him uncertainly, afraid he would suddenly go hostile and cold, but he was looking at her kindly. 'Will you take me over to Tregorlan Farm now, please, Spencer? We could ride double. I must see Andrew. I'm sure Jacka and Joan won't mind if I stayed the night to save you the trouble of bringing me back, and I want to thank Tressa.'

'Of course I'll take you. I'm only sorry I couldn't get here sooner but travelling is slow and I first went back to Rosemerryn to see if Vicki and Ince were all right.'

'And are they?' she smiled wanly.

'They're fine.'

Daisy had been standing in the kitchen doorway and had witnessed most of what had passed between them. She didn't know what had happened to Spencer to give him this new tenderness, especially where Laura was concerned, but she was grateful for it. Her heart quickened when she thought of all the misery Laura had gone through in her young life, so much of it undeservedly, and knowing that she herself had a guilty secret which she was keeping from Laura.

'Well, I've heard the good news,' she said brightly, coming into the front room with an armful of logs, her face all smiles. 'I'll put the kettle on. We'll have to tell Sergeant Beatty Andrew's all right. I expect he'll want to question Andrew.'

'Beatty's a policeman?' Spencer said, shaking his head in surprise. 'What's been going on? I only know part of the story.'

'You and all the village. Ada Prisk's going to have a field day trying to put the pieces together,' Daisy chuckled. 'I'll leave these logs and make us all a hot drink.'

When Daisy was in the kitchen, Laura looked Spencer in the face and risked asking, 'Are you sure Vicki didn't mind you leaving her to come here?'

'Not when I told her it was to stop you from worrying all through the night.' His eyes met hers fully. 'She misses you. When the lanes are clear, you're welcome to come to the farm to see her.'

Laura fought back another flood of tears as a fresh force of emotion caught her unawares. 'Wh-what changed your mind?'

'I've been thinking,' he replied. 'You were right about my over-possessiveness of Vicki being bad for her and I was wrong. Let's leave it at that, shall we?'

She knew she ought not to press him but she couldn't help herself. 'And Felicity?'

'Let me take one step at a time,' he said rather stiffly. 'This doesn't mean you and I are the best of friends. Ince sends you his love, by the way. He wanted to tell you about Macarthur but as I'd been involved, and because I wanted to tell you I feel differently about you seeing Vicki, it was better that I came.' He gazed at Laura with a touch of something she couldn't define at the back of his eyes. 'I'm sure you'd rather it had been Ince.'

'It doesn't matter, as long as Andrew is safe,' she told him. 'If you'll excuse me, I'll help Daisy in the kitchen.'

'Fine,' he said, moving so she could stand up. 'I'll go over to the pub and phone the doctor for advice on Macarthur and tell the Penhaligons and the policeman what's happened. Laura,' he had a sudden thought, 'I know Macarthur was kidnapped. Are you in any kind of danger? Will those thugs come back for him?'

'No, if they hadn't got what they wanted they would have killed Andrew and not left him to die.' She told Spencer the full story. 'Sergeant Beatty said as soon as Andrew's found, the villains in London will be arrested and so will the kidnappers when they get back. Attempted murder will be added to kidnap and extortion and they'll go to prison for a very long time.'

Spencer shook his head slowly in amazement then frowned. 'That's some tale. You're a brave woman. Aren't you worried about what they might do in the future?'

'At first I said I wouldn't testify against them but Sergeant Beatty assured me that the Morrisons wouldn't dare harm me or anyone close to me again because the finger would point straight at them.'

When he left, Laura felt heartened by the concern he'd shown her but she was under no illusions. Spencer had made it plain that he wasn't fully holding out an olive branch but that didn't matter; she wasn't looking to be friends with him. The Morrisons would be brought to justice for their crimes, Andrew was alive and well and she could see Vicki again. After the last harrowing two days, she couldn't have felt happier.

Cecil Roach hadn't been able to sleep but rather than tossing and turning, he welcomed the opportunity to slip away to his attic study. Padding up there in his dressing gown and slippers, he lit a paraffin heater and used a primus stove to make a cup of tea. After he had drunk the tea, he settled down by the light of an oil lantern in his armchair and turned over the pages of his most graphic illegal magazine. His favourite girl was in here, Etta, a big-breasted continental girl who struck poses that would make a gymnast weep. Within moments his body had heated up to fever pitch and he was giving full vent to his feelings. With the first release over, he lay back, leaving himself exposed, to await the next delicious moments at his leisure.

Barbara woke at a more hospitable hour and thankful not to find her husband beside her, she dashed out of bed. She dressed rapidly and was soon preparing breakfast. Tomorrow the new school term started but unless the snow thawed quickly and things returned to normal, the children would not be able to attend and it would mean another day's delay before her vile husband was given the news she and Marianne were dreading having to tell him.

At eight o'clock Marianne came down for breakfast. She was dressed in slacks, which she couldn't zip up at the side, the opening covered with a long thick jumper. She'd always loved the snow and although she was keeping away from people, Barbara knew she would go out in the garden after breakfast to tread through it.

'Where's Father?' Marianne yawned.

'Up in his study,' Barbara replied, putting a soft boiled egg and toasted soldiers in front of her daughter. 'It's quiet, he's probably fallen asleep.'

'Good.'

Barbara didn't reprimand her. They did not want his company. Since Marianne had revealed her pregnancy, mother and daughter had formed a close relationship and actually enjoyed one another's company. Cecil spoiled it with his constant petty criticisms and superior attitude. Both women had thought about how better their lives would be if he dropped dead or was killed in an accident. They hadn't admitted it to each other but they didn't feel guilty that such ideas had passed through their minds, their loathing of him was so great.

Now Marianne had accepted she couldn't dispose of her baby and had felt it moving and growing inside her, she wanted to keep it and Barbara had promised her that she would; somehow she would see her first grandchild grow up. Barbara's half-sister, Marta, a childless young widow who lived at Barnstaple in Devon, might be persuaded to take Marianne in until the child was born. Marta was well off and generous and lived in a large house. She might consider giving Marianne a permanent home and perhaps Barbara could follow her daughter later. Then somehow the two of them and the baby could set up home together. Barbara had never considered leaving Cecil until now but the baby had given her new hope of life without him and his bullying.

But Marianne needed money to get away. She had selfishly spent all her wages and Cecil only gave Barbara enough to buy the groceries and have her hair done. She had never been able to save and there was no one they could ask to borrow money from. Barbara had considered asking Laura to lend her money, knowing it was a terrible cheek but believing Laura would be glad to have the mother of her husband's illegitimate child out of the village. But it was known that the young widow had been left very little money. Doubtless Cecil would throw his wayward daughter out, not wanting her disgrace to become public and embarrass him, but they hoped and prayed he would give her the money to go. They trembled when they thought of the moment when they would tell him. For now they were content to enjoy a chat.

'I hope that Mr Macarthur has been found,' Barbara said, refilling their teacups. 'He seems such a nice man.'

'Yes, it would be a terrible waste, a handsome man like him dying on the moor. You'd think with the experience he must have gained working on Tregorlan Farm he'd have been more careful.'

'Well, even an experienced farmer has been known to get lost half a mile from his own front door in the mist or snow. Ada Prisk says he's after Tressa Davey.'

'Tressa! Tressa? Don't be silly, Mum. She may be pretty but a man like Andrew Macarthur wouldn't be interested in the likes of her.'

Barbara smiled. 'Because you've been staying out of other people's way lately you haven't been keeping up with the gossip, my girl.'

'Tressa Davey's a lucky girl then. Wow! I'd give anything to have a man like him after me.'

Up in his study, Cecil woke up. The paraffin had run out in the heater and he was cold. He moved sluggishly as he covered himself up, put his magazine away in its hiding place, then climbed down the ladder to take a much needed bath. He was in a good mood and was humming 'We'll Gather Lilacs in the Spring' as he passed Marianne's room. The door was ajar and he could see the room was messy, with the bed unmade and clothes strewn about on the floor. He tut-tutted. This would never do. He'd have to have a word with her mother. He went into the room to see just how bad it was.

Clothes and coat hangers were lying on the floor, shoes were all over the place, items of make-up and perfume bottles were strewn higgledy-piggledy on the dressing table. Lipstick had stained the lace runner. Hair was clogging up the hairbrush. On the bedside table books were stacked in a tall untidy pile. Cecil swiped each one off the pile. What trash! Ridiculous titles. *Love's Young Dream. Heart's Desire. Forever My Love. Dr Springfield's Mother and Baby Manual.* What on earth was this?

Cecil thrust open the first page. It described the symptoms of morning sickness; some of them were underlined. He turned more pages. There was a diagram of a sixteen-week baby in the womb. Written beside it in Marianne's writing were the words, 'The size of my baby.'

'What?' he roared. It all fell into place now. Marianne's mystery virus. Her refusal to go to work and out with her friends. The furtive whispering that went on between her and her wretched mother. The way Barbara had refused to let her lift a heavy basket of laundry the other day.

Cecil was seething mad. He was shaking. He was red in the face. He had business with his slut of a daughter and her lying bitch of a mother. But not in his dressing gown. First he would get dressed and then he would bring coals of fire down upon their heads.

'Help me clear the table for your father's breakfast, Marianne,' Barbara said, resigned that this period of respite was over. 'I can hear him coming down the stairs. I don't want you in his way.'

Cecil appeared in the kitchen and the two women were amazed to see him dressed in his second-best suit and black tie, not his old pair of flannel trousers and sweater that he would wear to clear the snow from the paths. The remains of his hair was Brylcreemed and severely parted.

Barbara sensed deep trouble. She put a hand on Marianne's arm and stepped in front of her. 'Are you going somewhere, dear?'

'No,' he spat venomously, 'but she is.' He pointed a stiffly held finger at Marianne. 'Whore! Slut! Get out of my house this minute. I'll have no bastard-bearing trollops living under my roof.'

So he knew. Well, it saved the trouble of having to tell him. Barbara stepped forward and lifted her chin defiantly. She wasn't a meek wife putting up with whatever he cared to hand out now. She was a mother fighting for the future of her young. 'She needs some money before she can go,' Barbara said, sounding calmer than she felt. 'We can ask my half-sister, Marta, to take her in.'

Cecil looked so fierce that Marianne burst into tears and clung to her mother. 'I'm s-sorry, Father.'

He was unmoved. This girl was no longer his daughter. She was no better than the lowest of whores. 'It's no good being sorry, you bloody bitch. It's too late for that. Too late the moment you lay down for the filthy swine who got you like this. Get out of my house before I throw you out.'

He strode across the room and thrust Barbara aside, pulling on Marianne's arm. She began to wail and he struck her viciously in the face. Barbara grabbed hold of his arm and yanked on it. 'Let her go, Cecil. I won't let you treat her like this.'

'And I won't have the little whore under my roof a moment longer,' Cecil howled like a demented animal. He shoved Barbara away from him, then gripped the neck of Marianne's jumper. She choked as he hauled her to the outside door.

'Let her go! Let her go!' yelled Barbara, beating on his back and trying to force his hands away from Marianne. 'You can't throw your own daughter out into the snow!'

Cecil dragged his screaming daughter to the door and opening it wide he threw her outside. Marianne fell headlong into the snow-covered dustbin and it fell over, its contents spilling over the whiteness without making much sound. 'If I ever catch sight of you again, I'll kill you, I swear it!'

'Run, Marianne,' Barbara shouted, trying to get past her husband at the door. 'Run to Laura Jennings, she'll take you in.'

'Mum!' Marianne shouted back where she lay.

'Get up, Marianne. Go on, for your own sake,' Barbara cried, then she screamed in pain as Cecil yanked her back by the hair and slammed the door shut. He turned the key and hit her full in the face.

'This is all your fault, you useless bitch. Our daughter, our only child, bringing disgrace down on my head because you're no good as a mother.' His face was an ugly mask of evil as he drove the full force of his fist into Barbara's stomach before she could move away from him.

She fell, hitting the cupboard under the sink. 'It's not my fault,' she shouted, clutching herself. 'It's you, you're vile and you're filthy, Cecil Roach. You're disgusting and the police would be interested to learn of the beastly things you get up to. You're not fit to be a husband or a father and you're not fit to teach innocent little children. I hate you, you unspeakable bastard. I wish you were dead.' This was the first time Barbara had spoken out against him and once she started, it all came pouring out. She wanted this loathsome creature to know exactly how she felt about him. Then she cried out in fear.

His foot was raised and he thrust it towards her head. 'You bitch! I'll make you pay for every word you've just said!'

-

Andrew drifted in and out of consciousness. At times he felt freezing cold and was surrounded by blackness and thought he was still bound up in the back of the kidnappers' van or the place they had taken him to. Then he would smell the scent of jasmine floating on the air and he'd smile happily and murmur, 'Tressa.'

The last time she answered him. 'Yes, Andrew. I'm here. Can I get you anything?'

He opened his eyes and saw he was lying in one of a pair of twin beds with knobbly brass bedsteads in a strange room. Tressa was standing by the door. He wasn't interested in his surroundings, he only took in that they were rather grim and basic with pale green distempered walls and sparse furniture. It was warm and smoky from the peat fire. He patted the side of the bed. 'Come closer, Tressa. Don't worry, I won't ask you to kiss me again, but if you want to I won't stop you.' He grinned and the effort hurt his jaw and he became aware of a thudding headache. 'Ohhh,' he put up a hand, which was still encased in a glove, to his forehead.

Tressa went to him quickly. 'There's some aspirin on the chair by your bed. Sit up and I'll help you take some.'

'I can't sit up by myself.' It would have been a good ruse to get her to help him but he was telling the truth. He felt as weak as the proverbial kitten.

Sitting on the bed, she put her arms round him and pulled him up. He rested his head against her breast and breathed in her fresh feminine scent. There was the smell of jasmine on her. So she used his present frequently. He'd have to get her some more.

'Lie back on the pillows. I've plumped them up for you,' she said.

'I can't, my head's spinning. Will you hold me for a minute?'

'Just for a minute,' she stressed. 'Dad wouldn't like it if he saw us.'

'Bloody hell, Tressa. I'm not about to pull you into this bed and make love to you.' But how he wanted to.

'Don't swear, Andrew, and don't say things like that,' she chided him like a naughty child. 'Dad wouldn't like that either. Now lie back and take the aspirins and soon the pain will go away.'

He could have said a lot of intimate things, hoping she would put it down to weakness or pain but he felt she'd not allow any more liberties. He lay back and took three aspirins out of her hand and washed them down with the glass of water she held for him. He had nearly died

291

from the kidnapping but he was grateful it had brought him here under Tressa's care. 'Thanks. I don't remember much about yesterday after the men put me in this bed, except for Laura turning up and continually telling me how sorry she was. What's been happening?'

She looked at him as though she was relieved he was behaving himself. 'You've been sleeping most of the time. Aunty Joan, Laura and I have taken turns watching over you. Spencer has taken Laura home. It's nearly teatime now. We couldn't get you to the hospital yesterday and it would have been stupid to try to take you on to the pub.'

'I'll be fine here,' Andrew grinned. 'I must thank your father and Joan.' He recalled the efforts she had made getting him out of the smuggler's hide. 'Were you hurt, Tressa?'

She touched her sides. 'Just a few bruises here.'

He wanted to caress the places where her hands had just been but knew he daren't. 'I take it this is your brothers' room?'

'You're in Matty's bed. You're wearing his shirt.'

He looked at the small fireplace, topped with a narrow ledge where the Davey brothers' few childhood toys stood. 'You shouldn't have lit a fire for me. You can't afford the peat.'

'Peat is free, we have right of turbary. You just have to work hard digging for it. We've got lots so don't worry about it.'

'Nevertheless, I'll make it up to you and no arguments. I've got my pride too.' He held up his hands. 'Whose gloves are these? Can you take them off now? I feel like a baby with mittens on.'

She pulled the gloves off slowly. His hands were swollen and streaked red, blue and purple. Tressa took hold of them gently. 'Do they hurt?'

'A bit.' She squeezed and he grimaced. 'A lot. They'll be all right, won't they?'

'I should think so. It won't be long before you'll be back writing all that legal stuff at your desk.'

'Tressa, I might not be going back to London. What—'

'I have something to show you,' she interrupted before he could say any more. As usual she was dressed in her brothers' old clothes and she took a piece of paper out of her trousers. 'Dad got this on Saturday. It's about those grants you put him on to. It's a form. They want more details. When you feel up to it, perhaps you can check he's filled it out right.' She put it back into her pocket.

'The sooner he gets it back in the post the better,' Andrew said. He looked gloomily out of the high window which had almost colourless short curtains at them. The form could have waited. Tressa wasn't prepared to talk about anything that might involve the two of them. Perhaps when the mess the Morrisons had left was cleared up he would be going back to London after all.

'I'd better go,' Tressa said, getting up off the bed.

She didn't want to leave him but her father was downstairs and would be watching the clock to see how long she stayed up here. Jacka was pleased that Andrew was safe and he was welcome to enjoy the hospitality of their home until he was completely well. Jacka had thought things through and was sorry for accusing Andrew unjustly of being a Casanova, but all the talk about villains from London and kidnapping had hardened his resolve that no matter what Andrew's feelings were, he was not the man for his daughter. Tressa wasn't as sure about that as her father.

Chapter 28

'So I missed all the fun and games while I was in London, Mother?' Harry Lean drawled. He'd got back to Hawksmoor House in the early hours of Friday morning that week and was enjoying breakfast with Felicity. 'A kidnap, a dramatic rescue, a pregnant girl thrown out into the snow and her mother falling mysteriously down the stairs.' He sipped his coffee and smiled under his long dark eyelashes. 'It's heartbreaking.'

'It isn't funny, Harry,' Felicity chided. 'Laura must have been worried out of her mind before her friend was found.'

'Lucky him, being found by Tressa,' Harry observed, picturing the girl he still desired and the man who had more honourable feelings towards her in the little deserted farmhouse.

'Yes,' Felicity said drily, frowning disapprovingly. She hadn't forgiven him for his assault on Tressa Davey. 'Andrew Macarthur is back in the pub and almost recovered and Laura's jewellery has been retrieved. It's all so terribly dramatic. Hard to believe it happened on our doorstep.'

Harry helped himself to more toast and buttered and marmaladed it thickly. 'It'll keep the tongues wagging for months. Where's Marianne now?' He wasn't in the least bit concerned about her but he wanted to know if she was likely to be a nuisance to him again.

'She ran up to Laura's cottage for help but Spencer had taken her overnight to Tregorlan Farm to see Andrew Macarthur. She stayed there until Laura got back. The girl was in a terrible state. Laura got to work straight away and contacted Marianne's aunt in Barnstaple, who sent her some money. As soon as the snow thawed, she travelled up there on the next train.'

'Good. I mean good that Marianne had someone to take her in. And good on Laura. Makes you wonder how the village managed without her. I take my hat off to her.' Pity I wasn't around to comfort her during her ordeal, he thought, smiling to himself again. He had much to smile about today.

'Don't you see the significance of what I said, Harry?' Felicity leant forward and took his hand. 'It was Spencer who took Laura to Tregorlan Farm. He went to Little Cot to tell Laura that Andrew Macarthur had been found, and that's not all. He told her he'd been thinking, that he's changed his mind about her seeing Vicki after the last quarrel they had. She's hoping he will finally come round about Vicki where you and I are concerned.' Harry sprang up and hugged and kissed his mother. 'That would be wonderful! So that's why you're looking bright and chirpy this morning.'

'It would make my dreams come true and it would all be due to Laura for somehow breaking through Spencer's grief and stubbornness.' Felicity studied her son. 'You're looking rather pleased yourself, darling. Did your business in London go well?'

'Yes, it did, thank you, Mother. And I'm quite certain a little piece of business I've been setting up locally is about to come to fruition too.'

The children of Kilgarthen were finally able to start school that morning. Laura was outside the pub buying fresh fish from the van when the mothers and children started the first of their twice or thrice daily trips, depending on whether their offspring stayed for dinner at the school. She looked keenly at the few vehicles that drove through the village to deposit children and her heart gave a sharp flip when she saw Rosemerryn Farm's Ford saloon.

Spencer and Vicki swept past and the little girl waved enthusiastically to her. Laura stepped away from the van and waved back until the car was out of sight and although she had only glimpsed Vicki's face, the shine and excitement on her features had caused a lump to rise in her throat.

'He'll find it hard,' Ada Prisk said, coming up behind Laura. Ada always seemed to be behind her in any queue.

'What?' Laura turned round. 'I mean pardon, Mrs Prisk.'

'Spencer Jeffries.' Ada nodded after the car. 'Seeing your child off to school on its first day is an emotional time for any parent, but when it's your one and only and you're as possessive as he is…'

'Joy Miller will be feeling much the same way about Benjy, her youngest child,' Laura murmured thoughtfully.

'Course they never got on, you know.'

Laura frowned, puzzled. 'Benjy and Vicki?'

'No, your late husband and Spencer Jeffries. They didn't just dislike one another, hate would be a better word for it.'

There were just the two of them left now. Laura was having Andrew to lunch and she asked the fishman for some cod, then stepped back closer to Ada. 'Do you know why they fell out, Mrs Prisk?' Maybe the village oracle would answer the question nobody else seemed willing to.

Ada was delighted that at last she had been able to engage the newcomer in a serious chat. 'I don't know what was said exactly,' she told Laura, 'but they had a terrible row over Natalie, Spencer's poor late wife. You'd have liked Natalie, you have a lot in common being beautiful and sophisticated. Well, Spencer knocked on the door of Little Cot in the middle of the night and threatened to break Bill's back. They were shouting at the tops of their voices and woke up the whole village. A scuffle started in the road and Mike Penhaligon and the vicar had to prise them apart or it would have got much worse. Lucky for them Constable Geach wasn't involved.'

'Really?' Laura said, her brain ticking over. Why hadn't anybody mentioned this to her before? Presumably they didn't want to say anything detrimental about their benefactor. 'And you have no idea what the row was about?'

'None, other than that Natalie's name was mentioned a lot.'

Laura paid for her fish and the two women changed places. Laura continued with her questioning. 'When was this? I mean when did it happen?'

The fishman looked at Ada impatiently for her order; he had a package to deliver to School House. Cecil Roach had written to him telling him to leave it on the table and he would find his money inside the bread bin. Mr Roach had said there would be no one about; his wife was in bed with the flu. People would think he was only delivering fish but the fishman liked to get his other merchandise out of his van as soon as possible.

''Twas about a couple of weeks before the little maid was born.' Ada replied, ignoring the Ashman's twitching face. 'I remember Bill was down for the weekend and he went home for Christmas. Why don't you come back to my house for a cup of tea, Mrs Jennings?'

'No, thank you,' Laura said hastily; she didn't relish warding off the stringent attempts Ada would no doubt make to drag all her innermost secrets out of her. 'Perhaps some other time, Mrs Prisk.'

Laura hurried across the road, dumped the fish on the kitchen table then ran upstairs to root out Bill's diaries from where she had thrown them on top of the wardrobe of the spare room. She had forgotten all about them with so many things happening. Perhaps he'd written his secrets in his diaries and she would learn what the violent row with Spencer had been about. Anything that would clear the air between her and Spencer would be helpful in reestablishing her relationship with Vicki. With Andrew safe, it was what was most important to her now. She intended to just happen to be outside the school this afternoon when the children went home.

She took Bill's diaries out of the cloth bag and sat on the bed to read them. They started several years before he had left the village to seek his fortune. She put aside the earlier volumes. She flicked through some of the pages and read his triumphant gloating when he had bought Little Cot from Harry Lean: 'Paid over the odds but the old man wouldn't have sold the cottage to me at any price. Out from under Big Mouth's thumb.' Big Mouth was presumably Harry. She didn't want to read any more of his spite and moved on to the diary dated 1943. She flicked through the pages until she came to the end of the year. She read the entries for the week leading up to Christmas. It revealed what he'd been planning to buy her as a present – an ugly cut-glass punch bowl which she'd hated – and his plans for her father's company in the new year, all of which he had achieved mainly by underhand means.

The entry for Sunday, 20 December, was brief: 'Had a set-to with S.J. The swine woke me up. Stupid cow shouldn't have told him.'

The stupid cow probably referred to Natalie. What shouldn't she have told Spencer? There were no more clues on the next pages. She was none the wiser about what the quarrel was about.

–

In the middle of the afternoon Laura made her way to Johnny Prouse's cottage. She found him in his back garden contentedly watching his new bantam hens which Bert Miller had bought from Launceston market for him. He hadn't had the heart to get another dog after Admiral died.

'Afternoon to 'ee, m'dear.' Johnny doffed his flat cap and grinned from ear to ear. 'Come and have a look at my new arrivals. What do you think of 'em?'

'They're beautiful, Johnny,' she said, studying the red and brown birds as they pecked and scratched for the corn Johnny had just thrown to them. 'I particularly like the speckled one.'

'That's Patmos,' the old man said proudly.

'Patmos? You've named them all, Johnny?'

'Ais, they're all named after places I've seen or visited on board ship. I was in the merchant navy as well as the Royal Navy, you know. I've told you I've been all round the world, haven't I?' He pointed to the little bobbing hens in turn. 'That's Milan, that's Morocco, that's Sicily, that's Brittany and that big bugger there, he's the rooster, that's Nelson, not named after a place but it speaks for itself, don't it?'

'It does,' Laura agreed, pleased to see him so cheerful. 'Their names make them all rather exotic.'

'Do 'ee think so? When I have some chicks, how about I call one Laura?'

'I'd be very honoured. Now, you're not getting cold out here, are you?'

'Bless your heart,' Johnny laughed. 'You're a good maid. Don't worry. I shall be going in drekkly.'

Laura took a handful of corn from the small sack in Johnny's hands and scattered it through the wire netting for the hens. He noticed that she was looking serious. 'You got something on your mind, m'dear?'

She flushed a little because she was about to lie. 'I've just been reading some diaries of Bill's. I was astonished to find out why he'd fallen out with Spencer Jeffries.'

'I'm very sorry about that but if you mean to tell me, Laura, I'd rather not know. It must be very personal.' Johnny had gone serious now and Laura was sorry for dampening his spirits.

'You're right,' Laura said. It seemed that only a few people knew why Bill and Spencer had quarrelled. There was Ince, Daisy and Bunty but they weren't telling. 'The past is better left in the past. When do you expect the hens to start laying?'

'As soon as they're settled. You ever had a bantam's egg? 'Tis delicious. You'll have two from my first batch. I promise 'ee that.'

When she moved on towards her final destination, the school, Laura saw Ma Noon coming along the road with her pony and jingle. Laura waved to her. The cloaked and bonneted old woman pulled on the reins and brought the good-natured tawny pony to a halt. 'Good afternoon, Mrs Noon,' Laura said quickly. 'I'm Laura Jennings. I've seen you in the village a few times and I just wanted to introduce myself. How did you manage in the snow earlier this week?'

'It's very kind of you to ask. I managed like I always have done, perfectly well, thank you, Mrs Jennings,' Ma Noon replied and Laura was taken aback to be addressed by a cultured voice. She had expected the old woman's accent to be as Cornish as Johnny's or Daisy's. Under the bonnet her hair was snowy white and piled on top of her head, held fast by tortoiseshell combs. Although Laura had been told she must be nearing seventy years old, her skin was smooth and virtually wrinkle-free in her fat face; jewel-clear green eyes studied her.

Laura felt foolish. She had hoped Ma Noon would be more talkative and perhaps throw some light on Bill's quarrel with Spencer. Laura stepped out of the jingle's way, and taking this to mean that was all she had wanted to say, Ma Noon touched the pony's shoulder with the reins and journeyed on. Laura was now as curious to learn something about Ma Noon as she was to find out about Bill and Spencer's fight. People rarely spoke of Ma Noon, except to say she was mazed and one should stay away from her; the label 'Ma' didn't suit her and Laura realised it was meant disparagingly.

It was about twenty minutes before the schoolchildren were due to leave for home and Laura made her way to the Millers' house. She found Joy sitting dejectedly in her pinny in the kitchen, the room untidy, a basket of ironing unattended to, the floor not swept, the sink full of dishes.

'Are you feeling poorly, Joy?' she asked, taking in the neglected scene.

'Oh, I'm fine, Laura,' she replied as if she was extremely tired. 'I've done everything upstairs but lost heart when I got down here. It's been so horribly quiet without Benjy running about chattering all day. Even though all four of them came home for dinner, I've still missed him.'

'Why didn't you come up to me rather than sit here like this?'

Joy raised and lowered a heavy arm. 'I couldn't be bothered. Don't look so worried, Laura. I'll be fine tomorrow. I'm just mourning the end of an era, that's all. By the time the brats have their half-term I'll be tearing my hair out wanting them all back at school. I've been considering asking my old man if we can have another baby but we can't afford another mouth to feed. Oh well, I'll put the kettle on. We've just got time for a quick cuppa before I go and fetch Benjy. He won't like it. He'll want his brother and sisters to see him home but I'm darned if I'll miss his first day. I hope he got on all right but having the others there meant he wasn't very nervous.' She heaved her flabby body out of the chair. 'Heard any more news about that kidnapping business?'

'No, and I hope I won't.' The incident was well and truly over as far as Laura was concerned. 'I wonder how Vicki got on at school. She's not used to being away from the farm.'

'Aw, she'll be all right. She's a friendly little mite and she's got Benjy in her class. They went in this morning holding hands.'

'Did they?' Laura smiled, wishing she'd seen it. 'What was Spencer like?'

'Like a fish out of water, what else? But I don't think he noticed that he was in among a lot of women when he took off her coat and helped her change her shoes in the cloakroom. He gave her dinner money to Miss Knight then gave her thr'pence for tuck. He kept kissing her and I thought he was going to cry when he had to leave. Miss Knight had to keep reassuring him. He would have liked to pick her up and take her home for dinner but it wouldn't be practical with him and Ince working on the farm. At least with dinners being provided at school now he or Ince won't have to make a pasty every day for her.' As Joy handed Laura a mug of tea, she said meaningfully, 'Ince is picking her up. You seen much of him lately?'

'Ince is just a friend,' Laura said, her mind elsewhere. 'I'll walk with you to the school and ask Vicki how she enjoyed her first day. Spencer said I can talk to her now. I haven't been over to the farm yet because I didn't want to push my luck. I've bought her a birthday present for last Wednesday but I'm biding my time before I give it to her.'

'You've got very fond of Vicki, haven't you?'

'Yes.' Laura's face glowed. 'I first saw her on my second day here. I don't think I've ever seen a more beautiful child and when you get to know her, you realise she has a character to match.'

'I don't think Spencer will let you share her.'

'I don't want him to,' Laura said sharply, but she couldn't lie. 'Well, just a bit.'

When the women reached the school, they found Ince waiting with the horse and cart. He was leaning against the school wall with his hands in his pockets. He straightened up and said hello but didn't smile or move towards them. Laura knew he must be feeling hurt because she had made no attempt to contact him since the night of the dance; she'd turned her face away from him when he'd bent his head to kiss her goodnight. She was very fond of him, she had enjoyed their intimacy, but she was too wary to fall in love again, even with a man who was gentler and more sympathetic than most. If things had unfolded in the same way much later in their relationship, it might have been a different story. She excused herself to Joy and went over to him.

'Have you been waiting long?' she asked to break the ice.

'No.' He kept his eyes on the door the children would spill out of in about five minutes' time.

'I'm, um, sorry I haven't seen much of you late, Ince.'

'You needn't explain, Laura. I was there when you needed someone and now your feelings have moved on.' He looked at her briefly and his voice was soft and tender but pain was evident in his face.

She knew he was right. 'It seems you knew more about me than I did myself. I'm sorry if I've hurt you, Ince.' He kept his eyes rooted on the school door. 'You've got nothing to be sorry about. Your world was turned upside down before you came here and has been tossed and hurled about ever since. I shouldn't have expected you to fall in love with me. How could you in those circumstances? I should have stepped back and not put my own feelings on the line.'

Laura sighed, her heart sinking down to her boots where it had lived for so much of her adult life. 'I feel terrible, Ince. I don't regret what happened between us. I hope we can still be friends.'

He looked at her fully then and his smile was warm. 'Of course we'll still be friends. I just need a little time to adjust to thinking of us as only that.'

Neither of them could think of anything else to say so they looked back at the school and saw Cecil Roach opening the door. He positioned himself there as the children came filing out, their heads up and shoulders back, conscious of his stern gaze on them.

'Here she comes,' Ince said, taking Laura's arm and propelling her towards the children who had started a stampede towards the gate, Vicki among them with her golden hair flying behind her as she ran. 'The one you really care about.'

Chapter 29

The next morning Tressa was walking along Rosemerryn Lane. She was pulling a small cart behind her, taking two milk churns down to the platform to await collection from the milk company. The cylindrical churns, one marked with a capital E, half-filled with last evening's milk, and the other marked M for this morning's, clattered and banged together despite being lashed down with a rope, their ill-fitting lids threatening to fall off. She hoisted the churns up next to those of Rosemerryn Farm then loaded the two empty ones scored with the name Tregorlan on them.

She turned the cart round and began the journey home, paying no heed to the whirling and clashing of the empty churns which worsened when she turned off on to the farm track. She was thinking of the first time she had met Andrew. Here was the very spot where he had fallen over. She stopped and relived every moment of it; he was rarely out of her mind these days.

When she'd first encountered him here she had thought him an irritating idiot. When she had deliberately made him walk through the boggy patch on the moor, she had thought him a nuisance and was eager to get rid of him. When he'd gone back to London she'd felt strangely sorry for her unkind and offhand behaviour towards him, and when he'd unexpectedly come back and seemed always to be around her, she had eventually got used to him. It had been a bit like having a brother again. His declaration that he adored her in Reddacoombe's farmhouse had shocked her.

When she and Spencer had got him safely back to Tregorlan Farm, she'd had time to think about what he had said. Her feelings were new, raw and quite frightening, but she had enjoyed exploring them. She had liked the feeling of holding him in her arms when she'd helped him to sit up in her brother's bed. He had spoken of making love and when, lying in her narrow bed, she had tried to imagine what it would be like with him, it had excited and alarmed her. At every opportunity she had slipped into his bedroom and gazed at him as he'd slept, taken up his meals and fetched him books when he was awake. She had allowed him to win at a game of draughts and her heart had thumped loudly in her ears when he'd laughed gleefully at his triumph and his face had shone with happiness. She liked to look at all the moods displayed on his handsome face. She liked being with him.

Three days after she had found him, the snow started to thaw and the doctor, satisfied with his progress, had driven Andrew back to the pub. She had wanted to visit him there, but Jacka always seemed to have urgent jobs for her on the farm. Andrew had sent word via Laura that he was strong enough to come to the farm today and Tressa was looking forward to seeing him again. She didn't want him to go back to London.

She was still in the same spot when the sounds of a squeaky bicycle told her the postwoman was bumping up behind her. Tressa went to meet her.

"'Tis a treat meeting you down here,' the cheery middle-aged post-woman said as she sorted through a handful of mail. 'You'll save me a bit of a journey and a muddy pawing from your dog. Here you are, my luvver, a letter for your father.'

Jacka was already sitting at the kitchen table waiting for his breakfast when she got there. It had begun to pour with rain and she shook her mane of wet hair. She took off her dripping coat, scarf and overalls and washed her hands at the sink, then encircling her father's broad neck with her arms, she kissed his ruddy cheek. 'You all right, Dad?'

'Yes, my handsome,' he replied, breathing heavily. 'Did 'ee get the milk down to the platform all right?'

'Yes. The yield was up again this morning.' She hoped the good news would soften him. 'Andrew's coming over later.'

'He won't be strong enough to help about the place yet,' Joan said, turning over rashers of bacon sizzling in the huge black frying pan.

Jacka very carefully said nothing.

'You don't mind him coming over here, do you, Dad?' Tressa asked, watching her father from the corner of her dark eyes as she laid the table with the oddments of cutlery.

''Tis all the same to me what he does,' Jacka muttered grumpily, studying his fingernails on outstretched hands. 'Must be about time he went back to London. Be nice to see un again before he goes, I s'pose.'

'Andrew told me he might not be going back to London,' Tressa said, still watching Jacka's face.

'Why ever not!' Jacka exclaimed accusingly, banging his fist on the table and making his knife and fork jump. 'There's nothing for he down here.'

'What have you got against Andrew?' Tressa demanded defiantly, putting her rough hands on her slender hips. 'I don't understand you, Dad. He's been really good to us. It's not like you to be so ungrateful.'

'Don't you talk to me like that!' Jacka shouted, jumping to his feet and slapping a hand to his head because the quick movement had made him feel dizzy. His heart started thudding uncomfortably, as it often did, and he broke into a sweat. 'You're getting bloody cheeky, my girl, and I won't have it, do you hear? I'll smack 'ee one round the bleddy ear.'

'Calm down, Jacka,' Joan said worriedly, pulling on his arm to try to get him back on his chair. 'Tressa's got a point. Andrew's a good man. You've said so often enough to me yourself. Ever since the vicar mentioned he had a fancy for Tressa you've turned against un. I thought you'd be pleased. After all, it was you who's been telling the maid to look for a husband. Now as soon as a man's interested in her, you've gone like this. It don't add up. It isn't as if she's thrown herself into his arms. You know Tressa's not like that.'

His face white, his large body trembling, Jacka sat down. He took the tea towel lying over Joan's shoulder and used it to mop his hot wet brow. Through tight lips he mumbled, 'I just don't want to see her hurt, that's all.'

'Whatever Andrew does, he would never hurt me,' Tressa said quietly. Jacka grunted and she and Joan exchanged worried looks.

He didn't look at all well and these episodes of bad temper followed by physical debility were getting more frequent.

'Why don't we just wait and see what happens,' Joan said wisely, returning to the frying pan. 'If you ask me, Jacka, you're jealous of another man showing he cares for your daughter, despite your wishes for her future.'

The family ate their breakfast in an uncomfortable silence. Jacka got up first from the table. 'I s'pose you want to stay in the yard this morning then?' he muttered at Tressa. 'You can stack that hay that's fallen down in the barn.'

'Thanks, Dad,' she replied, wanting to hug him and make him feel better. She remembered the letter and got up from the table and pulled it out of her coat pocket. 'I forgot all about this. It's for you, Dad. It looks official.'

'Must be from the bank, your receipt for the mortgage money you sent off, Jacka,' Joan said, her eyes on the long buff envelope. She and Tressa watched Jacka open it; letters were rare on Tregorlan Farm and they always stirred eager interest.

Jacka unfolded the white piece of paper inside and read its contents. Suddenly he gasped and gurgled, making a horrible long rattling noise, and clutched at his chest. 'It's not right... I sent it, I—' The next moment he thumped down on the floor, the letter grasped in his fist as a spasm of pain gripped his heart.

'Dad!' Tressa rushed and knelt over him. 'What's the matter? Get up!'

Joan grabbed Tressa's shoulder. 'He's very ill, Tressa. Run and call for the doctor. Quick! Hurry!' She pulled Tressa to her feet and shoved her towards the door. 'Run, Tressa!'

Tressa was stunned. She stood there watching her father moaning and writhing in agony. Her brain couldn't take in what was happening.

'Run, Tressa! For goodness sake!' Joan screamed at her as she pulled open Jacka's shirt buttons.

Tressa sprang back to life and tore out of the door. She pulled on her boots. Out in the yard she shouted at Meg to stay put then ran at full pelt down the muddy track. The rain was heavy and she hadn't stopped to get her coat; she was soaked through to the skin in moments and splashed nearly all the way up her legs with mud. All she could think of was her father's face, masked in pain and despair, his life in obvious danger.

As she ran, she gasped in mouthfuls of air. Very soon her lungs felt that they would burst but she didn't slow down. Suddenly she was falling. She hit the tarmaced lane and bounced and skidded along, ripping her trousers and bruising her knees, skinning her arms, knocking the last little bit of breath out of her. She pulled herself to a sitting position, her knees raised, her upper body hunched over them. She panted to regain some strength, cursing herself for falling.

Moments later she was up on her feet again. She couldn't run as fast and limped from the pain in her knees. She made several yards then a stitch attacked her side but she ran on despite the agony. She stopped once to take in some deep breaths and to push the wet hair out of her eyes. The rain was coming down so fiercely it was pummelling her head, running through her hair and dripping off her nose and chin. Her despair at her father's situation was growing and she held back the need to burst into tears. She was off once more, ignoring the pain in her knees and the rawness in her chest, running as fast as she could.

She made the top of the village hill and rather than looking at the shop or the public telephone, her eyes homed in on the pub.

Andrew was sitting with Pat and Mike round the kitchen table. Mike took several local and national newspapers every week and they were all reading as they finished their breakfast of toast and dark thick-cut marmalade and a second cup of tea.

Andrew turned the page of a local paper he was reading gingerly – his hands were still sore and didn't have a good grip. He searched the columns of Situations Vacant then his eyes were drawn to a boxed advertisement for the position of a partner in a law practice in Bodmin. He made a mental note of the telephone number. It wouldn't hurt to speak to the partners. He hadn't given up on Tressa, in fact she was getting quite friendly, and Jacka's change in attitude had done nothing to put him off. He was hopeful he could persuade Jacka he was not a cad only after her maidenly virtue.

There was a terrific crash on the outside pub doors, which had already been unlocked.

Mike rose to his feet.

'Don't say, there's been another accident,' Pat gasped, clutching the corner of the table.

Andrew threw the paper down and joined Mike. They could hear someone running down the passage. Before either of them could reach the kitchen door, it flew open and a very dishevelled Tressa spilled through it.

Andrew beat Mike to her by pushing the burly landlord out of the way. He grabbed her by the shoulders and her hands flew up to grip his shirt. 'What is it, darling? What's happened?'

Her eyes were bulging, her breath came in ragged noisy gasps, her mouth was gaping open and it was several moments before speech would come. 'Dad... collapsed... doctor,' she implored him. Then her strength left her, her knees buckled and she passed out. Andrew gathered her up in his arms.

'I'll phone for the doctor,' Mike said, taking charge. 'Andrew, take her through to our sitting room. Pat, get blankets and dry clothes.'

Tressa came to moments later to find herself being carried in Andrew's arms. 'Andrew...' she moaned.

'It's all right, Tressa,' he said tenderly. 'Mike's phoned for the doctor. Just relax and you'll feel better in a moment. Pat's getting you some dry clothes.' He was holding her closely against his body and his shirt was wet from her sopping clothes and hair.

'No!' Tressa struggled as she came fully too. 'Must get back to Dad. He needs me. Will you take me back? Please, Andrew.' He looked helplessly at Pat.

'You'd better do as she wants or she's going to work herself up into a frenzy. Here, take this.' Pat threw a blanket round her. 'I'll get the car keys.'

The Penhaligons' car had been found abandoned in a lane. Andrew put Tressa in the front passenger seat then took his coat from Pat who was standing with it under an umbrella.

When they sped off, Tressa huddled down in the blanket and wiped her wet face with it. She stared out of the window, willing the car to take wings and fly. 'Thanks, Andrew. Drive as fast as you can.' Her voice came out in a whimper and she was shivering with cold.

'What happened to Jacka?' he asked softly.

She told him in slow sentences. 'You know he hasn't been well for ages. He got a bit bothered at the breakfast table and just before he left to go back to work I remembered he got a letter. When he read it he shouted out something and then fell to the floor. He's in terrible pain and was clutching his chest. Oh, please hurry.'

Andrew took the next bend at a faster speed than was wise and the car lurched across the road before righting itself. He swore under his breath and slowed down; better to arrive a little later than not at all. It sounded like Jacka had suffered a heart attack but he didn't mention it. Tressa was very upset already.

He pulled up sharply in front of the farmhouse door and before he could help Tressa out of the car, she had opened the door and was running inside with the blanket dragging in the dirt. She charged into the kitchen with Andrew on her heels. Jacka was lying unconscious on his back where he had fallen in front of the dresser. The sound of his laboured breathing filled the room, his chest was rising and falling harshly. His face was a sickly grey colour. Joan had put a cushion under his head and covered him with coats. She was kneeling beside him, crooning to him that everything was going to be all right and he must hold on.

'Dad,' Tressa called loudly, hoping for a response. 'Dad. I'm back. The doctor is coming.'

'You can't do anything for him, Tressa, but you must take care of yourself,' Andrew said firmly, taking hold of her gently and pushing her in front of the range. 'You won't be any good to Jacka if you get pneumonia.' He took a dry towel off the washing line that hung across the kitchen from beam to beam and rubbed at her hair. Tressa let him do it but she turned her back to him so she wouldn't have to take her eyes off her father.

'It would be better if you turned him over on his side, Joan,' Andrew said, remembering some rules of first aid.

Joan did so and Jacka groaned feebly.

'Where's the doctor?' Tressa wailed despairingly after a couple more minutes. 'Why isn't he here yet?'

'I'm sure he's coming as fast as he can, darling,' Andrew said, trying to reassure her. Satisfied that her hair wouldn't drip, he put the towel on her shoulders and wrapped his arms round her. She didn't object, she was glad of the warmth and comfort.

Joan eyed them but said nothing about it. 'Tressa, I think we should get your father upstairs before the doctor gets here,' she said. 'We can manage between the three of us but we'll have to be careful. Then I want you to dry yourself and change your clothes.'

'But I want to stay with him, Aunty Joan,' Tressa protested, pulling herself free from Andrew's embrace.

'Now listen to me, Tressa,' Joan went on in the same no-nonsense tone, getting to her feet. 'If Jacka comes round and sees you like that he'll take poorly again. If we're going to get through this we must all be sensible.'

They carried Jacka upstairs and laid him in his bed. Tressa knelt down and kissed her father's brow. When she stood up, Andrew put his arm round her. 'He'll be all right, Tressa.'

'I hope so, oh, I do hope so.'

She jumped when a car pulled up in a spin then raced downstairs to let Dr Palmer in.

'What's the matter with him?' she asked when the doctor had made a preliminary examination.

'Looks like a mild coronary, a heart attack, but I'll know more when I've had a closer look.' He smiled encouragingly.

Her aunt gave her a pointed look and Tressa left the room reluctantly to change. Joan pushed something into Andrew's hand. 'Show her this when she's ready.'

Andrew joined her in the kitchen. She was sniffing back tears. He noticed a pile of ironing on a chair, shirts draped over the back. 'Come on now. Change into something clean and dry and you'll feel much better.'

She stood in front of the range, her small face puckered up as she tried not to cry. She knew he was right; she had to be strong for her father and aunt's sake. She raised her arms to the top button of her shirt.

Andrew put the kettle on to boil and was about to leave the room when Tressa cried out in pain. 'What is it?' he said anxiously.

'My arms.' She whistled through her teeth as her grazed flesh stung like thousands of bee stings. 'I fell over. I forgot all about it. My knees are hurting too.'

There were no buttons on her shirt sleeves and he gently rolled them up. The skin had been skimmed off from wrist nearly to elbow in a narrow patch on both arms. It was wonderful to tend to her, to be comforting her, and he had an overwhelming desire to kiss her arms better. 'Poor love, they'll need bathing. You get changed and we'll see what you've done to your knees.' Again he made to leave the room.

Tressa was trembling with shock and cold which seemed to be gnawing its way into her bones. Her fingers were clumsy and she couldn't get the buttons of her shirt undone. 'Andrew,' she groaned, 'I can't do it, my fingers won't work.'

He came back to her. 'Do you want me to help you?'

'I can't ask Aunty Joan at the moment and I can't stay like this. I trust you to behave.' She felt almost too weary to care but she did feel safe with him.

'I'm glad you trust me, Tressa,' he smiled, feeling rather shy that he was actually going to help undress her.

The buttons were tight in the wet cloth and with his sore fingers he had to tug on each one until they were free. He tugged the shirt out of her trousers and pulled each sleeve down carefully over her arms. She was saving the bra Laura had given her for best and was wearing a man's flannel vest.

'It's warmer,' she said, in case he thought it odd. Although he would have seen more bare flesh, she wished she was wearing the bra; she wanted him to find her feminine.

She might think the vest was plain and unflattering but with the wet flannel plastered against her small, firm breasts, her nipples standing out prominently, it was a sight that was certainly feminine. Andrew tore his eyes away. He had a lot of difficulty with the knotted tie at her waist, which held up her baggy trousers. He helped her get her boots off then pulled the trousers down carefully over her knees. She held on to his arms and stepped out of them.

'You've got bruises and scratches and your left knee is swollen a little,' he said, running his eyes up her perfect legs. The vest covered her knickers and rested wetly on her thighs. He could see how tiny she was but her figure was perfectly proportioned. 'You had better hurry up and get off your feet then your knees won't hurt so much.' His hands hovered about her hips for a moment, then he gave way to temptation. He gripped the end of her vest in both hands. 'Ready?' His voice had dropped to a husky whisper.

She put her hands over his. Their eyes met and clashed and she prevailed – as much over herself as over him because she had been tempted to allow him to remove the vest. 'I can manage,' she said softly. 'Get me some clothes from that chair, will you, please?'

He let go of the vest at once; he'd never do anything to hurt or offend her. He did as he was bidden and when he turned round with an armful of clothes for her to sift through, she had her back to him and had pulled the wet vest off. He had a glimpse of her smooth wet back before she wrapped a towel round herself. 'I'll put them on the table,' he said, not wanting to embarrass her or compromise her trust in him. 'I'll make the tea.'

He kept his back to her until the rustling of clothes being discarded and others put on was over. He turned to find her dressed in a shirt, her knees bare so they could be bathed. She was staring at him.

'I would have left the room,' he pointed out.

She gave a little shake of her head. 'I'm so glad you're here, Andrew.'

'I'll be here as long as you need me.' He held out his arms to her.

She remained where she was for a moment, then running on her bare feet she threw herself into his arms. He gathered her in and held her tightly. She buried her face deep against his chest and sobbed her heart out. He was elated. He had waited so long to hold her soft small body to his and it didn't matter that she only wanted comfort from him.

He stroked her hair. He caressed her back and neck. He planted a kiss on top of her head.

Tressa moved her head and looked up at him, hot tears falling down her face. 'I'm sorry. I've cried all over your shirt.'

'I don't mind, darling.' It was so natural to call her darling and she didn't seem to mind.

'I'm so frightened, Andrew. I had words with Dad this morning. I've been making him angry lately. If anything happens to him I'll never forgive myself.'

'It isn't your fault, Tressa. You could never hurt Jacka.'

Her eyes glittered with fresh tears as she gazed up at him. He smoothed strands of hair away from her face. He smiled and she smiled back. His longing to kiss her was so strong it was almost tangible. She kept looking back into his eyes. He moved his face closer to hers. Their lips were very close. Then she closed her eyes. It was several seconds before he realised she wanted him to kiss her. He pressed his lips tenderly on hers. This was her first kiss. She didn't move her lips at first, wanting to feel his tenderness and strength, then she responded tentatively to this new experience which she wanted as much as he did. It was a long kiss in which they gave each other all their warmth.

When their lips separated, he held her even closer. It had been the sweetest moment of his life. 'Tressa darling, I've wanted to do that since the first day we met.'

She looked at him with a new life and depth shining from her dark eyes. 'I wish I'd felt this way about you before. It scares me to think of what I would have missed if you'd not come back again.'

'You are worth fighting for, darling. Let's not waste any more time.'

They kissed passionately, reluctant to let each other go but her wounds had to be attended to.

'What will you do if you father objects to us?' Andrew asked as he bathed her knees.

'I think Dad will come round. I just hope he'll live so he'll have the chance to consider it,' she answered in a choked voice.

'We'll take one step at a time. We won't rush him.' He smiled tenderly. 'This might not be the most romantic time to repeat myself but I do love you, Tressa. I won't rush you either. When we know how Jacka is and everything has settled down again, I hope you'll find your feelings are the same for me.'

She stroked his shoulder and bent forward and kissed his cheek. She was already quite sure she knew how she felt about him.

He bound her grazed knees and arms with strips of gauze bandage. They drank some sweet tea then Tressa went upstairs to dress properly.

'The doctor's just left,' she said when she came back. 'He said Dad has to have at least four weeks' bed rest. Aunty Joan and I are going to take turns sitting with him for the first few days. She wants me to get on with some work but first can we drive over to Rosemerryn Farm and ask Spencer if he and Ince can take turns helping us out for the next few days. It's what we usually do when a farmer's laid up. I know you can do some jobs but I don't want you doing the heaviest work.'

He had taken the piece of paper out of his pocket Joan had given to him and was scanning the contents. 'I'll do anything you say, darling. Come to me a minute. This is the letter your father received. When you read it, you'll see what upset him so much.'

She went to him and he held her. Feeling alarmed by his grave face, she read the letter. 'But Dad paid half of the arrears the bank was demanding!' she exclaimed. '"No choice but to evict you…" He sent it off well before January the first. He went down specially to the village to post it himself.'

'Try not to worry, darling. I'll drive into Launceston and see the bank manager myself.'

Tressa's eyes filled with tears. 'But even if you do put things right, Andrew, it won't help Dad. If he survives this heart attack, he'll never be well enough to farm again, he'll feel his life has come to an end anyway.'

He kissed her brow. 'Jacka doesn't need to worry. If you'll let me, I'll see to the future for all of us.'

Chapter 30

Laura cycled over to Tregorlan Farm with Mike and Pat Penhaligon. The Rosemerryn Farm cart had just pulled up and the small army of helpers piled off their vehicles. Laura was thrilled to see Vicki was with Spencer and Ince.

Vicki let go of Spencer's hand and started to run towards her, a bright sunny smile on her little face. Then she stopped, frowned, and looked uncertainly at her father.

'It's all right, pipkin, you come inside with Laura,' he said. He strode off to meet Tressa and Andrew at the door. Ince followed him after giving Laura a brief smile.

Vicki started running again and Laura rushed to her and swept her up into her arms. 'Hello, Vicki.' She kissed both her rosy cheeks. 'How are you?'

Vicki wound her arms tightly round her neck. She put a peck on her cheek and said peevishly, 'You mustn't fall out with Daddy ever again. Then he won't tell you to stay away.'

'I won't,' Laura said, cuddling her tightly. 'I promise.'

Tressa and Andrew greeted them. 'Aunty Joan's upstairs with Dad,' Tressa said. 'The doctor's coming back this evening. He said the next forty-eight hours are going to be critical.'

'Now you're not to worry, my handsome,' Mike said. 'There's plenty of us here ready and willing to help. More will be up from the village throughout the day. You don't have to do any work so you can stay close to the house. And best of all,' he winked at Andrew, 'you've got Andrew here with you.'

They all went into the kitchen to discuss a working plan. Andrew stationed himself protectively at Tressa's side. 'I want to pop in and see Dad often,' Tressa said.

'I've got all day to spare,' Laura said. 'I can do the cooking.'

'And I'll do some housework,' Pat volunteered.

'I'll draw up a rota of field and beast work, if you like, Tressa,' Spencer said. He looked from the girl to Laura and his intense grey eyes made her colour slightly. 'Perhaps Vicki could stay here with Laura and then Ince and I will be able to put in more hours outside.'

'I'd love to have her here with me,' Laura said, and Vicki ran excitedly to her and climbed up onto her lap. Laura was pleased it was a Saturday and Vicki wouldn't have to go to school.

When everything was settled, Mike took Spencer aside. 'It's good of you to come. Pat's just reminded me that it's the anniversary of Natalie's death today.'

Spencer's face set like granite and he looked down at the floor. 'Life has to go on, they say. Jacka's life is in danger and his family needs my help. I'll do my grieving later privately. Please don't mention it to anyone else.'

Spencer and Ince left to complete some work on Rosemerryn Farm before one of them returned to be joined by Bert Miller later in the morning. When they were trotting back up the lane, Spencer glanced at Ince.

'I thought Laura would have been over to the farm to see Vicki before now. Has something happened between you and her? Could that be the reason? I couldn't help but notice you weren't particularly friendly just now.'

'No, that's the point,' Ince said, sighing and gazing at the road disappearing under the horse's hooves. 'Nothing has happened. My hopes for a romance with her have fizzled out.'

'I'm sorry, mate. I wanted to warn you, with her only being recently widowed, but felt it was none of my business.'

'You've also probably guessed that after her bad marriage she wasn't ready for a new relationship. Things happened too fast between us. Oh well, it probably wasn't meant to be anyway.'

'With her being church and you being chapel, you mean?'

That amused Ince. 'I don't think that would have been a factor,' he grinned. 'I don't know really. I think I was dazzled by her beauty and after years of a quiet village life she was so different to any other woman I know.' He was aware of the special sadness his friend was feeling today but thought it was about time he admitted something that had been on his mind for a long time before Laura arrived in Kilgarthen. 'I want a wife and family of my own, Spencer. I think it's only fair to tell you that I might not be living at the farm for ever.'

Spencer felt brave enough to accept that there might be another loss in the future but it wasn't as if Ince had said he'd go away and not be working on the farm any more. 'Vicki and I will miss you if you do go, Ince, but I wish you well and hope you find the right woman some day soon.'

–

'Right then,' Laura said to Vicki when Mike had left and Pat had gone upstairs with a duster, polish and broom. 'We've had a look at what's in the cupboards and larder. Shall we make a rabbit pie, mashed potatoes, cabbage and carrots? Followed by a steamed pudding for afters?'

Vicki nodded enthusiastically. 'Can I rub the fat into the flour? I did it the other day with Daddy.' She didn't mention she had made a terrible mess and covered half the table with flour and it had taken Spencer ages to wash her greasy hands clean.

Laura was willing to let her do anything she wanted. 'Of course you can, sweetheart. I'll prepare the meat and peel the vegetables then we'll stir the pudding together. First, let's see if we can find some aprons.'

The two of them spent a happy hour carrying food to the large table and preparing the meal. Vicki managed not to make quite as much mess as she had with her father. When all the preparations were finished, they sat at the table making shapes with the leftover pastry.

Pat bustled into the kitchen carrying an armful of washing. 'I had to creep about not to disturb Jacka. He's sleeping at the moment.

I'll take a cup of tea up to Joan. You two look like you're enjoying yourselves. I'll take this lot home and put it through the copper and handwash with mine. There isn't an item of women's clothing in Tressa's things but even her brother's clothes can't disguise how pretty she is, can they? You can see why Andrew's falling so heavily for her. They seemed very close, don't you think, before they went out to work? I hope with Jacka ill she isn't turning to him for the wrong reasons.'

'I've been thinking about that too,' Laura said, passing Vicki the rolling pin and a scone cutter. 'It's difficult but we'll just have to stand back and leave them to their own lives, but it was Andrew she ran to raise the alarm about Jacka. It was him she wanted to drive her back here.'

'Yes, there is that,' Pat admitted, feeling more optimistic. 'You've got the kettle on, good. I'll call them inside, they must be parched by now.'

'Are you staying to eat, Pat?' Laura asked, admiring Vicki's handiwork.

'Bless you, no. Mike's coming back soon and we'll ride home together.'

She smiled when Laura ducked as Vicki swung the rolling pin in the air and Laura laughed and said patiently, 'Careful, sweetheart. You nearly knocked my block off.'

'You'd make a good mother, Laura,' Pat stated.

Mike came with Bunty just before midday and they carried in a large box of groceries made up of various little gifts the villagers had wanted passed on. Bunty raised her eyebrows to see Vicki there. 'The vicar's on his way,' she said. 'How are you getting on here? How's Tressa bearing up? I saw her this morning from my bedroom window tearing down the hill to the pub in a terrible state. It gave me quite a turn, I can tell you.'

'Everything's under control,' Laura replied, packing up Vicki's pastry shape of a hedgehog and untying the little girl's makeshift apron. 'Tressa's taking it hard but she's better working outside. Will you tell Aunty Daisy I'll pop in and see her this evening, please?'

'Certainly I will.' Bunty looked as if she was chewing something over. 'Is Andrew with Tressa?'

Laura smiled to herself, she knew what Bunty was getting at. 'Yes, he hasn't left her side all day.' She knew that would provide a juicy morsel to pass on to Daisy.

And sure enough Bunty was in a hurry to leave. 'Are you ready, Pat and Mike? We'd best be going and let them eat their dinner here in peace.'

When dinner was over, Spencer was the next on the scene. Tressa and Andrew had no more work to do for a while and had taken mugs of tea into the sitting room. Vicki was sitting on Laura's lap while Laura plaited her hair, tying the ends with scraps of wool from Joan's knitting bag. Laura looked guiltily at Spencer; she never felt comfortable in his presence.

Vicki didn't get down and rush to him like she usually did but if Spencer was put out, he didn't show it. 'Is Bert Miller here yet?'

'I haven't seen or heard him,' Laura replied.

'I'll wait for him here.' He sat down in Jacka's chair on the other side of the range.

'Me and Laura made rabbit pie and a lovely pudding, Daddy,' Vicki piped up. 'You must get her to cook some for you.'

'That would be nice,' he said, noting the charming scene the two of them made. Vicki looked thoroughly at home on her perch having her hair plaited. Laura Jennings was exceedingly beautiful, even more so since country living had dispersed the pale, gaunt look she'd had when he'd first seen her. He felt sorry for Ince. He knew what it was like to lose the woman he loved and losing a woman such as this one would be very hard.

Laura tied the last piece of wool in Vicki's hair then said, 'Don't forget you've got something you made from the pastry to show Daddy. It's in the back kitchen keeping cool. Why don't you run along and fetch it?'

Vicki skipped off obediently and Laura turned to Spencer. He could see she was going to ask him something and he raised his fair brows. 'I was wondering if you would mind if I gave Vicki a present for her birthday. I know it's late but I wanted to ask you first. It's nothing showy, just a plain cardigan.'

'I can't see anything wrong with that. You seemed almost too afraid to ask me.'

'Things haven't been easy between us.'

'True, but seeing how much Vicki likes you, we must make sure that changes, mustn't we?'

In the evening, Andrew carried an armchair upstairs so Joan and Tressa in turn could sit and keep their vigil more comfortably.

'Would you like to stay at the farm until we learn one way or the other about Jacka?' Joan said, her voice weary from the long day. 'Tressa needs you to be close and I'd be glad to have you here too. It would be strange without a man about the place.'

Andrew was delighted and said so. 'I told Tressa today that I love her. I think she feels a lot for me too. But what about Jacka? If all goes well, and I pray to God it does, do you think if he's against us settling down, she'll follow his wishes? I couldn't bear to lose her, Joan.'

'I think Jacka's main worry is what sort of future Tressa will have with you. If you got married and lived in London she wouldn't be happy mixing with strangers she'd have nothing in common with. She said something this morning about you maybe not going back to London. Would you be happy down here, living a totally different kind of life, Andrew?'

'I love Tressa for what she is and wouldn't dream of taking her away from her beloved moor. I could set up in practice locally. I've got some savings and I'd sell my flat. I'll buy her a farm of her own if that's what she wants and we'll work the land together, it's got a strong hold over me now. In fact, I could sort out the problem with the bank and buy Tregorlan Farm and we could all live here together. The farm's big enough and we can always make some alterations. When Jacka gets better, he can potter around to his heart's content and not risk his health. It would be the answer to all our problems, Joan.'

Joan wiped a tear from her eye and put a hand on his arm. 'You're a good man, Andrew Macarthur. You go ahead and put a ring on Tressa's finger with my blessing. Jacka will feel the same way, I'm sure, but if he doesn't, you just leave him to me.'

Joan insisted she would sit up with Jacka the first night. Tressa couldn't sleep. She lay in her bed staring out of the window at the starlit sky. She went over every moment of Jacka's symptoms leading up to his heart attack and blamed herself for not seeing how ill he was. She regretted every cross word she'd said to him recently even though there were only a few. She thought of Joan and their worries for the future, although her aunt seemed more serene since the few moments she'd spent talking with Andrew. She thought about Andrew. Not the things that had already happened between them, not even the way they had stolen a long passionate kiss goodnight. She was thinking about him lying in the next room and how she wanted and needed his arms round her, his closeness, his love. She knew she couldn't live without him now.

She endured her loneliness another hour then got out of bed. She crept out onto the landing, passed her brothers' room and stopped and listened outside her father's room. She could hear Joan snoring. She peeped inside and saw that her father was sleeping; he had hardly roused during the day. She tiptoed back to her brothers' room and slowly lifted the latch. She had done this on many nights as a small girl when she had felt frightened after a bad dream, or when the wind on the moor was particularly fierce, and had crept into Jimmy's or Matty's bed and they had comforted her. She was seeking a different sort of comfort tonight.

Andrew hadn't been able to sleep either and sat up in surprise. He waited for her slender form in the thin nightdress to reach him. 'What's the matter, darling?' he whispered through the darkness.

'Nothing. I can't sleep,' she whispered back. 'I-I want to be with you.'

'You'll get cold if you stay there. You're welcome to come in with me but I've got nothing on. I won't be fetching my things until tomorrow.'

'It doesn't matter.' She shivered but she wasn't cold. 'I won't be able to see anything.'

'That wasn't what I was thinking of.' He held back the covers. He had been noble enough to point out that they would have only the barrier of her nightdress between them, but he didn't want her to change her mind.

She slipped in under the covers beside him. They lay on their sides facing each other, their faces on the pillow, their arms around each other.

'I was tempted to come to you but I was afraid it would upset you and if Joan caught me she'd get out a shotgun,' he said, grinning.

'We'll have to be very quiet. If Aunty Joan wakes up, she'll be horrified with me.'

He caressed her cheek. 'Why did you come to me?'

'I used to climb in with Matty or Jimmy when I was frightened as a girl.'

'I'm not one of your brothers, Tressa.'

She ran a hand over his broad shoulder and rested the palm on his bare chest. 'I know.'

He gathered her in close to him and she could hear his heart beating wildly and she could feel that he wanted her. 'Sorry,' he murmured, kissing her hair, 'but you can't really blame me. Don't worry, I can keep control.'

She rested her face on his chest, breathing in his wonderful male scent and luxuriating in the feeling of being in contact with him all the way down his strong lean body. 'It's all right to do it if you're in love, isn't it?' she whispered, making him shiver deliciously where her warm breath caressed his flesh.

He put his hand under her chin and lifted her face to his. 'Are you saying you love me? And do you want to make love?'

'Yes, I love you, Andrew. I've been thinking about how I feel all day.' She kissed his lips.

He wanted to shout for joy but kept his voice to an emotional whisper. 'Apart from Jacka taking ill, this has been the best day of my life. What about my other question?'

Tressa was fighting with herself, but she had been brought up to do things in their proper sequence. 'I want to but it wouldn't be right with Dad and Aunty Joan in the next room, but when the time is right...'

Andrew blinked away tears of pure happiness. He crushed her to him. 'Just holding you here like this is enough for now, darling. And the time will be right when I meet you in the village church and make you my wife as soon as I possibly can.'

Chapter 31

'They fell for it. What twerps grown-ups are. Old man Lean played
into my hands.' These were words from Bill's first diary dated 1932,
when he was twelve years old.

Now that the frights of Andrew's kidnapping and Jacka's heart
attack were over, and Jacka was recovering, Laura had picked up her
husband's diaries again. It was a cold, brisk day early in February and
she was going to take her first ride on a Hawksmoor pony later in the
day. She felt that if she read anything unpalatable, the moor and fresh
air would cleanse it from her mind.

What had Bill been referring to? The obvious answer was that it
had something to do with William Lean being his father. Many of
Bill's entries showed spite and gloating and would have made sense
only to himself. She had read several pages from all the diaries. What
he'd written about her had made her shiver with repugnance. In an
early entry: 'Thank God I can come down here to get away from her.
Her adoration makes me sick.' Then later: 'I can't stand her feeble face
of suffering.'

It made uncomfortable reading and Laura knew she had been
married to a thoroughly despicable man with no conscience. She
felt consoled in the knowledge that nothing she had done had made
him the obnoxious individual he'd turned out to be. He had written
scathing things about most of the villagers; some, it seemed, he'd hated.
'These pathetic people think I'm wonderful. They're so moral and
upright, but money always talks. Bloody hypocrites! My father did as
much for them but they never fell at his feet.' Laura was puzzled by
that last statement. Had William Lean not been so horrible after all?

Even Aunty Daisy hadn't escaped his spite, he had referred to her as 'that silly interfering woman'.

As Laura had suspected, Bill had splashed money round the village only to show off. An entry about the war memorial read: 'They loved the decorative chains for the war memorial. Actually felt sorry for me because I couldn't join up. (Not much wrong with my eyes.) The Davey boys and the others were idiots and they think I was honouring them.' Honouring yourself, more like, Laura thought.

The only genuine thing about him had been his love for the moorland and its unique wildness and beauty. It had been this that had brought him back here, a salve for his rotten soul.

As she closed the volume Laura knew she would get no answers to her questions from the diaries; Bill had used them as an outlet for his sneering envy and contempt, not to record facts.

As she set off for her riding excursion, Ma Noon was coming up the hill towards her.

Laura nodded a greeting but didn't attempt to stop the jingle. She was surprised when the old lady brought the pony to a halt.

'How is Mr Davey progressing?' she asked from within the confines of her big ribboned bonnet.

Once again her polished voice was a shock to Laura and she hoped her face didn't betray it. 'He's allowed out of bed for an hour a day and the doctor and district nurse are looking in on him. He's a bit depressed but that's only to be expected. If he's careful and doesn't try to overdo his work in the future, the doctor says he should avoid another attack.' Laura knew that despite Andrew's reassurances that he was going to make sure everything would work out all right, Jacka was still worried about being evicted from his home, but Laura kept that to herself.

'The poor man. I am glad to hear he is getting better though.' Ma Noon regarded Laura with a critical eye, taking in her riding clothes and boots. The old woman might keep herself almost entirely to herself but Laura felt sure her shrewd green eyes didn't miss much. 'You look as if you're going somewhere.'

'I am, to Hawksmoor stables. I'm borrowing a pony to trek over the moor.'

'Hop up. I'll drive you there, if you like.'

Laura wasn't going to miss this opportunity to get to know the mysterious Ma Noon and perhaps discover some information about Bill's past. She climbed up and squeezed herself beside Ma Noon's bulk. She held her knapsack on her lap. 'I'm taking a flask of tea, some food, a light raincoat and a good map,' she explained.

'Very sensible,' Ma Noon commented, making the pony walk on. 'I see you have dressed sensibly. The moor won't be trifled with.' Like all the locals, she spoke of the moor as if it was a living thing.

'Have you lived in Kilgarthen all your life, Mrs Noon?' Laura asked, smiling with false charm at Ada Prisk who stared at them with her mouth wide open as they passed her.

'Only since I married. Like all parts of the moor, Kilgarthen has changed a lot since those days. Life probably seems primitive to you but when I was a bride we had no shop and no sub-post office, and until the roads were tarmacked we had no delivery vans plying their wares. There was no coal as an alternative to turf and we used to live almost entirely on potatoes and salt pork.' She looked at Laura through the corners of her eyes. 'We cared nothing for fashion.'

Laura would have liked to ask her many personal questions but felt she couldn't on such a short acquaintance; hopefully there would be another time. She brought up the subject of Bill. In his diaries he'd referred to the old lady simply as Ma and logged the times he had called on her. 'I understand Bill came to your smallholding often.'

'He did. People think me rather strange and perhaps I am, but no matter, I live my life as I choose to. Bill wasn't afraid of me like the other children. I caught him one day throwing stones at my goats. I asked him not to do it again. He was surprised that I didn't shout at him or threaten to get the constable after him – that's never been my way. When he said he was sorry, I asked him into the house to take tea with me, something I'd never done before, and our friendship grew from there. He was a very mixed-up child and I didn't mind that he used to boast that he wasn't afraid of me to the other children. He came often and did little jobs for me and I was very grateful for all that he did for me as a man. Each time he came back to the village, after he'd seen his aunt, Mrs Tamblyn, he called on me. He used to confide in me and although he made a success of his life, I sensed he was often unhappy.

'Before I say any more about him, I ought to add that I knew of his dark side. As a boy and youth he used to get frustrated and fly into terrible rages. He never took them out on me but used me as a sounding board. I knew he could be ruthless and although he rarely spoke of you, I was sure that he never treated you right. I'm sorry Bill turned out the way he did. I never went to his funeral, but then I haven't set foot in the graveyard since I laid my husband to rest there thirty-five years ago, but I do miss Bill.'

Laura detected emotion in Mrs Noon's throat and she kept silent until they had passed by the Methodist chapel and driven on several more yards. 'I've been told that Bill resented his humble life and felt he should be treated better as he was really William Lean's son.'

'So you've heard those rumours. Bill should never have started them.'

Laura stared at Ma Noon. 'You mean Bill started them himself? But why?'

'I don't know why, Mrs Jennings. I pleaded with him to put the matter right but he never did.'

'But that's a terrible thing to do.' Laura was outraged and could hardly trust herself to carry on with the conversation.

'He paid for his sins,' Mrs Noon said, her voice sharpening, shoulders stiffening. 'He died very young. I would think that punishment enough if I were you.'

The other woman's loyalty to Bill was obviously unshakable. 'I won't say anything, if that's what you're hinting at, Mrs Noon, but you can hardly expect me to respect Bill's memory.'

'Why not? You married him for better or worse. My husband was the devil incarnate and I stood by him through thick and thin. He was also taken young. I was left free to do as I pleased after that. You're in the same position. Take my advice and do the same.'

'I am, but we'll have to agree to differ on some of your views.' Laura was thinking of Barbara Roach. Laura didn't believe the stories of Barbara falling down the stairs and having flu. Bruises caused by what had obviously been a vicious beating had still been visible on her face yesterday when she'd dared to show her face in the shop for the first time since Cecil had thrown Marianne out in the snow. Barbara had refused to stop and talk, not even responding when she was asked how Marianne was. Laura hoped Barbara hadn't heard the speculations about who the father of Marianne's baby was. Ada Prisk had declared that one of several men could be responsible, 'after all, the girl has always been a flighty piece'.

Laura was glad when Hawksmoor House appeared just up ahead. Mrs Noon might not be mad as some villagers thought she was but she was certainly very strange. 'Thank you, Mrs Noon. It was kind of you to go out of your way for me.' She got down and waited for the old lady to turn the jingle round.

Ma Noon studied her for a moment. 'Like I said, Mrs Jennings, I do precisely what I want to. Good afternoon to you.'

As the jingle ambled back down the lane, Laura was left with the thought that there went a contrary character. She said she had stuck by her husband, but how willingly? Had she turned bitter and passed it on to Bill? She shrugged her shoulders. No matter. She didn't expect to be invited to the Noon smallholding and the old lady was unlikely to play a part in her future life.

The Hawksmoor stable boy had Laura's mount, a dark, quiet mare named Honesty, ready for her. He gave a few instructions and asked her what route she intended to take and what time she would bring the pony back, then he tweaked his cap and left the stableyard. Laura led Honesty into the yard and walked her up and down to get the measure of her, talking to get her used to the sound of her voice. She put her riding hat on, her foot in the stirrup to mount when a pair of hands on her waist made her shriek and whirl round.

'Harry Lean!' She was horrified he was there, she had chosen a day when Felicity said he would be sure to be at his office. He was dressed in a suit and she suspected he had come home early to proposition her. 'What do you think you're doing? How dare you creep up on me and touch me like that.'

'No need to go on so,' he laughed, much amused. 'I wasn't about to try to have my wicked way with you, Laura.'

'I don't believe you,' she snorted. 'I haven't forgotten how you molested Tressa Davey. She told me what you offered her.'

He raised a dark sardonic eyebrow. 'Whatever she may have told you, she got it all wrong. I never meant her any harm. I was only trying to help her father. How is Jacka? I hear they may be evicted because he couldn't pay his mortgage or something.'

'You needn't worry about the Daveys, Harry,' she told him in no uncertain terms. 'Andrew Macarthur has been to see the bank manager and is sorting it all out for them. In his position, he is sure to be successful. Now if you'll excuse me, I want to go riding. The air is getting damper and I want to get on.'

Harry's face had darkened. He was seething; it seemed his plan to have the Daveys evicted was about to be ruined. Then, looking at Laura, he rallied. Well, never mind, one must be sporting about these things. Macarthur was likely to succeed where he had failed; he hoped Tressa Davey would go the same way as Marianne Roach. This young widow would do in Tressa's place. He rearranged his features into a pleasant smile. 'I'm glad to hear Macarthur's being helpful. I was able to get away earlier than I expected today. Give me a minute and I'll change my clothes and join you.'

'No, thank you, Harry,' she said emphatically. 'I want to ride alone.'

He moved closer and put his arm over the mare's saddle. 'Oh, but I insist. You don't know the moor and you might get lost.'

'I have a lot of thinking to do,' Laura snapped. 'If I can't go alone then I won't go at all.'

Harry knew he wouldn't get anywhere with her if he didn't comply with her wishes. He put on an innocent expression. 'Oh, very well. As you wish, Laura. Just trying to be friendly.' He moved away from the pony.

On a sudden impulse she turned to him. 'Harry, have you ever heard the rumours that Bill was fathered by your father?'

'Hah!' Harry laughed evilly. 'I wondered how long it would take before you heard that and brought it up. It was all Bill's doing. The bastard thought he could wring money out of the old man by offering to scotch the rumours himself My father whipped him that day with his riding crop.'

'Why didn't your father ever deny it? He didn't, to my knowledge.'

'There wouldn't have been any point. A denial would have been almost as good as an admission. There's no smoke without fire, people would only have said. He left the rumours to die a natural death and I don't care what the blasted villagers think.'

'Would you stay here if it wasn't for your mother, Harry?' she was curious to know.

'Why? You interested in running off with me to start a new life?'

'Hardly.'

'I've also got a niece on the other side of the village, remember. You're well in with Spencer now, so I hear. When do you think it likely that a miracle for Mother will occur?' On this he was as serious as a judge in court.

'Soon, I hope. That's all I can say at the moment.'

–

Laura was glad to get away from Hawksmoor. The air on the moor was bracing and the solitude freshened her mind in a way nothing else could. Using the map for guidance, she trotted along the course of the Withey Brook where a great variety of water weeds grew in all shades of brown, green and red; in many places they gave the appearance of seaside rock pools. From out of their weedy hiding places small trout darted. She moved over thick, sweeping patches of bracken which were interspersed with rough grassland and stunted bushes bending to the prevailing east wind. Here and there some yellow was bursting forth on the budding gorse bushes.

From her vantage point on the pony's back she could see the tracks that foxes and other wildlife had made. She crossed the brook over a narrow wooden bridge, brushing away midge-like insects which bombarded her face. The track she was following had been used in ancient times and was marked by a weathered granite cross. Every few minutes she stopped and scoured the landscape and looked up at the tors and craggy rocks that rose up like silent sentinels. Two big black crows cawed to each other from a pair of boulders as if they were discussing this visitor on horseback. A kestrel, magnificent on the wing, wheeled overhead and Laura felt it was watching her.

Trotting on, she came across some unbroken ponies a few hands shorter than Honesty and dismounted to approach them. There were a dozen in all, in a variety of colours. Some were cautious, but when one trotted up to her, its wide head nodding as if in greeting, the others followed suit. She stroked their shaggy coats and tangled manes and they nuzzled her, hoping for a titbit of food. When she remounted, she was followed for some time by the inquisitive ponies.

Back on the track again, she soon located a Bronze Age settlement on Bastreet Downs. The remains of many of these ancient communities were scattered across the whole of the moorland. Laura could make out the circles where their huts had once stood and the site of a barrow where a chieftain had been buried and where his bones and worldly possessions probably still remained unexcavated. It was strange to think of those hardy pre-Celtic tribes living and working in this very spot.

Sitting at the foot of the burial mound, she drank from her flask and ate her sandwiches. She was content with life and felt it was beginning anew at last. She was more able to think out here on the moor; the air was fresh and clean, the wind invigorating. Staying to live in Kilgarthen had been the wisest move of her life. If she had gone back to London she would have been surrounded by bad memories and probably become bitter. Although she had chosen to live in Bill's village, his influence on her life had all but vanished. She had met new people and become involved in their lives. She had found comfort in Ince's arms, proving to her that one day she could form a proper relationship with a man, and although she was sorry she had hurt him, she was glad that he understood she needed to be unattached for now. She had watched Andrew's innocent romance unfold before her eyes. Best of all she had found Vicki.

A snatch of chilly wind suddenly tugged at her clothes and she looked up at the sky. It had turned a gloomy grey and even as she looked a thick mist began to descend. A prickle of alarm made her gather up the knapsack and hasten to the pony.

'Come on, Honesty, we must head for home. The weather's changing fast.'

She headed the pony back the way they had come, a niggle of fear sitting on her back. She had been told often that the weather could change with frightening speed on the moor but she didn't realise it could happen in mere seconds. She urged Honesty on but the track was narrow and they couldn't canter for fear of stumbling on the tufts of long grass and the jutting rocks. She told herself she had nothing to fear, she wasn't far from Hawksmoor, about two miles.

The distance she could see up ahead was steadily getting shorter. If she could make it to the bridge she could dismount, and although she would have to beware of boggy patches, she could follow the course of the Withey Brook and with luck find her way back to Hawksmoor. Moments later the ragged hems of the mist sank down to meet the moorland floor and she couldn't see past the pony's head. All she could do was to let the reins drop loose and allow Honesty to walk at will, hoping and praying she would find the way home.

It was strangely silent, there were no sounds of wildlife or the rustle of grass; even the wind had stopped blowing although the mist swirled eerily all around her. Her head bent low over the saddle, she strained for sounds of rushing water that would mean the Withy Brook was not far away. She was wet through and shivering and continually had to wipe moisture from her eyelashes. Never had she felt more alone. Fear and desolation were mounting inside her by the second. She had found a new life, but how long was she going to live it?

Time passed; it seemed like hours. She looked at her watch and saw that it was over an hour since she had started back. In that time they had splashed through streams and rounded sudden outcrops of granite, the moorland growth pulling at the pony's hooves and unsettling it. At times Laura was forced to dismount and lead Honesty through an almost impenetrable ground of tangled brambles or tightly packed gorse and dead bracken. She was desperate to come across a deserted farm to shelter in until the mist cleared, her terror growing that she would have to spend the night on the open moor. Unwary people had been lost before and not survived. The solitude she had enjoyed earlier had turned into a feeling of bleak aloneness.

Honesty suddenly whinnied nervously and reared up. She backed up and Laura grasped the reins tightly. She panicked when she realised the mare's hooves were sinking into marshy ground. They had not passed over ground like this on the way to the Bronze Age settlement. She knew they were hopelessly lost.

They were slipping down a waterlogged slope. Honesty couldn't keep her footing and Laura made to dismount. Honesty bucked violently and she was thrown from the saddle. She hit the ground with a squelchy thump, screaming at the pony to come back as it tore off in fear, leaving her face and clothes splashed with thick mud. Laura sat up to get her breath and her insides froze as she heard Honesty whinnying in terror and struggling. The pony had run into a bog and was sinking fast.

Chapter 32

Felicity hurried out of her car and dashed into the kitchen of Rose-merryn Farm. Spencer and Vicki, who were peeling potatoes together at the sink, turned round in surprise.

'Before you say anything, Spencer,' Felicity blurted out, holding up her hands to still his protests, 'Laura's out on the moor in this mist. I've just come back from the hairdresser's to find she had gone riding to Bastreet Downs to look at the settlements. That was about three hours ago. She wouldn't have had time to get back before the mist came down and now it's getting dark. When I left Hawksmoor, there was no sign of her. I'm terribly worried. If she hasn't stayed in one place she's almost certainly lost by now. I'm worried she might have wandered onto Redmoor Marsh and come a cropper. Could you go and look for her? Harry's gone to Truro on business and the stable boy's not experienced enough so I daren't send him.'

Spencer's mouth was agape. Drying his hands, he lifted Vicki down off the stool she was kneeling on. It was strange having this woman back in his house after so many years but that didn't matter. He was sorry now that he had dragged his heels over telling Vicki about her grandmother and had not spoken to Felicity as he had intended to do. 'Ince won't be back for a while. He's attending a calving. Will you stay with Vicki so I can leave straightaway?'

'Of course I will,' Felicity said, smiling at her granddaughter who was holding on to her father's leg with a sulky face. 'You don't need to ask that, Spencer.' Spencer lowered himself down and put his hands on Vicki's waist. 'Do you understand what's happening, pipkin? Laura could be in danger and it's very important that I go at once to find her. My horse is used to all weather conditions on the moor. This lady is called Felicity, you've seen her about the village. She's going to stay with you until Uncle Ince comes in or Daddy gets back. Now you be a good girl for her.' He kissed his daughter's cheek. 'I have to go now and get ready.'

Vicki hugged him and reluctantly let him go. 'Hurry, Daddy, find Laura. I want her to be my new mummy.' Spencer made no remark. A strained look passed between him and Felicity. He left the room to change into wet weather clothing.

Smiling uncertainly at Vicki, who was glaring at her frostily, Felicity took off her headscarf and coat; her hairdo was quite ruined. 'Were you and Daddy making supper, Vicki?' she said. 'Perhaps I can help you instead?'

Vicki folded her arms and put up her chin. It was something Natalie used to do when cross and Felicity was overcome with emotion. She felt out of place as her granddaughter stood defiantly in her little pinny in the middle of the room and Spencer rushed about picking up items he might need. When he had finally gone, Vicki marched back to the sink and climbed up onto the stool. She picked up a potato and the knife and Felicity rushed over to her.

'I don't think you ought to be using that knife, Vicki. Why don't I peel the potatoes like your Daddy was and you carry on with what you were doing.'

'He was passing me the spuds to put in the saucepan.' Vicki's voice was loud and decidedly surly.

'I see he's already done carrots, parsnips, turnip and onions. What was he going to cook?'

'Stew.'

'Do you like stew, dear?' Felicity asked, passing her granddaughter a peeled potato.

Vicki held it up high and dropped it into the saucepan so it made a loud plop and splashed water over the sides. 'No, I don't like stew,' she retorted rudely. 'If you make it I won't eat it and don't call me dear.'

'Vicki,' Felicity implored her, 'why are you behaving like this?'

Vicki scrambled down from the stool and pulling off her pinny threw it on the floor. 'I don't like you!' she stormed.

335

Stung to the depths of her heart, Felicity left the sink and asked her daughter's only child, 'But why not, Vicki?'

'Benjy Miller said you are my granny and you don't love me. His granny gives him presents and knits him jumpers and comes to see him and has him back to her place to stay overnight. You don't want anything to do with me. You don't love me.' Vicki ended by stamping her foot.

Tears of grief welled up in Felicity's eyes. 'That's not true, Vicki. Perhaps when your daddy comes back he'll explain things to you. Why don't you play with your toys while I carry on with the supper?'

Her little face still dark and heated, Vicki went huffily to her doll's cot. She wanted to ignore this stranger but there was something she didn't want to miss out on. She stood close to Felicity as she put the chopped beef on the range to boil.

'Yes, Vicki? Do you want something?' Felicity asked cautiously.

'Daddy said I could see the new calf,' she muttered ungraciously. 'He was going to take me out to Uncle Ince in the barn. They put her in there 'cos of the weather. I'm not allowed to go by myself 'cos I might get in the way.'

'Well, this meat isn't going to boil for ages. Why don't we put our coats on and go to the barn now, then we can see how much longer it will be before the calf is born.'

Vicki refused to be helped into her outdoor clothes and when they were both ready, she stuffed her hands into her pockets. She reminded Felicity so much of Natalie; she hadn't been afraid to speak her mind and get on her high horse either. It was almost pitch dark and by the light of Felicity's torch they made their way across the mist-shrouded yard. Vicki pushed open the barn door, ushered Felicity inside, then closed it as she had been taught to do.

Ince was at the back of the barn, at the tail end of the cow, pulling on the protruding front legs of the emerging calf. One mighty pull, a long loud moan from the cow and the calf slithered out in its birth sac. Ince lowered it safely onto the straw. He wiped the calf's mouth then pulled it round to its mother who immediately began licking it clean.

'Uncle Ince! Uncle Ince! I saw it. I came in time,' Vicki shrieked, jumping up and down.

'I didn't hear you come in, sweetheart. You're just in time to name the calf,' Ince said without looking round at the newcomers. ''Tis a fine healthy calf, mate,' he added with much satisfaction, thinking he was talking to Spencer.

'Laura,' Vicki almost shouted. 'I want to call the calf Laura.'

'Now why does that come as no surprise to me?' Ince turned round with a big smile on his gentle face. 'Mrs Lean! You're the last person I expected to see here.'

'I'm here because Laura's out on the moor in the mist. Spencer's gone to look for her,' Felicity explained, the strain of the worry and Vicki's hostility plain on her face. Her dishevelled hair bothered Ince. He had only ever seen her immaculately groomed.

Vicki climbed over the bales of straw Ince had put up as a draught excluder for the cow and calf, and squeezing herself between him and the calf she put her arms round his neck looking for comfort. 'Daddy will find Laura, won't he, Uncle Ince? He won't let her stay out all night?'

'Daddy will do his best, sweetheart, don't worry.' He cuddled her in close and Felicity felt jealous that he could give her grandchild the comfort that she could not.

'Shall I leave Vicki with you while I go back and look after the supper?' she asked in a small, defeated voice.

'It might be best,' Ince replied sombrely. He had correctly summed up the situation between them. 'Poor Laura. First Andrew Macarthur is kidnapped, Jacka Davey has a heart attack and now this.'

–

Spencer held the lantern high and shouted for the umpteenth time. 'Laura! Laura!' He listened for an answering voice or the whinny of a pony but there was nothing in response except the wail of the bone-chilling wind that had whipped up and was thankfully dispersing the mist.

337

He had crossed the wooden bridge over the Withey Brook and was on Bastreet Downs. In the growing darkness, vision was limited to five feet. Splendour, his sleek black stallion, was accustomed to the popular moorland tracks and they followed the route Laura had taken to the ancient settlement. Occasionally Spencer saw a hoof print in the black mud and felt encouraged that he was on the right track.

When he reached the settlement, he circled it calling to her. At the foot of the barrow, something caught his eye and he dismounted. He had found Laura's red chiffon scarf which she hadn't picked up in her hurry to leave. It smelled of her familiar musky perfume. He pushed it into his pocket.

'So you were here. But where are you now?'

Back in the saddle, he stroked Splendour's strong neck. 'Where is she, boy? My guess is that she would have let Honesty try to find the way home. So what went wrong?' His guts were knotting by the moment. If he didn't find her tonight, a daylight search would probably only discover a body. He urged Splendour on. All he could do was hope he'd come across her by chance.

He could see Vicki's sweet face and knew what it would do to her if she lost Laura. He didn't want Laura to be lost either, that beautiful, vital woman who had become a small part of his life too.

He was on East Moor now where the dreaded Redmoor Marsh was to be found. Loose stones did not scuttle away from the horse's feet here because they were embedded in the soft muddy ground. Splendour was trained to avoid the dangers of the marsh; if he came to soft ground he would lower his head and snort agitatedly but would have no difficulty in skirting it. Nevertheless, Spencer was scared, his pulse rate had heightened and nervous sweat trickled down his back.

He pulled the stallion up suddenly. He thought he had heard something. He put his hands round his mouth and shouted as loudly as he could. 'Laura! Laura!'

There it was again. It might be the call of a small animal, a murmur on the wind or a cry for help. His boots sank into deep mud as he dismounted and led Splendour by the reins in the general direction of the noise, stopping and shouting at regular intervals, warily testing the ground. If it was Laura out there, his shouts would encourage her. He stopped once more to listen.

'Help...'

He made out the cry that time. 'Laura! It's all right. I'm coming for you.'

'Help me!'

Fairly sure of her location, he got on the stallion and urged it over the slippery turf. After several yards, Splendour came to a halt and refused to go on, shaking his magnificent head. Trusting the horse's instincts Spencer let it walk at will but kept it in the direction of the cries.

'Laura! Where are you? Stay calm and keep shouting so I can follow the sound of your voice.'

'Help me. I'm over here.' Her voice was weak but unmistakable. 'Careful, the ground is marshy.'

With the lantern at face level, he scanned the gloomy surroundings. 'Find a stone and throw it in front of you, Laura! I'll listen for where it falls.'

A cry of exertion was quickly followed by a dull thud about ten feet away. Within a few minutes he had reached Laura. Putting the lantern on the ground, he found her huddled in a sitting position, her white face tilted up to him. She was not far from a saucer-like depression of deep marsh. Keeping Splendour close by, he knelt down beside her and she leaned into him. 'Oh, Spencer. Thank God you've come. I was afraid to move. I thought I was going to die out here all alone.'

He pulled a small lightweight blanket out of his bag and put it round her shoulders. 'I'll get you onto my horse,' he said soothingly, using a voice he often employed with Vicki. 'You'll feel better away from the wet ground. Do you think you can walk?' He lifted her to her feet and she groaned as she straightened her stiff limbs. 'I'll gladly carry you but you'll warm up a little if you can walk.'

She gripped his coat and cried, 'Honesty's dead. I heard her drown in the marsh.'

He gave her a small hug. 'There's nothing we can do about that now. The best thing is to get you home safe and warm. You wandered way off the track. We've got a long way to go.'

She had no strength in her legs and he held her upright as he walked her the short distance to where Splendour was patiently waiting.

'What's the time? How long have I been out here?'

'It's about six o'clock. What time did you set off?'

'One thirty,' she groaned. 'It feels as if I've been out here for ever.'

'Never mind that now. I'll soon have you home.'

He lifted her up on to Splendour's back then swung up in the saddle behind her. She leaned against him and holding the reins with one hand, he used the other to clasp her to him.

'I was so frightened,' Laura whispered, reliving every bitter lonely moment since Honesty's terrified whinnies had stopped. 'How did you know I was in danger?'

'Felicity came to the farm. I left her there with Vicki because Ince was helping a calf into the world.'

This made Laura think of something other than her ordeal. 'I'm glad it was Felicity. It will give them a chance to get to know each other.'

'I haven't said anything to Vicki yet, and judging by her face when I left, it wasn't going very well, but we can't worry about that now. It's important to get you home and warm and dry. My horse is trained to cope with all moorland conditions. He should have no trouble finding his way back off the moor.'

Journeying slowly in the hazardous conditions, it took another two hours before they trotted into the village. Feeling secure, Laura had dozed off to sleep and she woke up with a start when Spencer lifted her down. He left Splendour tied to the lych gate.

'It looks like paradise in here,' she mumbled as she looked round the front room of Little Cot from his strong arms.

Laura had long learned how to feed the range in the kitchen and it never went out. Spencer carried her into the cosy room. He put her down on a chair and pulled the kettle across to boil for tea. He looked at her pale, drawn face. 'You'd better get out of those wet clothes.'

'The bathroom's through there,' she murmured, pointing feebly. 'I won't be long.'

'How do you feel now?' he asked gently when she came back clad in her bathrobe with a towel round her head. 'I've brought a blanket downstairs for you.'

She sat down and gratefully took a cup of hot steaming tea from him. 'Thanks, I'm much better now but I feel terrible about Honesty. I'd only ridden her for a couple of hours but she had such a steady nature. How am I going to tell Felicity? How am I going to tell Harry? It was his pony.'

'It wasn't your fault, Laura. Even seasoned moor dwellers have been caught out in sudden weather changes on the moor. I have. Ince has.'

'But you probably knew what to do. You probably stayed where you knew it was reasonably safe and didn't wander off and risk an animal's life.' Tears of wretchedness filled her eyes and she let them slide unchecked down her cheeks. 'I shall never forgive myself for what happened. If you had been hurt or had died, then Vicki would have lost her father as well as her mother.'

Spencer knelt beside her and wiped her tears away with his fingers. 'You're making too much of this, Laura. I wasn't at risk,' he lied, 'and Vicki would have been distraught if anything had happened to you. I had to find you as much for her sake as your own.'

Laura's face lit up. 'Do I mean that much to her?'

'You're special to all of us. Now drink your tea, it'll warm you up. Do you want something to eat?'

She shook her head. He stood up and busied himself making a hot water bottle. 'Which room do you sleep in?'

'Up the top of the stairs, second on the right.' It felt strangely lonely when he went upstairs with the hot water bottle, not the terrible aching loneliness she'd suffered on the moor, but she was left with a longing for human companionship and his was as good as anybody's; in fact she was glad it was him.

'Do you want to go to bed now?' he asked when he reappeared. 'You look all in.'

'I should have a bath and wash my hair but it'll have to wait until tomorrow. I think I will go up now.' She rose and her knees immediately trembled and refused to take her weight.

Spencer lifted her up in his arms. He carried her to her bedroom and sat her on the bed. She couldn't be bothered to put on her nightdress; keeping the blanket round her, she climbed into bed.

'Before I go home I'll pop up the hill to Daisy's and get her to sit with you,' Spencer said, putting the covers over her.

'I'm cold,' she shuddered suddenly, complaining like a recalcitrant child. 'I've never felt so cold in all my life. I don't think I'll ever feel warm again.'

'You will. Try to get some sleep.'

'I don't feel sleepy now I'm in bed.'

He gazed at her for some moments. Her blonde hair was splayed on the pillows round her pale face, making her look ethereal and even more beautiful. Her blue eyes were just as bold and bright. This woman was so very desirable. She'd only been widowed for three months and already Ince, the most unlikely male candidate in the village to chase after her, had loved and lost her. It wouldn't be long before the next man would step forward and make his feelings plain. If she did marry again, he hoped it wouldn't affect her growing relationship with Vicki. It had taken him a long time to admit it, and it had been a bitter pill to swallow, but Vicki needed Laura Jennings. He'd have to take care she stayed around for his beloved daughter's sake.

He said gently, 'Would you like me to hold you for a while?'

'Yes,' she nodded, not wanting him to leave her.

'I'll stay until you're sleeping.'

He half lay on the bed and slipping his arms under the covers, nestled her against his chest. She pressed her face to his thick jumper, feeling his warmth through the soft wool.

'Thank you for saving my life, Spencer.' With him there she was able to put the terrors of the day to the back of her mind and close her eyes. Long after she had drifted off to sleep, he was still there.

Chapter 33

The following Sunday Laura was invited to Hawksmoor House for tea. So was Daisy, Spencer, Vicki and Ince, but Ince declined the invitation. They arrived together in Spencer's car.

Felicity was looking her usual elegant self but ten years younger and full of vitality now that five years of unexpressed grief and an unfair burden had been lifted from her. When Spencer had got back to the farm after Laura's rescue, he had taken Vicki aside and explained how the estrangement between her and her grandmother had been entirely his fault, that Felicity had always longed to see her and do all the things grandmothers did. Vicki had taken most of it in and dropped her surliness but Felicity was still a stranger and she had kept her distance. Felicity didn't mind that, she had all the years ahead to build up a loving relationship with her.

'What a pity Ince hasn't come,' Felicity said gaily, showing her guests to their seats in the dining room, putting Vicki next to her and Laura on the other side of Vicki. It was hard to come to terms with another woman taking part of her dead daughter's place in Vicki's life, but Felicity cared deeply for Laura and acknowledged that if it hadn't been for her, this day would never have come.

'Ince felt it was something of a family occasion,' Spencer said, sitting down opposite Laura and admiring her figure in a fitted blouse and straight skirt. 'And he's always kept to himself.'

'As long as he doesn't feel left out,' Felicity said. Another person came into the room and she met him at the door, threading her arm proudly through his. 'This is your Uncle Harry, Vicki. Would you like to come and say hello to him, dear?'

Vicki viewed the tall dark man in the doorway. She was feeling rather shy and shook her head.

'Perhaps she will a little later,' Laura said.

Harry sat at the head of the table. 'We'll have tea first to break the ice, eh?' he said jovially, winking at Vicki. He looked lingeringly at Laura. 'Good to see you looking the picture of health, Laura.' Then he turned to Daisy. 'She gave us all a scare, didn't she, Mrs Tamblyn? I feel guilty. I should have noticed the way the weather was changing before she set off. I was most alarmed when I drove back from Truro and into the mist but luckily by then Spencer had everything in hand.'

'She's been up to all sorts since she's lived down here,' Daisy laughed, but she refused to look at Harry; he was a menace to any decent woman, in her opinion. 'I can't keep up with her. Thank goodness Spencer found her in time.'

Everyone was looking at her and Laura felt embarrassed. 'Thank you for the flowers you sent me, Harry.' She was still upset over Honesty's death and hadn't had the chance to talk to Harry about it yet. She hoped to do so today.

'My pleasure,' Harry drawled. He noticed that although Vicki was sitting patiently, she was gazing longingly at a plateful of iced, cherry-topped cakes.

'Here you are, poppit,' he said. He put a cake on her plate and then took the cherries off all the other cakes and added them to hers. 'Tuck in and after that Uncle Harry will give you a huge plateful of strawberry trifle.'

Vicki laughed gleefully and popped a cherry into her mouth.

'You will not!' Spencer said disapprovingly; he would never stop loathing Harry.

'You'll make her sick,' Laura tut-tutted.

'You shouldn't have done that,' Daisy muttered, looking down over her nose.

'It would have been better if she had started with a sandwich, Harry,' Felicity pointed out.

Unconcerned, Vicki bit into the soft sponge and white icing. She giggled as Harry winked at her. 'Take no notice of the fuddy-duddies,

Vicki,' he laughed, taking a ham sandwich for himself, then adding in a W.C. Fields voice, 'Stick with Uncle Harry, my dear, and you'll have a rip-roaring time.'

'Well,' Felicity said smiling impishly, seeing the funny side. 'Do start, the rest of you. I'll pour the tea.

'You're quite sure you've no after-effects from being out so long in the wet and cold, Laura?' she asked.

'Yes, no aches and pains, I promise you. Spencer looked after me very well.' He was looking at her as he took a sandwich from the plate Daisy was offering him and she smiled at him. He smiled back. It was only the merest lift of the corners of his wide mouth but it amazed her at how much kinder it made him look. 'Now I've got my strength back, it's time I looked for a job. I've got my jewellery but I want to keep it as a nest egg and I don't want to use up all my small savings.'

'You were your father's personal assistant before you married. Harry could find you something, couldn't you, darling?' Felicity said. She was pleased with the way he had conquered Vicki's shyness of him.

'Absolutely, leave it with me,' Harry replied, pulling funny faces at Vicki and making her laugh.

'You can work in the shop with me,' Daisy put in hastily and somewhat forcibly. 'I'd love to have you. Bunty's finding it hard with her arthritis and I'm not as young as I was. It wouldn't be as much pay as a personal assistant but it would save you the drive into Launceston or one of the other towns every day. It would only be about five hours, Monday to Friday, and every other Saturday morning. You'd have plenty of time to do other things.' She was hinting at time to spend with Vicki and visiting people like Joy Miller and Johnny Prouse.

'It sounds ideal, Aunty Daisy,' Laura exclaimed enthusiastically. She had no particular desire for a high-flown job. 'The perfect answer to all our problems.'

'It will be lovely having you handy in the village,' Felicity said, putting down her teacup. She had begun to show her face again in the village since things had been sorted out with Spencer. 'What about your friend, Andrew Macarthur? Has he made any plans to return to London yet?'

'Oh, didn't you know? Andrew's emigrating down here too. He's taking up a partnership in a Bodmin law practice at the end of the month.'

'And all he needs now is for a certain maid to say she will marry him,' Daisy added, beaming round the table. 'I'm sure you all know who I'm talking about.'

'Is he going to give Jacka and Joan a home too?' Spencer asked tartly. 'Or will he leave them on the streets when they're evicted?'

'Andrew would never do that,' Laura retorted, annoyed. It seemed Spencer's distrustful nature hadn't mellowed much. 'He's been to the bank to try to sort things out and should be hearing from them soon. But even if he doesn't succeed, he'll provide a home for all the Daveys. He's very fond of Jacka and Joan.'

'Aye, he'll see them all right,' Daisy observed, looking at Spencer. 'He's a good man, kindness itself, and he adores that dear maid. Be a wedding soon, I shouldn't wonder. That'll give us all something to look forward to.'

Spencer made an impatient sound and Laura was reminded of his grumpy disposition. It was a pity he couldn't be more relaxed about life, even act silly at times, like Harry.

Harry had gone quiet. It still irked him that he had failed to bring Tressa Davey to the gutter if not his bed. A small hand tugged on his shirt cuff.

'Can I see your horses please, Uncle Harry?' Vicki had plucked up the courage to ask but she didn't want to go alone. 'And Laura, can she come too?'

'Certainly, you both can,' Harry replied heartily, tweaking her nose. 'As soon as you've stuffed yourself full of trifle.'

When tea was over, Felicity showed Daisy over the house while Spencer went alone to the drawing room to mull over the times he had spent there with Natalie. Laura helped Vicki into her hat and coat and they accompanied Harry to the stables.

Vicki allowed Harry to hold her other hand. 'Why have you got so many horses, Uncle Harry?' she wanted to know.

'I hire them out to holidaymakers to ride. We're quite remote here, a long way from the towns, but lots of people like to go pony trekking.

346

In the summer I hire a trained guide to go with them.' He added over Vicki's head, 'I wish I'd had a guide the day you went out, Laura.'

When Vicki was standing halfway up the gate of a stall, held safely by Harry, absorbed in stroking Harry's own mount Charlie Boy, Laura tapped his arm. He immediately gave her his attention.

'Harry, I've been wanting to talk to you about Honesty. I'm so sorry she died, I feel responsible. She must have been valuable to you. Is there any way I can compensate you?'

Oh yes, he thought, looking deeply into her eyes, I can think of one very special way. He wouldn't suggest what was on his mind. Felicity liked and respected Laura, and they both had reason to be grateful to her over Vicki; he'd just have to rely on his charm to achieve his ends.

'Laura, I want you to forget about doing any such thing. What happened was an accident. If you're worried about the financial side of things, then don't. I have insurance for that sort of thing. Look, I know I've come on strong with you and you don't trust me after what I did to Tressa, but if you ever want to go riding again and don't want to go by yourself, I hope you will consider letting me accompany you. I make no bones about the fact that I like the ladies but you have my word you can trust me.'

'Thanks, Harry,' Laura said. 'If and when I ride again, I won't go alone.'

They were suddenly aware of Vicki looking at them with a strange expression on her face.

'What's the matter, darling?' Laura asked anxiously. 'Are you afraid of the horse?'

'No, I like Charlie Boy. Uncle Harry is a nice man to show him to me. My granny is a nice lady. Daddy said he kept me away from them. Is my daddy a horrible man?'

Laura was appalled. 'Oh no, your daddy's a very nice man, Vicki. He got very upset when your mummy died and sometimes grown-ups behave in ways children can't understand. He loves you very much, Vicki, never forget that.'

Spencer had come out to the stable and had overheard. He coughed to gain attention and gave Laura a quick look of gratitude. 'I'm afraid we'll have to break the tea party up. Bunty was just on the phone. The shop has been broken into and Daisy has to go home.'

'Oh no,' Laura said, lifting Vicki down and holding her in her arms.

'She's in a state of shock,' Spencer said. 'I'll drive you and Daisy back.' He held out his hand. 'Come along with me, pipkin.'

'If Vicki would like to, why don't you let her stay here with me and Mother?' Harry offered.

Spencer looked very doubtful and Laura seized the opportunity to let Vicki be fully united with her grandmother and uncle. 'Things could be upsetting at the shop, Spencer.'

With a submissive sigh, Spencer said, 'Would you like to stay with Granny and Uncle Harry, pipkin?'

'For a little while,' Vicki replied quietly.

'I'll be back in an hour,' Spencer promised her.

Laura kissed Vicki goodbye and handed her over to Harry. Daisy was waiting in Spencer's car, shaking and sobbing and being comforted by Felicity. They drove to the shop quickly to find Mike Penhaligon and Andrew waiting inside with Bunty, who was also distressed.

'Constable Geach is on his way,' Andrew said, leading Daisy to her chair in the kitchen. 'I was on my way to Tregorlan Farm to pick Jacka up to take him to evensong. I thought I saw someone at a window and as I knew you were going to Hawksmoor House for tea with Laura, I asked Miss Buzza if you had changed your mind. I got Mike and we found the back door had been forced open. We checked over the house to make sure the burglar wasn't still here and then Miss Buzza was able to check your stock. Cigarettes have been taken and I'm afraid yesterday's takings and all the post office takings have gone too.'

'But who could have done it?' Daisy sobbed. 'There were a couple of burglaries, including a post office, in Bodmin during the war but we've never had nothing like this round here before.'

'You leave that to the constable, m'dear,' Mike said.

Spencer and Andrew exchanged a look. 'If you want to get away, Macarthur, I can stay with Mike and the ladies.'

Andrew nodded gratefully. Eager to make a good impression, he wanted to sit with Jacka through the service. After assuring Daisy he would do all he could for her tomorrow, he left.

'Love's young dream,' Spencer said drily.

'There's no need to be like that,' Laura said, wanting to dig him in the ribs, then she remembered she also wanted to congratulate him. 'It was good of you to leave Vicki at Hawksmoor. Are you finding it difficult?'

'I'll survive,' he growled under his breath so the others in the room couldn't hear. 'My personal feelings are my own business.'

'Don't worry,' she replied moving away from him. 'I won't forget it again.'

They had been warned not to touch anything until the constable arrived and there was nothing else to do but sit and drink tea, laced with a tot of brandy which Mike had brought with him.

PC Reginald Geach walked into the room, notebook and pencil at the ready, some twenty minutes later. A stocky middle-aged man, he was breathless from the long bicycle ride from his home on the other side of Lewannick, and had to have a cup of tea before he could start his inquiries.

'Now then, as I understand it, Mr Macarthur raised the alarm when he saw someone in the house. You shouldn't have let him leave here. I'll have to have a word with he after the church service. I'm afraid you'll have the CID swarming all over the place tomorrow, Mrs Tamblyn. There's been a spate of sub-post offices being broken into in this area. Would you like to come with me now and see exactly what's been taken?'

They went through to the shop with Bunty and Mike; Laura and Spencer stayed put, not wanting to crowd the small shop.

'The men didn't say whether anything had been taken from the house,' Spencer said. 'Shall we take a look and see if anything has been disturbed?'

'Good idea. Let's start in the sitting room.'

Laura saw at once that two brass candlesticks were missing and some ornaments from a small glass cupboard. 'Daisy will never get over this,' she breathed, feeling sick to her stomach. 'Some of the things missing were sent to her from abroad by her children, the only contact she has with them.'

'Look at this,' Spencer said angrily. 'The silver photograph frame of Vicki as a baby is gone and the photograph left all screwed up.'

Laura took the photograph from him and straightened it out but the creases had ruined the picture. 'You've probably got another one at home. You can have a copy done for her. Vicki was a beautiful baby, anyone who could screw up a photo like this must have a cruel mentality.'

'Yes,' Spencer agreed. 'It's a good job Daisy didn't decide to stay at home.' He had a sudden thought. 'You'd better put it down, Laura, there might be fingerprints on it. Let's look upstairs.'

The bedroom Laura had slept in on her first few nights in the village looked undisturbed but in Daisy's room all the drawers and cupboards had obviously been opened; none of them were quite closed. Some papers were scattered on the chest of drawers.

'They've probably taken what they wanted and left the rest,' Spencer said grimly.

Laura looked down at the papers. Most of them were old letters and receipts and Daisy's insurance policies. A document caught her eye and when she read it she gasped.

'What is it?' Spencer asked.

'It's this,' she uttered. 'It's a will.' Her voice was raw and painful. 'It says here that the shop was left to Daisy and her sister Faith, that's Bill's mother. That means when his mother died, Bill would have inherited half the shop. He never said anything about this. He couldn't have known. His mother couldn't have known. It looks like Daisy kept it a secret. I'm going to ask her about it.'

As she made to leave the bedroom, Spencer restrained her. 'I don't think now is the time, Laura. If it turns out to be what you fear, it's a criminal offence and there is a policeman in the house. You don't want to get Daisy into trouble, do you? Leave it until tomorrow.'

Laura folded up the will and put it in her coat pocket. She said grimly, 'I can't stay here. I'm taking this home now to study it. I'll make some excuse to Daisy. Will you come with me?'

'Of course.'

Inside Little Cot, Laura read the will very carefully and handed it to Spencer. He shook his head disbelievingly as he read it. 'Well, there's no doubt that unless there's a later will, half the shop and its income should have gone to Faith Jennings, then Bill, and as Bill's widow, to you. You're entitled to a lot of back income, Laura.'

'I don't care about that!' Laura snapped, furious now the full implications of the document had hit her. 'Don't you see what this means, Spencer? Bill's cruel behaviour stemmed from the fact that he baulked against his father being a poor groom. If his mother had owned half the shop and shared half the takings he would have had some standing in the village. He would have felt better with himself. He might not have been so ambitious, so ruthless. He might not have treated me the way he did because he was clawing his way up from feeling like a nobody.' She was shouting now, rage making her shake from head to foot. 'No wonder she wanted me to work in the shop. She wanted to salve her conscience! And to think that I once thought of giving her Little Cot. I trusted and loved that woman and now it seems she's a liar and a thief. This sort of thing is frightening, it rocks your world and turns it upside down.'

'I have to go back for Vicki soon,' Spencer said gently. 'But I'm not leaving you here like this. You can come back to the farm with us and put her to bed. Would you like that?'

'I'd like nothing more,' she replied, grateful for his understanding.

For a few moments he held her and she rested in his arms.

Chapter 34

The next day Andrew was knocking on the shop door an hour before it was due to open at eight thirty. Bunty answered in her dressing gown and slippers; she had stayed the night.

'What do you want, Mr Macarthur?' she asked warily.

'I was wondering if the postwoman had called yet. Are you all right, Miss Buzza? How about Mrs Tamblyn? Is there anything I can do?'

'Everything's under control, thank you. The postwoman should be here within the next half-hour. Now if you'll excuse me, I'm going to coax Mrs Tamblyn to eat some breakfast.'

Andrew left, puzzled. He expected Bunty to be upset over what had happened to her friend but she had seemed as jumpy as if she thought he was the burglar come back. He went on to Little Cot, having noticed that lights were on there too.

'Do you want to join me for breakfast, Andrew, or have you eaten?' Laura asked, as she carried toast to the kitchen table.

'You're another one,' he exclaimed, ignoring her question. 'You look as if you've seen a ghost. Miss Buzza looked just the same when I called at the shop just now. Anyone would think Mrs Tamblyn had been murdered in her bed. Has something happened that I don't know about? The constable seemed to think it was a straightforward burglary.'

'Sit down, Andrew. I've got something to tell you.'

He was astonished at the tale of the will and Daisy keeping the contents secret.

'Daisy had lost her husband and was living in the shop when her parents died. As the elder daughter, she must have taken it upon herself

352

to wind up her parents' affairs and she lied about the contents of the will.'

'If there isn't a later will, are you going to sue her?'

'I don't think I could do that. I'll wait until I've spoken to her then I'll decide what to do.' She looked Andrew over. He was dressed in what he called his working clothes. 'Why are you up so early? As if I didn't know.'

'I'm hoping to hear from the bank today concerning my offer to buy Tregorlan Farm. Speaking of which, I'd better get back to the pub and wait for the post. Will you be all right alone?'

Laura made a wry face. 'I've coped with everything so far that's been thrown at me. Run along but make sure I'm the first to know when you have good news.'

Daisy was on the doorstep soon after Andrew left. She had dressed hurriedly, her coat was flapping open and her cardigan was buttoned up wrongly. Her face was twisted in worry. 'Please let me come in, Laura. I must speak to you. I haven't slept a wink all night and it had nothing to do with the break-in.'

Laura said nothing and stood aside to let Daisy in. They sat down in the front room. Daisy twisted her hands agitatedly in her lap. 'My will was taken yesterday. Was it you?'

'Yes,' Laura said coolly. She picked up the document she had taken from Daisy's bedroom. 'Is there a later one to this one?'

'No,' Daisy admitted in a croaky voice. 'I cheated my sister all those years ago, I cheated Bill and I've been cheating you.'

'Why?' Laura asked. 'It seems so unlike you.'

Daisy sobbed into a hanky, looking down at her trembling hands. 'I-it was jealousy. Although Ron didn't bring in much money, Faith had everything I wanted. Her own home and a loving husband. My husband, Sidney, didn't die as people thought. He ran off with another woman. He'd gone off with women all our married life. He left me in debt and I had to come home with my children and live with my parents in the shop. I was left bitter, Laura, and I hated to see how happy Faith and Ron were. I was so lonely. My son and daughters left home at fourteen to work and I've hardly seen them since.

'When my mother died, Father showed me the will so I would know what would happen when he died. Three months later he died and I… I suggested to Faith that they wanted me to have everything, to make up for what I had lost. Faith was happy with her life and didn't seem too bothered. I sweetened her up by saying she could have free groceries. I gave her some keepsakes and kept the will hidden. Soon afterwards I felt guilty and suggested to Faith that she take over half of the shop, but she wouldn't hear of it. She said if me being sole owner of the shop was our parents' wishes she wouldn't go against them. I desperately wanted to but I couldn't put things right. I've felt so guilty over the years. It's been a terrible burden on me. All because of a few moments of jealousy.

'I tried to put things right in small ways. I paid for Faith's and Ron's funerals. I paid for Billy to go to London and bought his clothes until he made some money of his own. I was so relieved when he became rich – I didn't know then that he was taking it from you and your father. A little village shop and sub-post office seemed so little by comparison.' Daisy's mouth worked like a cow's chewing the cud. 'Well, now the truth is out. What are you going to do, Laura?'

Laura sighed. 'Nothing for the moment, Daisy. I couldn't do anything that would get you into trouble, if that's what you're worried about.'

'Well, I was but that isn't the main issue. I'll make it up to you as much as I can, of course. I have some savings, that will go part of the way to what I owed Faith and Bill and now you.'

'I don't want your money, Daisy,' Laura said emphatically. The very idea was repugnant to her.

'Will you disown me?' Daisy broke into a fresh bout of sobbing. 'I don't expect you'll want to have anything to do with me from now on.'

'I need a day or two to think about it,' Laura said. 'I'll come up to see you then.'

'Of course.' Daisy got up. 'I must go and get ready to open the shop. I've got some post office officials coming later. Thank you, Laura. You've been very understanding.'

When she'd gone, Laura was left with the image of Daisy's distraught face on her mind. It was usually cheerful and kindly. Daisy was a genuinely kind woman. She had been good to Laura from the day of Bill's funeral. She had supported her through the times she had fallen out with Spencer and when Andrew had been kidnapped. Her story was a sad one and it was easy to see how a moment of weakness had led to years of deceit.

It kept running through Laura's head that the police, the post office officials and every other villager would be in the shop today asking endless questions. How was Daisy going to cope if Bunty was unable to offer her her usual comfort and support? What Daisy had done had started long ago in the past and Laura had learned that the past shouldn't be allowed to spoil the present and future.

Putting on her coat, she went up the hill and into the shop. Daisy watched uncertainly as she took off her coat and carried it through to the kitchen. Then she came back with her sleeves rolled up and an apron tied round her waist.

'Come on, Aunty Daisy,' she said briskly. 'If we're going to open on time and get ready for a busy day, we've got a lot of clearing up to do.'

–

Andrew saw Laura walking up to the shop from the pub window and he sighed in relief. It would have been a shame if there had been a rift between the two women. He moved to another window and rubbed condensation off it.

'You'll rub a hole in the glass soon,' Pat said, coming through to the bar to join him with a duster and carpet sweeper. 'You're like a cat on hot bricks this morning, Andrew. What's the matter with 'ee?'

'I'm waiting for the postwoman,' he answered impatiently, gazing up the hill in the direction she would come.

'So that's why you're late going over to Tregorlan this morning. Jacka will be docking your wages,' Pat joked.

'Here she comes!' Andrew whooped and he rushed from the room, almost sweeping Pat off her feet.

He met the postwoman halfway up the hill. 'Have you got a letter for a Mr A. Macarthur, care of the Tremewan Arms, please?'

'I might have,' the postwoman said cagily, free-wheeling down the hill on her bicycle.

Andrew ran to keep up with her. 'I'm Andrew Macarthur. I'm staying at the pub. Could you stop and see if you've got a letter for me?'

'If I have then I will put it through the letter box as I'm paid to do,' she said stubbornly.

Andrew stopped running and made a face at her back. Ada Prisk at the water pump had witnessed his fool's errand and was making her way determinedly towards him.

'Good morning, Mr Macarthur,' she called long before she reached him so he would have no choice but to stop and talk to her.

He smiled wider than was necessary. 'Ah, Mrs Prisk. Good morning to you.' He edged nearer the pub but she kept coming.

'It is true what I heard? That poor Mrs Tamblyn had a break-in yesterday? What a shameful affair. I saw the constable talking to you after evensong. Were you able to help him at all?'

She was like a hunter bearing down on wounded prey and he knew he wasn't going to get away from her until she was satisfied she'd pumped him dry. The postwoman put a handful of letters through the pub letter box. Pat opened the door and they were chatting. He was on tenterhooks to see whether he had a letter.

'There was very little I could tell Constable Geach, Mrs Prisk. Apparently it was a straightforward burglary.'

'I see. Off to Tregorlan again, are you? I can't help but notice how you're dressed.'

'Yes, Mrs Prisk.'

'I thought Jacka was looking well last night. He must be finding you a great help on the farm now he can't do any work.'

'I hope so, Mrs Prisk.'

Ada cocked her head to the side and Andrew knew he was going to be asked a very personal question. 'You interested in Tressa? Is that why you're still in the village?'

He put his hands behind his back and crossed his fingers. 'No, I'm not interested in her at all, Mrs Prisk.'

'That's not what I heard,' she returned disbelievingly.

'Really, Mrs Prisk? How odd.'

Mrs Sparnock was crossing the road for water and Ada left him for fresh pastures. Andrew tore into the pub. Pat was in the bar polishing the tables.

'Pat! Was there—'

She took two letters out of her apron pocket and waved them in the air. He snatched them out of her hand. One was from London from his old partners and he tossed it on a table unread. The other one had a Launceston postmark. He ripped open the envelope and taking out the letter inside went over to the window to read it. Pat was joined by Mike and they watched him anxiously.

'I've done it!' The letter was thrown up in the air and deftly caught. 'They've accepted my offer!' He sat down and became absolutely serious. 'Give me a small whisky, Mike. I'm going to ask Jacka for Tressa's hand in marriage.'

–

Joan was hanging up washing in the garden and Andrew went to her first. 'Is Tressa out in the fields, Joan?'

'Yes,' she replied, hiding a pair of her voluminous drawers behind her back. 'She went out with Ince first thing. It's his turn to help her this morning.'

'I'm glad she's not here,' he said, hopping about nervously. 'I can do what I'm about to do better without her hanging about looking hopeful. I've received good news from the bank. All I've got to do now is get Jacka's approval. Say a prayer for me.'

Jacka was reclining in his chair in front of the range in the kitchen. He had been advised to give up his pipe but he was taking one of his twice daily puffs.

'You're here then?' Jacka said drily.

'Yes, I'm here.' Andrew had never felt so nervous. Jacka's treatment of him varied, depending on his mood. When he was depressed he hardly said a word, unless it was to mutter grumpily. In lighter moods he'd expressed his gratitude for Andrew's unpaid help and how he was trying to keep the roof over his family's head, but he never mentioned Tressa and Andrew's relationship, despite their obvious love for one another. He watched them like hawks, demanding Tressa stay close to him when not in the fields and giving them very little time together. It seemed a long time since Andrew had last kissed her more than hurriedly. But he had been happy to wait patiently for the news he'd received this morning. And if that hadn't worked out, he would have suggested building another property in Kilgarthen. 'Do you mind if I sit down for a minute, Jacka?'

Jacka nodded absentmindedly. 'Free country.'

'You're probably wondering why I wasn't here early enough to go out with Tressa this morning.'

'No, she's got enough help. You've got your own life to lead.'

'I was waiting for this letter to arrive from the bank.' Andrew produced it from his trouser pocket.

'Oh?' Jacka leaned forward, more interested now. 'What does it say then?'

'Well, as you know, they didn't receive the postal order you sent them until several days after their deadline, the first of January. Although they acknowledge the postal order itself was dated late December, there is no proof of when you sent it, the postmark is smudged. They were sympathetic but insisted their deadlines must be honoured. They said they had received a good offer for the farm. I told them that whatever they had been offered, I would top it by five hundred pounds. This is what this letter is about. They've accepted my offer. Are you following me, Jacka?'

'Aye, I think so. What does it mean?'

Andrew felt uncomfortable. 'When I've signed the necessary papers, it means that Tregorlan Farm belongs to me.'

Jacka took his pipe out of his mouth and looked down at it dejectedly. 'So after years of owning me own farm, you're now my landlord.'

'Better me than the other person who put in an offer,' Andrew pointed out.

'Who was that then?'

'I don't know and there's no way of finding out. The reason why I've bought the farm...' Suddenly Andrew had had enough of pussy-footing around. 'You know why I've bought the farm, Jacka, and why I've stayed so long in Kilgarthen. I'm in love with Tressa. I adore her. I worship the ground she walks on. I can't say it any plainer than that. Against my wildest dreams, she returns my love. We want to get married, Jacka, and we want to have your blessing. Joan knows how we feel and she's happy for us and wants to see us married. I've given up my partnership in London and have taken on a new one in a law firm in Bodmin. I couldn't leave Kilgarthen now any more than I could give up breathing. If Tressa and I get married, I'm sure we could all live here happily, with a bit of give and take. I'll provide you, Joan and Tressa with everything you want.' As if he had run out of steam, Andrew stopped talking.

'Have you finished?' Jacka asked as if he was breathless too.

'Yes, I—'

'Thank goodness for that. Ruddy embarrassing listening to all that sort of stuff.'

'Well? What do you say, Jacka?'

'Tressa and Joan are all I've got.' He puffed on his pipe and disappeared behind a cloud of smoke. Andrew wanted to wave his arms about and clear the air between them. 'I wouldn't give either of 'em up easily. I wasn't keen on you being interested in my maid. I couldn't see she leaving her way of life and being happy in London and although you said you might stay down here I was worried you weren't really serious and you'd come to resent it. But if you've already changed your job, well, that shows me you're determined to do right by Tressa. Like you said, 'tis better you owning the farm than someone else who'd evict us to farm it himself, and it means I haven't got to move my old bones and start a new life and I won't have no money worries any more.'

Jacka seemed to have stopped without completing his ruminations and Andrew was still in an agony of doubt. 'Does that mean you won't mind if Tressa and I get married?'

Jacka wrinkled up his face and rubbed his stubbly jaw. 'You might as well, boy. You spend nearly every blinking day and night here anyway.'

Andrew still wasn't sure until he saw Jacka grin. Then he leaped from his chair and pumped his future father-in-law's hand. 'You won't regret this, Jacka. I'll make Tressa happy, I promise. I'll make all of us happy.'

Stopping to give Joan the good news as she came in from the garden, Andrew raced across the fields and moor to where Tressa and Ince were working with the cattle. She stopped working and ran to meet him. He gathered her up in his arms and swung her round and round until they fell over laughing in a dizzy heap.

Tressa held his face in both hands. 'You've heard from the bank? And Dad's said we can get married?'

'Yes, yes, yes!' he shouted, kissing her. 'As soon as you've finished here, I'm taking you down to the vicarage to arrange our wedding date with Mr Farrow.'

'Congratulations,' Ince said, smiling down on them. 'You can go now, if you like. I don't mind finishing up here.'

'You're an angel, Ince,' Andrew said gratefully, leading Tressa away.

'Not an angel,' Ince said wistfully, returning to the cattle. 'Just a man wanting the same as you.'

'We'll give this village the biggest wedding it's ever seen,' Andrew said, eyeing Tressa, half expecting the girl who had lived for so long in men's clothing to object.

'I can't wait,' she said happily, hugging him tightly as they walked over the turf. 'You look so handsome in a suit.'

'I thought you'd want a quiet do, darling. No fuss at all.'

'Andrew Macarthur, after what we've been through together, when I think how I could have lost you at Reddacoombe Farm and if you hadn't persisted with me, I want the whole world to know how much I love you.'

Chapter 35

Having had a particularly good night with his obscene magazines, Cecil Roach was in a chirpy mood as he sat down for breakfast. Barbara put a piping hot plateful of scrambled eggs in front of him and a rack of golden toast cut in perfect triangles. They did not speak. Hardly a word had passed between them since he'd thrown Marianne out and given Barbara a merciless beating. But this morning Cecil felt like talking.

'I hear the Davey girl is getting married,' he said, stuffing a mouthful of food between his thin cruel lips.

Barbara never watched him eat; he had more than one vile habit and it made her feel physically sick. She avoided sitting at the table with him and had eaten her breakfast earlier. She was forced to turn round and face him. Why had he mentioned Tressa Davey? Barbara had also been in church on Sunday and heard the first banns being called.

'So I understand,' she replied in the blandest voice she could find.

'The Jeffries girl is doing well at school. Excellent at arithmetic. Inclined to chat a lot to that Miller boy so she's often standing in the corner. I shall have to make sure they don't sit together.'

'Has Benjamin settled down well?' Barbara asked, remembering to call the boy by his full given name.

'Not too bad, not much of a scholar but good at physical jerks. He should do well in the school sports day in the summer.'

'That's good.' And you'll take all the credit as usual.

'Are you going to attend to that mess on the landing this morning?' He gulped down a mouthful of tea and licked the drips off the side of the cup with one long swipe of his tongue. He hated to see tea stains on the crockery.

Barbara suppressed a shudder. 'Yes, I am.' Of course I am. That's the third time you've mentioned that tiny spot of dirt since you noticed it last evening.

'Well, then, I'd better be off.' He belched. 'I have a lot to do this morning. The men are arriving to put the maypole up and as it's a dry day, the children can learn a new dance.'

'The children will like that.' The children will hate it, but you don't care that it's bitterly cold outside with a biting south-easterly wind.

Before leaving the room, Cecil gave her a firm kiss on the cheek. Barbara slumped into a chair. This meant he would want to have his way with her again. The one blessed relief of the savage beating she'd received was that he had left her alone. Now the whole beastly business would begin all over again, and judging by the sounds that had emanated from his study last night he probably had some new ideas to try out on her.

Cecil put on his coat and carefully positioned his hat and scarf. He picked up his briefcase to leave the house then remembered he had taken some papers up to the study last night to read and sign before he enjoyed himself. He went up to his study. He picked up the papers but before he put them in his briefcase he noticed Etta, the continental beauty, smiling beguilingly at him from a centrefold.

Cecil glanced at his watch. He had just enough time...

At eight forty-five Barbara called up to him. 'Cecil, are you aware of the time?'

He came back fully to the real world and hastily piled papers into his briefcase. He dashed to the bathroom, washed his hands and hurried off to the school.

As soon as he was out of the house, Barbara went to the public telephone box; she daren't run up a bill at home. She asked the operator to get her a number in Barnstaple in Devon.

'Mum?' Marianne answered at once. 'You're a bit late ringing. I was getting worried about you.'

'Your father was late leaving the house. How are you, dear? And Aunt Marta?'

'We're both fine, Mum. When are you coming, to join us? Aunt Marta sent the train fare down to you weeks ago.'

'I'll get away as soon as I can,' Barbara said, trying to sound convincing. She couldn't tell Marianne that Cecil had threatened that if she ever left him to join her, he would track them down and cause as much trouble as he could. A schoolmaster with a wayward daughter was bad enough, a deserting wife could cost him his position. Marta had been delighted to have Marianne, and soon the baby, live with her in her big house. She wanted Barbara to join them so they could make a fresh start in a safe environment, but although Barbara longed to go, how could she put Marianne and her grandchild at risk?

'You keep saying that, Mum,' Marianne pressured her. 'If you're afraid to make the break, ask Laura Jennings to help you. I'm sure she would hide your suitcases and help you get to the railway station.'

'It's difficult, dear. You know what your father is like. I promise I'll come as soon as I can. It's you I'm ringing about. What did the midwife say?'

'She said everything is going well. Do come up soon, Mum. I want you with me for the birth. I can't wait to show you all the little things I've made for the baby since I've learned to knit. Aunt Marta has got your room ready. All we need is you.'

'I must go now, dear. I've run out of money to put into the telephone box. I'll ring you next week.' Barbara put the receiver down and wept quietly for a few moments before going out into the cold air.

—

After assembly, Cecil took Class One for their daily arithmetic. He chalked up some simple sums on the blackboard and told the children to copy them into their books and work out the correct answers. 'In neat writing that I am able to read clearly, don't forget, children, then Miss Knight will be here to supervise half an hour at the sandpit for those of you who are good.'

Vicki and Benjy had been separated and she was sitting at a little single desk in front of him. With her head bent studiously over her work, she completed her sums in half the set time.

'What's the answer to the second one?' Benjy whispered to her.

'That's easy,' Vicki hissed back scornfully. 'Six and four equals ten.'

Cecil looked up from some exercise books he was marking. 'Victoria Jeffries, are you talking again?'

'Y-yes, sir.'

'Stand up when you talk to me, girl!'

Vicki had forgotten one of the golden rules she'd had drummed into her since starting school. She shot to her feet. 'Yes, sir. Sorry, sir.'

'Have you finished your work?'

'Yes, sir.'

He beckoned to her. 'Bring it here.'

Vicki put her exercise book nervously on his desk. Cecil flicked through her answers. They were all correct. Rather than getting the telling off she had feared, Mr Roach seemed pleased with her and gave her a beaming smile. 'I can see why your attention wandered. You need more of a challenge in this subject because you are very good at it, Victoria. I shall have a word with your father and suggest I set some harder work for you. I'm sure you won't let me down, will you?'

Vicki shook her head then remembered another golden rule, to answer a teacher's question with clear speech. 'No, sir.'

'I'm sure you will pass the county examination with flying colours. Do the school proud.' He patted her on the head, which Vicki hated. 'I would have let you play in the sandpit all on your own but as you were talking, you must return to your desk and stay there until the last child has finished.' He passed her a clean sheet of white paper. 'You may draw and colour in a picture of your father's farm for him and the other parents to see.' Cecil liked the parents to believe he was encouraging art among their offspring.

Vicki returned to her seat, lifted the lid of her desk and took out her crayons. She drew a picture of the farm, with cattle in the fields and herself, her father, Ince and Laura in the yard.

Cecil got up to tend to the open fire at the front of the classroom. It irked him that he had to use his valuable time on such a menial task, but he didn't want to badger the authority for an oil heating system while the possibility remained that the school might be closed down to merge with another for financial reasons.

He opened his briefcase to extract his papers and put them out for the secretary who came in once a week. To his horror he saw that in his haste to leave his study he had put one of his private magazines in with them. He shut his briefcase quickly. A few moments later desire caught hold of him. Did he dare take one crafty little look? Piercing the children with his beady eyes for several moments, which ensured all young heads were bent over their exercise books, he returned to the fire holding his briefcase. With his back to the children, he took out the magazine.

The lead of Benjy Miller's pencil broke. He was worried. If he didn't finish his sums at the same time as the other children, Mr Roach would be very cross. He got up from his desk and nervously approached the schoolmaster. 'P-please, Mr Roach—'

'Oh!' Cecil threw the magazine on the fire in fright. He whirled round and grabbing Benjy by the arm marched him to his desk. 'How dare you startle me like that, boy!'

The classroom door opened and Cecil received another fright. It was Miss Knight. 'The secretary has arrived and is waiting for you in your office, Mr Roach.'

Cecil hastily composed himself. 'Thank you, Miss Knight. I will be along in a moment. I'm just slipping out of the room for a few minutes, children,' he said in his most authoritative voice. 'Be sure that when I come back you are getting on with your work. Woe betide you if you are not. As for you, Benjamin Miller,' he scowled down on the unfortunate little boy, 'stand in the corner next to my desk until I get back and then your explanation had better be a good one.'

When Mr Roach had followed Miss Knight out of the room, Vicki looked sympathetically at Benjy's quaking back, then the fire took her attention. The magazine had made the flames dance, sending crazy shadows over the walls. She watched them for a while then looked back at the cavorting flames. Mr Roach had forgotten to put the fireguard back and sitting at the front of the classroom she had a wonderful view. It was as good as bonfire night. The magazine unfolded and slipped off the coals. It hit the floor and within moments the mat in front of the fire was ablaze.

–

Laura had done her housework and was walking up the hill to do her daily stint in the shop. The atmosphere had been tense for the first few days after the revelation that Daisy had cheated two generations of Jenningses out of their share of the shop, but an agreement had been worked out and things were back to normal now. Daisy had savings of one thousand pounds and she was to give Laura half of it. Laura was to receive half of the takings from the shop from now on and have her say in running it. The burglar had been apprehended while attempting a similar robbery in Bodmin and a few of Daisy's valuables had been returned. The two women now only wanted to put the episode behind them.

Laura's new life looked set in a solid and enjoyable pattern. She saw her friends and Vicki often, and today she was to collect her from school. They would have tea together before Laura took her home. She had a wedding to look forward to and had been charged with helping Tressa to choose her dress on a day trip to Plymouth.

'Good morning, Mrs Jennings.'

Laura stopped. 'Hello, Mrs Prisk, rather parky today,' she said, rubbing her hands together.

'That's your soft city-dwelling life telling on you,' Ada said bitingly. 'How are the wedding plans going?'

'Are you referring to Andrew's and Tressa's?' Laura asked mischievously.

Ada grabbed her arm. 'Why? Is somebody else getting married?'

'No, Mrs Prisk, I was just teasing you. Are you walking up to the shop? That's where I'm going. The wedding plans are going well. The cakes have been made and the hall's booked for the reception. Everyone in the village is going to be invited.'

'That's nice of Mr Macarthur, but then I've always said what a fine young man he is,' Ada stated as they walked on. 'Are you going to be one of those matrons-of-honour or whatever they call it?'

'No, Tressa won't be having any bridesmaids.'

'Really?' Ada gave Laura a nudge. 'I thought Vicki Jeffries might be one. I suppose one of his London friends will be best man.'

'Andrew's got a brother, actually, but as it will be a long, tiring journey for him and he has a young family, Mike Penhaligon—' Laura stopped and sniffed the air. 'Can you smell something?'

Ada sniffed and snorted. 'Smells like someone's got a chimney fire.'

Laura stepped out into the middle of the road to get a better view of the village. What she saw almost made her heart stop. 'It's the school! It's on fire!' Then she was tearing back down the hill. 'Vicki! Oh, God help me! Vicki!'

Chapter 36

Laura rushed into the school as some of the older children were spilling out of the building to safety under the charge of Miss Knight.

Laura clutched the teacher's arm. 'Where's Vicki Jeffries? Are the little ones out yet?'

'They're trapped in their classroom,' Miss Knight cried, coughing as black smoke overtook them.

Laura plunged on. She saw Cecil Roach running towards her. 'Get out! Get out!' He waved his arms at her.

'But the children!' Laura screamed.

'We can't do anything for them. The door's on fire,' Cecil shouted and he broke into a fit of coughing.

He ran outside and Laura raced after him. She grabbed hold of him so violently he nearly lost his footing. 'You can't just leave them in there, you coward. Go back inside and do something.'

'That would be madness. My wife has rung for the fire brigade.' He thrust her away indignantly. 'There's nothing we can do but wait for them to deal with it.'

'But it will take ages for them to get here down the lanes.'

Mothers were turning up in both playgrounds. Some were gratefully taking their children away while others were distraught for those still inside. And there were screams. The screams of the little children trapped in their burning classroom.

Laura ran to the window. It was about five feet off the ground, triangular in shape with a granite sill and six large panes rising up to the roof. Joy Miller and Ada Prisk joined her and Laura turned desperately to them.

'Their only chance is for one of us to climb in through the window and pass them out. We need something to stand on.'

'The dustbins,' Ada cried. 'We can empty one out and turn it upside down.'

'I'll get it,' Joy said, running off.

Laura put her hands on the sill and peered inside. She couldn't make out much in the smoke and the flames which were consuming the wall of the fireplace, but from the children's screams she guessed they had crowded away from the door and were huddled down in a heap under the window out of sight.

'Vicki! Vicki! Can you hear me!' she shouted, abject fear making adrenalin course through her veins and giving her a heady strength and feeling of steely determination.

'Laura,' a small, terrified voice called back.

'It's all right, Vicki. I'm coming in to get you and the others. Just stay where you are and keep down low where there is less smoke.'

Joy Miller was back with the dustbin. Laura climbed up on it and peered in through the window. She could just see the tops of the children's heads. With dismay she realised she would have to get them away from the window so they wouldn't be showered with glass when she broke it. She would have to rely on Vicki to trust her and keep a clear head.

'Hurry, Laura,' Joy Miller pleaded with her. 'Benjy gets asthma. He won't last as long as the others.'

'Vicki, listen to me,' Laura shouted. 'Get the children to move along the wall and away from the window. I have to break the glass. Did you hear me, darling?'

'Yes,' Vicki murmured fearfully.

The children were all holding hands. Vicki was at the end of the line and she tugged them along after her, shouting at them to follow her. Smoke billowed over her face and she started coughing.

Laura ripped off her coat and wound it round her arm. She smashed one of the lowest panes and knocked out the remaining shards of glass. Then she hauled herself through the opening and dropped down on the floor. One quick look told her she had only a few moments to get the children out. She knew there were ten children in Vicki's class and one was at home today with a cold.

'Don't worry, children,' she said, waving at smoke wafting towards them. 'You'll soon be safe.'

She pushed a desk under the window and climbing up on it held out her arms. Her immediate thought was to get Vicki out first but this was also the safest choice since she had already shown some bravery and the other children were more likely to follow her and not stay put in a panic.

'Vicki! Come to me quickly. I'm going to lift you out to Mrs Miller.'

Vicki ran to her, bringing Benjy with her, and the line of children followed on. Laura grabbed Vicki none too gently and lifting her up high thrust her into Joy's waiting arms. Joy passed her to Ada who passed her on to another mother who led her away from the burning building. Benjy was out next and then the next child. Four, five, six. The line was broken as a sheet of flame spread across the ceiling, blowing Laura off the desk. The remaining children fell back screaming.

Cecil Roach had got a grip on himself and he demanded he take Joy's place on the dustbin. Ada pushed him away roughly. 'Bugger off, you! You weren't no use before and we can manage better without you now.'

Joy was shouting desperately at Laura. 'Get up, Laura! You have to get out, the fire's spreading.'

Laura's arm hurt badly but she scrambled across the room on all fours towards the three remaining children. She wrapped her arms round them and dragged them towards the desk. She clutched the backs of the cardigans of two sobbing little girls and with a cry of pain and effort she heaved them up for Joy who got a grip on their fronts. Joy yanked them out so hard she fell off the dustbin with them. Two mothers came forward and pulled their daughters to safety.

Ada got up on the dustbin, paying no regard to her age and arthritis. She saw that Laura was swaying as she coughed and choked. 'Laura! Don't give up now. Take hold of the boy. Come on, you can do it.'

Laura bent down, reaching for the terrified little boy. She touched the boy's head and lowering her hands she put them under his armpits just as the boy passed out. He was a dead weight to lift. Somehow she got him up to her chest level and threw the top half of his body over the window frame. Ada grabbed him and realising Laura was about to buckle and fall off the desk, she shot out her other arm and grabbed her hair.

'Help me, someone!'

Spencer and Ince, like many of the farmers working outside had seen the smoke billowing up in the sky. They had driven to the village at speed, knowing there was a fire but doubly horrified to find it was the school.

'Daddy! Daddy!' Vicki screamed shrilly, freeing herself from the mother looking after her and running up to him. 'Get Laura! Get Laura!'

Spencer saw Ada's predicament at the same time he heard her shout for help. Thrusting Vicki into Ince's arms he sprinted across the playground and leaped up onto the dustbin, beating the boy's mother to it. He pulled the little boy out over the top of the window and dropped him into his mother's arms. He got a tight grip on Laura's shoulders and just before the first tongues of flames could reach her he dragged her out.

Barbara Roach helped Ada down off the dustbin and led the old lady outside the school walls where everyone else had moved for greater safety. Spencer jumped down with Laura lying limp in his arms. He carried her away from the building to join those watching helplessly as smoke and flames poured out of every window and door and through the roof. The ringing of the fire engine could be heard but it would be too late to save the school.

Andrew and Tressa had arrived, with Daisy on their heels. They pushed their way through to where Spencer was laying Laura gently on a coat on the ground. 'Did she breathe in much smoke?' Andrew asked anxiously, looking at her blackened face. 'I'll give her mouth to mouth resuscitation.'

Spencer pushed him away. 'I know how to do it.' He tilted Laura's head back and put his mouth over hers and breathed into her. Her

371

chest rose and fell but she didn't seem to be breathing on her own. He breathed into her five more times and then she coughed and spluttered. She gasped for air and Spencer sat her up against his chest.

'Is she going to be all right, Daddy?' Vicki asked tearfully from Ince's arms.

'I think so, pipkin. Has someone rung for an ambulance?' Spencer looked at all the staring, concerned faces. It was easy to tell which of the children had been trapped and rescued, their faces and clothes were blackened, the whites of their eyes gleaming like snow. Then he realised that Vicki's face was blackened too. 'Oh, my God.' He held his arms out to her and Ince passed her to him. He cried unashamedly over the woman leaning against his chest who was now gazing up weakly at him. 'Thank you, Laura. How can I ever thank you.'

'I've rung for an ambulance, Mr Jeffries,' Barbara said, kneeling down beside them and rubbing Laura's wrist. 'It's no good asking my husband to do anything at a time like this.'

There were similar mutters in the crowd. Questions had revealed that Cecil Roach had only left the classroom moments before the fire began and most people held him responsible. Cecil scowled and slunk away. He had to think of a way out of this.

'Be careful with her other arm,' Barbara said as she ministered to Laura. 'It looks as if it's broken.'

'All these children would have died if it wasn't for Laura,' Daisy said, sniffing back tears as she voiced what was on everyone's mind. 'And Mrs Prisk and Mrs Miller.'

'It was a glad day for the village when that maid come here,' Johnny Prouse added emotionally.

Laura regained full consciousness. 'Vicki! Vicki!' She tried to get up but Spencer and Barbara held her gently down.

'I'm here, Laura,' Vicki murmured, the full extent of her frightful ordeal now hitting her.

'Thank God,' Laura croaked, her voice husky from the smoke, holding out her arms to her.

Vicki wriggled out of Spencer's arms and placed her head on Laura's shoulder. Laura put her good arm round her. 'Thank God she survived,' she whispered to Spencer. 'I don't know what I would have done if anything had happened to her. What about the boy? The other children?'

'They're all right, thanks to you,' Felicity Lean said, smiling down encouragingly on them. 'I've been checking up on all of them. They'll all have to go to hospital just to be sure. You're the one who has suffered the most, Laura.'

'What about Mrs Prisk?' Laura gasped, mindful that she was an old woman. 'She saved my life.'

'I'm fine, m'dear.' Ada pushed her head through the milling crowd and grinned down on her. 'Take more than that to stop my yap.'

Laura smiled, then cuddling the child she loved more than anyone in the world, completely worn out, she fell asleep in Spencer's arms.

Chapter 37

Cecil Roach looked at the smouldering ruins of his school. His life was in ruins too. Any hopes that the authorities would give him even a humble teaching position would be lost in the recriminations of the many angry parents who despised him anyway. There would be an inquiry. There would be newspaper reporters knocking on his door. The constable might want to ask questions. He thought of the magazine that had been responsible for the fire and turned for home. He had to get rid of his illicit collection.

He passed through the kitchen, spitefully pushing Barbara out of the way; he would deal with her later for the disloyal way she had spoken about him in front of all those wretched people. Up in his study he began piling his precious magazines and postcards together. He'd burn them in the garden. It would be a terrible wrench to get rid of them but when he was settled again, he'd begin another collection. He'd have to leave this house and village.

He gathered up an armful of Etta and her playmates to put them in a cardboard box. A strange numbing feeling that started in his head and spread quickly through his body made him stagger. His vision blurred. His strength left him and he dropped his dirty books. He felt dizzy. Sweat broke out all over him and he tried to get to his chair to sit down. He didn't make it and fell to the floor. He wet himself. He couldn't move. He couldn't speak. All he could do was stare straight ahead at a picture of a totally naked Etta.

Barbara thought it strange that Cecil didn't come down for tea but because he hated being disturbed when in his study she didn't call him. She had been thinking over her position. How could she go on living with a man like him? He was cruel. He was a coward. He was vile. He was perverted. Cecil Roach should never be allowed near a child again. In a few months' time her grandchild would be born and he had sworn to make trouble for that innocent little soul if she left. Barbara was suddenly full of indignant fury. Like hell he would! She'd protect that child at all costs. Her mind was clear. She'd leave her despicable husband this very minute and if he made any attempt to come near her, Marianne and the baby, she'd go to the police and tell them about his filthy secrets. All she had to do now was to tell Cecil, and she had the outrage and courage running through her veins to do it. She picked up the poker. Heaven help him if he tried any violence this time.

She climbed the stairs and stood for a moment at the bottom of the study steps. He would be furious with her for setting foot in his precious domain, he had never allowed her even to dust up there and she had never dared to venture inside it before.

As she went up the steps, she realised it was strangely quiet. She called to him. There was no answer, not even the usual abuse. She remembered the sudden bump she had heard hours earlier. If he had been any other sort of man she might have thought he'd been so upset over the school fire he had done something drastic.

She turned the handle of the study door, pushed it open while resolutely tightening her grip on the poker. She saw Cecil lying on the floor, his mouth open, eyes glazed as they stared ahead. She thought he was dead at first then she noticed him twitching.

'Cecil, what's happened to you?'

Then she saw his filthy pictures. Wanton women with huge breasts and bottoms seemed to be leering at her from every angle of the room. They were mocking her. It was them that had led him to want to do so many beastly things to her.

'You bastard,' she shouted at Cecil contemptuously, holding back the urge to kick him. 'So this is what you get up to up here? I knew it was something filthy but I never guessed you went this far.'

She could see now what had happened to him. He had suffered a massive stroke. Barbara looked down at him with no emotion. He seemed to be silently pleading to her for help.

'If you think that after all you've put me through, all the terrible things you've done to make me suffer, that I'm going to nurse you for the rest of your life while you're as helpless as a baby, then you're very wrong, Cecil Roach.' Her voice was ice-cold. 'I came up here to tell you I'm leaving you. Who will blame me, even with you like this? They all know in the village what a bastard you are. I'm going to Marianne and her baby, my grandchild, the one you don't want. You can't come after us and even if you could, I'd never let you hurt us again.' She made to go and he made a frantic gargling noise. 'Oh, don't worry, Cecil. Someone will find you eventually. They've got nice little seaside institutions for cases like you, although when they see this filth they might find another place to put you.'

She hurried to her bedroom and packed her suitcases. She telephoned Marianne, and then ordered a taxi to pick her up at the top of the village hill. She dashed off two notes. One was to Cecil, saying she'd had enough of his cruelty and was leaving him. It wouldn't be found by him, of course, but by the people who would have to arrange to have him carted away. They would assume she had left him before he'd had the stroke and knew nothing about it. The other note was to Laura Jennings, thanking her for all her help and kindness. She would put it through Little Cot's letter box when she left this house to start her new life.

Chapter 38

'All ready to go home, Mrs Jennings?' the tall straight-backed sister on Laura's ward in Launceston Hospital asked in her efficient manner.

'Yes, Sister,' Laura replied, her voice hoarse, her throat sore. She was sitting on the bed, dressed except for her shoes. 'It's good to be wearing clean clothes but even after a hair wash and bath I still feel dirty and gritty. I can still smell the smoke.'

'That will fade and your throat will soon be less sore. I've just received a telephone call from your family. They're on their way to collect you. Now, you are to go home and get straight into bed and rest for the next few days. You've got a broken arm, your lungs took in some smoke and you badly strained yourself pulling those children out of danger. Your body needs plenty of rest to recover properly.' The sister smiled and put her hand on Laura's shoulder, a gesture she had never made to a patient before. 'I've never had a heroine on my ward before. Good luck to you, dear.'

The sister left her and like so many times since she had been brought here two days ago, Laura felt weepy. Her eyes stung as hot tears hit her eyelids and she sniffed into a hanky.

'Never mind, my luvver,' the jolly woman in the next bed said to her. 'You'll feel better when you get home.'

Laura smiled gratefully for the words of comfort. Although all the children had been saved, and Benjy Miller had quickly recovered from an asthma attack brought on as a result of the trauma, she kept thinking about the children being suffocated or burned to death. Their screams echoed through her mind. In her imagination she could see their little blackened faces turned up to her from the schoolroom floor, begging her to get them out. She saw herself standing on the dustbin, unable to break the glass, unable to climb through the window, unable to reach them, unable to coax them to come to her. She couldn't understand why she was thinking this way. They were all safe; Vicki had cuddled into her all the way to the hospital to prove it.

Laura looked at the handkerchief she was almost shredding with the fingers of her good hand. Each corner was embroidered with tiny flowers and in one corner was the letter A. Laura remembered coming round as she was being put into the ambulance and a thin elderly face, topped with an untidy iron-grey bun, looming over her and a familiar voice exclaiming, 'You can't go without one of these, dear.' Ada Prisk. She had given the hanky to the ambulance man to pass on to her when she was cleaned up. 'It'll take more than that to shut up my yap,' Ada had said stoutly.

Laura knew that when she got home everything apart from the village having no school would be the same. Ada would be chasing her for gossip and all the other villagers would be the same familiar characters. But all of them would be closer. She dried her eyes and practised a bright smile, ready for when her 'family' arrived on the ward. She assumed Andrew and Aunty Daisy were coming for her.

A pair of running light feet heading towards her made her face shine with delight. 'Vicki, darling! What are you doing here?' She held out her arm and Vicki climbed up on the bed and hugged her tightly. 'How are you?' She saw scratches on Vicki's face.

'Never mind me. Are you feeling better, Laura?' Vicki asked, peering at her face with a wisdom beyond her years. 'You look tired but just as beautiful. Doesn't she, Daddy?'

'Yes, she does, pipkin.'

'Spencer, what a surprise,' Laura exclaimed. She hadn't noticed him following close behind Vicki. 'I wasn't expecting you and Vicki.'

'I asked Andrew and Daisy if we could come for you,' Spencer said, putting down a huge bunch of flowers and a box of chocolates on the bedside cabinet. He looked at her closely, much as his daughter had done. 'You look pale, but as soon as you're able to get about, a little moorland air will put the colour back in your cheeks.'

'Is your arm poorly?' Vicki said, gingerly touching the plaster on Laura's broken arm.

'Yes, but it will soon get better. You can be the first to write your name on it.'

A nurse came with a wheelchair. 'Here, you are, Mrs Jennings. I'm to escort you safely off the premises. Has your husband brought you a coat?' she asked, bending down to put Laura's shoes on.

'Mrs Jennings is a friend,' Spencer corrected the nurse, lifting a bag he had with him up on the bed. 'A very special friend. I have everything she needs. A scarf and gloves as well as a blanket to wrap her up in.'

'I shall feel like a newborn baby,' Laura laughed.

'We're going to look after you,' Vicki piped up determinedly.

'I'll enjoy that,' Laura replied, caressing the little girl's hair.

The sister accompanied them to the hospital doors and Laura was put safely in the car. Vicki sat beside her and held her hand. As they waved goodbye to the sister, Laura was already feeling tired.

'Vicki was right when she said we're going to look after you,' Spencer said as he drove out of the hospital grounds. 'We're taking you to Rosemerryn Farm.'

Laura was thrilled but there were other people to consider. 'What will Daisy say about that?'

'It's all been agreed. Vicki won't be going to school until it's been decided where the children will go from now on, probably to Lewannick. It's unlikely there will ever be a school in Kilgarthen again. You'll recover better with Vicki around you. Daisy and the others will be dropping in regularly to help out so all you have to do is rest and get well.'

'Thanks, Spencer,' Laura said, feeling overwhelmed with joy. 'You don't know how much this means to me.'

He looked over Vicki's head and smiled at her. 'Oh, but I do. You're part of Vicki's life now, part of everyone's in Kilgarthen, including mine.'

'I never thought I'd ever hear you say that.'

'Nor did I.'

As soon as they arrived at Rosemerryn Farm, Laura was bundled up to bed in Vicki's room; a camp bed was going to be put up beside it for Vicki for the next few days.

'Ince offered his room,' Spencer said as he knocked and came in with a tray of tea. 'But it's a bit basic for a woman to sleep in and I thought you wouldn't mind sharing with Vicki.'

'And Lizzie,' Vicki said, putting her doll in the bed beside Laura for company.

'I can't think of anything better,' Laura said, warmed through.

'Are you comfortable?' Vicki asked, copying the nurse's tone of voice. 'Can I get you anything?'

'Why don't you go downstairs and get some of those delicious chocolate biscuits for Laura, pipkin?' Spencer said, nodding at the door.

Laura was about to protest that she wasn't hungry but she sensed that he wanted to talk to her alone. 'What is it?' she asked when Vicki had dutifully trotted off.

He started to pace the room, one moment pushing his hands into his pockets, the next pulling them out and clenching his fists. 'I think before we go on there is one thing that we ought to clear up.' He stood still and gazed at her from the foot of the bed. 'It's about Bill. You want to know why Bill and I quarrelled. It was over Natalie. I find it hard even thinking about it, it makes me feel so sick, angry and bitter.'

'You don't have to tell me, Spencer. It's not important any more.'

'I think it's better out in the open.' He took a deep breath. 'Not long before Vicki was born, Natalie met up with Bill in Launceston. She was shopping for baby things. She felt faint for a few moments and he took her into a cafe for a glass of water then he offered to drive her home. She was grateful to him because it meant she wouldn't have to ride in the bone-shaker bus.' Spencer broke off to contain his growing emotion.

'And then what happened?' Laura prompted him softly, dreading the answer.

'On... on the journey home he propositioned her. Can you imagine a man doing anything lower than that? Asking a heavily pregnant woman who he believed was his half-sister to go to bed with him?'

380

'No, I can't.' Laura's cheeks suffused with bright colour as a wave of contempt for the man she had been married to swept over her. 'But I can imagine him doing it.'

Spencer swallowed and raised his eyes to the ceiling. There was more to the tale. 'He-he stopped the car and grabbed her... Natalie had to fight him off. I think it was only her pregnancy that saved her in the end. Now can you see why I hate him so much? Natalie was so upset. She became depressed. I think it was the reason why she went into premature labour and... and why she died.'

Laura felt a special closeness to Spencer, and not just because he had saved her life twice and was Vicki's father. She wanted to put her arms round him and give him comfort. What she said felt very inadequate. 'I'm very sorry, Spencer. You're only one of a lot of people who have suffered at Bill's hands.'

He came closer to her. 'I want you to know, Laura, that I don't blame you, not now.'

She reached out to stroke his arm and he took her hand and held it. 'I'm glad you've told me, Spencer, but there's something you don't know. I hope that in some small way it will make it easier for you to bear. Bill wasn't William Lean's son, he was in no way related to Natalie. Mrs Noon told me that it was Bill himself who started the rumours as a means to blackmail William Lean but it didn't work. I asked Harry about it and he confirmed it was true.'

Spencer sat on the bed. 'Natalie and I never talked about the rumours. It didn't seem important with her father long dead when we married.' After a pause, in which he dried his eyes, he managed a brief smile. 'Vicki will be back in a minute. I just wanted to clear the air between us.'

He studied a picture on the wall above Laura's head as if it was a lifeline. He held her hand a little tighter and Laura wondered what was to come. 'I've been thinking. I... I know that you love Vicki dearly and she loves you. I acknowledge that without her own mother she'll need you more and more. Perhaps one day we ought to think about making some sort of permanent arrangement for Vicki's sake. What do you say?'

Laura was stunned. The proposition was totally unexpected. She had little hope of falling in love and getting married again, but could she marry Spencer for Vicki's sake? 'You mean have what people call an understanding?'

'Yes, for Vicki's sake,' he stressed. He'd do anything for Vicki and he was afraid if Laura married again she'd have children of her own and Vicki would take a back seat, but the proposition was partly for himself. He hadn't sorted out his feelings for the woman who had saved his daughter's life but they were very strong.

They heard Vicki's feet pitter-pattering up the stairs. She came into the room with a plate piled high with chocolate biscuits.

'Goodness me!' Laura exclaimed, laughing. 'I don't think I can eat that much.'

Vicki moved past her father and climbed up on the bed beside Laura. Laura indulgently took a biscuit off the plate. She knew Spencer was waiting for her answer. What she wanted most in all the world was to receive his little girl's endless love. She looked into his eyes, smiled, nodded and hugged Vicki happily to her.

The Kilgarthen Sagas

Kilgarthen
Rosemerryn